MW01623393

The Bloody Crown of
CONAN

THE FULLY ILLUSTRATED ROBERT E. HOWARD LIBRARY
from Del Rey Books

The Coming of Conan the Cimmerian

The Savage Tales of Solomon Kane

The Bloody Crown of Conan

*Bran Mak Morn: The Last King**

*The Conquering Sword of Conan**

*forthcoming

GIANNI

The Bloody Crown of CONAN

ROBERT E. HOWARD

ILLUSTRATED BY GARY GIANNI

BALLANTINE BOOKS • NEW YORK

A Del Rey® Book
Published by The Random House Publishing Group

Design: Marcelo Anciano
Typography: Stuart Williams
Editor: Patrice Louinet
Series Editor: Rusty Burke

Published in the United States by Del Rey Books, an imprint of The Random House Publishing Group, a division of Random House, Inc., New York. Previously published in Great Britain by Wandering Star, Ltd., London, in 2003.

This edition published by arrangement with Wandering Star Books, Ltd.

Library of Congress Control Number: 2004103781

ISBN 0-7394-4971-0

Manufactured in the United States of America

The illustrations in this book are dedicated
to Margaret and Louis Gianni

Gary Gianni

The People of the Black Circle
first published *Weird Tales*, September, October and November 1934

The Hour of the Dragon
first published *Weird Tales*, December 1935 and January, February, March and April 1936

A Witch Shall Be Born
first published *Weird Tales*, December 1934

Contents

Plates

Foreword

When I was a kid, I watched a man knock down a house with a sledge hammer. It wasn't a house exactly – a shack would be a more apt description. I can recall the afternoon vividly, the neighbourhood boys assembled in my friend Joe's yard because his father was about to demolish an old shack which stood at the end of their property. What eight year old wouldn't want to witness that?

When I arrived, Mr. Lill was already sizing up the job with the large sledge hammer perched over his broad shoulders. The structure leant towards him in a show of defiance. Perhaps the man sensed the mockery for he exploded into action. He was an engine of destruction. With arms spinning like a windmill he delivered crashing blows to insure maximum damage to his teetering opponent. The clouds of dust combined with the groaning timbers created an illusion of a fantastic battle taking place. I, for one, was enthralled by the spectacle and I wonder now how many of those kids vicariously waged the fight with gritted teeth and clenched fists.

When the last perpendicular post was hurled onto the pile of wreckage, the man climbed atop the heap, leaned on his sledge hammer and grimly surveyed his handiwork.

In retrospect it was a transcendent moment, a real life brush with the embodiment of John Henry, Hercules and Samson. We have all had experiences similar to this in one form or another and these memories can best be described as "Heroic Realism," a term coined by the writer Louis Menand. The fantasy elements aside, this is the quality I am chiefly interested in with my work with Conan – the sense of real danger, romance and intrigue grounded in a tangible reality.

As a teenager, years after that shack came crashing down, I came upon a paperback book with a cover painting of a man leaning on a broadsword standing atop a pile of vanquished opponents. Somehow in the deep recesses of my memories this picture had a familiar feel to it.

I thought of that afternoon and the thrill came rushing over me. The power of images.

The book, of course, was *Conan the Adventurer* by Robert E. Howard and the cover was painted by Frank Frazetta. It was my introduction to Howard's fictional barbarian.

That was a long time ago and many talented artists have portrayed Conan's adventures. I was content to stand aside and enjoy their work but the opportunity presented itself after I had illustrated two of the other great Robert E. Howard heroes – Solomon Kane and Bran Mak Morn. How could I resist?

I feel privileged in depicting these characters and I now join the list of eminent illustrators who have had a crack at depicting Conan. It is a fitting tribute to the writing ability of Robert E. Howard that regardless of how many artists add to the mythos of Conan in books, comics and movies, it is the original stories themselves and the powerful imagery they evoke that will ultimately thrill the reader.

Gary Gianni
2003

Introduction

"There is no literary work, to me, half as zestful as rewriting history in the guise of fiction," wrote Robert E. Howard to his friend H.P. Lovecraft. This certainly helps to explain some of the zest to be found in his tales of the indomitable Conan of Cimmeria, for here is history as vivid, dramatic fiction.

What? Conan as history? Surely this is fantasy, isn't it? This world, "the Hyborian Age," is merely a figment of Howard's imagination, right? Well, yes and no. Certainly it is Howard's unique literary creation – but into its creation he has poured all his love of history and legend and romance.

Robert E. Howard was an extraordinarily gifted but emphatically commercial writer. Storytelling apparently came naturally to him: friends of his youth attest that he was directing their play as early as age ten, and friends of his young manhood tell us that he was a spellbinding storyteller. Of course, we have the testament of his fiction to tell us that, too. And while he himself disavowed any particular artistic motives, there is in his best work genuine artistry. As Lovecraft noted, "He was greater than any profit-making policy that he could adopt."

But Howard put his natural storytelling talent to work in wresting a living for himself, so it was important to him that his work find a market. In the early 1930s, with the Great Depression settling upon the land, his markets, the pulp magazines, were struggling. Those that survived sometimes did so by cutting rates, or reducing their frequency (and thus demand for new material). As much as he loved the historical tales he had been writing for *Oriental Stories*, mostly set during the Crusades or the eras of Mongol or Islamic conquests, and the stories of ancient Irish warriors for which he had not found a market, they required a lot of research, and that was time he could ill afford. "Every page of history teems with dramas that should be put on paper," he wrote. "A single paragraph may be packed with action and drama enough to fill a whole volume of fiction work. I could never make a living writing such things, though; the markets are too scanty, with requirements too narrow, and it takes me so long to complete one."

Howard's interest in history, as strong as it was, did not extend to "civilized" peoples. "When a race – almost any race – is emerging from barbarism, or not yet emerged, they hold my interest. I can seem to understand them, and to write intelligently of them. But as they progress toward civilization, my grip on them begins to weaken, until at last it vanishes entirely, and I find their ways and thoughts and ambitions perfectly alien and baffling. Thus the first Mongol conquerors of China and India inspire in me the most intense interest and appreciation; but a few generations later when they have adopted the civilization of their subjects, they stir not a hint of interest in my mind. My study of history has been a continual search for newer barbarians, from age to age."

During the early months of 1932, on a trip to Mission, Texas, in the Rio Grande Valley, the answer came to him: the Hyborian Age, a period lying between the sinking of Atlantis and the cataclysms that shaped our modern world, populated by the forebears – the veritable archetypes – of all the barbarians he so loved to study. The character Conan "stalked full grown out of oblivion and set me at work recording the saga of his adventures." These exploits took place in a world populated by Elizabethan pirates, Irish reavers, and Barbary corsairs; American frontiersmen and Cossack raiders; Egyptian sorcerers and followers of Roman mystery cults; medieval knights and Assyrian armies. All were given disguises, but with no attempt to actually hide their identities. In fact, Howard tried to give them names that would allow the reader to guess their identities without too much effort – he wanted us to recognize them instantly, but with the wink that says, "We know this is a story, right? On with it!" Can any reader fail to recognize that Afghulistan is Afghanistan, or that Vendhya is India? Surely not!

With his creation of the Hyborian Age, Howard had created a world in which his beloved historical barbarians could run riot, and he could weave those tales packed with action and drama that he loved to tell. It's a brilliant concept, and one I believe may have been suggested to him by G.K. Chesterton, whose epic poem *The Ballad of the White Horse* was one of Howard's favorites, to judge not only from his effusive comments in two different letters to his friend Clyde Smith in 1927, but from his frequent use of quotations from the poem as epigrams or verse headings for his stories, and the fact that he was still quoting from it in letters as late as 1935. *The Ballad of the White Horse* tells of King Alfred and the Battle of Ethandune, but Chesterton admits that "All of it that is not frankly fictitious, as in any prose romance about the past, is meant to emphasize tradition rather than history." Because the work he wants to celebrate, the fight "for the Christian civilization against the heathen nihilism," was "really done by generation after generation," he created fictitious Roman, Celtic, and Saxon heroes to share in the glory of victory with Alfred. "It is the chief value of legend," he wrote, "to mix up the centuries while preserving the sentiment; to see all ages in a sort of splendid foreshortening. That is the use of tradition: it telescopes history."

Chesterton, of course, was hardly the first to create such a literary work: the Arthurian romances of Chrétien de Troyes and Sir Thomas Malory come to mind, and earlier still the Norse sagas and the ancient legend of Beowulf. But Chesterton's statement of rationale may have wormed its way into Howard's consciousness to emerge years later as the Hyborian Age. Howard did write an epic poem, *The Ballad of King Geraint*, that was an echo of Chesterton's: he depicted a valiant last stand of the Celtic tribes of Britain and Ireland against the invading Anglo-Saxons. But it wasn't until his creation of the Hyborian Age in 1932 that he was able to put this telescoping idea to really effective use, turning history into what Lovecraft termed "vivid artificial legendry."

Because Howard wrote a lengthy history of the Hyborian Age, and took pains to make it a self-consistent world, some critics have placed him within what is termed the "imaginary worlds" tradition of fantasy, exemplified by such inventive writers as George Macdonald, William Morris, Lord Dunsany, and J.R.R. Tolkien. But the Hyborian Age is historical, not imaginary: it is simply a nexus where elements from different historical eras may come together for the sake of the story. Part of the appeal of the Conan stories is that they seem so real, because we recognize the world in which Conan moves. And Howard was not a literary stylist in the manner of these "imaginary worlds" writers: he was a storyteller, who preferred clear, direct, simple language with a minimum of description. There is, to be sure, considerable poetry in his best prose, as the opening chapter of *The Hour of the Dragon* amply demonstrates. Howard was raised on poetry, which his mother read to him, and was himself perhaps the best poet among writers of the fantastic. As Steve Eng says, "Howard may have sensed that poetry suited his imagination better than did prose. His fictional Sword-and-Sorcery heroes and foes would seem to be more naturally chanted or sung about than portrayed in paragraphs."

But there was another element to Howard's fiction: "every urge in me," he told E. Hoffmann Price, "is to write realism." This may seem incongruous coming from an author best known for his fantasies, but in surveying the corpus of his work, we find a "realistic" novel, a great number of boxing stories, many historical and western stories – in other words, a good deal of realism. Jack London was perhaps his favorite writer: best known today for his outdoor adventures, London was a noted socialist as well, whose semi-autobiographical *Martin Eden*, the model for Howard's own *Post Oaks and Sand Roughs*, has been suggested as the first existentialist novel. Another writer Howard thought highly of was Jim Tully, whose fictionalizations of his life as hobo, circus roustabout, boxer and journalist find echoes in Howard's work. Both London and Tully were "road kids," and Howard frequently wrote of characters, including Conan, who had left home to roam the world as youngsters.

In his seminal essay, 'Robert E. Howard: Hard-Boiled Heroic Fantasist,' George Knight suggests that Howard was bringing to fantasy something of the same sensibility that his contemporary Dashiell Hammett and others were bringing to the detective story: a gritty, tough attitude toward life, expressed in simple, vigorously direct prose (not without poetry), with violence as the dark heart of the tale. Conan in his Hyborian Age has much in common with the Continental Op on the mean streets of San Francisco: he is a freelance operator, with a cynical, worldly-wise attitude tempered by his own strict moral code. He feels no loyalty to rules imposed by authority or tradition, choosing to live by rules that help him "maintain order in a world tilting into insanity." He can be hired, but he cannot be bought. He is, as Charles Hoffman has noted, 'Conan the Existentialist': "The consummate self-determining man, alone in a hostile universe." Conan, says Hoffman, knows that life is meaningless: "There is no hope here or hereafter in the cult of my people," he says in *Queen of the Black Coast*. "In this world men struggle and suffer vainly...." Yet this knowledge of the ultimate meaninglessness of man's actions does not cause Conan despair: he "demonstrates how a strong-willed man can create goals, values, and meaning for himself."

Herein, I think, lies a good part of Conan's appeal. Our destiny, he says, does not lie in the stars, or in our noble blood, but in our willingness to create ourselves. The stories in the present volume are all excellent illustrations: in each, Conan is confronted with choices, and he makes his decisions not on the basis of some "noble destiny" to be fulfilled but on what seems, to him, the right course of action at the time. He seizes opportunities to get what he wants, and turns down opportunities that other men would unhesitatingly grasp. He is his own man, and he does things his own way, guided by little more than his whim of the moment and his sense of right and wrong.

But of course, above all the appeal of Robert E. Howard's Conan stories lies in his gifts as a storyteller. He is unsurpassed in his ability to sweep the reader up and bring him *into* the story. So turn the page, and get ready for an exhilarating journey through the historical wonderland of the Hyborian Age.

Rusty Burke
2003

The People of the Black Circle

The People of the Black Circle

I

Death Strikes a King

The king of Vendhya was dying. Through the hot, stifling night the temple gongs boomed and the conchs roared. Their clamor was a faint echo in the gold-domed chamber where Bunda Chand struggled on the velvet-cushioned dais. Beads of sweat glistened on his dark skin; his fingers twisted the gold-worked fabric beneath him. He was young; no spear had touched him, no poison lurked in his wine. But his veins stood out like blue cords on his temples, and his eyes dilated with the nearness of death. Trembling slave-girls knelt at the foot of the dais, and leaning down to him, watching him with passionate intensity, was his sister, the Devi Yasmina. With her was the *wazam*, a noble grown old in the royal court.

She threw up her head in a gusty gesture of wrath and despair as the thunder of the distant drums reached her ears.

"The priests and their clamor!" she exclaimed. "They are no wiser than the leeches who are helpless! Nay, he dies and none can say why. He is dying now – and I stand here helpless, who would burn the whole city and spill the blood of thousands to save him."

"Not a man of Ayodhya but would die in his place, if it might be, Devi," answered the *wazam*. "This poison – "

"I tell you it is not poison!" she cried. "Since his birth he has been guarded so closely that the cleverest poisoners of the East could not reach him. Five skulls bleaching on the Tower of the Kites can testify to attempts which were made – and which failed. As you well know, there are ten men and ten women whose sole duty is to taste his food and wine, and fifty armed warriors guard his chamber as they guard it now. No, it is not poison; it is sorcery – black, ghastly magic – "

She ceased as the king spoke; his livid lips did not move, and there was no recognition in his glassy eyes. But his voice rose in an eery call, indistinct and far away, as if he called to her from beyond vast, wind-blown gulfs.

"Yasmina! Yasmina! My sister, where are you? I can not find you. All is darkness, and the roaring of great winds!"

"Brother!" cried Yasmina, catching his limp hand in a convulsive grasp. "I am here! Do you not know me – "

Her voice died at the utter vacancy of his face. A low confused moaning waned from his mouth. The slave-girls at the foot of the dais whimpered with fear, and Yasmina beat her breast in her anguish.

In another part of the city a man stood in a latticed balcony overlooking a long street in which torches tossed luridly, smokily revealing upturned dark faces and the whites of gleaming eyes. A long-drawn wailing rose from the multitude.

The man shrugged his broad shoulders and turned back into the arabesqued chamber. He was a tall man, compactly built, and richly clad.

"The king is not yet dead, but the dirge is sounded," he said to another man who sat cross-legged on a mat in a corner. This man was clad in a brown camel-hair robe and sandals, and a green turban was on his head. His expression was tranquil, his gaze impersonal.

"The people know he will never see another dawn," this man answered.

The first speaker favored him with a long, searching stare.

"What I can not understand," he said, "is why I have had to wait so long for your masters to strike. If they have slain the king now, why could they not have slain him months ago?"

"Even the arts you call sorcery are governed by cosmic laws," answered the man in the green turban. "The stars direct these actions, as in other affairs. Not even my masters can alter the stars. Not until the heavens were in the proper order could they perform this necromancy." With a long, stained finger-nail he mapped the constellations on the marble-tiled floor. "The slant of the moon presaged evil for the king of Vendhya; the stars are in turmoil, the Serpent in the House of the Elephant. During such juxtaposition, the invisible guardians are removed from the spirit of Bhunda Chand. A path is opened in the unseen realms, and once a point of contact was established, mighty powers were put in play along that path."

"Point of contact?" inquired the other. "Do you mean that lock of Bhunda Chand's hair?"

"Yes. All discarded portions of the human body still remain part of it, attached to it by intangible connections. The priests of Asura have a dim inkling of this truth, and so all nail-trimmings, hair and other waste products of the persons of the royal family are carefully reduced to ashes and the ashes hidden. But at the urgent entreaty of the princess of Khosala, who loved Bhunda Chand vainly, he gave her a lock of his long black hair as a token of remembrance. When my masters decided upon his doom, the lock, in its golden, jewel-crusted case, was stolen from under her pillow while she slept, and another substituted, so like the first that she never knew the difference. Then the genuine lock travelled by camel-caravan up the long, long road to Peshkhauri, thence up the Zhaibar Pass, until it reached the hands of those for whom it was intended."

"Only a lock of hair," murmured the nobleman.

"By which a soul is drawn from its body and across gulfs of echoing space," returned the man on the mat.

The nobleman studied him curiously.

"I do not know if you are a man or a demon, Khemsa," he said at last. "Few of us are what we seem. I, whom the Kshatriyas know as Kerim Shah, a prince from Iranistan, am no greater a masquerader than most men. They are all traitors in one way or another, and half of them know not whom they serve. There at least I have no doubts; for I serve King Yezdigerd of Turan."

"And I the Black Seers of Yimsha," said Khemsa; "and my masters are greater than yours, for they have accomplished by their arts what Yezdigerd could not with a hundred thousand swords."

Outside, the moan of the tortured thousands shuddered up to the stars which crusted the sweating Vendhyan night, and the conchs bellowed like oxen in pain.

In the gardens of the palace the torches glinted on polished helmets and curved swords and gold-chased corselets. All the noble-born fighting-men of Ayodhya were gathered in the great palace or about it, and at each broad-arched gate and door fifty archers stood on guard, with bows in their hands. But Death stalked through the royal palace and none could stay his ghostly tread.

On the dais under the golden dome the king cried out again, racked by awful paroxysms. Again his voice came faintly and far away, and again the Devi bent to him, trembling with a fear that was darker than the terror of death.

"Yasmina!" Again that far, weirdly dreeing cry, from realms immeasurable. "Aid me! I am far from my mortal house! Wizards have drawn my soul through the wind-blown darkness. They seek to snap the silver cord that binds me to my dying body. They cluster around me; their hands are taloned, their eyes are red like flame burning in darkness. *Aie*, save me, my sister! Their fingers sear me like fire! They would slay my body and damn my soul! What is this they bring before me? – *Aie!*"

At the terror in his hopeless cry Yasmina screamed uncontrollably and threw herself bodily upon him in the abandon of her anguish. He was torn by a terrible convulsion; foam flew from his contorted lips and his writhing fingers left their marks on the girl's shoulders. But the glassy blankness passed from his eyes like smoke blown from a fire, and he looked up at his sister with recognition.

"Brother!" she sobbed. "Brother – "

"Swift!" he gasped, and his weakening voice was rational. "I know now what brings me to the pyre. I have been on a far journey and I understand. I have been ensorceled by the wizards of the Himelians. They drew my soul out of my body and far away, into a stone room. There they strove to break the silver cord of life, and thrust my soul into the body of a foul night-weird their sorcery summoned up from hell. Ah! I feel their pull upon me now! Your cry and the grip of your fingers brought me back, but I am going fast. My soul clings to my body, but its hold weakens. Quick – kill me, before they can trap my soul for ever!"

"I can not!" she wailed, smiting her naked breasts.

"Swiftly, I command you!" There was the old imperious note in his failing whisper. "You have never disobeyed me – obey my last command! Send my soul clean to Asura! Haste, lest you damn me to spend eternity as a filthy gaunt of darkness. Strike, I command you! *Strike!*"

Sobbing wildly, Yasmina plucked a jeweled dagger from her girdle and plunged it to the hilt in his breast. He stiffened and then went limp, a grim smile curving his dead lips. Yasmina hurled herself face-down on the rush-covered floor, beating the reeds with her clenched hands. Outside, the gongs and conchs brayed and thundered and the priests gashed themselves with copper knives.

II

A Barbarian from the Hills

Chunder Shan, governor of Peshkhauri, laid down his golden pen and carefully scanned that which he had written on parchment that bore his official seal. He had ruled Peshkhauri so long only because he weighed his every word, spoken or written. Danger breeds caution, and only a wary man lives long in that wild country where the hot Vendhyan plains meet the crags of the Himelians. An hour's ride westward or northward and one crossed the border and was among the hills where men lived by the law of the knife.

The governor was alone in his chamber, seated at his ornately-carven table of inlaid ebony. Through the wide window, open for the coolness, he could see a square of the blue Himelian night, dotted with great white stars. An adjacent parapet was a shadowy line, and further crenelles and embrasures were barely hinted at in the dim starlight. The governor's fortress was strong, and situated outside the walls of the city it guarded. The breeze that stirred the tapestries on the wall brought faint noises from the streets of Peshkhauri – occasional snatches of wailing song, or the thrum of a cithern.

The governor read what he had written, slowly, with his open hand shading his eyes from the bronze butter-lamp, his lips moving. Absently, as he read, he heard the drum of horses' hoofs outside the barbican, the sharp staccato of the guards' challenge. He did not heed, intent upon his letter. It was addressed to the *wazam* of Vendhya, at the royal court of Ayodhya, and it stated, after the customary salutations:

> "Let it be known to your excellency that I have faithfully carried out your excellency's instructions. The seven tribesmen are well guarded in their prison, and I have repeatedly sent word into the hills that their chief come in person to bargain for their release. But he has made no move, except to send word that unless they are freed he will burn Peshkhauri and cover his saddle with my hide, begging your excellency's indulgence. This he is quite capable of attempting, and I have tripled the numbers of the lance guards. The man is not a native of Ghulistan. I can not with certainty predict his next move. But since it is the wish of the Devi – "

He was out of his ivory chair and on his feet facing the arched door, all in one instant. He snatched at the curved sword lying in its ornate scabbard on the table, and then checked the movement.

It was a woman who had entered unannounced, a woman whose gossamer robes did not conceal the rich garments beneath any more than they concealed the suppleness and beauty of her tall, slender figure. A filmy veil fell below her breasts, supported by a flowing head-dress bound about with a triple gold braid and adorned with a golden crescent. Her dark eyes regarded the astonished governor over the veil, and then with an imperious gesture of her white hand, she uncovered her face.

"Devi!" The governor dropped to his knee before her, his surprize and confusion somewhat spoiling the stateliness of his obeisance. With a gesture she motioned him to rise, and he hastened to lead her to the ivory chair, all the while bowing level with his girdle. But his first words were of reproof.

"Your majesty! This was most unwise! The border is unsettled. Raids from the hills are incessant. You came with a large attendance?"

"An ample retinue followed me to Peshkhauri," she answered. "I lodged my people there and came on to the fort with my maid, Gitara."

Chunder Shan groaned in horror.

"Devi! You do not understand the peril. An hour's ride from this spot the hills swarm with barbarians who make a profession of murder and rapine. Women have been stolen and men stabbed between the fort and the city. Peshkhauri is not like your southern provinces – "

"But I am here, and unharmed," she interrupted with a trace of impatience. "I showed my signet ring to the guard at the gate, and to the one outside your door, and they admitted me unannounced, not knowing me, but supposing me to be a secret courier from Ayodhya. Let us not now waste time.

"You have received no word from the chief of the barbarians?"

"None save threats and curses, Devi. He is wary and suspicious. He deems it a trap, and perhaps he is not to be blamed. The Kshatriyas have not always kept their promises to the hill people."

"He must be brought to terms!" broke in Yasmina, the knuckles of her clenched hands showing white.

"I do not understand." The governor shook his head. "When I chanced to capture these seven hillmen, I reported their capture to the *wazam*, as is the custom, and then, before I could hang them, there came an order to hold them and communicate with their chief. This I did, but the man holds aloof, as I have said. These men are of the tribe of Afghulis, but he is a foreigner from the west, and he is called Conan. I have threatened to hang them tomorrow at dawn, if he does not come."

"Good!" exclaimed the Devi. "You have done well. And I will tell you why I have given these orders. My brother – " she faltered, choking, and the governor bowed his head, with the customary gesture of respect for a departed sovereign.

"The king of Vendhya was destroyed by magic," she said at last. "I have devoted my life to the destruction of his murderers. As he died he gave me a clue, and I have followed it. I have read the Book of Skelos, and talked with nameless hermits in the caves below Jhelai. I learned how, and by whom, he was destroyed. His enemies were the Black Seers of Mount Yimsha."

"Asura!" whispered Chunder Shan, paling.

Her eyes knifed him through. "Do you fear them?"

"Who does not, your majesty?" he replied. "They are black devils, haunting the uninhabited hills beyond the Zhaibar. But the sages say that they seldom interfere in the lives of mortal men."

"Why they slew my brother I do not know," she answered. "But I have sworn on the altar of Asura to destroy them! And I need the aid of a man beyond the border. A Kshatriya army, unaided, would never reach Yimsha."

"Aye," muttered Chunder Shan. "You speak the truth there. It would be a fight every step of the way, with hairy hillmen hurling down boulders from every height, and rushing us with their long knives in every valley. The Turanians fought their way through the Himelians once, but how many returned to Khurusun? Few of those who escaped the swords of the Kshatriyas, after the king, your brother, defeated their host on the Jhumda River, ever saw Secunderam again."

"And so I must control men across the border," she said, "men who know the way to Mount Yimsha – "

"But the tribes fear the Black Seers and shun the unholy mountain," broke in the governor.

"Does the chief, Conan, fear them?" she asked.

"Well, as to that," muttered the governor, "I doubt if there is anything that devil fears."

"So I have been told. Therefore he is the man I must deal with. He wishes the release of his seven men. Very well; their ransom shall be the heads of the Black Seers!" Her voice thrummed with hate as she uttered the last words, and her hands clenched at her sides. She looked an image of incarnate passion as she stood there with her head thrown high and her bosom heaving.

Again the governor knelt, for part of his wisdom was the knowledge that a woman in such an emotional tempest is as perilous as a blind cobra to any about her.

"It shall be as you wish, your majesty." Then as she presented a calmer aspect, he rose and ventured to drop a word of warning. "I can not predict what the chief Conan's action will be. The tribesmen are always turbulent, and I have reason to believe that emissaries from the Turanians are stirring them up to raid our borders. As your majesty knows, the Turanians have established themselves in Secunderam and other northern cities, though the hill tribes remain unconquered. King Yezdigerd has long looked southward with greedy lust and perhaps is seeking to gain by treachery what he could not win by force of arms. I have thought that Conan might well be one of his spies."

"We shall see," she answered. "If he loves his followers, he will be at the gates at dawn, to parley. I shall spend the night in the fortress. I came in disguise to Peshkhauri, and lodged my retinue at an inn instead of the palace. Besides my people, only yourself knows of my presence here."

"I shall escort you to your quarters, your majesty," said the governor, and as they emerged from the doorway, he beckoned the warrior on guard there, and the man fell in behind them, spear held at salute. The maid waited, veiled like her mistress, outside the door, and the group traversed a wide, winding corridor, lighted by smoky torches, and reached the quarters reserved for visiting notables – generals and viceroys, mostly; none of the royal family had ever honored the fortress before. Chunder Shan had a perturbed feeling that the suite was not suitable to such an exalted personage as the Devi, and though she sought to make him feel at ease in her presence, he was glad when she dismissed him and he bowed himself out. All the menials of the fort had been summoned to serve his royal guest – though he did not divulge her identity – and he stationed a squad of spearmen before her doors, among them the warrior who had guarded his own chamber. In his preoccupation he forgot to replace the man.

The governor had not been gone long from her, when Yasmina suddenly remembered something else which she had wished to discuss with him, but had forgotten until that moment. It concerned the past actions of one Kerim Shah, a nobleman from Iranistan, who had dwelt for awhile in Peshkhauri before coming on to the court at Ayodhya. A vague suspicion concerning the man had been stirred by a glimpse of him in Peshkhauri that night. She wondered if he had followed her from Ayodhya. Being a truly remarkable Devi, she did not summon the governor to her again, but hurried out into the corridor alone, and hastened toward his chamber.

Chunder Shan, entering his chamber, closed the door and went to his table. There he took the letter he had been writing and tore it to bits. Scarcely had he finished when he heard something drop softly onto the parapet adjacent to the window. He looked up to see a figure loom briefly against the stars, and then a man dropped lightly into the room. The light glinted on a long sheen of steel in his hand.

"Shhhh!" he warned. "Don't make a noise, you bastard, or I'll send the devil a henchman!"

The governor checked his motion toward the sword on the table. He was within reach of the yard-long Zhaibar knife that glittered in the intruder's fist, and he knew the desperate quickness of a hillman.

The invader was a tall man, at once strong and supple. He was dressed like a hillman, but his dark features and blazing blue eyes did not match his garb. Chunder Shan had never seen a man like him; he was not an Easterner, but some barbarian from the West. But his aspect was as untamed and formidable as any of the hairy tribesmen who haunt the hills of Ghulistan.

"You come like a thief in the night," commented the governor, recovering some of his composure, although he remembered that there was no guard within call. Still, the hillman could not know that.

"I climbed a bastion," snarled the intruder. "A guard thrust his head over the battlement in time for me to rap it with my knife hilt."

"You are Conan?"

"Who else? You sent word into the hills that you wished for me to come and parley with you. Well, by Crom, I've come! Keep away from that table or I'll gut you."

"I merely wish to seat myself," answered the governor, carefully sinking into the ivory chair, which he wheeled away from the table. Conan moved restlessly before him, glancing suspiciously at the door, thumbing the razor edge of his three-foot knife. He did not walk like an Afghuli, and was bluntly direct where the East is subtle.

"You have seven of my men," he said abruptly. "You refused the ransom I offered. What the devil do you want?"

"Let us discuss terms," answered Chunder Shan cautiously.

"Terms?" There was a timbre of dangerous anger in his voice. "What do you mean? Haven't I offered you gold?"

Chunder Shan laughed.

"Gold? There is more gold in Peshkhauri than you ever saw."

"You're a liar," retorted Conan. "I've seen the *suk* of the goldsmiths in Khurusun."

"Well – more than any Afghuli ever saw," amended Chunder Shan. "And it is but a drop of all the treasure of Vendhya. Why should we desire gold? It would be more to our advantage to hang these seven thieves."

Conan ripped out a sulphurous oath and the long blade quivered in his grip as the muscles rose in ridges on his brown arm.

"I'll split your head like a ripe melon!"

A wild blue flame flickered in the hillman's eyes, but Chunder Shan shrugged his shoulders, though keeping an eye on the keen steel.

"You can kill me easily, and probably escape over the wall afterwards. But that would not save the seven tribesmen. They would surely hang them. And these men are headmen among the Afghulis."

"I know it," snarled Conan. "The tribe is baying like wolves at my heels because I have not secured their release. Tell me in plain words what you want, because by Crom, if there's no other way, I'll raise a horde and lead it to the very gates of Peshkhauri!"

Looking at the man as he stood squarely, knife in fist and eyes glaring, Chunder Shan did not doubt that he was capable of it. The governor did not believe any hill-horde could take Peshkhauri, but he did not wish a devastated countryside.

"There is a mission you must perform," he said, choosing his words with as much care as if they had been razors. "There – "

Conan had sprung back, wheeling to face the door at the same instant, lips asnarl. His barbarian ears had caught the sound noiseless to Chunder Shan – the quick tread of soft slippers outside the door. The next instant the door was thrown open and a slim, silk-robed form entered hastily, pulling the door shut – then stopping short at the sight of the hillman.

Chunder Shan sprang up, his heart jumping into his mouth.

"Devi!" he cried involuntarily, losing his head momentarily in his fright.

"Devi!" It was like an explosive echo from the hillman's lips. Chunder Shan saw recognition and intent flame up in the fierce blue eyes. The governor shouted desperately and caught at his sword, but the hillman moved with the devastating speed of a hurricane. He sprang, knocked the governor sprawling with a savage blow of his knife hilt, swept up the astounded Devi in one brawny arm and leaped for the window. Chunder Shan, struggling frantically to his feet, saw the man poise an instant on the sill, in a flutter of silken skirts and white limbs that was his royal captive, and heard his fierce, exultant snarl: "*Now* dare to hang my men!" and then Conan leaped to the parapet and was gone. A wild scream floated back to the governor's ears.

"Guard! *Guard!*" screamed the governor, struggling up and running drunkenly

to the door. He tore it open and reeled into the hall. His shouts re-echoed along the corridors and warriors came running, gaping to see the governor holding his broken head, from which the blood streamed.

"Turn out the lancers!" he roared. "There has been an abduction!" Even in his frenzy he had enough sense left to withhold the full truth. He stopped short as he heard a sudden drum of hoofs outside, a frantic scream and a wild yell of barbaric exultation.

Followed by the bewildered guardsmen, the governor raced for the stair. In the courtyard of the fort a force of lancers always stood by saddled steeds, ready to ride at an instant's notice. Chunder Shan sent this squadron flying after the fugitive, though his head swam so he had to hold with both hands to the saddle. He did not divulge the identity of the victim, but said merely that the noblewoman who had borne the royal signet-ring had been carried away by the chief of the Afghulis. The abductor was out of sight and hearing, but they knew the path he would strike – the road that runs straight to the mouth of the Zhaibar. There was no moon; peasant huts rose dimly in the starlight. Behind them fell away the grim bastion of the fort, and the towers of Peshkhauri. Ahead of them loomed the black walls of the Himelians.

III

Khemsa uses Magic

In the confusion that reigned in the fortress while the guard was being turned out, no one noticed that the girl who had accompanied the Devi slipped out the great arched gate and vanished in the darkness. She ran straight for the city, her garments tucked high. She did not follow the open road, but cut straight through fields and over slopes, avoiding fences and leaping irrigation ditches as surely as if it were broad daylight, and as easily as if she were a trained masculine runner. The hoof-drum of the guardsmen had faded away up the hill road before she reached the city wall. She did not go to the great gate, beneath whose arch men leaned on spears and craned their necks into the darkness, discussing the unwonted activity about the fortress. She skirted the wall until she reached a certain point where the spire of a tower was visible above the battlements. Then she placed her hands to her mouth and voiced a low weird call that carried strangely.

Almost instantly a head appeared at an embrasure and a rope came wriggling down the wall. She seized it, placed a foot in the loop at the end, and waved her arm. Then quickly and smoothly she was drawn up the sheer stone curtain. An instant later she scrambled over the merlons and stood up on a flat roof which covered a house that was built against the wall. There was an open trap there, and a man in a camel-hair robe who silently coiled the rope, not showing in any way the strain of exertion from hauling a full-grown woman up a forty foot wall.

"Where is Kerim Shah?" she gasped, panting after her long run.

"Asleep in the house below. You have news?"

"Conan has stolen the Devi out of the fortress and carried her away into the hills!" She blurted out her news in a rush, the words stumbling over each other.

Khemsa showed no emotion, but merely nodded his turbaned head.

"Kerim Shah will be glad to hear that," he said.

"Wait!" The girl threw her supple arms about his neck. She was panting hard, but not only from exertion. Her eyes blazed like black jewels in the starlight. Her upturned face was close to Khemsa's, but though he submitted to her embrace, he did not return it.

"Do not tell the Hyrkanian!" she panted. "Let us use this knowledge ourselves! The governor has gone into the hills with his riders, but he might as well chase a ghost. He has not told anyone that it was the Devi who was kidnapped. None in Peshkhauri or the fort knows it except us!"

"But what good does it do us?" the man expostulated. "My masters sent me with Kerim Shah to aid him in every way – "

"Aid yourself!" she cried fiercely. "Shake off your yoke!"

"You mean – disobey my masters?" he gasped, and she felt his whole body turn cold under her arms.

"Aye!" she shook him in the fury of her emotion. "You too are a magician! Why will you be a slave, using your powers only to elevate others? Use your arts for yourself!"

"That is forbidden!" He was shaking as if with an ague. "I am not one of the Black Circle. Only by the command of the masters do I dare to use the knowledge they have taught me."

"But you *can* use it!" she argued passionately. "Do as I beg you! Of course Conan has taken the Devi to hold as hostage against the seven tribesmen in the governor's prison. Destroy them, so Chunder Shan can not use them to buy back the Devi. Then let us go into the mountains and take her from the Afghulis. They can not stand against your sorcery with their knives! The treasure of the Vendhyan kings will be ours as ransom – and then when we have it in our hands, we can trick them, and sell her to the king of Turan. We shall have wealth beyond our maddest dreams! With it we can buy warriors! We will take Khorbhul, oust the Turanians from the hills, and send our hosts southward; become king and queen of an empire!"

Khemsa too was panting, shaking like a leaf in her grasp; his face showed grey in the starlight, beaded with great drops of perspiration.

"I love you!" she cried fiercely, writhing her body against his, almost strangling him in her wild embrace, shaking him in her abandon. "I will make a king of you! For love of you I betrayed my mistress; for love of me betray your masters! Why fear the Black Seers? By your love for me you have broken one of their laws already! Break the rest! You are strong as they!"

A man of ice could not have withstood the searing heat of her passion and fury. With an inarticulate cry he crushed her to him, bending her backward and showering gasping kisses on her eyes, face and lips.

"I'll do it!" His voice was thick with laboring emotions. He staggered like a drunken man. "The arts they have taught me shall work for me, not for my masters. We shall be rulers of the world – of the world – "

"Come then!" Twisting lithely out of his embrace, she seized his hand and led him toward the trap-door. "First we must make sure that the governor does not exchange those seven Afghulis for the Devi."

He moved like a man in a daze, until they had descended a ladder and she paused in the chamber below. Kerim Shah lay on a couch motionless, an arm across his face as though to shield his sleeping eyes from the soft light of a brass lamp. She plucked Khemsa's arm and made a quick gesture across her own throat. Khemsa lifted his hand, then his expression changed and he drew away.

"I have eaten his salt," he muttered. "Besides he can not interfere with us." He led the girl through a door that opened on a winding stair. After their soft tread had faded into silence, the man on the couch sat up. Kerim Shah wiped the sweat from his face. A knife thrust he did not dread, but he feared Khemsa as a man fears a poisonous reptile.

"People who plot on roofs should remember to lower their voices," he muttered. "But as Khemsa has turned against his masters, and as he was my only contact with them, I can count on their aid no longer. From now on I play the game in my own way."

Rising to his feet he went quickly to a table, drew pen and parchment from his girdle and scribbled a few succinct lines.

"To Khosru Khan, governor of Secunderam: the Cimmerian Conan has carried the Devi Yasmina to the villages of the Afghulis. It is an opportunity to get the Devi into our hands, as the king has so long desired. Send three thousand horsemen at once. I will meet them in the valley of Gurashah with native guides." And he signed it with a name that was not in the least like Kerim Shah.

Then from a golden cage he drew forth a carrier pigeon, to whose leg he made fast the parchment, rolled into a tiny cylinder and secured with gold wire. Then he went quickly to a casement and tossed the bird into the night. It wavered on fluttering wings, balanced, and was gone like a flitting shadow. Catching up helmet, sword and cloak, Kerim Shah hurried out of the chamber and down the winding stair.

The prison quarters of Peshkhauri were separated from the rest of the city by a massive wall, in which was set a single iron-bound door under an arch. Over the arch burned a lurid red cresset, and beside the door stood – or squatted – a warrior with spear and shield.

This warrior, leaning on his spear, and yawning from time to time, started suddenly to his feet. He had not thought he had dozed, but a man was standing before him, a man he had not heard approach. The man wore a camel-hair robe and a green turban. In the flickering light of the cresset his features were shadowy, but a pair of lambent eyes shone surprizingly in the lurid glow.

"Who comes?" demanded the warrior, presenting his spear. "Who are you?"

The stranger did not seem perturbed, though the spear point touched his bosom. His eyes held the warrior's with strange intensity.

"What are you obliged to do?" he asked, strangely.

"To guard the gate!" The warrior spoke thickly and mechanically; he stood rigid as a statue, his eyes slowly glazing.

"You lie! You are obliged to obey me! You have looked into my eyes, and your soul is no longer your own. Open that door!"

Stiffly, with the wooden features of an image, the guard wheeled about, drew a great key from his girdle, turned it in the massive lock and swung open the door. Then he stood at attention, his unseeing stare straight ahead of him.

A woman glided from the shadows and laid an eager hand on the mesmerist's arm.

"Bid him fetch us horses, Khemsa," she whispered.

"No need of that," answered the Rakhsha. Lifting his voice slightly he spoke to the guardsman. "I have no more use for you. Kill yourself!"

Like a man in a trance the warrior thrust the butt of his spear against the base of the wall, and placed the keen head against his body, just below the ribs. Then slowly, stolidly, he leaned against it with all his weight, so that it transfixed his body and came out between his shoulders. Sliding down the shaft he lay still, the spear jutting above him its full length, like a horrible stalk growing out of his back.

The girl stared down at him in morbid fascination, until Khemsa took her arm and led her through the gate. Torches lighted a narrow space between the outer wall and a lower inner one, in which were arched doors at regular intervals. A warrior paced this enclosure, and when the gate opened he came sauntering up, so secure in his knowledge of the prison's strength that he was not suspicious until Khemsa and the girl emerged from the archway. Then it was too late. The Rakhsha did not waste time in hypnotism, though his action savored of magic to the girl. The guard lowered his spear threateningly, opening his mouth to shout an alarm that would bring spearmen swarming out of the guard-rooms at either end of the alley-way. Khemsa flicked the spear aside with his left hand, as a man might flick a straw, and his right flashed out and back, seeming gently to caress the warrior's neck in passing. And the guard pitched on his face without a sound, his head lolling on a broken neck.

Khemsa did not glance at him, but went straight to one of the arched doors and placed his open hand against the heavy bronze lock. With a rending shudder the portal buckled inward. As the girl followed him through, she saw that the thick teak wood hung in splinters, the bronze bolts were bent and twisted from their sockets, and the great hinges broken and disjointed. A thousand pound battering ram with forty men to swing it could have shattered the barrier no more completely. Khemsa was drunk with freedom and the exercise of his power, glorying in his might and flinging his strength about as a young giant exercises his thews with unnecessary vigor in the exultant pride of his prowess.

The broken door let them into a small courtyard, lit by a cresset. Opposite the door was a wide grille of iron bars. A hairy hand was visible, gripping one of these bars, and in the darkness behind them glimmered the whites of eyes.

Khemsa stood silent for a space, gazing into the shadows from which those glimmering eyes gave back his stare with burning intensity. Then his hand went into his robe and came out again, and from his opening fingers a shimmering feather of sparkling dust sifted to the flags. Instantly a flare of green fire lighted the enclosure. In the brief glare the forms of seven men, standing motionless behind the bars, were limned in vivid detail; tall, hairy men in ragged hillmen's garments. They did not speak, but in their eyes blazed the fear of death, and their hairy fingers gripped the bars.

The fire died out but the glow remained, a quivering ball of lambent green that pulsed and shimmered on the flags before Khemsa's feet. The wide gaze of the tribesmen was fixed upon it. It wavered, elongated; it turned into a luminous green smoke spiralling upward. It twisted and writhed like a great shadowy serpent, then broadened and billowed out in shining folds and whorls. It grew to a cloud moving silently over the flags – straight toward the grille. The men watched its coming with dilated eyes; the bars quivered with the grip of their desperate fingers. Bearded lips parted but no sound came forth. The green cloud rolled on the bars and blotted them from sight; like a fog it oozed through the grille and hid the men within. From the enveloping folds came a strangled gasp, as of a man plunged suddenly under the surface of water. That was all.

Khemsa touched the girl's arm, as she stood with parted lips and dilated eyes. Mechanically she turned away with him, looking back over her shoulder. Already the mist was thinning; close to the bars she saw a pair of sandalled feet, the toes turned upward – she glimpsed the indistinct outlines of seven still, prostrate shapes –

"And now for a steed swifter than the fastest horse ever bred in a mortal stable," Khemsa was saying. "We will be in Afghulistan before dawn."

IV

An Encounter in the Pass

Yasmina Devi could never clearly remember the details of her abduction. The unexpectedness and violence stunned her; she had only a confused impression of a whirl of happenings – the terrifying grip of a mighty arm, the blazing eyes of her abductor, and his hot breath burning on her flesh. The leap through the window to the parapet, the mad race across battlements and roofs when the fear of falling froze her, the reckless descent of a rope bound to a merlon – he went down almost at a run, his captive folded limply over his brawny shoulder – all this was a befuddled tangle in the Devi's mind. She retained a more vivid memory of him running fleetly into the shadows of the trees, carrying her like a child, and vaulting into the saddle of a fierce Bhalkhana stallion which reared and snorted. Then there was a sensation of flying, and the racing hoofs were striking sparks of fire from the flinty road as the stallion swept up the slopes.

As the girl's mind cleared, her first sensations were furious rage and shame. She was appalled. The rulers of the golden kingdoms south of the Himelians were considered little short of divine; and she was the Devi of Vendhya! Fright was submerged in regal wrath. She cried out furiously and began struggling. She, Yasmina, to be carried on the saddle-bow of a hill chief, like a common wench of the market-place! He merely hardened his massive thews slightly against her writhings, and for the first time in her life she experienced the coercion of superior physical strength. His arms felt like iron about her slender limbs. He glanced down at her and grinned hugely. His teeth glimmered whitely in the starlight. The reins lay loose on the stallion's flowing mane, and every thew and fiber of the great beast strained as he hurtled along the boulder-strewn trail. But Conan sat easily, almost carelessly, in the saddle, riding like a centaur.

"You hill-bred dog!" she panted, quivering with the impact of shame, anger and the realization of helplessness. "You dare – you *dare*! Your life shall pay for this! Where are you taking me?"

"To the villages of Afghulistan," he answered, casting a glance over his shoulder. Behind them, beyond the slopes they had traversed, torches were tossing on the walls of the fortress and he glimpsed a flare of light that meant the great gate had been opened. And he laughed, a deep-throated boom gusty as the hill wind.

"The governor has sent his riders after us," he laughed. "By Crom, we will lead him a merry chase! What do you think, Devi – will they pay seven lives for a Kshatriya princess?"

"They will send an army to hang you and your spawn of devils," she promised him with conviction. He laughed gustily and shifted her to a more comfortable position in his arms. But she took this as a fresh outrage, and renewed her vain struggles, until she saw that her efforts were only amusing him. Besides, her light silken garments, floating on the wind, were being outrageously disarranged by her struggles. She concluded that a scornful submission was the better part of dignity, and lapsed into a smoldering quiescence.

She felt even her anger being submerged by awe as they entered the mouth of the Pass, lowering like a black well mouth in the blacker walls that rose like colossal ramparts to bar their way. It was as if a gigantic knife had cut the Zhaibar out of walls of solid rock. On either hand sheer slopes pitched up for thousands of feet, and the mouth of the Pass was dark as hate. Even Conan could not see with any accuracy, but he knew the road, even by night. And knowing that armed men were racing through the starlight after him, he did not check the stallion's speed. The great brute was not yet showing fatigue. He thundered along the road that followed the valley bed, labored up a slope, swept along a low ridge where treacherous shale on either hand lurked for the unwary, and came upon a trail that followed the lap of the left-hand wall.

Not even Conan could spy, in that darkness, an ambush set by Zhaibar tribesmen. It was as they swept past the black mouth of a gorge that opened into the Pass that a javelin swished through the air and thudded home behind the stallion's straining shoulder. The great beast let out his life in a shuddering sob and stumbled, going headlong in full mid-stride. But Conan had recognized the flight and stroke of the javelin, and he acted with spring-steel quickness.

As the horse fell he leaped clear, holding the girl aloft to guard her from

striking boulders. He hit on his feet like a cat, thrust her into a cleft of rock, and wheeled toward the outer darkness, drawing his knife.

Yasmina, confused by the rapidity of events, not quite sure just what had happened, saw a vague shape rush out of the darkness, bare feet slapping softly on the rock, ragged garments whipping on the wind of his haste. She glimpsed the flicker of steel, heard the lightning crack of stroke, parry and counter-stroke, and the crunch of bone as Conan's long knife split the other's skull.

Conan sprang back, crouching in the shelter of the rocks. Out in the night men were moving and a stentorian voice roared: "What, you dogs! Do you flinch? In, curse you, and take them!"

Conan started, peered into the darkness and lifted his voice.

"Yar Afzal! Is it you?"

There sounded a startled imprecation, and the voice called warily.

"Conan? Is it you, Conan?"

"Aye!" The Cimmerian laughed. "Come forth, you old war-dog. I've slain one of your men."

There was movement among the rocks, a light flared dimly, and then a flame appeared and came bobbing toward him, and as it approached, a fierce bearded countenance grew out of the darkness. The man who carried it held it high, thrust forward, and craned his neck to peer among the boulders it lighted, the other hand gripping a great curved tulwar. Conan stepped forward, sheathing his knife, and the other roared a greeting.

"Aye, it is Conan! Come out of your rocks, dogs! It is Conan!"

Others pressed into the wavering circle of light – wild, ragged, bearded men, with eyes like wolves, and long blades in their fists. They did not see Yasmina, for she was hidden by Conan's massive body. But peeping from her covert, she knew icy fear for the first time that night. These men were more like wolves than human beings.

"What are you hunting in the Zhaibar by night, Yar Afzal?" Conan demanded of the burly chief. He grinned like a bearded ghoul.

"Who knows what might come up the Pass after dark? We Wazulis are night hawks. But what of you, Conan?"

"I have a prisoner," answered the Cimmerian. And moving aside he disclosed the cowering girl. Reaching a long arm into the crevice he drew her trembling forth. Her imperious bearing was gone. She stared timidly at the ring of bearded faces that hemmed her in, and was grateful for the strong arm that clasped her possessively. The torch was thrust close to her, and there was a sucking intake of breath about the ring.

"She is my captive," Conan warned, glancing pointedly at the feet of the man he had slain, just visible within the ring of light. "I was taking her to Afghulistan, but now you have slain my horse, and the Kshatriyas are close behind me."

"Come with us to my village," suggested Yar Afzal. "We have horses hidden in the gorge. They can never follow us in the darkness. They are close behind you, you say?"

"So close that I hear now the clink of their hoofs on the flint," answered Conan grimly. Instantly there was movement; the torch was dashed out and the ragged shapes melted like phantoms into the darkness. Conan swept up the Devi in his arms, and she did not resist. The rocky ground hurt her slim feet in their soft slippers and she felt very small and helpless in that brutish, primordial blackness among those colossal, nighted crags.

Feeling her shiver in the wind that moaned down the defiles, Conan jerked a ragged cloak from its owner's shoulders and wrapped it about her. He also hissed a warning in her ear, ordering her to make no sound. She did not hear the distant clink of shod hoofs on rock that warned the keen-eared hillmen; but she was far too frightened to disobey, in any event.

She could see nothing but a few faint stars far above, but she knew by the deepening darkness when they entered the gorge mouth. There was a stir about them, the uneasy movement of horses. A few muttered words, and Conan mounted the horse of the man he had killed, lifting the girl up in front of him. Like phantoms except for the click of their hoofs, the band swept away up the shadowy gorge. Behind them on the trail they left the dead horse and the dead man, which were found less than half an hour later by the riders from the fortress, who recognized the man as a Wazuli and drew their own conclusions accordingly.

Yasmina, snuggled warmly in her captor's arms, grew drowsy in spite of herself. The motion of the horse, though it was uneven, uphill and down, yet possessed a certain rhythm which combined with weariness and emotional exhaustion to force sleep upon her. She had lost all sense of time or direction. They moved in soft thick darkness, in which she sometimes glimpsed vaguely gigantic walls sweeping up like black ramparts, or great crags shouldering the stars; at times she sensed echoing depths beneath them, or felt the wind of dizzy heights blowing cold about her. Gradually these things faded into a dreamy unwakefulness in which the clink of hoofs and the creak of saddles were like the irrelevant sounds in a dream.

She was vaguely aware when the motion ceased and she was lifted down and carried a few steps. Then she was laid down on something soft and rustling, and something – a folded coat perhaps – was thrust under her head, and the cloak in which she was wrapped was carefully tucked about her. She heard Yar Afzal laugh.

"A rare prize, Conan; fit mate for a chief of the Afghulis."

"Not for me," came Conan's answering rumble. "This wench will buy the lives of my seven headmen, blast their souls."

That was the last she heard as she sank into dreamless slumber.

She slept while armed men rode through the dark hills, and the fate of kingdoms hung in the balance. Through the shadowy gorges and defiles that night there rang the hoofs of galloping horses, and the starlight glimmered on helmets and curved blades, until the ghoulish shapes that haunt the crags stared into the darkness from ravine and boulder and wondered what things were afoot.

A band of these sat gaunt horses in the black pit-mouth of a gorge as the hurrying hoofs swept past. Their leader, a well-built man in a helmet and gilt-braided cloak, held up his hand warningly, until the riders had sped on. Then he laughed softly.

"They must have lost the trail! Or else they have found that Conan has already reached the Afghuli villages. It will take many riders to smoke out that hive. There will be squadrons riding up the Zhaibar by dawn."

"If there is fighting in the hills there will be looting," muttered a voice behind him, in the dialect of the Irakzai.

"There will be looting," answered the man with the helmet. "But first it is our business to reach the valley of Gurashah and await the riders that will be galloping southward from Secunderam before daylight."

He lifted his reins and rode out of the defile, his men falling in behind him – thirty ragged phantoms in the starlight.

V
The Black Stallion

The sun was well up when Yasmina awoke. She did not start and stare blankly, wondering where she was. She awoke with full knowledge of all that had occurred. Her supple limbs were stiff from her long ride, and her firm flesh still seemed to feel the contact of the muscular arms that had borne her so far.

She was lying on a sheepskin covering a pallet of leaves on a hard-beaten dirt floor. A folded sheepskin coat was under her head, and she was wrapped in a ragged cloak. She was in a large room, the walls of which were crudely but strongly built of uncut rocks, plastered with sun-baked mud. Heavy beams supported a roof of the same kind, in which showed a trap-door up to which led a ladder. There were no windows in the thick walls, only loop-holes. There was one door, a sturdy bronze affair that must have been looted from some Vendhyan border tower. Opposite it was a wide opening in the wall, with no door, but several strong wooden bars in place. Beyond them Yasmina saw a magnificent black stallion munching a pile of dried grass. The building was fort, dwelling-place and stable in one.

At the other end of the room a girl in the vest and baggy trousers of a hillwoman squatted beside a small fire, cooking strips of meat on an iron grid laid over blocks of stone. There was a sooty cleft in the wall a few feet from the floor, and some of the smoke found its way out there. The rest floated in blue wisps about the room.

The hill-girl glanced at Yasmina over her shoulder, displaying a bold, handsome face, and then continued her cooking. Voices boomed outside, then the door was kicked open, and Conan strode in. He looked more enormous than ever with the morning sunlight behind him, and Yasmina noted some details that had escaped her the night before. His garments were clean and not ragged. The broad Bakhariot girdle that supported his knife in its ornamented scabbard would have matched the robes of a prince, and there was a glint of fine Turanian mail under his shirt.

"Your captive is awake, Conan," said the Wazuli girl, and he grunted, strode up to the fire and swept the strips of mutton off into a stone dish. The squatting girl laughed up at him, with some spicy jest, and he grinned wolfishly, and hooking a toe under her haunches, tumbled her sprawling onto the floor. She seemed to derive considerable amusement from this bit of rough horse-play, but Conan paid no more heed to her. Producing a great hunk of bread from somewhere, with a copper jug of wine, he carried the lot to Yasmina, who had risen from her pallet and was regarding him doubtfully.

"Rough fare for a Devi, girl, but our best," he grunted. "It will fill your belly, at least."

He set the platter on the floor and she was suddenly aware of a ravenous hunger. Making no comment she seated herself cross-legged on the floor, and taking the dish in her lap, she began to eat, using her fingers, which were all she had in the way of table utensils. After all, adaptability is one of the tests of true aristocracy. Conan stood looking down at her, his thumbs hooked in his girdle. He never sat cross-legged, after the Eastern fashion.

"Where am I?" she asked abruptly.

"In the hut of Yar Afzal, the chief of the Khurum Wazulis," he answered. "Afghulistan lies a good many miles further on to the west. We'll hide here awhile. The Kshatriyas are beating up the hills for you – several of their squads have been cut up by the tribes already."

"What are you going to do?" she asked.

"Keep you until Chunder Shan is willing to trade back my seven cow-thieves," he grunted. "Women of the Wazulis are crushing ink out of *shoki* leaves, and after awhile you can write a letter to the governor."

A touch of her old imperious wrath shook her, as she thought how maddeningly her plans had gone awry, leaving her captive of the very man she had plotted to get into her power. She flung down the dish, with the remnants of her meal, and sprang to her feet, tense with anger.

"I will not write a letter! If you do not take me back, they will hang your seven men, and a thousand more besides!"

The Wazuli girl laughed mockingly, Conan scowled, and then the door opened and Yar Afzal came swaggering in. The Wazuli chief was as tall as Conan, and of greater girth, but he looked fat and slow beside the hard compactness of the Cimmerian. He plucked his red-stained beard and stared meaningly at the Wazuli

girl, and that wench rose and skurried out without delay. Then Yar Afzal turned to his guest.

"The damnable people murmur, Conan," quoth he. "They wish me to murder you and take the girl to hold for ransom. They say that anyone can tell by her garments that she is a noble lady. They say why should the Afghuli dogs profit by her, when they take the risk of guarding her?"

"Lend me your horse," said Conan. "I'll take her and go."

"Pish!" boomed Yar Afzal. "Do you think I can't handle my own people? I'll have them dancing in their shirts if they cross me! They don't love you – or any outlander – but you saved my life once, and I will not forget. Come out, though, Conan; a scout has returned."

Conan hitched at his girdle and followed the chief outside. They closed the door after them, and Yasmina peeped through a loop-hole. She looked out on a level space before the hut. At the further end of that space there was a cluster of mud and stone huts, and she saw naked children playing among the boulders, and the slim, erect women of the hills going about their tasks.

Directly before the chief's hut a circle of hairy, ragged men squatted, facing the door. Conan and Yar Afzal stood a few paces before the door, and between them and the ring of warriors another man sat cross-legged. This one was addressing his chief in the harsh accents of the Wazuli which Yasmina could scarcely understand, though as part of her royal education she had been taught the languages of Iranistan and the kindred tongues of Ghulistan.

"I talked with a Dagozai who saw the riders last night," said the scout. "He was lurking near when they came to the spot where we ambushed the lord Conan. He overheard their speech. Chunder Shan was with them. They found the dead horse, and one of the men recognized it as Conan's. Then they found the man Conan slew, and knew him for a Wazuli. So it seemed to them that Conan had been slain and the girl taken by the Wazuli, so they turned aside from their purpose of following to Afghulistan. But they did not know from which village the dead man was come, and we had left no trail a Kshatriya could follow.

"So they rode to the nearest Wazuli village, which was the village of Jugra, and burnt it and slew many of the people. But the men of Khojur came upon them in darkness and slew some of them, and wounded the governor. So the survivors retired down the Zhaibar in the darkness before dawn. But they returned with reinforcements before sunrise, and there has been skirmishing and fighting in the hills all morning. It is said that a great army is being raised to sweep the hills about the Zhaibar. The tribes are whetting their knives and laying ambushes in every pass from here to Gurashah valley. Moreover, Kerim Shah has returned to the hills."

A grunt went around the circle and Yasmina leaned closer to the loop-hole at the name she had begun to mistrust.

"Where went he?" demanded Yar Afzal.

"The Dagozai did not know; with him were thirty Irakzai of the lower villages. They rode into the hills and disappeared."

"These Irakzai are jackals that follow a lion for crumbs," growled Yar Afzal. "They have been lapping up thc coins Kerim Shah scatters among the border tribes to buy men like horses. I like him not, for all hc is our kinsman from Iranistan."

"He's not even that," said Conan. "I know him of old. He's an Hyrkanian, a spy of Yezdigerd's. If I catch him I'll hang his hide to a tamarisk."

"But the Kshatriyas!" clamored the men in the semi-circle. "Are we to squat on our haunches until they smoke us out? They will learn at last in which Wazuli village the wench is held! We are not loved by the Zhaibari; they will help the Kshatriyas hunt us out."

"Let them come," grunted Yar Afzal. "We can hold the defiles against a host."

One of the men leaped up and shook his fist at Conan.

"Are we to take all the risks while he reaps the rewards?" he howled. "Are we to fight his battles for him?"

With a stride Conan reached him and bent slightly to stare full into his hairy face. The Cimmerian had not drawn his long knife, but his left hand grasped the scabbard, jutting the hilt suggestively forward.

"I ask no man to fight my battles," he said softly. "Draw your blade if you dare, you yapping dog!"

The Wazuli started back, snarling like a cat.

"Dare to touch me and here are fifty men to rend you apart!" he screeched.

"What!" roared Yar Afzal, his face purpling with wrath. His whiskers bristled, his belly swelled with his rage. "Are you chief of Khurum? Do the Wazulis take orders from Yar Afzal, or from a low-bred cur?"

The man cringed before his invincible chief, and Yar Afzal, striding up to him, seized him by the throat and choked him until his face was turning black. Then he hurled the man savagely against the ground and stood over him with his tulwar in his hand.

"Is there any who questions my authority?" he roared, and his warriors looked down sullenly as his bellicose glare swept their semi-circle. Yar Afzal grunted scornfully and sheathed his weapon with a gesture that was the apex of insult. Then he kicked the fallen agitator with a concentrated vindictiveness that brought howls from his victim.

"Get down the valley to the watchers on the heights and bring word if they have seen anything," commanded Yar Afzal, and the man went, shaking with fear and grinding his teeth with fury.

Yar Afzal then seated himself ponderously on a stone, growling in his beard. Conan stood near him, legs braced apart, thumbs hooked in his girdle, narrowly watching the assembled warriors. They stared at him sullenly, not daring to brave Yar Afzal's fury, but hating the foreigner as only a hillman can hate.

"Now listen to me, you sons of nameless dogs, while I tell you what the lord Conan and I have planned to fool the Kshatriyas –" the boom of Yar Afzal's bull-like voice followed the discomfited warrior as he slunk away from the assembly.

The man passed by the cluster of huts, where women who had seen his defeat laughed at him and called stinging comments, and hastened on along the trail that wound among spurs and rocks toward the valley head.

Just as he rounded the first turn that took him out of sight of the village, he stopped short, gaping stupidly. He had not believed it possible for a stranger to enter the valley of Khurum without being detected by the hawk-eyed watchers along the heights, yet a man sat cross-legged on a low ledge beside the path – a man in a camel-hair robe and a green turban.

The Wazuli's mouth gaped for a yell, and his hand leaped to his knife hilt. But at that instant his eyes met those of the stranger and the cry died in his throat, his fingers went limp. He stood like a statue, his own eyes glazed and vacant.

For minutes the scene held motionless, then the man on the ledge drew a cryptic symbol in the dust on the rock with his forefinger. The Wazuli did not see him place anything within the compass of that emblem, but presently something gleamed there – a round, shiny black ball that looked like polished jade. The man in the green turban took this up and tossed it to the Wazuli who mechanically caught it.

"Carry this to Yar Afzal," he said, and the Wazuli turned like an automaton and went back along the path, holding the black jade ball in his outstretched hand. He did not even turn his head to the renewed jeers of the women as he passed the huts. He did not seem to hear.

The man on the ledge gazed after him with a cryptic smile. A girl's head rose above the rim of the ledge and she looked at him with admiration and a touch of fear that had not been present the night before.

"Why did you do that?" she asked.

He ran his fingers through her dark locks caressingly.

"Are you still dizzy from your flight on the *horse-of-air* that you doubt my wisdom?" he laughed. "As long as Yar Afzal lives, Conan will bide safe among the Wazuli fighting-men. It would be easier, even for me, to trap the Cimmerian as he flees alone with the girl, than to seek to slay him and take her from among them. It takes no wizard to predict what the Wazulis will do, and what Conan will do, when my victim hands the globe of Yezud to the chief of Khurum."

Back before the hut, Yar Afzal halted in the midst of some tirade, surprized and displeased to see the man he had sent up the valley, pushing his way through the throng.

"I bade you go to the watchers!" the chief bellowed. "You have not had time to come from them!"

The other did not reply; he stood woodenly, staring vacantly into the chief's face, his palm outstretched holding the jade ball. Conan, looking over Yar Afzal's shoulder, murmured something and reached to touch the chief's arm, but as he did so, Yar Afzal, in a paroxysm of anger, struck the man with his clenched fist and felled him like an ox. As he fell the jade sphere rolled to Yar Afzal's foot and the chief, seeming to see it for the first time, bent and picked it up. The men, staring perplexedly at their senseless comrade, saw their chief bend, but they did not see what he picked up from the ground.

Yar Afzal straightened, glanced at the jade, and made a motion to thrust it into his girdle.

"Carry that fool to his hut," he growled. "He has the look of a lotus-eater. He returned me a blank stare. I – *aie!*"

In his right hand, moving toward his girdle, he had suddenly felt movement where movement should not be. His voice died away as he stood and glared at nothing; and inside his clenched right hand he felt the quivering of *change*, of *motion*, of *life*. He no longer held a smooth shining sphere in his fingers. And he dared not look; his tongue clove to the roof of his mouth, and he could not open his hand. His astonished warriors saw Yar Afzal's eyes distend, the color ebb from his face. Then suddenly a bellow of agony burst from his bearded lips, he swayed and fell as if struck by lightning, his right arm tossed out in front of him. Face down he lay, and from between his opening fingers crawled a spider – a hideous, black, hairy-legged monster whose body shone like black jade. The men yelled and gave back suddenly, and the creature scuttled into a crevice of the rocks and disappeared.

The warriors started up, glaring wildly, and a voice rose above their clamor, a far-carrying voice of command which came from none knew where. Afterwards each man there – who still lived – denied that he had shouted, but all there heard it.

"Yar Afzal is dead! Kill the outlander!"

That shout focussed their whirling minds as one. Doubt, bewilderment and fear vanished in the uproaring surge of the blood-lust. A furious yell rent the skies as the tribesmen responded instantly to the suggestion. They came headlong across the open space, cloaks flapping, eyes blazing, knives lifted.

Conan's action was as quick as theirs. As the voice shouted he sprang for the hut door. But they were closer to him than he was to the door, and with one foot on the sill he had to wheel and parry the swipe of a yard-long blade. He split the man's skull – ducked another swinging knife and gutted the wielder – felled a man with his left fist and stabbed another in the belly – and heaved back mightily against the closed door with his shoulders. Hacking blades were nicking chips out of the jambs about his ears, but the door flew open under the impact of his shoulders, and he went stumbling backward into the room. A bearded tribesman, thrusting with all his fury as Conan sprang back, over-reached and pitched head-first through the doorway. Conan stooped, grasped the slack of his garments and hauled him clear, and slammed the door in the faces of the men who came surging into it. Bones snapped under the impact, and the next instant Conan slammed the bolts into place and whirled with desperate haste to meet the man who sprang from the floor and tore into action like a madman.

Yasmina cowered in a corner, staring in horror as the two men fought back and forth across the room, almost trampling her at times; the flash and clangor of their blades filled the room, and outside the mob clamored like a wolf-pack, hacking deafeningly at the bronze door with their long knives, and dashing huge rocks against it. Somebody fetched a tree trunk, and the door began to stagger under the thunderous assault. Yasmina clasped her ears, staring wildly. Violence and fury within, cataclysmic madness without. The stallion in his stall neighed and reared, thundering with his heels against the walls. He wheeled and launched his hoofs through the bars just as the tribesman, backing away from Conan's murderous swipes, stumbled against them. His spine cracked in three places like a rotten branch and he was hurled headlong against the Cimmerian, bearing him backward so they both crashed to the beaten floor. Yasmina cried out and ran forward; to her dazed sight it seemed that both were slain. She reached them just as Conan threw aside the corpse and rose. She caught his arm, trembling from head to foot.

"Oh, you live! I thought – I thought you were dead!"

He glanced down at her quickly, into the pale, upturned face and the wide staring dark eyes.

"Why are you trembling?" he demanded. "Why should you care if I live or die?"

A vestige of her poise returned to her, and she drew away, making a rather pitiful attempt at playing the Devi.

"You are preferable to those wolves howling without," she answered, gesturing toward the door, the stone sill of which was beginning to splinter away.

"That won't hold long," he muttered, then turned and went swiftly to the stall of the stallion. Yasmina clenched her hands and caught her breath as she saw him tear aside the splintered bars and go into the stall with the maddened beast. The stallion reared above him, neighing terribly, hoofs lifted, eyes and teeth flashing and ears laid back, but Conan leaped and caught his mane and with a display of sheer strength that seemed impossible, dragged the beast down on his forelegs. The steed snorted and quivered, but stood still while the man bridled him and clapped on the gold-worked saddle, with the wide silver stirrups.

Wheeling the beast around in the stall, Conan called quickly to Yasmina, and the girl came, sidling nervously past the stallion's heels. Conan was working at the stone wall, talking swiftly as he worked.

"A secret door in the wall here, that not even the Wazuli know about. Yar Afzal showed it to me once when he was drunk. It opens out into the mouth of the ravine behind the hut. Ha!"

As he tugged at a projection that seemed casual, a whole section of the wall slid back on oiled iron runners. Looking through, the girl saw a narrow defile opening in a sheer stone wall within a few feet of the hut's back wall. Then Conan sprang into the saddle and hauled her up before him. Behind them the great door groaned like a living thing and crashed in and a yell rang to the roof as the entrance was instantly flooded with hairy faces and knives in hairy fists. And then the great stallion went through the wall like a javelin from a catapult, and thundered into the defile, running low, foam flying from the bit-rings.

That move came as an absolute surprize to the Wazulis. It was a surprize, too, to those stealing down the ravine. It happened so quickly – the hurricane-like charge of the great horse – that a man in a green turban was unable to get out of the way. He went down under the frantic hoofs, and a girl screamed. Conan got one glimpse of her as they thundered by – a slim, dark girl in silk trousers and a jeweled breast-band, flattening herself against the ravine wall. Then the black horse and his riders were gone up the gorge like the spume blown before a storm, and the men who came tumbling through the wall into the defile after them met that which changed their yells of blood-lust to shrill screams of fear and death.

VI

The Mountain of the Black Seers

"Where now?" Yasmina was trying to sit erect on the rocking saddle bow, clutching to her captor. She was conscious of a recognition of shame that she should not find unpleasant the feel of his muscular flesh under her fingers, but under that too was a wicked little tingle that would not be denied.

"To Afghulistan," he answered. "It's a perilous road, but the stallion will carry us easily, unless we fall in with some of your friends, or my tribal enemies. Now that Yar Afzal is dead, those damned Wazulis will be on our heels. I'm surprized we haven't sighted them behind us already."

"Who was that man you rode down?" she asked.

"I don't know. I never saw him before. He's no Ghuli, that's certain. What the devil he was doing there is more than I can say. There was a girl with him, too."

"Yes." Her gaze was shadowed. "I can not understand that. That girl was my maid, Gitara. Do you suppose she was coming to aid me? That the man was a friend? If so, the Wazulis have captured them both."

"Well," he answered, "there's nothing we can do. If we go back, they'll skin us both. I can't understand how a girl like that could get this far into the mountains with only one man – and he a robed scholar, for that's what he looked like. There's something infernally queer in all this. That fellow Yar Afzal beat and sent away – he moved like a man walking in his sleep. I've seen the priests of Zamora perform their abominable rituals in their forbidden temples, and their victims had a stare like that man. The priests looked into their eyes and muttered incantations, and then the people became like walking dead men, with glassy eyes, doing as they were ordered.

"And then I saw what the fellow had in his hand, which Yar Afzal picked up. It was like a big black jade bead, such as the temple girls of Yezud wear when they dance before the black stone spider which is their god. Yar Afzal held it in his hand, and he didn't pick up anything else. Yet when he fell dead a spider, like the god at Yezud, only smaller, ran out of his fingers. And then, when the Wazulis stood uncertain there, a voice cried out for them to kill me, and I know that voice didn't come from any of the warriors, nor from the women who watched by the huts. It seemed to come from *above*."

Yasmina did not reply. She glanced at the stark outlines of the mountains all about them and shuddered. Her soul shrank from their gaunt brutality. This was a grim, naked land where anything might happen. Age-old traditions invested it with shuddersome horror for anyone born in the hot, luxuriant southern plains.

The sun was high, beating down with fierce heat, yet the wind that blew in fitful gusts seemed to sweep off slopes of ice. Once she heard a strange rushing above them that was not the sweep of the wind, and from the way Conan looked up, she knew it was not a common sound to him, either. She thought that a strip of the cold blue sky was momentarily blurred, as if some all but invisible object had swept between it and herself, but she could not be sure. Neither made any comment, but Conan loosened his knife in his scabbard.

They were following no marked trail, but dipping down into ravines so deep the sun never struck bottom, laboring up steep slopes where loose shale threatened to slide from beneath their feet, and following knife-edge ridges with blue-hazed echoing depths on either hand.

The sun had passed its zenith when they came to a narrow trail winding among the crags. Conan reined the horse aside and followed it southward, going almost at right angles to their former course.

"A Galzai village is at one end of this trail," he explained. "Their women follow it to a well, for water. You need new garments."

Glancing down at her filmy attire, Yasmina agreed with him. Her cloth-of-gold slippers were in tatters, her robes and silken under-garments torn to shreds that scarcely held together decently. Garments meant for the streets of Peshkhauri were scarcely appropriate for the crags of the Himelians.

Coming to a crook in the trail, Conan dismounted, helped Yasmina down and waited. Presently he nodded, though she heard nothing.

"A woman coming along the trail," he remarked. In sudden panic she clutched his arm.

"You will not – not kill her?"

"I don't kill women ordinarily," he grunted; "though some of these hill women are she-wolves. No," he grinned as at a huge jest. "By Crom, I'll *pay* for her clothes! How is that?" He displayed a handful of gold coins, and replaced all but the largest. She nodded, much relieved. It was perhaps natural for men to slay and die; her flesh crawled at the thought of watching the butchery of a woman.

Presently a woman appeared around the crook of the trail – a tall, slim Galzai girl, straight as a young sapling, bearing a great empty gourd. She stopped short and the gourd fell from her hands when she saw them; she wavered as though to run, then realized that Conan was too close to her to allow her to escape, and so stood still, staring at them with an expression mixed of fear and curiosity.

Conan displayed the gold coin.

"If you will give this woman your garments," he said, "I will give you this money."

The response was instant. The girl smiled broadly with surprize and delight, and, with the disdain of a hill woman for prudish conventions, promptly yanked off her sleeveless embroidered vest, slipped down her wide trousers and stepped out of them, twitched off her wide-sleeved shirt, and kicked off her sandals. Bundling them all in a bunch, she proffered them to Conan, who handed them to the astonished Devi.

"Get behind that rock and put these on," he directed, further proving himself no native hillman. "Fold your robes up into a bundle and bring them to me when you come out."

"The money!" clamored the hill girl, stretching out her hands eagerly. "The gold you promised me!"

Conan flipped the coin to her, she caught it, bit, then thrust it into her hair, bent supplely and caught up the gourd and went on down the path, as devoid of self-consciousness as of garments. Conan waited with some impatience while the Devi, for the first time in her pampered life, dressed herself. When she stepped from behind the rock he swore in surprize, and she felt a curious rush of emotions at the unrestrained admiration burning in his fierce blue eyes. She felt shame, embarrassment, yet a stimulation of vanity she had never before experienced, and the same naughty tingling she had felt before when meeting the impact of his eyes or the grasp of his arms. He laid a heavy hand on her shoulder and turned her about, staring avidly at her from all angles.

"By Crom!" said he. "In those smoky, mystic robes you were aloof and cold and far-off as a star! Now you are a woman of warm flesh and blood! You went behind that rock as the Devi of Vendhya; you come out as a hill girl – though a thousand times more beautiful than any wench of the Zhaibar! You were a goddess – now you are real!"

He spanked her resoundingly, and she, recognizing this as merely another expression of admiration, did not feel particularly outraged. It was indeed as if the changing of her garments had wrought a change in her personality. The feelings and sensations she had suppressed rose to domination in her now, as if the queenly robes she had cast off had been material shackles and inhibitions.

But Conan, in his renewed admiration, did not forget that peril lurked all about them. The further they drew away from the region of the Zhaibar, the less likely he was to encounter any Kshatriya troops. On the other hand he had been listening all throughout their flight for sounds that would tell him the vengeful Wazulis of Khurum were on their heels.

Swinging the Devi up, he followed her into the saddle and again reined the stallion westward. The bundle of garments she had given him, he hurled over a cliff, to fall into the depths of a thousand-foot gorge.

"Why did you do that?" she asked. "Why did you not give them to the girl?"

"The riders from Peshkhauri are combing these hills," he said. "They'll be ambushed and harried at every turn, and by way of reprisal they'll destroy every village they can take. They may turn westward any time. If they found a girl wearing your garments, they'd torture her into talking, and she might put them on my trail."

"What will she do?" asked Yasmina.

"Go back to her village and tell her people that a stranger stripped her and raped her," he answered. "She'll have them on our track, alright. But she had to go on and get the water first; if she dared go back without it, they'd whip the skin off her. That gives us a long start. They'll never catch us. By nightfall we'll cross the Afghuli border."

"There are no paths or signs of human habitation in these parts," she commented. "Even for the Himelians this region seems singularly deserted. We have not seen a trail since we left the one where we met the Galzai woman."

For answer he pointed to the northwest, where she glimpsed a peak in a notch of the crags.

"Yimsha," grunted Conan. "The tribes build their villages as far from that mountain as they can."

She was instantly rigid with attention.

"Yimsha!" she whispered. "The mountain of the Black Seers!"

"So they say," he answered. "This is as near as I ever approached it. I have swung north to avoid any Kshatriya troops that might be prowling through the hills. The regular trail from Khurum to Afghulistan lies further south.

She was staring at the distant peak with avid intentness. Her nails bit into her pink palms.

"How long would it take to reach Yimsha from this point?"

"All the rest of the day, and all night," he answered, and grinned. "Do you want to go there? By Crom, it's no place for an ordinary human, from what the hill people say."

"Why do they not gather and destroy the devils that inhabit it?" she demanded.

"Wipe out wizards with swords? Anyway, they never interfere with people, unless the people interfere with them. I never saw one of them, though I've talked with men who swore they had. They say they've glimpsed people from the tower among the crags at sunset or sunrise – tall, silent men in black robes."

"Would you be afraid to attack them?"

"I?" The idea seemed a new one to him. "Why, if they imposed upon me, it would be my life or theirs. But I have nothing to do with them. I came to these mountains to raise a following of human beings, not to war with wizards."

Yasmina did not at once reply. She stared at the peak as at a human enemy, feeling all her anger and hatred stir in her bosom anew. And another feeling began to take dim shape. She had plotted to hurl against the masters of Yimsha the man in whose arms she was now carried. Perhaps there was another way, besides the method she had planned, to accomplish her purpose. She could not mistake the look that was beginning to dawn in this wild man's eyes as they rested on her. Kingdoms have fallen when a woman's slim white hands pulled the strings of destiny – suddenly she stiffened, pointing.

"Look!"

Just visible on the distant peak there hung a cloud of peculiar aspect. It was a frosty crimson in color, veined with sparkling gold. This cloud was in motion; it rotated, and as it whirled it contracted. It dwindled to a spinning taper that flashed in the sun. And suddenly it detached itself from the snow-tipped peak, floated out over the void like a gay-hued feather, and became invisible against the cerulean sky.

"What could that have been?" asked the girl uneasily, as a shoulder of rock shut the distant mountain from view; the phenomenon had been disturbing, even in its beauty.

"The hillmen call it Yimsha's Carpet, whatever the devil that means," answered Conan. "I've seen five hundred of them running as if the devil were at their heels, to hide themselves in caves and crags, because they saw that crimson cloud float up from the peak. What the hell!"

They had advanced through a narrow, knife-cut gash between turreted walls, and emerged upon a broad ledge, flanked by a series of rugged slopes on one hand, and a gigantic precipice on the other. The dim trail followed this ledge, bent around a shoulder and reappeared at intervals far below, working a tedious way downward. And emerging from the gut that opened upon the ledge, the black stallion halted short, snorting. Conan urged him on impatiently, and the horse snorted and threw his head up and down, quivering and straining as if against an invisible barrier.

Conan swore and swung off, lifting Yasmina down with him. He went forward, with a hand thrown out before him as if expecting to encounter unseen resistance, but there was nothing to hinder him, though when he tried to lead the horse, it neighed shrilly and jerked back. Then Yasmina cried out, and Conan wheeled, hand starting to knife hilt.

Neither of them had seen him come, but he stood there, with his arms folded, a man in a camel-hair robe and a green turban. Conan grunted with surprize to recognize the man the stallion had spurned in the ravine outside the Wazuli village.

"Who the devil are you?" he demanded.

The man did not answer. Conan noticed that his eyes were wide, fixed, and of a peculiar luminous quality. And those eyes held his like a magnet.

Khemsa's sorcery was based on hypnotism, as is the case with most Eastern magic. The way has been prepared for the hypnotist for untold centuries of generations who have lived and died in the firm conviction of the reality and power of hypnotism, building up, by mass thought and practise, a colossal though intangible atmosphere against which the individual, steeped in the traditions of the land, finds himself helpless.

But Conan was not a son of the East. Its traditions were meaningless to him; he was the product of an utterly alien atmosphere. Hypnotism was not even a myth in Cimmeria. The heritage that prepared a native of the East for submission to the mesmerist was not his.

He was aware of what Khemsa was trying to do to him; but he felt the impact of the man's uncanny power only as a vague impulsion, a tugging and pulling that he could shake off as a man shakes spider webs from his garments.

Aware of hostility and black magic, he ripped out his long knife and lunged, as quick on his feet as a mountain lion.

But hypnotism was not all of Khemsa's magic. Yasmina, watching, did not see by what roguery of movement or illusion the man in the green turban avoided the terrible disembowelling thrust. But the keen blade whickered between side and lifted arm, and to Yasmina it seemed that Khemsa merely brushed his open palm lightly against Conan's bull-neck. But the Cimmerian went down like a slain ox.

Yet Conan was not dead; breaking his fall with his left hand, he slashed at Khemsa's legs even as he went down, and the Rakhsha avoided the scythe-like swipe only by a most unwizardly bound backward. Then Yasmina cried out sharply as she saw a woman she recognized as Gitara glide out from among the rocks and come up to the man. The greeting died in the Devi's throat as she saw the malevolence in the girl's beautiful face.

Conan was rising slowly, shaken and dazed by the cruel craft of that blow which, delivered with an art forgotten of men before Atlantis sank, would have broken like a rotten twig the neck of a lesser man. Khemsa gazed at him cautiously and a trifle uncertainly. The Rakhsha had learned the full flood of his own power when he faced at bay the knives of the maddened Wazulis in the ravine behind

Khurum village; but the Cimmerian's resistance had perhaps shaken his new-found confidence a trifle. Sorcery thrives on success, not on failure.

He stepped forward, lifting his hand – then halted as if frozen, head tilted back, eyes wide open, hand raised. In spite of himself Conan followed his gaze, and so did the women – the girl cowering by the trembling stallion, and the girl beside Khemsa.

Down the mountain-slopes, like a whorl of shining dust blown before the wind, a crimson, conoid cloud came dancing. Khemsa's dark face turned ashen; his hand began to tremble, then sank to his side. The girl beside him, sensing the change in him, stared at him inquiringly.

The crimson shape left the mountain-slope and came down in a long arching swoop. It struck the ledge between Conan and Khemsa, and the Rakhsha gave back with a stifled cry. He backed away, pushing the girl Gitara back with groping, fending hands.

The crimson cloud balanced like a spinning top for an instant, whirling in a dazzling sheen on its point. Then without warning it was gone, vanished as a bubble vanishes when burst. There on the ledge stood four men. It was miraculous, incredible, impossible, yet it was true. They were not ghosts or phantoms. They were four tall men, with shaven, vulture-like heads, and black robes that hid their feet. Their hands were concealed by their wide sleeves. They stood in silence, their naked heads nodding slightly in unison. They were facing Khemsa, but behind them Conan felt his own blood turning to ice in his veins. Rising he backed stealthily away, until he felt the stallion's shoulder trembling against his back, and the Devi crept into the shelter of his arm. There was no word spoken. Silence hung like a stifling pall.

All four of the men in black robes stared at Khemsa. Their vulture-like faces were immobile, their eyes introspective and contemplative. But Khemsa shook like a man in an ague. His feet were braced on the rock, his calves straining as if in physical combat. Sweat ran in streams down his dark face. His right hand locked on something under his brown robe so desperately that the blood ebbed from that hand and left it white. His left hand fell on the shoulder of Gitara and clutched in agony like the grasp of a drowning man. She did not flinch or whimper, though his fingers dug like talons into her firm flesh.

Conan had witnessed hundreds of battles in his wild life, but never one like this, wherein four diabolical wills sought to beat down one lesser but equally devilish will that opposed them. But he only faintly sensed the monstrous quality of that hideous struggle. With his back to the wall, driven to bay by his former masters, Khemsa was fighting for his life with all the dark power, all the frightful knowledge they had taught him through long, grim years of neophytism and vassalage.

He was stronger than even he had guessed, and the free exercise of his powers in his own behalf had tapped unsuspected reservoirs of forces. And he was nerved to super-energy by frantic fear and desperation. He reeled before the merciless impact of those hypnotic eyes, but he held his ground. His features were distorted into a bestial grin of agony from which dripped bloody sweat, and his limbs were twisted as in a rack. It was a war of souls, of frightful brains steeped in lore forbidden to men for a million years, of mentalities which had plumbed the abysses and explored the dark stars where spawn the shadows.

Yasmina understood this better than did Conan. And she dimly understood why Khemsa could withstand the concentrated impact of those four hellish wills which might have blasted into atoms the very rock on which he stood. The reason was the girl that he clutched with the strength of his despair. She was like an anchor to his staggering soul, battered by the waves of those psychic emanations. His weakness was now his strength. His love for the girl, violent and evil though it might be, was yet a tie that bound him to the rest of humanity, providing an earthly leverage for his will, a chain that his inhuman enemies could not break. At least not break through Khemsa.

They realized that before he did. And one of them turned his gaze from the Rakhsha full upon Gitara. There was no battle there. The girl shrank and wilted like a leaf in the drouth. Irresistibly impelled, she tore herself from her lover's arms before he realized what was happening. Then a hideous thing came to pass. She began to back toward the precipice, facing her tormentors, her eyes wide and blank as dark gleaming glass from behind which a lamp has been blown out. Khemsa groaned and staggered toward her, falling into the trap set for him. A divided mind could not maintain the unequal battle. He was beaten, a straw in their hands. The girl went backward, walking like an automaton, and Khemsa reeled drunkenly after her, hands vainly outstretched, groaning, slobbering in his pain, his feet moving heavily like dead things.

On the very brink she paused, standing stiffly, her heels on the edge, and he fell on his knees and crawled whimpering toward her, groping for her, to drag her back from destruction. And just before his clumsy fingers touched her, one of the wizards laughed, like the sudden, bronze note of a bell in hell. The girl reeled suddenly, and consummate climax of exquisite cruelty, reason and understanding flooded back into her eyes which flared with awful fear. She screamed, clutched wildly at her lover's straining hands, and then, unable to save herself, fell headlong with a moaning cry.

Khemsa hauled himself to the edge and stared over, haggardly, his lips working as he mumbled to himself. Then he turned and stared for a long minute at his torturers, with wide eyes that held no human light. And then with a cry that almost burst the rocks, he reeled up and came rushing toward them, a knife lifted in his hand.

One of the Rakhshas stepped forward and stamped his foot, and as he stamped, there came a rumbling that grew swiftly to a grinding roar. Where his foot struck, a crevice opened in the solid rock that widened instantly. Then, with a deafening crash, a whole section of the ledge gave way. There was a last glimpse of Khemsa, with arms wildly upflung, and then he vanished amidst the roar of the avalanche that thundered down into the abyss.

The four looked contemplatively at the ragged edge of rock that formed the new rim of the precipice, and then turned suddenly. Conan, thrown off his feet by the shudder of the mountain, was rising, lifting Yasmina. He seemed to move as slowly as his brain was working. He was befogged and stupid. He realized that there was desperate need for him to lift the Devi on the black stallion, and ride like the wind, but an unaccountable sluggishness weighted his every thought and action.

And now the wizards had turned toward him; they raised their arms, and to his horrified sight, he saw their outlines fading, dimming, becoming hazy and nebulous, as a crimson smoke billowed around their feet and rose about them. They were blotted out by a sudden whirling cloud – and then he realized that he too was enveloped in a blinding crimson mist – he heard Yasmina scream and the stallion cried out like a woman in pain. The Devi was torn from his arm and as he lashed out with his knife blindly, a terrific blow like a gust of storm wind knocked him sprawling against a rock. Dazedly he saw a crimson conoid cloud spinning up and over the mountain slopes. Yasmina was gone, and so were the four men in black. Only the terrified stallion shared the ledge with him.

VII
On to Yimsha

As mists vanish before a strong wind, the cobwebs vanished from Conan's brain. With a searing curse he leaped into the saddle and the stallion reared neighing beneath him. He glared up the slopes, hesitated, and then turned down the trail in the direction he had been going when halted by Khemsa's trickery. But now he did not ride at a measured gait. He shook loose the reins and the stallion went like a thunder-bolt, as if frantic to lose hysteria in violent physical exertion. Across the ledge and around the crag and down the narrow trail threading the great steep they plunged at break-neck speed. The path followed a fold of rock, winding interminably down from tier to tier of striated escarpment, and once, far below, Conan got a glimpse of the ruin that had fallen – a mighty pile of broken stone and boulders at the foot of a gigantic cliff.

The valley floor was still far below him when he reached a long and lofty ridge that led out from the slope like a natural causeway. Out upon this he rode, with an almost sheer drop on either hand. He could trace ahead of him the trail he had to follow; far ahead it dropped down from the ridge, and made a great horseshoe back into the river-bed at his left hand. He cursed the necessity of traversing those miles, but it was the only way. To try to descend to the lower lap of the trail here would be to attempt the impossible. Only a bird could get to the river-bed with a whole neck.

So he urged on the wearying stallion, until a clink of hoofs reached his ears, welling up from below. Pulling up short and reining to the lip of the cliff, he stared down into the dry river-bed that wound along the foot of the ridge. Along that gorge rode a motley throng – bearded men on half-wild horses, five hundred strong, bristling with weapons. And Conan shouted suddenly, leaning over the edge of the cliff, three hundred feet above them.

At his shout they reined back, and five hundred bearded faces were tilted up toward him; a deep, clamorous roar filled the canyon. Conan did not waste words.

"I was riding for Ghor!" he roared. "I had not hoped to meet you dogs on the trail. Follow me as fast as your nags can push! I'm going to Yimsha, and – "

"Traitor!" The howl was like a dash of ice water in his face.

"What?" He glared down at them, jolted speechless. He saw wild eyes blazing up at him, faces contorted with fury, fists brandishing blades.

"Traitor!" they roared back, whole-heartedly. "Where are the seven chiefs held captive in Peshkhauri?"

"Why, in the governor's prison, I suppose," he answered.

A blood-thirsty yell from a hundred throats answered him, with such a waving of weapons and a clamor that he could not understand what they were saying. He beat down the din with a bull-like roar, and bellowed: "What devil's play is this? Let one of you speak, so I can understand what you mean!"

A gaunt old chief elected himself to this position, shook his tulwar at Conan as a preamble, and shouted accusingly: "You would not let us go raiding Peshkhauri to rescue our brothers!"

"No, you fools!" roared the exasperated Cimmerian. "Even if you'd breached the wall, which is unlikely, they'd have hanged the prisoners before you could reach them."

"And you went alone to traffic with the governor!" yelled the Afghuli, working himself into a frothing frenzy.

"Well?"

"Where are the seven chiefs?" howled the old chief, making his tulwar into a glimmering wheel of steel about his head. "Where are they? Dead!"

"What!" Conan nearly fell off his horse in his surprize.

"Aye, dead!" Five hundred blood-thirsty voices assured him. The old chief brandished his arms and got the floor again. "They were not hanged!" he screeched. "A Wazuli in another cell saw them die! The governor sent a wizard to slay them by craft!"

"That must be a lie," said Conan. "The governor would not dare. Last night I talked with him – "

The admission was unfortunate. A yell of hate and accusation split the skies.

"Aye! You went to him alone! To betray us! It is no lie. The Wazuli escaped through the doors the wizard burst in his entry, and told the tale to our scouts whom he met in the Zhaibar. They had been sent forth to search for you, when you did not return. When they heard the Wazuli's tale, they returned with all haste to Ghor, and we saddled our steeds and girt our swords!"

"And what do you fools mean to do?" demanded the Cimmerian.

"To avenge our brothers!" they howled. "Death to the Kshatriyas! Slay him, brothers, he is a traitor!"

Arrows began to rattle around him. Conan rose in his stirrups, striving to make himself heard above the tumult, and then, with a roar mingled of rage, defiance and disgust, he wheeled and galloped back up the trail. Behind him and below him the Afghulis came pelting, mouthing their rage, too furious even to remember that the only way they could reach the height whereon he rode was to traverse the river-bed in the other direction, make the broad bend and follow the twisting trail up over the ridge. When they did remember this, and turned back, their repudiated chief had almost reached the point where the ridge joined the escarpment.

At the cliff he did not take the trail by which he had descended, but turned off on another, a mere trace along a rock-fault, where the stallion scrambled for footing. He had not ridden far when the stallion snorted and shied back from something lying in the trail. Conan stared down on the travesty of a man, a broken, shredded, bloody heap that gibbered and gnashed splintered teeth.

Only the dark gods that rule over the grim destinies of wizards know how Khemsa dragged his shattered body from beneath that awful cairn of fallen rocks and up the steep slope to the trail.

Impelled by some obscure reason, Conan dismounted and stood looking down at the ghastly shape, knowing that he was witness of a thing miraculous and opposed to nature. The Rakhsha lifted his gory head and his strange eyes, glazed with agony and approaching death, rested on Conan with recognition.

"Where are they?" It was a racking croak not even remotely resembling a human voice.

"Gone back to their damnable castle on Yimsha," grunted Conan. "They took the Devi with them."

"I will go!" muttered the man. "I will follow them! They killed Gitara; I will kill them – the acolytes, the Four of the Black Circle, the Master himself! Kill – kill them all!" He strove to drag his mutilated frame along the rock, but not even his indomitable will could animate that gory mass longer, where the splintered bones hung together only by torn tissue and ruptured fiber.

"Follow them!" raved Khemsa, drooling a bloody slaver. "Follow!"

"I'm going to," growled Conan. "I went to fetch my Afghulis, but they've turned on me. I'm going on to Yimsha alone. I'll have the Devi back if I have to tear down that damned mountain with my bare hands. I didn't think the governor would dare kill my headmen, when I had the Devi, but it seems he did. I'll have his head for that. She's no use to me now as a hostage, but – "

"The curse of Yizil on them!" gasped Khemsa. "Go! I am dying. Wait – take my girdle." He tried to fumble with a mangled hand at his tatters, and Conan, understanding what he sought to convey, bent and drew from about his gory waist a girdle of curious aspect.

"Follow the golden vein through the abyss," muttered Khemsa. "Wear the girdle. I had it from a Stygian priest. It will aid you, though it failed me at last. Break the crystal globe with the four golden pomegranates. Beware of the Master's transmutations – I am going to Gitara – she is waiting for me in hell – *aie, ya Skelos yar!*" And so he died.

Conan stared down at the girdle. The hair of which it was woven was not horse-hair. He was convinced that it was woven of the thick black tresses of a woman. Set in the thick mesh were tiny jewels such as he had never seen. The buckle was strangely made, in the form of a golden serpent head, flat, wedge-shaped and scaled with curious art. A strong shudder shook Conan as he handled it, and he turned as though to cast it over the precipice; then he hesitated, and finally buckled it about his waist, under the Bakhariot girdle. Then he mounted and pushed on.

The sun had sunk behind the crags. He climbed the trail in the vast shadow of the cliffs that was thrown out like a dark blue mantle over valleys and ridges far below. He was not far from the crest when, edging around the shoulder of a jutting crag, he heard the clink of shod hoofs ahead of him. He did not turn back. Indeed, so narrow was the path that the stallion could not have wheeled his great body upon it. He rounded the jut of the rock and came onto a portion of the path that broadened somewhat. A chorus of threatening yells broke on his ear, but his stallion pinned a terrified horse hard against the rock, and Conan caught the arm of the rider in an iron grip, checking the lifted sword in mid-air.

"Kerim Shah!" muttered Conan, red glints smoldering luridly in his eyes. The Turanian did not struggle; they sat their horses almost breast to breast, Conan's fingers locking the other's sword-arm. Behind Kerim Shah filed a group of lean Irakzai on gaunt horses. They glared like wolves, fingering bows and knives, but rendered uncertain because of the narrowness of the path and the perilous proximity of the abyss that yawned beneath them.

"Where is the Devi?" demanded Kerim Shah.

"What's it to you, you Hyrkanian spy?" snarled Conan.

"I know you have her," answered Kerim Shah. "I was on my way northward with some tribesmen when we were ambushed by enemies in Shalizah Pass. Many of my men were slain, and the rest of us harried through the hills like jackals. When we had beaten off our pursuers, we turned westward, toward Amir Jehun Pass, and this morning we came upon a Wazuli wandering through the hills. He was quite mad, but I learned much from his incoherent gibberings before he died. I learned that he was the sole survivor of a band which followed a chief of the Afghulis and a captive Kshatriya woman into a gorge behind Khurum village. He babbled much of a man in a green turban whom the Afghuli rode down, but who, when attacked by the Wazulis who pursued, smote them with a nameless doom that wiped them out as a gust of wind-driven fire wipes out a cluster of locusts.

"How that one man escaped, I do not know, nor did he; but I knew from his maunderings that Conan of Ghor had been in Khurum with his royal captive. And as we made our way through the hills, we overtook a naked Galzai girl bearing a gourd of water, who told us a tale of having been stripped and ravished by a giant foreigner in the garb of an Afghuli chief, who, she said, gave her garments to a Vendhyan woman who accompanied him. She said you rode westward."

Kerim Shah did not consider it necessary to explain that he had been on his way to keep his rendezvous with the expected troops from Secunderam when he found his way barred by hostile tribesmen. The road to Gurashah valley through Shalizah Pass was longer than the road that wound through Amir Jehun Pass, but the latter traversed part of the Afghuli country, which Kerim Shah had been anxious to avoid until he came with an army. Barred from the Shalizah road, however, he had turned to the forbidden route, until news that Conan had not yet reached Afghulistan with his captive had caused him to turn southward and push on recklessly in the hope of overtaking the Cimmerian in the hills.

"So you had better tell me where the Devi is," suggested Kerim Shah. "We outnumber you – "

"Let one of your dogs nock a shaft and I'll throw you over the cliff," Conan promised. "It wouldn't do you any good to kill me, anyhow. Five hundred Afghulis are on my trail, and if they find you've cheated them, they'll flay you alive. Anyway, I haven't got the Devi. She's in the hands of the Black Seers of Yimsha."

"Tarim!" swore Kerim Shah softly, shaken out of his poise for the first time. "Khemsa – "

"Khemsa's dead," grunted Conan. "His masters sent him to hell on a landslide. And now get out of my way. I'd be glad to kill you if I had the time, but I'm on my way to Yimsha."

"I'll go with you," said the Turanian abruptly.

Conan laughed at him. "Do you think I'd trust you, you Hyrkanian dog?"

"I don't ask you to," returned Kerim Shah. "We both want the Devi. You know my reason; King Yezdigerd desires to add her kingdom to his empire, and herself to his seraglio. And I knew you, in the days when you were a *hetman* of the *kozak* steppes, so I know your ambition is wholesale plunder. You want to loot Vendhya, and to twist out a huge ransom for Yasmina. Well, let us for the time being, without any illusions about one another, unite our forces, and try to rescue the Devi from the Seers. If we succeed, and live, we can fight it out to see who keeps her."

Conan narrowly scrutinized the other for a moment, and then nodded, releasing the Turanian's arm. "Agreed; what about your men?"

Kerim Shah turned to the silent Irakzai and spoke briefly: "This chief and I are going to Yimsha to fight the wizards. Will you go with us, or stay here to be flayed by the Afghulis who are following this man?"

They looked at him with eyes grimly fatalistic. They were doomed and they knew it – had known it ever since the singing arrows of the ambushed Dagozai had driven them back from the pass of Shalizah. The men of the lower Zhaibar had too many reeking blood-feuds among the crag-dwellers. They were too small a band to fight their way back through the hills to the villages of the border, without the guidance of the crafty Turanian. They counted themselves as dead already, so they made the reply that only dead men would make: "We will go with thee and die on Yimsha."

"Then in Crom's name let us begone," grunted Conan, fidgeting with impatience as he stared into the blue gulfs of the deepening twilight. "My wolves were hours behind me, but we've lost a devilish lot of time."

Kerim Shah backed his steed from between the black stallion and the cliff, sheathed his sword and cautiously turned the horse. Presently the band was filing up the path as swiftly as they dared. They came out upon the crest nearly a mile east of the spot where Khemsa had halted the Cimmerian and the Devi. The path they had traversed was a perilous one, even for hillmen, and for that reason Conan had avoided it that day when carrying Yasmina, though Kerim Shah, following him, had taken it supposing the Cimmerian had done likewise. Even Conan sighed with relief when the horses scrambled up over the last rim. They moved like phantom riders through an enchanted realm of shadows. The soft creak of leather, the clink of steel marked their passing, then again the dark mountain slopes lay naked and silent in the starlight.

VIII
Yasmina knows Stark Terror

Yasmina had time but for one scream when she felt herself enveloped in that crimson whorl and torn from her protector with appalling force. She screamed once, and then she had no breath to scream. She was blinded, deafened, rendered mute and eventually senseless by the terrific rushing of the air about her. There was a dazed consciousness of dizzy height and numbing speed, a confused impression of natural sensations gone mad, and then vertigo and oblivion.

A vestige of these sensations clung to her as she recovered consciousness so she cried out and clutched wildly as though to stay a headlong and involuntary flight. Her fingers closed on soft fabric and a relieving sense of stability pervaded her. She took cognizance of her surroundings.

She was lying on a dais covered with black velvet. This dais stood in a great, dim room whose walls were hung with dusky tapestries across which crawled dragons reproduced with repellant realism. Floating shadows merely hinted at the lofty ceiling, and gloom that lent itself to illusion lurked in the corners. There seemed to be neither windows nor doors in the walls, or else they were concealed by the nighted tapestries. Where the dim light came from, Yasmina could not determine. The great room was a realm of mysteries, of shadows, and shadowy shapes in which she could not have sworn to observe movement, yet which invaded her mind with a dim and formless terror.

But her gaze fixed itself on a tangible object. On another, smaller dais of jet, a few feet away, a man sat cross-legged, gazing contemplatively at her. His long black velvet robe, embroidered with gold thread, fell loosely about him, masking his figure. His hands were folded in his sleeves. There was a velvet cap upon his head. His face was calm, placid, not unhandsome, his eyes lambent and slightly oblique.

He did not move a muscle as he sat regarding her, nor did his expression alter when he saw she was conscious.

Yasmina felt fear crawl like a trickle of ice water down her supple spine. She lifted herself on her elbows and stared apprehensively at the stranger.

"Who are you?" she demanded; her voice sounded brittle and inadequate.

"I am the Master of Yimsha." The tone was rich and resonant, like the mellow notes of a temple bell.

"Why did you bring me here?" she demanded.

"Were you not seeking me?"

"If you are one of the Black Seers – yes!" she answered recklessly, believing that he could read her thoughts anyway.

He laughed softly and chills crawled up and down her spine again.

"You would turn the wild children of the hills against the Seers of Yimsha!" he smiled. "I have read it in your mind, princess. Your weak, human mind, filled with petty dreams of hate and revenge."

"You slew my brother!" A rising tide of anger was vying with her fear; her hands were clenched, her lithe body rigid. "Why did you persecute him? He never harmed you. The priests say the Seers are above meddling in human affairs. Why did you destroy the king of Vendhya?"

"How can an ordinary human understand the motives of a Seer?" returned the Master equably. "My acolytes in the temples of Turan, who are the priests behind the priests of Tarim, urged me to bestir myself in behalf of Yezdigerd. For reasons of my own, I complied. How can I explain my mystic reasons to your puny intellect? You could not understand."

"I understand this: that my brother died!" Tears of grief and rage shook in her voice. She rose upon her knees and stared at him with wide blazing eyes, as supple and dangerous as a she-panther in that moment.

"As Yezdigerd desired," agreed the Master calmly. "For awhile it was my whim to further his ambitions."

"Is Yezdigerd your vassal?" Yasmina tried to keep the timbre of her voice unaltered. She had felt her knee pressing something hard and symmetrical under a fold of velvet. Subtly she shifted her position, moving her hand under the fold.

"Is the dog that licks up the offal in the temple yard the vassal of the god?" returned the Master. He did not seem to notice the actions she sought to dissemble. Concealed by the velvet, her fingers closed on what she knew was the golden hilt of a dagger. She bent her head to hide the light of triumph in her eyes.

"I am weary of Yezdigerd," said the Master. "I have turned to other amusements – ha!"

With a fierce cry Yasmina sprang like a jungle cat, stabbing murderously. Then she stumbled and slid to the floor, where she cowered staring up at the man on the dais. He had not moved; his cryptic smile was unchanged. Tremblingly she lifted her hand and stared at it with dilated eyes. There was no dagger in her fingers; they grasped a stalk of golden lotus, the crushed blossoms drooping on the bruised stem.

She dropped it as if it had been a viper, and scrambled away from the proximity of her tormentor. She returned to her own dais, because that was at least more dignified for a queen than grovelling on the floor at the feet of a sorcerer, and eyed him apprehensively, expecting reprisals.

But the Master made no move.

"All substance is one to him who holds the key of the cosmos," he said cryptically. "To an adept nothing is immutable. At will steel blossoms bloom in unnamed gardens, or flower-swords flash in the moonlight."

"You are a devil," she sobbed.

"Not I!" he laughed. "I was born on this planet, long ago. Once I was a common man, nor have I lost all human attributes in the numberless eons of my adept-ship. A human steeped in the dark arts is greater than a devil. I am of human origin, but I rule demons. You have seen the Lords of the Black Circle – it would blast your soul to hear from what far realm I summoned them and from what doom I guard them with ensorcelled crystal and golden serpents.

"But only I can rule them. My foolish Khemsa thought to make himself great – poor fool, bursting material doors and hurtling himself and his mistress through the air from hill to hill! Yet if he had not been destroyed his power might have grown to rival mine."

He laughed again. "And you, poor, silly thing! Plotting to send a hairy hill chief to storm Yimsha! It was such a jest that I myself could have designed, had it occurred to me, that you should fall in his hands. And I read in your childish mind an intention to seduce by your feminine wiles to attempt your purpose, anyway.

"But for all your stupidity, you are a woman fair to look upon. It is my whim to keep you for my slave."

The daughter of a thousand proud emperors gasped with shame and fury at the word.

"You dare not!"

His mocking laughter cut her like a whip across her naked shoulders.

"The king dares not trample a worm in the road! Little fool, do you not realize that your royal pride is no more to me than a straw blown on the wind? I, who have known the kisses of the queens of Hell! You have seen how I deal with a rebel!"

Cowed and awed, the girl crouched on the velvet-covered dais. The light grew dimmer and more phantom-like. The features of the Master became shadowy. His voice took on a newer tone of command.

"I will never yield to you!" Her voice trembled with fear but it carried a ring of resolution.

"You will yield," he answered with horrible conviction. "Fear and pain shall teach you. I will lash you with horror and agony to the last quivering ounce of your endurance, until you become as melted wax to be bent and molded in my hands as I desire. You shall know such discipline as no mortal woman ever knew, until my slightest command is to you as the unalterable will of the gods. And first, to humble your pride, you shall travel back through the lost ages, and view all the shapes that have been you. *Aie, yil la khosa!*"

At these words the shadowy room swam before Yasmina's affrighted gaze. The roots of her hair prickled her scalp, and her tongue clove to her palate. Somewhere a gong sounded a deep, ominous note. The dragons on the tapestries glowed like blue fire, and then faded out. The Master on his dais was but a shapeless shadow. The dim light gave way to soft, thick darkness, almost tangible, that pulsed with strange radiations. She could no longer see the Master. She could see nothing. She had a strange sensation that the walls and ceiling had withdrawn immensely from her.

Then somewhere in the darkness a glow began, like a firefly that rhythmically dimmed and quickened. It grew to a golden ball, and as it expanded its light grew more intense, flaming whitely. It burst suddenly, showering the darkness with white sparks that did not illumine the shadows. But like an impression left in the gloom, a faint luminance remained, and revealed a slender dusky shaft shooting up from the shadowy floor. Under the girl's dilated gaze it spread, took shape; stems and broad leaves appeared, and great black poisonous blossoms that towered above her as she cringed against the velvet. A subtle perfume pervaded the atmosphere. It was the dread figure of the black lotus that had grown up as she watched, as it grows in the haunted, forbidden jungles of Khitai.

The broad leaves were murmurous with evil life. The blossoms bent toward her like sentient things, nodding serpent-like on pliant stems. Etched against soft, impenetrable darkness it loomed over her, gigantic, blackly visible in some mad way. Her brain reeled with the drugging scent and she sought to crawl from the dais. Then she clung to it as it seemed to be pitching at an impossible slant. She cried out with terror and clung to the velvet, but she felt her fingers ruthlessly torn away. There was a sensation as of all sanity and stability crumbling and vanishing. She was a quivering atom of sentiency driven through a black, roaring, icy void by a thundering wind that threatened to extinguish her feeble flicker of animate life like a candle blown out in a storm.

Then there came a period of blind impulse and movement, when the atom that was she mingled and merged with myriad other atoms of spawning life in the yeasty morass of existence, molded by formative forces until she emerged again a conscious individual, whirling down an endless spiral of lives.

In a mist of terror she relived all her former existences, recognized and *was* again all the bodies that had carried her ego throughout the changing ages. She bruised her feet again over the long, long weary road of life that stretched out behind her into the immemorial Past. Back beyond the dimmest dawns of Time she crouched shuddering in primordial jungles, hunted by slavering beasts of prey. Skin-clad, she waded thigh-deep in rice-swamps, battling with squawking water-fowl for the precious grains. She labored with the oxen to drag the pointed stick through the stubborn soil, and she crouched endlessly over looms in peasant huts.

She saw walled cities burst into flame, and fled screaming before the slayers. She reeled naked and bleeding over burning sands, dragged at the slaver's stirrup, and she knew the grip of hot, fierce hands on her writhing flesh, the shame and agony of brutal lust. She screamed under the bite of the lash, and moaned on the rack; mad with terror she fought against the hands that forced her head inexorably down on the bloody block.

She knew the agonies of child-birth, and the bitterness of love betrayed. She suffered all the woes and wrongs and brutalities that man has inflicted on woman throughout the eons; and she endured all the spite and malice of woman for woman. And like the flick of a fiery whip throughout was the consciousness she retained of her Devi-ship. She was all the women she had ever been, yet in her knowing she was Yasmina. This consciousness was not lost in the throes of reincarnation. At one and the same time she was a naked slave wench grovelling under the whip, and the proud Devi of Vendhya. And she suffered not only as the slave girl suffered, but as Yasmina, to whose pride the whip was like a white hot brand.

Life merged into life in flying chaos, each with its burden of woe and shame and agony, until she dimly heard her own voice screaming unbearably, like one long-drawn cry of suffering echoing down the ages.

Then she awakened on the velvet-covered dais in the mystic room.

In a ghostly grey light she saw again the dais and the cryptic robed figure seated upon it. The hooded head was bent, the high shoulders faintly etched against the uncertain dimness. She could make out no details clearly, but the hood, where the velvet cap had been, stirred a formless uneasiness in her. As she stared, there stole over her a nameless fear that froze her tongue to her palate – a feeling that it was not the Master who sat so silently on that black dais.

Then the figure moved and rose upright, towering above her. It stooped over her and the long arms in their wide black sleeves bent about her. She fought against them in speechless fright, surprized by their lean hardness. The hooded head bent down toward her averted face. And she screamed, and screamed again in poignant fear and loathing. Bony arms gripped her lithe body, and from that hood looked forth a countenance of death and decay – features like rotting parchment on a moldering skull. She screamed again, and then, as those champing, grinning jaws bent toward her lips, she lost consciousness.

IX

The Castle of the Wizards

The sun had risen over the white Himelian peaks. At the foot of a long slope a group of horsemen halted and stared upward. High above them a stone tower poised on the pitch of the mountain side. Beyond and above that gleamed the walls of a greater keep, near the line where the snow began that capped Yimsha's pinnacle. There was a touch of unreality about the whole – purple slopes pitching up to that fantastic castle, toy-like with distance, and above it the white glistening peak shouldering the cold blue.

"We'll leave the horses here," grunted Conan. "That treacherous slope is safer for a man on foot. Besides, they're done."

He swung down from the black stallion which stood with wide-braced legs and drooping head. They had pushed hard throughout the night, gnawing at scraps from saddle bags, and pausing only to give the horses the rests they had to have.

"That first tower is held by the acolytes of the Black Seers," said Conan. "Or so men say; watch dogs for their masters – lesser sorcerers. They won't sit sucking their thumbs as we climb this slope."

Kerim Shah glanced up the mountain, then back the way they had come; they were already far up on Yimsha's side, and a vast expanse of lesser peaks and crags spread out beneath them. Among those labyrinths the Turanian sought in vain for a movement of color that would betray men. Evidently the pursuing Afghulis had lost their chief's trail in the night.

"Let us go, then." They tied the weary horses in a clump of tamarisk and without further comment turned up the slope. There was no cover. It was a naked incline, strewn with boulders not big enough to conceal a man. But they did conceal something else.

The party had not gone fifty steps when a snarling shape burst from behind a rock. It was one of the gaunt savage dogs that infested the hill villages, and its eyes glared redly, its jaws dripped foam. Conan was leading, but it did not attack him. It dashed past him and leaped at Kerim Shah. The Turanian leaped aside, and the great dog flung itself upon the Irakzai behind him. The man yelled and threw up his arm, which was torn by the brute's fangs as it bore him backward, and the next instant half a dozen tulwars were hacking at the beast. Yet not until it was literally dismembered did the hideous creature cease its efforts to seize and rend its attackers.

Kerim Shah bound up the wounded warrior's gashed arm, looked at him narrowly, and then turned away without a word. He rejoined Conan and they renewed the climb in silence.

Presently Kerim Shah said: "Strange to find a village dog in this place."

"There's no offal here," grunted Conan. Both turned their heads to glance back at the wounded warrior toiling after them among his companions. Sweat glistened on his dark face and his lips were drawn back from his teeth in a grimace of pain. Then both looked again at the stone tower squatting above them.

A slumberous quiet lay over the uplands. The tower showed no sign of life, nor did the strange pyramidal structure beyond it. But the men who toiled upward went with the tenseness of men walking on the edge of a crater. Kerim Shah had unslung the powerful Turanian bow that killed at five hundred paces, and the Irakzai looked to their own lighter and less lethal bows.

But they were not within bow-shot of the tower when something shot down out of the sky without warning. It passed so close to Conan that he felt the wind of the rushing wings, but it was an Irakzai who staggered and fell, blood jetting from a severed jugular. A hawk with wings like burnished steel shot up again, blood dripping from the scimitar-beak, to reel against the sky as Kerim Shah's bow-string twanged. It dropped like a plummet, but no man saw where it struck the earth.

Conan bent over the victim of the attack, but the man was already dead. No one spoke; useless to comment on the fact that never before had a hawk been known to swoop on a man. Red rage began to vie with fatalistic lethargy in the wild souls of the Irakzai. Hairy fingers nocked arrows and men glared vengefully at the tower whose very silence mocked them.

But the next attack came swiftly and direct. They all saw it – a white puff-ball of smoke that tumbled over the tower-rim and came drifting and rolling down the slope toward them. Others followed it. They seemed harmless, mere woolly globes of cloudy foam, but Conan stepped aside to avoid contact with the first. Behind him one of the Irakzai reached out and thrust his sword into the unstable mass. Instantly a sharp report shook the mountain-side. There was a burst of blinding flame, and then the puff-ball had vanished, and of the too-curious warrior remained only a heap of charred and blackened bones. The crisped hand still gripped the ivory sword hilt, but the blade was gone – melted and destroyed by that awful heat. Yet men standing almost within reach of the victim had not suffered except to be dazzled and half-blinded by the sudden flare.

"Steel touches it off," grunted Conan. "Look out – here they come!"

The slope above them was almost covered by the billowing spheres. Kerim Shah bent his bow and sent a shaft into the mass, and those touched by the arrow burst like bubbles in spurting flame. His men followed his example and for the next few minutes it was as if a thunderstorm raged on the mountain slope, with bolts of lightning striking and bursting in showers of flame. When the barrage ceased, only a few arrows were left in the quivers of the archers.

They pushed on grimly, over soil charred and blackened, where the naked rock had in places been turned to lava by the explosion of those diabolical bombs.

Now they were within easy arrow-flight of the silent tower, and they spread their line, nerves taut, ready for any horror that might descend upon them.

On the tower appeared a single figure, lifting a ten-foot bronze horn. Its strident bellow roared out across the echoing slopes, like the blare of trumpets on Judgment Day. And it began to be fearfully answered. The ground trembled under the feet of the invaders, and rumblings and grindings welled up from subterranean depths.

The Irakzai screamed, reeling like drunken men on the shuddering slope, and Conan, eyes glaring, charged recklessly up the incline, knife in hand, straight at the door that showed in the tower-wall. Above him the great horn roared and bellowed in brutish mockery. And then Kerim Shah drew a shaft to his ear and loosed.

Only a Turanian could have made that shot. The bellowing of the horn ceased suddenly, and a high, thin scream shrilled in its place. The green-robed figure on the tower staggered, clutching at the long shaft which quivered in its bosom, and then pitched across the parapet. The great horn tumbled upon the battlement and hung precariously, and another robed figure rushed to seize it, shrieking in horror. Again the Turanian bow twanged, and again it was answered by a death-howl. The second acolyte, in falling, struck the horn with his elbow and knocked it clatteringly over the parapet to land shatteringly on the rocks far below.

At such headlong speed had Conan covered the ground, that before the clattering echoes of that fall had died away, he was hacking at the door. Warned by his savage instinct suddenly, he gave back as a tide of molten lead splashed down from above. But the next instant he was back again, attacking the panels with redoubled fury. He was galvanized by the fact that his enemies had resorted to earthly weapons. The sorcery of the acolytes was limited. Their necromantic resources might well be exhausted. Kerim Shah was hurrying up the slope, his hillmen behind him in a straggling crescent. They loosed as they ran, their arrows splintering against the walls or arching over the parapet.

The heavy teak portal gave way beneath the Cimmerian's assault, and he peered inside warily, expecting anything. He was looking into a circular chamber from which a stair wound upward. On the opposite side of the chamber a door gaped open, revealing the outer slope – and the backs of half a dozen green-robed figures in full retreat.

Conan yelled, took a step into the tower, and then native caution jerked him back, just as a great block of stone fell crashing to the floor where his foot had been an instant before. Shouting to his followers he raced around the tower.

The acolytes had evacuated their first line of defense. As Conan rounded the tower he saw their green robes twinkling up the mountain ahead of him. He gave chase, panting with earnest blood-lust, and behind him Kerim Shah and the Irakzai came pelting, the latter yelling like wolves at the flight of their enemies, their fatalism momentarily submerged by temporary triumph.

The tower stood on the lower edge of a narrow plateau whose upward slant was barely perceptible. A few hundred yards away this plateau ended abruptly in a chasm which had been invisible further down the mountain. Into this chasm the acolytes apparently leaped without checking their speed. Their pursuers saw the green robes flutter and disappear over the edge.

A few moments later they themselves were standing on the brink of the mighty moat that cut them off from the castle of the Black Seers. It was a sheer-walled ravine that extended in either direction as far as they could see, apparently girdling the mountain, some four hundred yards in width and five hundred feet deep. And in it, from rim to rim, a strange, translucent mist sparkled and shimmered.

Looking down, Conan grunted. Far below him, moving across the glimmering floor, which shone like burnished silver, he saw the forms of the green-robed acolytes. Their outline was wavering and indistinct, like figures seen under deep water. They walked single file, moving toward the opposite wall.

Kerim Shah nocked an arrow and sent it singing downward. But when it struck the mist that filled the chasm it seemed to lose momentum and direction, wandering widely from its course.

"If they went down, so can we!" grunted Conan, while Kerim Shah stared after his shaft in amazement. "I saw them last at this spot – "

Squinting down he saw something shining like a golden thread across the canyon floor far below. The acolytes seemed to be following this thread, and there suddenly came to him Khemsa's cryptic words – "Follow the golden vein!" On the brink, under his very hand as he crouched, he found it – a thin vein of sparkling gold running from an outcropping of ore to the edge and down, across the silvery floor. And he found something else, which had before been invisible to him, because of the peculiar refraction of the light. The gold vein followed a narrow ramp which slanted down into the ravine, fitted with niches for hand and foot hold.

"Here's where they went down," he grunted to Kerim Shah. "They're no adepts, to waft themselves through the air! We'll follow them – "

It was at that instant that the man who had been bitten by the mad dog cried out horribly and leaped at Kerim Shah, foaming and gnashing his teeth. The Turanian, quick as a cat on his feet, sprang aside and the madman pitched head-first over the brink. The others rushed to the edge and glared after him in amazement. The maniac did not fall plummet-like. He floated slowly down through the rosy haze like a man sinking in deep water. His limbs moved like a man trying to swim, and his features were purple and convulsed beyond the contortions of his madness. Far down at last on the shining floor his body settled and lay still.

"There's death in that chasm," muttered Kerim Shah, drawing back from the rosy mist that shimmered almost at his feet. "What now, Conan?"

"On!" answered the Cimmerian grimly. "Those acolytes are human; if the mist doesn't kill them, it won't kill me." He hitched his belt, and his hands touched the girdle Khemsa had given him; he scowled, then smiled bleakly. He had forgotten that girdle; yet thrice had death passed him by to strike another victim.

The acolytes had reached the further wall and were moving up it like great green flies. Letting himself upon the ramp he descended warily. The rosy cloud lapped about his ankles, ascending as he lowered himself. It reached his knees, his thighs, his waist, his arm-pits. He felt it as one feels a thick heavy fog on a damp night. With it lapping about his chin he hesitated, and then ducked under. Instantly his breath ceased; all air was shut off from him and he felt his ribs caving in on his vitals. With a frantic effort he heaved himself up, fighting for life. His head rose above the surface and he drank air in great gulps.

Kerim Shah leaned down toward him, spoke to him, but Conan neither heard nor heeded. Stubbornly, his mind fixed on what the dying Khemsa had told him, the Cimmerian groped for the gold vein, and found that he had moved off it in his descent. Several series of hand-holds were niched in the ramp. Placing himself directly over the thread, he began climbing down once more. The rosy mist rose about him, engulfed him. Now his head was under, but he was still drinking pure air. Above him he saw his companions staring down at him, their features blurred by the haze that shimmered over his head. He gestured for them to follow, and went down swiftly, without waiting to see whether they complied or not.

Kerim Shah sheathed his sword without comment and followed, and the Irakzai, more fearful of being left alone than of the terrors that might lurk below, scrambled after him. Each man clung to the golden thread as they saw the Cimmerian do.

Down the slanting ramp they went to the ravine floor, and moved out across the shining level, treading the gold vein like rope walkers. It was as if they walked along an invisible tunnel through which air circulated freely. They felt death pressing in on them above and on either hand, but it did not touch them.

The vein crawled up a similar ramp on the other wall up which the acolytes had disappeared, and up it they went with taut nerves, not knowing what might be waiting for them among the jutting spurs of rock that fanged the lip of the precipice.

It was the green-robed acolytes who awaited them, with knives in their hands. Perhaps they had reached the limits to which they could retreat. Perhaps the Stygian girdle about Conan's waist could have told why their necromantic spells had proven so weak and so quickly exhausted. Perhaps it was knowledge of death decreed for failure that sent them leaping from among the rocks, eyes glaring and knives glittering, resorting in their desperation to material weapons.

There among the rocky fangs on the precipice lip was no war of wizard craft. It was a whirl of blades, where real steel bit and real blood spurted, where sinewy arms dealt forthright blows that severed quivering flesh, and men went down to be trodden under foot as the fight raged over them.

One of the Irakzai bled to death among the rocks, but the acolytes were down – slashed and hacked asunder or hurled over the edge to float sluggishly down to the silver floor that shone so far below.

Then the conquerors shook blood and sweat from their eyes, and looked at each other. Conan and Kerim Shah still stood upright, and four of the Irakzai.

They stood among the rocky teeth that serrated the precipice brink and from that spot a path wound up a gentle slope to a broad stair, consisting of half a dozen steps, a hundred feet across, cut out of a green jade-like substance. They led up to a broad stage or roofless gallery of the same polished stone, and above it rose, tier upon tier, the castle of the Black Seers. It seemed to have been carved out of the sheer stone of the mountain. The architecture was faultless, but unadorned. The many casements were barred and masked with curtains within. There was no sign of life, friendly or hostile.

They went up the path in silence, and warily as men treading the lair of a serpent. The Irakzai were dumb, like men marching to a certain doom. Even Kerim Shah was silent. Only Conan seemed not aware what a monstrous dislocating and uprooting of accepted thought and action their invasion constituted, what an unprecedented violation of tradition. He was not of the East; and he came of a breed who fought devils and wizards as promptly and matter-of-factly as they battled human foes.

He strode up the shining stairs and across the wide green gallery straight toward the great golden-bound teak door that opened upon it. He cast but a single glance upward at the higher tiers of the great pyramidal structure towering above him. He reached a hand for the bronze prong that jutted like a handle from the door – then checked himself, grinning hardly. The handle was made in the shape of a serpent, head lifted on arched neck; and Conan had a suspicion that that metal head would come to grisly life under his hand.

He struck it from the door with one blow, and its bronze clink on the glassy floor did not lessen his caution. He flipped it aside with his knife point, and again turned to the door. Utter silence reigned over the towers. Far below them the mountain slopes fell away into a purple haze of distance. The sun glittered on snow-clad peaks on either hand. High above a vulture hung like a black dot in the cold blue of the sky. But for it the men before the gold-bound door were the only evidence of life, tiny figures on a green jade gallery poised on the dizzy height, with that fantastic pile of stone towering above them.

A sharp wind off the snow slashed them, whipping their tatters about. Conan's long knife splintering through the teak panels roused the startled echoes. Again and again he struck, hewing through polished wood and metal bands alike. Through the sundered ruins he glared into the interior, alert and suspicious as a wolf. He saw a broad chamber, the polished stone walls untapestried, the mosaic floor uncarpeted. Square, polished ebon stools and a stone dais formed the only furnishings. The room was empty of human life. Another door showed in the opposite wall.

"Leave a man on guard outside," grunted Conan. "I'm going in."

Kerim Shah designated a warrior for that duty, and the man fell back toward the middle of the gallery, bow in hand. Conan strode into the castle, followed by the Turanian and the three remaining Irakzai. The one outside spat, grumbled in his beard, and started suddenly as a low mocking laugh reached his ears.

He lifted his head and saw, on the tier above him, a tall, black-robed figure, naked head nodding slightly as he stared down. His whole attitude suggested mockery and malignity. Quick as a flash the Irakzai bent his bow and loosed, and the arrow streaked upward to strike full in the black-robed breast. The mocking smile did not alter. The Seer plucked out the missile and threw it back at the bowman, not as a weapon is hurled, but with a contemptuous gesture. The Irakzai dodged, instinctively throwing up his arm. His fingers closed on the revolving shaft.

Then he shrieked. In his hand the wooden shaft suddenly *writhed*. Its rigid outline became pliant, melting in his grasp. He tried to throw it from him, but it was too late. He held a twisting serpent in his naked hand and already it had coiled about his wrist and its wicked wedge-shaped head darted at his muscular arm. He screamed again and his eyes became distended, his features purple. He went to his knees shaken by an awful convulsion, and then lay still.

The men inside had wheeled at his first cry. Conan took a swift stride toward the open doorway, and then halted short, baffled. To the men behind him it seemed that he strained against empty air. But though he could see nothing, there was a slick, smooth, hard surface under his hands, and he knew that a sheet of crystal had been let down in the doorway. Through it he saw the Irakzai lying motionless on the glassy gallery, an ordinary arrow sticking in his arm. Naturally, he could not see the man on the tier below.

Conan lifted his knife and smote, and the watchers were dumbfounded to see his blow checked apparently in mid-air, with the loud clang of steel that meets an unyielding substance. He wasted no more effort. He knew that not even the legendary tulwar of Amir Khurum could shatter that invisible curtain.

In a few words he explained the matter to Kerim Shah, and the Turanian shrugged his shoulders. "Well, if our exit is barred, we must find another. In the meanwhile our way lies forward, does it not?"

With a grunt the Cimmerian turned and strode across the chamber to the opposite door, with a feeling of treading on the threshold of doom. As he lifted his knife to shatter the door, it swung silently open as if of its own accord. He strode into a great hall, flanked with tall glassy columns. A hundred feet from the door began the broad jade-green steps of a stair that tapered toward the top like the side of a pyramid. What lay beyond that stair he could not tell. But between him and its shimmering foot stood a curious altar of gleaming black jade. Four great golden serpents twined their tails about this altar and reared their wedge-shaped heads in the air, facing the four quarters of the compass like the enchanted guardians of a fabled treasure. But on the altar, between the arching necks, stood only a crystal globe filled with a cloudy smoke-like substance, in which floated four golden pomegranates.

The sight stirred some dim recollection in his mind; then Conan heeded the altar no longer, for on the lower steps of the stair stood four black-robed figures. He had not seen them come. They were simply there, tall, gaunt, their vulture-heads nodding in unison, their feet and hands hidden by their flowing garments.

One lifted his arm and the sleeve fell away revealing his hand – and it was not a hand at all. Conan halted in mid-stride, compelled against his will. He had encountered a force differing subtly from Khemsa's mesmerism, and he could not advance, though he felt it in his power to retreat if he wished. His companions had likewise halted, and they seemed even more helpless than he, unable to move in either direction.

The Seer whose arm was lifted beckoned to one of the Irakzai, and the man moved toward him like one in a trance, eyes staring and fixed, blade hanging in limp fingers. As he pushed past Conan, the Cimmerian threw an arm across his breast to arrest him. Conan was so much stronger than the Irakzai that in ordinary circumstances he could have broken his spine between his hands. But now the muscular arm was brushed aside like a straw and the Irakzai moved toward the stair, treading jerkily and mechanically. He reached the steps and knelt stiffly, proffering his blade and bending his head. The Seer took the sword. It flashed as he swung it up and down. The Irakzai's head tumbled from his shoulders and thudded heavily on the black marble floor. An arch of blood jetted from the severed arteries and the body slumped over and lay with arms spread wide.

Again a malformed hand lifted and beckoned, and another Irakzai stumbled stiffly to his doom. The ghastly drama was re-enacted and another headless form lay beside the first.

As the third tribesman clumped his way past Conan to his death, the Cimmerian, his veins bulging in his temples with his efforts to break past the unseen barrier that held him, was suddenly aware of allied forces, unseen, but waking into life about him. This realization came without warning, but so powerfully he could not doubt his instinct. His left hand slid involuntarily under his Bakhariot belt and closed on the Stygian girdle. And as he gripped it he felt new strength and power flood his numbed limbs; the will to live was a pulsing white-hot fire, matched by the intensity of his burning rage.

The third Irakzai was a decapitated corpse, and the hideous finger was lifting again when Conan felt the bursting of the invisible barrier. A fierce, involuntary cry burst from his lips as he leaped with the explosive suddenness of pent-up ferocity. His left hand gripped the sorcerer's girdle as a drowning man grips a floating log, and the long knife was a sheen of light in his right. The men on the steps did not move. They watched calmly, cynically; if they felt surprize they did not show it. Conan did not allow himself to think what might chance when he came within knife-reach of them. His blood was pounding in his temples, a mist of crimson swam before his sight. He was afire with the urge to kill – to drive his knife deep into flesh and bone, and twist the blade in blood and entrails.

Another dozen strides would carry him to the steps where the sneering demons stood. He drew his breath deep, his fury rising redly as his charge gathered momentum. He was hurtling past the altar with its golden serpents when like a levin-flash there shot across his mind again as vividly as if spoken in his external ear, the cryptic words of Khemsa: "*Break the crystal ball!*"

His reaction was almost without his own volition. Execution followed impulse so spontaneously that the greatest sorcerer of the age would not have had time to read his mind and prevent his action. Wheeling like a cat from his headlong charge, he brought his knife crashing down upon the crystal. Instantly the air vibrated with a peal of terror – whether from the stairs, the altar, or the crystal itself he could not tell. Hisses filled his ears as the golden serpents, suddenly vibrant with hideous life, writhed and smote at him. But he was fired to the speed of a maddened tiger. A whirl of steel sheared through the hideous trunks that waved toward him, and he smote the crystal sphere again and yet again. And the globe burst with a noise like a thunder-clap, raining fiery shards on the black marble, and the gold pomegranates, as if released from captivity, shot upward toward the lofty roof and were gone.

A mad screaming, bestial and ghastly, was echoing through the great hall. On the steps writhed four black-robed figures, twisting in convulsions, froth dripping from their livid mouths. Then with one frenzied crescendo of inhuman ululation they stiffened and lay still, and Conan knew they were dead. He stared down at the altar and the crystal shards. Four headless golden serpents still coiled about the altar, but no alien life now animated the dully gleaming metal.

Kerim Shah was rising slowly from his knees whither he had been dashed by some unseen force. He shook his head to clear the ringing from his ears.

"Did you hear that crash when you struck? It was as if a thousand crystal panels shattered all over the castle as that globe burst. Were the souls of the wizards imprisoned in those golden balls? – Ha!"

Conan wheeled as Kerim Shah drew his sword and pointed.

Another figure stood at the head of the stair. His robe, too, was black, but of richly embroidered velvet, and there was a velvet cap on his head. His face was calm, and not unhandsome.

"Who the devil are you?" demanded Conan, staring up at him, knife in hand.

"I am the Master of Yimsha!" His voice was like the chime of a temple bell, but a note of cruel mirth ran through it.

"Where is Yasmina?" demanded Kerim Shah.

The Master laughed down at him.

"What is that to you, dead man? Have you so quickly forgotten my strength, once lent to you, that you come armed against me, you poor fool? I think I will take your heart, Kerim Shah!"

He held out his hand as if to receive something, and the Turanian cried out sharply like a man in mortal agony. He reeled drunkenly, and then, with a splintering of bones, a rending of flesh and muscle and a snapping of mail-links, his breast *burst* outward with a shower of blood, and through the ghastly aperture something red and dripping shot through the air into the Master's outstretched hand, as a bit of steel leaps to the magnet. The Turanian slumped to the floor and lay motionless, and the Master laughed and hurled the object to fall before Conan's feet – a still quivering human heart.

With a roar and a curse Conan charged the stair. From Khemsa's girdle he felt strength and deathless hate flow into him to combat the terrible emanation of power that met him on the steps. The air filled with a shimmering steely haze through which he plunged like a swimmer through surf, head lowered, left arm bent about his face, knife gripped low in his right hand. His half-blinded eyes, glaring over the crook of his elbow, made out the hated shape of the Seer before and above him, the outline wavering as a reflection wavers in disturbed water.

He was racked and torn by forces beyond his comprehension, but he felt a driving power outside and beyond his own lifting him inexorably upward and onward, despite the wizard's strength and his own agony.

Now he had reached the head of the stairs, and the Master's face floated in the steely haze before him, and a strange fear shadowed the inscrutable eyes. Conan waded through the mist as through a surf, and his knife lunged upward like a live thing. The keen point ripped the Master's robe as he sprang back with a low cry. Then before Conan's gaze the wizard vanished – simply disappeared like a burst bubble, and something long and undulating darted up one of the smaller stairs that led up to left and right from the landing.

Conan charged after it, up the left-hand stair, uncertain as to just what he had seen whip up those steps, but in a berserk mood that drowned the nausea and horror whispering at the back of his consciousness.

He plunged out into a broad corridor whose uncarpeted floor and untapestried walls were of polished jade, and something long and swift whisked down the corridor ahead of him, and into a curtained door. From within the chamber rose a scream of urgent terror. The sound lent wings to Conan's flying feet and he hurtled through the curtains and headlong into the chamber within.

A frightful scene met his glare. Yasmina cowered on the further edge of a velvet covered dais, screaming her loathing and horror, an arm lifted as if to ward off attack, while before her swayed the hideous head of a giant serpent, shining neck arching up from dark gleaming coils. With a choked cry Conan threw his knife.

Instantly the monster whirled and was upon him like the rush of wind through tall grass. The long knife quivered in its neck, point and a foot of blade showing on one side, and the hilt and a hand's breadth of steel on the other, but it only seemed to madden the giant reptile. The great head towered above the man who faced it, and then darted down, the venom-dripping jaws gaping wide. But Conan had plucked a dagger from his girdle and he stabbed upward as the head dipped down. The point tore through the lower jaw and transfixed the upper, pinning them together. The next instant the great trunk had looped itself about the Cimmerian as the snake, unable to use its fangs, employed its remaining form of attack.

Conan's left arm was pinioned among the bone-crushing folds, but his right was free. Bracing his feet to keep upright, he stretched forth his hand, gripped the hilt of the long knife jutting from the serpent's neck, and tore it free in a shower of blood. As if divining his purpose with more than bestial intelligence, the snake

writhed and knotted, seeking to cast its loops about his right arm. But with the speed of light the long knife rose and fell, shearing half-way through the reptile's giant trunk.

Before he could strike again, the great pliant loops fell from him and the monster dragged itself across the floor, gushing blood from its ghastly wounds. Conan sprang after it, knife lifted, but his vicious swipe cut empty air as the serpent writhed away from him and struck its blunt nose against a panelled screen of sandalwood. One of the panels gave inward and the long, bleeding barrel whipped through it and was gone.

Conan instantly attacked the screen. A few blows rent it apart and he glared into the dim alcove beyond. No horrific shape coiled there; there was blood on the marble floor, and bloody tracks led to a cryptic arched door. Those tracks were of a man's bare feet –

"Conan!" He wheeled back into the chamber just in time to catch the Devi of Vendhya in his arms as she rushed across the room and threw herself upon him, catching him about the neck with a frantic clasp, half hysterical with terror and gratitude and relief.

His own wild blood had been stirred to its uttermost by all that had passed. He caught her to him in a grasp that would have made her wince at another time, and crushed her lips with his. She made no resistance; the Devi was drowned in the elemental woman. She closed her eyes and drank in his fierce, hot, lawless kisses with all the abandon of passionate thirst. She was panting with his violence when he ceased for breath, and glared down at her lying limp in his mighty arms.

"I knew you'd come for me," she murmured. "You would not leave me in this den of devils."

At her words recollection of their environments came to him suddenly. He lifted his head and listened intently. Silence reigned over the castle of Yimsha, but it was a silence impregnated with menace. Peril crouched in every corner, leered invisibly from every hanging.

"We'd better go while we can," he muttered. "Those cuts were enough to kill any common beast – or *man* – but a wizard has a dozen lives. Wound one, and he writhes away like a crippled snake to soak up fresh venom from some source of sorcery."

He picked up the girl and carrying her in his arms like a child, he strode out into the gleaming jade corridor and down the stairs, nerves tautly alert for any sign or sound.

"I met the Master," she whispered, clinging to him and shuddering. "He worked his spells on me to break my will. The most awful was a moldering corpse which seized me in its arms – I fainted then and lay as one dead, I do not know how long. Shortly after I regained consciousness I heard sounds of strife below, and cries, and then that snake came slithering through the curtains – ah!" She shook at the memory of that horror. "I knew somehow that it was not an illusion, but a real serpent that sought my life."

"It was not a shadow, at least," answered Conan cryptically. "He knew he was beaten, and chose to slay you rather than let you be rescued."

"What do you mean, *he*?" she asked uneasily, and then shrank against him, crying out, and forgetting her question. She had seen the corpses at the foot of the stairs. Those of the Seers were not good to look at; as they lay twisted and contorted, their hands and feet were exposed to view, and at the sight Yasmina went livid and hid her face against Conan's powerful shoulder.

X

Yasmina and Conan

Conan passed through the hall quickly enough, traversed the outer chamber and approached the door that let upon the gallery with uncertainty. Then he saw the floor sprinkled with tiny, glittering shards. The crystal sheet that had covered the doorway had been shivered to bits, and he remembered the crash that had accompanied the shattering of the crystal globe. He believed that every piece of crystal in the castle had broken at that instant, and some dim instinct or memory of esoteric lore vaguely suggested the truth of the monstrous connection between the Lords of the Black Circle and the golden pomegranates. He felt the short hairs bristle chilly at the back of his neck and put the matter hastily out of his mind.

He breathed a deep sigh of relief as he stepped out upon the green jade gallery. There was still the gorge to cross, but at least he could see the white peaks glistening in the sun, and the long slopes falling away into the distant blue hazes.

The Irakzai lay where he had fallen, an ugly blotch on the glassy smoothness. As Conan strode down the winding path, he was surprized to note the position of the sun. It had not yet passed its zenith; and yet it seemed to him that hours had passed since he plunged into the castle of the Black Seers.

He felt an urge to hasten, not a mere blind panic, but an instinct of peril growing behind his back. He said nothing to Yasmina, and she seemed content to nestle her dark head against his arching breast and find content in the clasp of his iron arms. He paused an instant on the brink of the chasm, frowning down. The haze which danced in the gorge was no longer rose-hued and sparkling. It was smoky, dim, ghostly, like the life-tide that flickered thinly in a wounded man. The thought came vaguely to Conan that the spells of magicians were more closely bound to their personal beings than were the actions of common men to the actors.

But far below the floor shone like tarnished silver, and the gold thread sparkled undimmed. Conan shifted Yasmina across his shoulder where she lay docilely, and began the descent. Hurriedly he descended the ramp, and hurriedly he fled across the echoing floor. He had a conviction that they were racing with time; that their chance of survival depended upon crossing that gorge of horrors before the wounded Master of the castle should regain enough power to loose some other doom upon them.

When he toiled up the further ramp and came out upon the crest, he breathed a gusty sigh of relief, and stood Yasmina upon her feet.

"You walk from here," he told her, "it's downhill all the way."

She stole a glance at the gleaming pyramid across the chasm; it reared up against the snowy slope like the citadel of silence and immemorial evil.

"Are you a magician, that you have conquered the Black Seers of Yimsha, Conan of Ghor?" she asked, as they went down the path, with his heavy arm about her supple waist.

"It was a girdle Khemsa gave me before he died," Conan answered. "Yes, I found him on the trail. It is a curious one which I'll show you when I have time. Against some spells it was weak, but against others it was strong, and a good knife is always a hearty incantation."

"But if the girdle aided you in conquering the Master," she argued, "why did it not aid Khemsa?"

He shook his head. "Who knows? But Khemsa had been the Master's slave; perhaps that weakened its magic. He had no hold on me as he had on Khemsa. Yet I can't say that I conquered him. He retreated, but I have a feeling that we haven't seen the last of him. I want to put as many miles between us and his lair as we can."

He was further relieved to find the horses tethered among the tamarisks as he had left them. He loosed them swiftly and mounted the black stallion, swinging the girl up before him. The others followed, freshened by their rest.

"And what now?" she asked. "To Afghulistan?"

"Not just now!" He grinned hardly. "Somebody – maybe the governor – killed my seven headmen. My idiotic followers think I had something to do with it, and unless I am able to convince them otherwise, they'll hunt me like a wounded jackal."

"Then what of me? If the headmen are dead, I am useless to you as a hostage. Will you slay me, to avenge them?"

He looked down at her, with eyes fiercely aglow, and laughed at the suggestion.

"Then let us ride to the border," she said. "You'll be safe from the Afghulis there – "

"Yes, on a Vendhyan gibbet."

"I am queen of Vendhya," she reminded him with a touch of her old imperiousness. "You have saved my life and at least partly avenged my brother. You shall be rewarded."

She did not intend it as it sounded, but he growled in his throat, ill-pleased.

"Keep your bounty for your city-bred dogs, princess! If you're a queen of the plains, I'm a chief of the hills, and not one foot toward the border will I take you!"

"But you would be safe – " she began bewilderedly.

"And you'd be the Devi again," he broke in. "No, girl; I prefer you as you are now – a woman of flesh and blood, riding on my saddle bow."

"But you can't *keep* me!" she cried. "You can't – "

"Watch and see!" he advised her grimly.

"But I will pay you a vast ransom – "

"Devil take your ransom," he answered roughly, his arms hardening about her supple figure. "The kingdom of Vendhya could give me nothing I desire half as much as I desire you. I took you at the risk of my neck; if your courtiers want you back, let them come up the Zhaibar and fight for you."

"But you have no followers now!" she protested. "You are hunted! How can you preserve your own life, much less mine?"

"I still have friends in the hills," he answered. "There is a chief of the Khurakzai who will keep you safely while I bicker with the Afghulis. If they will have none of me, by Crom I will ride northward with you to the steppes of the *kozaki*. I was a *hetman* among the Free Companions before I rode southward. I'll make you a queen on the Zaporoska River!"

"But I can not!" she objected. "You must not hold me – "

"If the idea's so repulsive," he demanded, "why did you yield yourself so willingly?"

"Even a queen is human," she answered, coloring. "But because I am a queen, I must consider my kingdom. Do not carry me away into some foreign country. Come back to Vendhya with me!"

"Would you make me your king?" he asked sardonically.

"Well, there are customs – " she stammered, and he interrupted her with a hard laugh.

"Yes, civilized customs that won't let you do as you wish. You'll marry some withered old king of the plains, and I can go my way with only the memory of a few kisses snatched from your lips. Ha!"

"But I must return to my kingdom!" she repeated helplessly.

"Why?" he demanded angrily. "To chafe your rump on gold thrones, and listen to the plaudits of smirking, velvet-skirted fools? Where is the gain? Listen: I was born in the Cimmerian hills where the people are all barbarians. I have been a mercenary soldier, a corsair, a *kozak*, and a hundred other things. What king has roamed the countries, fought the battles, loved the women, and won the plunder that I have?

"I came into Ghulistan to raise a horde and plunder the kingdoms to the south – your own among them. Being chief of the Afghulis was only a start. If I can conciliate them, I'll have a dozen tribes following me within a year. But if I can't I'll ride back to the steppes and loot the Turanian borders with the *kozaki*. And you'll go with me. To the devil with your kingdom; they fended for themselves before you were born."

She lay in his arms looking up at him, and she felt a tug at her spirit, a lawless, reckless urge that matched his own and was by it called into being. But a thousand generations of sovereignship rode heavy upon her.

"I can't! I can't!" she repeated helplessly.

"You haven't any choice," he assured her. "You – what the devil!"

They had left Yimsha some miles behind them, and were riding along a high ridge that separated two deep valleys. They had just topped a steep crest where they could gaze down into the valley on their right hand. And there a running fight was in progress. A strong wind was blowing away from them, carrying the sound from their ears, but even so the clashing of steel and thunder of hoofs welled up from far below.

They saw the glint of the sun on lance-tip and spired helmet. Three thousand mailed horsemen were driving before them a ragged band of turbaned riders, who fled snarling and striking like fleeing wolves.

"Turanians!" muttered Conan. "Squadrons from Secunderam. What the devil are they doing here?"

"Who are the men they pursue?" asked Yasmina. "And why do they fall back so stubbornly? They can not stand against such odds."

"Five hundred of my mad Afghulis," he growled, scowling down into the vale. "They're in a trap, and they know it."

The valley was indeed a cul-de-sac at that end. It narrowed to a high walled gorge, opening out further into a round bowl, completely rimmed with lofty, unscalable walls.

The turbaned riders were being forced into this gorge, because there was nowhere else for them to go, and they went reluctantly, in a shower of arrows and a whirl of swords. The helmeted riders harried them, but did not press in too rashly. They knew the desperate fury of the hill tribes, and they knew too that they had their prey in a trap from which there was no escape. They had recognized the hillmen as Afghulis, and they wished to hem them in and force a surrender. They needed hostages for the purpose they had in mind.

Their emir was a man of decision and initiative. When he reached Gurashah valley, and found neither guides nor emissary waiting for him, he pushed on, trusting to his own knowledge of the country. All the way from Secunderam there had been fighting, and tribesmen were licking their wounds in many a crag-perched village. He knew there was a good chance that neither he nor any of his helmeted spearmen would ever ride through the gates of Secunderam again, for the tribes would all be up behind him now, but he was determined to carry out his orders – which were to take Yasmina Devi from the Afghulis at all costs, and to bring her captive to Secunderam, or if confronted by impossibility, to strike off her head before he himself died.

Of all this, of course, the watchers on the ridge were not aware. But Conan fidgeted with nervousness.

"Why the devil did they get themselves trapped?" he demanded of the universe at large. "I know what they're doing in these parts – they were hunting me, the dogs! Poking into every valley – and found themselves penned in before they knew it. The damned fools! They're making a stand in the gorge, but they can't hold out for long. When the Turanians have pushed them back into the bowl, they'll slaughter them at their leisure."

The din welling up from below increased in volume and intensity. In the strait of the narrow gut the Afghulis, fighting desperately, were for the time being holding their own against the mailed riders who could not throw their whole weight against them.

Conan scowled darkly, moved restlessly, fingering his hilt, and finally spoke bluntly: "Devi, I must go down to them. I'll find a place for you to hide until I come back to you. You spoke of your kingdom – well, I don't pretend to look on those hairy devils as my children, but after all, such as they are, they're my henchmen. A chief should never desert his followers, even if they desert him first. They think they were right in kicking me out – hell, I won't be cast off! I'm still chief of the Afghulis, and I'll prove it! I can climb down on foot into the gorge."

"But what of me?" she queried. "You carried me away forcibly from *my* people; now will you leave me to die in the hills alone while you go down and sacrifice yourself uselessly?"

His veins swelled with the conflict of his emotions.

"That's right," he muttered helplessly. "Crom knows what I *can* do."

She turned her head slightly, a curious expression dawning on her beautiful face. Then –

"Listen!" she cried. "Listen!" A distant fanfare of trumpets was borne faintly to their ears. They stared into the deep valley on the left, and caught a glint of steel on the further side. A long line of lances and polished helmets moved along the vale, gleaming in the sunlight.

"The riders of Vendhya!" she cried exultingly. "Even at this distance I can not mistake them!"

"There are thousands of them!" muttered Conan. "It has been long since a Kshatriya host has ridden this far into the hills."

"They are searching for me!" she exclaimed. "Give me your horse! I will ride to my warriors! The ridge is not so precipitous on the left, and I can reach the valley floor. Go to your men and make them hold out a little longer. I will lead my horsemen into the valley at the upper end and fall upon the Turanians! We will crush them in the vise! Quick, Conan! Will you sacrifice your men to your own desire?"

The burning hunger of the steppes and the wintry forests glared out of his eyes, but he shook his head and swung off the stallion, placing the reins in her hands.

"You win!" he grunted. "Ride like the devil!"

She wheeled away down the left-hand slope and he ran swiftly along the ridge until he reached the long ragged cleft that was the defile in which the fight raged. Down the rugged wall he scrambled like an ape, clinging to projections and crevices, to fall at last, feet-first, into the mêlée that raged in the mouth of the gorge. Blades were whickering and clanging about him, horses rearing and stamping, helmet plumes nodding among turbans that were stained crimson.

As he hit, he yelled like a wolf, caught a gold-worked rein and dodging the sweep of a scimitar, drove his long knife upward through the rider's vitals. In another instant he was in the saddle, yelling ferocious orders to the Afghulis. They stared at him stupidly for an instant, then as they saw the havoc his steel was wreaking among their enemies, they fell to their work again, accepting him without comment. In that inferno of licking blades and spurting blood there was no time to ask or answer questions.

The riders in their spired helmets and gold-worked hauberks swarmed about the gorge mouth, thrusting and slashing, and the narrow defile was packed and jammed with horses and men, the warriors crushed breast to breast, stabbing with shortened blades, slashing murderously when there was an instant's room to swing a sword. When a man went down he did not get up from beneath the stamping, swirling hoofs. Weight and sheer strength counted heavily there, and the chief of the Afghulis did the work of ten. At such times accustomed habits sway men strongly, and the warriors who were used to seeing Conan in their vanguard, were heartened mightily, despite their distrust of him.

But superior numbers counted too. The pressure of the men behind forced the horsemen of Turan deeper and deeper into the gorge, in the teeth of the flickering tulwars. Foot by foot the Afghulis were shoved back, leaving the defile-floor carpeted with dead, on which the riders trampled. As he hacked and smote like a man possessed, Conan had time for some chilling doubts – would Yasmina keep her word? She had but to join her warriors, turn southward and leave him and his band to perish.

But at last, after what seemed centuries of desperate battling, in the valley outside there rose another sound above the clash of steel and yells of slaughter. And then with a burst of trumpets that shook the walls, and rushing thunder of hoofs, five thousand riders of Vendhya smote the hosts of Secunderam.

That stroke split the Turanian squadrons asunder, shattered, tore and rent them and scattered their fragments all over the valley. In an instant the surge had ebbed back out of the gorge; there was a chaotic, confused swirl of fighting, horsemen wheeling and smiting singly and in clusters, and then the emir went down with a Kshatriya lance through his breast, and the riders in their spired helmets turned their horses down the valley, spurring like mad and seeking to slash a way through the swarms which had come upon them from the rear. As they scattered in flight, the conquerors scattered in pursuit, and all across the valley floor, and up on the slopes near the mouth and over the crests streamed the fugitives and the pursuers. The Afghulis, those left to ride, rushed out of the gorge and joined in the harrying of their foes, accepting the unexpected alliance as unquestioningly as they had accepted the return of their repudiated chief.

The sun was sinking toward the distant crags when Conan, his garments hacked to tatters and the mail under them reeking and clotted with blood, his knife dripping and crusted to the hilt, strode over the corpses to where Yasmina Devi sat her horse among her nobles on the crest of the ridge, near a lofty precipice.

"You kept your word, Devi!" he roared. "By Crom, though, I had some bad seconds down in that gorge – *look out!*"

Down from the sky swooped a vulture of tremendous size with a thunder of wings that knocked men sprawling from their horses.

The scimitar-like beak was slashing for the Devi's soft neck, but Conan was quicker – a short run, a tigerish leap, the savage thrust of a dripping knife, and the vulture voiced a horribly human cry, pitched sideways and went tumbling down the cliffs to the rocks and river a thousand feet below. As it fell, its black wings thrashing the air, it took on the semblance, not of a bird, but of a black-robed human body that fell, arms in wide black sleeves thrown abroad.

Conan turned to Yasmina, his red knife still in his hand, his blue eyes smoldering, blood oozing from wounds on his thickly-muscled arms and thighs.

"You are the Devi again," he said, grinning fiercely at the gold-clasped gossamer robe she had donned over her hill-girl attire, and awed not at all by the imposing array of chivalry all about him. "I have you to thank for the lives of some three hundred and fifty of my rogues, who are at least convinced that I didn't betray them. You have put my hands on the reins of conquest again."

"I still owe you my ransom," she said, her dark eyes glowing as they swept over him. "Ten thousand pieces of gold I will pay you – "

He made a savage, impatient gesture, shook the blood from his knife and thrust it back in its scabbard, wiping his hands on his mail.

"I will collect your ransom in my own way, at my own time," he said. "I will collect it in your palace at Ayodhya, and I will come with fifty thousand men to see that the scales are fair."

She laughed, gathering her reins into her hands. "And I will meet you on the shores of the Jhumda with a hundred thousand!"

His eyes shone with fierce appreciation and admiration, and stepping back, he lifted his hand with a gesture that was like the assumption of kingship, indicating that her road was clear before her.

The Hour of the Dragon

The Hour of the Dragon

The Lion banner sways and falls in the horror haunted gloom;
A scarlet Dragon rustles by, borne on winds of doom.
In heaps the shining horsemen lie, where the thrusting lances break,
And deep in the haunted mountains the lost, black gods awake.
Dead hands grope in the shadows, the stars turn pale with fright,
For this is the Dragon's Hour, the triumph of Fear and Night.

I

O Sleeper, Awake!

The long tapers flickered, sending the black shadows wavering along the walls, and the velvet tapestries rippled. Yet there was no wind in the chamber. Four men stood about the ebony table on which lay the green sarcophagus that gleamed like carven jade. In the upraised right hand of each man a curious black candle burned with a weird greenish light. Outside was night and a lost wind moaning among the black trees.

Inside the chamber was tense silence, and the wavering of the shadows, while four pairs of eyes, burning with intensity, were fixed on the long green case across which cryptic hieroglyphics writhed, as if lent life and movement by the unsteady light. The man at the foot of the sarcophagus leaned over it and moved his candle as if he were writing with a pen, inscribing a mystic symbol in the air. Then he set down the candle in its black gold stick at the foot of the case, and, mumbling some formula unintelligible to his companions, he thrust a broad white hand into his fur-trimmed robe. When he brought it forth again it was as if he cupped in his palm a ball of living fire.

The other three drew in their breath sharply, and the dark, powerful man who stood at the head of the sarcophagus whispered: "The Heart of Ahriman!" The other lifted a quick hand for silence. Somewhere a dog began howling dolefully, and a stealthy step padded outside the barred and bolted door. But none looked aside from the mummy-case over which the man in the ermine-trimmed robe was now moving the great flaming jewel while he muttered an incantation that was old when Atlantis sank. The glare of the gem dazzled their eyes, so that they could not be sure of what they saw; but with a splintering crash, the carven lid of the sarcophagus burst outward as if from some irresistible pressure applied from within, and the four men, bending eagerly forward, saw the occupant – a huddled, withered, wizened shape, with dried brown limbs like dead wood showing through moldering bandages.

"Bring that thing *back*?" muttered the small dark man who stood on the right, with a short, sardonic laugh. "It is ready to crumble at a touch. We are fools – "

"Shhh!" It was an urgent hiss of command from the large man who held the jewel. Perspiration stood upon his broad white forehead and his eyes were dilated. He leaned forward, and, without touching the thing with his hand, laid on the breast of the mummy the blazing jewel. Then he drew back and watched with fierce intensity, his lips moving in soundless invocation.

It was as if a globe of living fire flickered and burned on the dead, withered bosom. And breath sucked in, hissing, through the clenched teeth of the watchers. For as they watched, an awful transmutation became apparent. The withered shape in the sarcophagus was expanding, was growing, lengthening. The bandages burst and fell into brown dust. The shriveled limbs swelled, straightened. Their dusky hue began to fade.

"By Mitra!" whispered the tall, yellow-haired man on the left. "He was *not* a Stygian. That part at least was true."

Again a trembling finger warned for silence. The hound outside was no longer howling. He whimpered, as with an evil dream, and then that sound, too, died away in silence, in which the yellow-haired man plainly heard the straining of the heavy door, as if something outside pushed powerfully upon it. He half turned, his hand at his sword, but the man in the ermine robe hissed an urgent warning: "Stay! Do not break the chain! And on your life do not go to the door!"

The yellow-haired man shrugged and turned back, and then he stopped short, staring. In the jade sarcophagus lay a living man: a tall, lusty man, naked, white of skin, and dark of hair and beard. He lay motionless, his eyes wide open, and blank and unknowing as a newborn babe's. On his breast the great jewel smoldered and sparkled.

The man in ermine reeled as if from some let-down of extreme tension.

"Ishtar!" he gasped. "It is Xaltotun! – *and he lives!* Valerius! Tarascus! Amalric! Do you see? Do you see? You doubted me – but I have not failed! We have been close to the open gates of hell this night, and the shapes of darkness have gathered close about us – aye, they followed *him* to the very door – but we have brought the great magician back to life."

"And damned our souls to purgatories everlasting, I doubt not," muttered the small, dark man, Tarascus.

The yellow-haired man, Valerius, laughed harshly.

"What purgatory can be worse than life itself? So we are all damned together from birth. Besides, who would not sell his miserable soul for a throne?"

"There is no intelligence in his stare, Orastes," said the large man.

"He has long been dead," answered Orastes. "He is as one newly awakened. His mind is empty after the long sleep – nay, he was *dead*, not sleeping. We brought his spirit back over the voids and gulfs of night and oblivion. I will speak to him."

He bent over the foot of the sarcophagus, and fixing his gaze on the wide dark eyes of the man within, he said, slowly: "Awake, Xaltotun!"

The lips of the man moved mechanically. "Xaltotun!" he repeated in a groping whisper.

"*You* are Xaltotun!" exclaimed Orastes, like a hypnotist driving home his suggestions. "You are Xaltotun of Python, in Acheron."

A dim flame flickered in the dark eyes.

"I was Xaltotun," he whispered. "I am dead."

"You *are* Xaltotun!" cried Orastes. "You are not dead! You live!"

"I am Xaltotun," came the eery whisper. "But I am dead. In my house in Khemi, in Stygia, there I died."

"And the priests who poisoned you mummified your body with their dark arts, keeping all your organs intact!" exclaimed Orastes. "But now you live again! The Heart of Ahriman has restored your life, drawn your spirit back from space and eternity."

"The Heart of Ahriman!" The flame of remembrance grew stronger. "The barbarians stole it from me!"

"He remembers," muttered Orastes. "Lift him from the case."

The others obeyed hesitantly, as if reluctant to touch the man they had recreated, and they seemed not easier in their minds when they felt firm muscular flesh, vibrant with blood and life, beneath their fingers. But they lifted him upon the table, and Orastes clothed him in a curious dark velvet robe, splashed with gold stars and crescent moons, and fastened a cloth-of-gold fillet about his temples, confining the black wavy locks that fell to his shoulders. He let them do as they would, saying nothing, not even when they set him in a carven throne-like chair with a high ebony back and wide silver arms, and feet like golden claws. He sat there motionless, and slowly intelligence grew in his dark eyes and made them deep and strange and luminous. It was as if long-sunken witchlights floated slowly up through midnight pools of darkness.

Orastes cast a furtive glance at his companions, who stood staring in morbid fascination at their strange guest. Their iron nerves had withstood an ordeal that might have driven weaker men mad. He knew it was with no weaklings that he conspired, but men whose courage was as profound as their lawless ambitions and capacity for evil. He turned his attention to the figure in the ebon-black chair. And this one spoke at last.

"I remember," he said in a strong, resonant voice, speaking Nemedian with a curious, archaic accent. "I am Xaltotun, who was high priest of Set in Python, which was in Acheron. The Heart of Ahriman – I dreamed I had found it again – where is it?"

Orastes placed it in his hand, and he drew breath deeply as he gazed into the depths of the terrible jewel burning in his grasp.

"They stole it from me, long ago," he said. "The red heart of the night it is, strong to save or to damn. It came from afar, and from long ago. While I held it, none could stand before me. But it was stolen from me, and Acheron fell, and I fled an exile into dark Stygia. Much I remember, but much I have forgotten. I have been in a far land, across misty voids and gulfs and unlit oceans. What is the year?"

Orastes answered him. "It is the waning of the Year of the Lion, three thousand years after the fall of Acheron."

"Three thousand years!" murmured the other. "So long? Who are you?"

"I am Orastes, once a priest of Mitra. This man is Amalric, baron of Tor, in Nemedia; this other is Tarascus, younger brother of the king of Nemedia; and this tall man is Valerius, rightful heir of the throne of Aquilonia."

"Why have you given me life?" demanded Xaltotun. "What do you require of me?"

The man was now fully alive and awake, his keen eyes reflecting the working of an unclouded brain. There was no hesitation or uncertainty in his manner. He came directly to the point, as one who knows that no man gives something for nothing. Orastes met him with equal candor.

"We have opened the doors of hell this night to free your soul and return it to your body because we need your aid. We wish to place Tarascus on the throne of Nemedia, and to win for Valerius the crown of Aquilonia. With your necromancy you can aid us."

Xaltotun's mind was devious and full of unexpected slants.

"You must be deep in the arts yourself, Orastes, to have been able to restore my life. How is it that a priest of Mitra knows of the Heart of Ahriman, and the incantations of Skelos?"

"I am no longer a priest of Mitra," answered Orastes. "I was cast forth from my order because of my delving in black magic. But for Amalric there I might have been burned as a magician.

"But that left me free to pursue my studies. I journeyed in Zamora, in Vendhya, in Stygia, and among the haunted jungles of Khitai. I read the iron-bound books of Skelos, and talked with unseen creatures in deep wells, and faceless shapes in black reeking jungles. I obtained a glimpse of your sarcophagus in the demon-haunted crypts below the black giant-walled temple of Set in the hinterlands of Stygia, and I learned of the arts that would bring back life to your shriveled corpse. From moldering manuscripts I learned of the Heart of Ahriman. Then for a year I sought its hiding-place, and at last I found it."

"Then why trouble to bring me back to life?" demanded Xaltotun, with his piercing gaze fixed on the priest. "Why did you not employ the Heart to further your own power?"

"Because no man today knows the secrets of the Heart," answered Orastes. "Not even in legends live the arts by which to loose its full powers. I knew it could restore life; of its deeper secrets I am ignorant. I merely used it to bring you back to life. It is the use of your knowledge we seek. As for the Heart, you alone know its awful secrets."

Xaltotun shook his head, staring broodingly into the flaming depths.

"My necromantic knowledge is greater than the sum of all the knowledge of other men," he said; "yet I do not know the full power of the jewel. I did not invoke it in the old days; I guarded it lest it be used against me. At last it was stolen, and in the hands of a feathered shaman of the barbarians it defeated all my mighty sorcery. Then it vanished, and I was poisoned by the jealous priests of Stygia before I could learn where it was hidden."

"It was hidden in a cavern below the temple of Mitra, in Tarantia," said Orastes. "By devious ways I discovered this, after I had located your remains in Set's subterranean temple in Stygia.

"Zamorian thieves, partly protected by spells I learned from sources better left unmentioned, stole your mummy-case from under the very talons of those which guarded it in the dark, and by camel-caravan and galley and ox-wagon it came at last to this city.

"Those same thieves – or rather those of them who still lived after their frightful quest – stole the Heart of Ahriman from its haunted cavern below the temple of Mitra, and all the skill of men and the spells of sorcerers nearly failed. One man of them lived long enough to reach me and give the jewel into my hands, before he died slavering and gibbering of what he had seen in that accursed crypt. The thieves of Zamora are the most faithful of men to their trust. Even with my conjurements, none but them could have stolen the Heart from where it has lain in demon-guarded darkness since the fall of Acheron, three thousand years ago."

Xaltotun lifted his lion-like head and stared far off into space, as if plumbing the lost centuries.

"Three thousand years!" he muttered. "Set! Tell me what has chanced in the world."

"The barbarians who overthrew Acheron set up new kingdoms," quoth Orastes. "Where the empire had stretched now rose realms called Aquilonia, and Nemedia, and Argos, from the tribes that founded them. The older kingdoms of Ophir, Corinthia and western Koth, which had been subject to the kings of Acheron, regained their independence with the fall of the empire."

"And what of the people of Acheron?" demanded Orastes. "When I fled into Stygia, Python was in ruins, and all the great, purple-towered cities of Acheron fouled with blood and trampled by the sandals of the barbarians."

"In the hills small groups of folk still boast descent from Acheron," answered Orastes. "For the rest, the tide of my barbarian ancestors rolled over them and wiped them out. They – my ancestors – had suffered much from the kings of Acheron."

A grim and terrible smile curled the Pythonian's lips.

"Aye! Many a barbarian, both man and woman, died screaming on the altar under this hand. I have seen their heads piled to make a pyramid in the great square in Python when the kings returned from the west with their spoils and naked captives."

"Aye. And when the day of reckoning came, the sword was not spared. So Acheron ceased to be, and purple-towered Python became a memory of forgotten days. But the younger kingdoms rose on the imperial ruins and waxed great. And now we have brought you back to aid us to rule these kingdoms, which, if less strange and wonderful than Acheron of old, are yet rich and powerful, well worth fighting for. Look!" Orastes unrolled before the stranger a map drawn cunningly on vellum.

Xaltotun regarded it, and then shook his head, baffled.

"The very outlines of the land are changed. It is like some familiar thing seen in a dream, fantastically distorted."

"Howbeit," answered Orastes, tracing with his forefinger, "here is Belverus, the capital of Nemedia, in which we now are. Here run the boundaries of the land of Nemedia. To the south and southeast are Ophir and Corinthia, to the east Brythunia, to the west Aquilonia."

"It is the map of a world I do not know," said Xaltotun softly, but Orastes did not miss the lurid fire of hate that flickered in his dark eyes.

"It is a map you shall help us change," answered Orastes. "It is our desire first to set Tarascus on the throne of Nemedia. We wish to accomplish this without strife, and in such a way that no suspicion will rest on Tarascus. We do not wish the land to be torn by civil wars, but to reserve all our power for the conquest of Aquilonia.

"Should King Nimed and his sons die naturally, in a plague for instance, Tarascus would mount the throne as the next heir, peacefully and unopposed."

Xaltotun nodded, without replying, and Orastes continued.

"The other task will be more difficult. We cannot set Valerius on the Aquilonian throne without a war, and that kingdom is a formidable foe. Its people are a hardy, war-like race, toughened by continual wars with the Picts, Zingarans and Cimmerians. For five hundred years Aquilonia and Nemedia have intermittently waged war, and the ultimate advantage has always lain with the Aquilonians.

"Their present king is the most renowned warrior among the western nations. He is an outlander, an adventurer who seized the crown by force during a time of civil strife, strangling King Namedides with his own hands, upon the very throne. His name is Conan, and no man can stand before him in battle.

"Valerius is now the rightful heir of the throne. He had been driven into exile by his royal kinsman, Namedides, and has been away from his native realm for years, but he is of the blood of the old dynasty, and many of the barons would secretly hail the overthrow of Conan, who is a nobody without royal or even noble blood. But the common people are loyal to him, and the nobility of the outlying provinces. Yet if his forces were overthrown in the battle that must first take place, and Conan himself slain, I think it would not be difficult to put Valerius on the throne. Indeed, with Conan slain, the only center of the government would be gone. He is not part of a dynasty, but only a lone adventurer."

"I wish that I might see this king," mused Xaltotun, glancing toward a silvery mirror which formed one of the panels of the wall. This mirror cast no reflection, but Xaltotun's expression showed that he understood its purpose, and Orastes nodded with the pride a good craftsman takes in the recognition of his accomplishments by a master of his craft.

"I will try to show him to you," he said. And seating himself before the mirror, he gazed hypnotically into its depths, where presently a dim shadow began to take shape.

It was uncanny, but those watching knew it was no more than the reflected image of Orastes' thought, embodied in that mirror as a wizard's thoughts are embodied in a magic crystal. It floated hazily, then leaped into startling clarity – a tall man, mightily shouldered and deep of chest, with a massive corded neck and heavily muscled limbs. He was clad in silk and velvet, with the royal lions of Aquilonia worked in gold upon his rich jupon, and the crown of Aquilonia shone on his square-cut black mane; but the great sword at his side seemed more natural to him than the regal accouterments. His brow was low and broad, his eyes a volcanic blue that smoldered as if with some inner fire. His dark, scarred, almost sinister face was that of a fighting-man, and his velvet garments could not conceal the hard, dangerous lines of his limbs.

"That man is no Hyborian!" exclaimed Xaltotun.

"No; he is a Cimmerian, one of those wild tribesmen who dwell in the gray hills of the north."

"I fought his ancestors of old," muttered Xaltotun. "Not even the kings of Acheron could conquer them."

"They still remain a terror to the nations of the south," answered Orastes. "He is a true son of that savage race, and has proved himself, thus far, unconquerable."

Xaltotun did not reply; he sat staring down at the pool of living fire that shimmered in his hand. Outside, the hound howled again, long and shudderingly.

II
A Black Wind Blows

The year of the Dragon had birth in war and pestilence and unrest. The black plague stalked through the streets of Belverus, striking down the merchant in his stall, the serf in his kennel, the knight at his banquet board. Before it the arts of the leeches were helpless. Men said it had been sent from hell as punishment for the sins of pride and lust. It was swift and deadly as the stroke of an adder. The victim's body turned purple and then black, and within a few minutes he sank down dying, and the stench of his own putrefaction was in his nostrils even before death wrenched his soul from his rotting body. A hot, roaring wind blew incessantly from the south, and the crops withered in the fields, the cattle sank and died in their tracks.

Men cried out on Mitra, and muttered against the king; for somehow, throughout the kingdom, the word was whispered that the king was secretly addicted to loathsome practises and foul debauches in the seclusion of his nighted palace. And then in that palace death stalked grinning on feet about which swirled the monstrous vapors of the plague. In one night the king died with his three sons, and the drums that thundered their dirge drowned the grim and ominous bells that rang from the carts that lumbered through the streets gathering up the rotting dead.

That night, just before dawn, the hot wind that had blown for weeks ceased to rustle evilly through the silken window curtains. Out of the north rose a great wind that roared among the towers, and there was cataclysmic thunder, and blinding sheets of lightning, and driving rain. But the dawn shone clean and green and clear; the scorched ground veiled itself in grass, the thirsty crops sprang up anew, and the plague was gone – its miasma swept clean out of the land by the mighty wind.

Men said the gods were satisfied because the evil king and his spawn were slain, and when his young brother Tarascus was crowned in the great coronation hall, the populace cheered until the towers rocked, acclaiming the monarch on whom the gods smiled.

Such a wave of enthusiasm and rejoicing as swept the land is frequently the signal for a war of conquest. So no one was surprized when it was announced that King Tarascus had declared the truce made by the late king with their western neighbors void, and was gathering his hosts to invade Aquilonia. His reason was candid; his motives, loudly proclaimed, gilded his actions with something of the glamor of a crusade. He espoused the cause of Valerius, "rightful heir to the throne"; he came, he proclaimed, not as an enemy of Aquilonia, but as a friend, to free the people from the tyranny of a usurper and a foreigner.

If there were cynical smiles in certain quarters, and whispers concerning the king's good friend Amalric, whose vast personal wealth seemed to be flowing into the rather depleted royal treasury, they were unheeded in the general wave of fervor and zeal of Tarascus's popularity. If any shrewd individuals suspected that Amalric was the real ruler of Nemedia, behind the scenes, they were careful not to voice such heresy. And the war went forward with enthusiasm.

The king and his allies moved westward at the head of fifty thousand men – knights in shining armor with their pennons streaming above their helmets, pikemen in steel caps and brigandines, crossbowmen in leather jerkins. They crossed the border, took a frontier castle and burned three mountain villages, and then, in the valley of the Valkia, ten miles west of the boundary line, they met the hosts of Conan, king of Aquilonia – forty-five thousand knights, archers and men-at-arms, the flower of Aquilonian strength and chivalry. Only the knights of Poitain, under Prospero, had not yet arrived, for they had far to ride up from the southwestern corner of the kingdom. Tarascus had struck without warning. His invasion had come on the heels of his proclamation, without formal declaration of war.

The two hosts confronted each other across a wide, shallow valley, with rugged cliffs, and a shallow stream winding through masses of reeds and willows down the middle of the vale. The camp-followers of both hosts came down to this stream for water, and shouted insults and hurled stones across at one another. The last glints of the sun shone on the golden banner of Nemedia with the scarlet dragon, unfurled in the breeze above the pavilion of King Tarascus on an eminence near the eastern cliffs. But the shadow of the western cliffs fell like a vast purple pall across the tents and the army of Aquilonia, and upon the black banner with its golden lion that floated above King Conan's pavilion.

All night the fires flared the length of the valley, and the wind brought the call of trumpets, the clangor of arms, and the sharp challenges of the sentries who paced their horses along either edge of the willow-grown stream.

It was in the darkness before dawn that King Conan stirred on his couch, which was no more than a pile of silks and furs thrown on a dais, and awakened. He started up, crying out sharply and clutching at his sword. Pallantides, his commander, rushing in at the cry, saw his king sitting upright, his hand on his hilt, and perspiration dripping from his strangely pale face.

"Your Majesty!" exclaimed Pallantides. "Is aught amiss?"

"What of the camp?" demanded Conan. "Are the guards out?"

"Five hundred horsemen patrol the stream, Your Majesty," answered the general. "The Nemedians have not offered to move against us in the night. They wait for dawn, even as we."

"By Crom," muttered Conan. "I awoke with a feeling that doom was creeping on me in the night."

He stared up at the great golden lamp which shed a soft glow over the velvet hangings and carpets of the great tent. They were alone; not even a slave or a page slept on the carpeted floor; but Conan's eyes blazed as they were wont to blaze in the teeth of great peril, and the sword quivered in his hand. Pallantides watched him uneasily. Conan seemed to be listening.

"Listen!" hissed the king. "Did you hear it? A furtive step!"

"Seven knights guard your tent, Your Majesty," said Pallantides. "None could approach it unchallenged."

"Not outside," growled Conan. "It seemed to sound *inside* the tent."

Pallantides cast a swift, startled look around. The velvet hangings merged with shadows in the corners, but if there had been anyone in the pavilion besides themselves, the general would have seen him. Again he shook his head.

"There is no one here, sire. You sleep in the midst of your host."

"I have seen death strike a king in the midst of thousands," muttered Conan. "Something that walks on invisible feet and is not seen – "

"Perhaps you were dreaming, Your Majesty," said Pallantides, somewhat perturbed.

"So I was," grunted Conan. "A devilish strange dream it was, too. I trod again all the long, weary roads I traveled on my way to the kingship."

He fell silent, and Pallantides stared at him unspeaking. The king was an enigma to the general, as to most of his civilized subjects. Pallantides knew that Conan had walked many strange roads in his wild, eventful life, and had been many things before a twist of Fate set him on the throne of Aquilonia.

"I saw again the battlefield whereon I was born," said Conan, resting his chin moodily on a massive fist. "I saw myself in a pantherskin loin-clout, throwing my spear at the mountain beasts. I was a mercenary swordsman again, a hetman of the *kozaki* who dwell along the Zaporoska River, a corsair looting the coasts of Kush, a pirate of the Barachan Isles, a chief of the Himelian hillmen. All these things I've been, and of all these things I dreamed; all the shapes that have been *I* passed like an endless procession, and their feet beat out a dirge in the sounding dust.

"But throughout my dreams moved strange, veiled figures and ghostly shadows, and a far-away voice mocked me. And toward the last I seemed to see myself lying on this dais in my tent, and a shape bent over me, robed and hooded. I lay unable to move, and then the hood fell away and a moldering skull grinned down at me. Then it was that I awoke."

"This is an evil dream, Your Majesty," said Pallantides, suppressing a shudder. "But no more."

Conan shook his head, more in doubt than in denial. He came of a barbaric race, and the superstitions and instincts of his heritage lurked close beneath the surface of his consciousness.

"I've dreamed many evil dreams," he said, "and most of them were meaningless. But by Crom, this was not like most dreams! I wish this battle were fought and won, for I've had a grisly premonition ever since King Nimed died in the black plague. Why did it cease when he died?"

"Men say he sinned – "

"Men are fools, as always," grunted Conan. "If the plague struck all who sinned, then by Crom, there wouldn't be enough left to count the living! Why should the gods – who the priests tell me are just – slay five hundred peasants and merchants and nobles before they slew the king, if the whole pestilence were aimed at him? Were the gods smiting blindly, like swordsmen in a fog? By Mitra, if I aimed my strokes no straighter, Aquilonia would have had a new king long ago.

"No! The black plague's no common pestilence. It lurks in Stygian tombs, and is called forth into being only by wizards. I was a swordsman in Prince Almuric's army that invaded Stygia, and of his thirty thousand, fifteen thousand perished by Stygian arrows, and the rest by the black plague that rolled on us like a wind out of the south. I was the only man who lived."

"Yet only five hundred died in Nemedia," argued Pallantides.

"Whoever called it into being knew how to cut it short at will," answered

Conan. "So I know there was something planned and diabolical about it. Someone called it forth, someone banished it when the work was completed – when Tarascus was safe on the throne and being hailed as the deliverer of the people from the wrath of the gods. By Crom, I sense a black, subtle brain behind all this. What of this stranger who men say gives counsel to Tarascus?"

"He wears a veil," answered Pallantides; "they say he is a foreigner; a stranger from Stygia."

"A stranger from Stygia!" repeated Conan scowling. "A stranger from hell, more like! – Ha! What is that?"

"The trumpets of the Nemedians!" exclaimed Pallantides. "And hark, how our own blare upon their heels! Dawn is breaking, and the captains are marshaling the hosts for the onset! Mitra be with them, for many will not see the sun go down behind the crags."

"Send my squires to me!" exclaimed Conan, rising with alacrity and casting off his velvet night-garment; he seemed to have forgotten his forebodings at the prospect of action. "Go to the captains and see that all is in readiness. I will be with you as soon as I don my armor."

Many of Conan's ways were inexplicable to the civilized people he ruled, and one of them was his insistence on sleeping alone in his chamber or tent. Pallantides hastened from the pavilion, clanking in the armor he had donned at midnight after a few hours' sleep. He cast a swift glance over the camp, which was beginning to swarm with activity, mail clinking and men moving about dimly in the uncertain light, among the long lines of tents. Stars still glimmered palely in the western sky, but long pink streamers stretched along the eastern horizon, and against them the dragon banner of Nemedia flung out its billowing silken folds.

Pallantides turned toward a smaller tent near by, where slept the royal squires. These were tumbling out already, roused by the trumpets. And as Pallantides called to them to hasten, he was frozen speechless by a deep fierce shout and the impact of a heavy blow inside the king's tent, followed by the heart-stopping crash of a falling body. There sounded a low laugh that turned the general's blood to ice.

Echoing the cry, Pallantides wheeled and rushed back into the pavilion. He cried out again as he saw Conan's powerful frame stretched out on the carpet. The king's great two-handed sword lay near his hand, and a shattered tent-pole seemed to show where his stroke had fallen. Pallantides' sword was out, and he glared about the tent, but nothing met his gaze. Save for the king and himself it was empty, as it had been when he left it.

"Your Majesty!" Pallantides threw himself on his knee beside the fallen giant.

Conan's eyes were open; they blazed up at him with full intelligence and recognition. His lips writhed, but no sound came forth. He seemed unable to move.

Voices sounded without. Pallantides rose swiftly and stepped to the door. The royal squires and one of the knights who guarded the tent stood there.

"We heard a sound within," said the knight apologetically. "Is all well with the king?"

Pallantides regarded him searchingly.

"None has entered or left the pavilion this night?"

"None save yourself, my lord," answered the knight, and Pallantides could not doubt his honesty.

"The king stumbled and dropped his sword," said Pallantides briefly. "Return to your post."

As the knight turned away, the general covertly motioned to the five royal squires, and when they had followed him in, he drew the flap closely. They turned pale at sight of the king stretched upon the carpet, but Pallantides' quick gesture checked their exclamations.

The general bent over him again, and again Conan made an effort to speak. The veins in his temples and the cords in his neck swelled with his efforts, and he lifted his head clear of the ground. Voice came at last, mumbling and half intelligible.

"The thing – the thing in the corner!"

Pallantides lifted his head and looked fearfully about him. He saw the pale faces of the squires in the lamplight, the velvet shadows that lurked along the walls of the pavilion. That was all.

"There is nothing here, Your Majesty," he said.

"It was there, in the corner," muttered the king, tossing his lion-maned head from side to side in his efforts to rise. "A man – at least he looked like a man – wrapped in rags like a mummy's bandages, with a moldering cloak drawn about him, and a hood. All I could see was his eyes, as he crouched there in the shadows. I thought he was a shadow himself, until I saw his eyes. They were like black jewels.

"I made at him and swung my sword, but I missed him clean – how, Crom knows – and splintered that pole instead. He caught my wrist as I staggered off balance, and his fingers burned like hot iron. All the strength went out of me, and the floor rose and struck me like a club. Then he was gone, and I was down, and – curse him! – I can't move! I'm paralyzed!"

Pallantides lifted the giant's hand, and his flesh crawled. On the king's wrist showed the blue marks of long, lean fingers. What hand could grip so hard as to leave its print on that thick wrist? Pallantides remembered that low laugh he had heard as he rushed into the tent, and cold perspiration beaded his skin. It had not been Conan who laughed.

"This is a thing diabolical!" whispered a trembling squire. "Men say the children of darkness war for Tarascus!"

"Be silent!" ordered Pallantides sternly.

Outside, the dawn was dimming the stars. A light wind sprang up from the peaks, and brought the fanfare of a thousand trumpets. At the sound a convulsive shudder ran through the king's mighty form. Again the veins in his temples knotted as he strove to break the invisible shackles which crushed him down.

"Put my harness on me and tie me into my saddle," he whispered. "I'll lead the charge yet!"

Pallantides shook his head, and a squire plucked his skirt.

"My lord, we are lost if the host learns the king has been smitten! Only he could have led us to victory this day."

"Help me lift him on the dais," answered the general.

They obeyed, and laid the helpless giant on the furs, and spread a silken cloak over him. Pallantides turned to the five squires and searched their pale faces long before he spoke.

"Our lips must be sealed for ever as to what happens in this tent," he said at last. "The kingdom of Aquilonia depends upon it. One of you go and fetch me the officer Valannus, who is a captain of the Pellian spearmen."

The squire indicated bowed and hastened from the tent, and Pallantides stood staring down at the stricken king, while outside trumpets blared, drums thundered, and the roar of the multitudes rose in the growing dawn. Presently the squire returned with the officer Pallantides had named – a tall man, broad and powerful, built much like the king. Like him, also, he had thick black hair. But his eyes were gray and he did not resemble Conan in his features.

"The king is stricken by a strange malady," said Pallantides briefly. "A great honor is yours; you are to wear his armor and ride at the head of the host today. None must know that it is not the king who rides."

"It is an honor for which a man might gladly give up his life," stammered the captain, overcome by the suggestion. "Mitra grant that I do not fail of this mighty trust!"

And while the fallen king stared with burning eyes that reflected the bitter rage and humiliation that ate his heart, the squires stripped Valannus of mail shirt, burganet and leg-pieces, and clad him in Conan's armor of black plate-mail, with the vizored salade, and the dark plumes nodding over the wivern crest. Over all they put the silken surcoat with the royal lion worked in gold upon the breast, and they girt him with a broad gold-buckled belt which supported a jewel-hilted broadsword in a cloth-of-gold scabbard. While they worked, trumpets clamored outside, arms clanged, and across the river rose a deep-throated roar as squadron after squadron swung into place.

Full-armed, Valannus dropped to his knee and bent his plumes before the figure that lay on the dais.

"Lord king, Mitra grant that I do not dishonor the harness I wear this day!"

"Bring me Tarascus's head and I'll make you a baron!" In the stress of his anguish Conan's veneer of civilization had fallen from him. His eyes flamed, he ground his teeth in fury and blood-lust, as barbaric as any tribesmen in the Cimmerian hills.

III

The Cliffs Reel

The Aquilonian host was drawn up, long serried lines of pikemen and horsemen in gleaming steel, when a giant figure in black armor emerged from the royal pavilion, and as he swung up into the saddle of the black stallion held by four squires, a roar that shook the mountains went up from the host. They shook their blades and thundered forth their acclaim of their warrior king – knights in gold-chased armor, pikemen in mail coats and basinets, archers in their leather jerkins, with their longbows in their left hand.

The host on the opposite side of the valley was in motion, trotting down the long gentle slope toward the river; their steel shone through the mists of morning that swirled about their horses' feet.

The Aquilonian host moved leisurely to meet them. The measured tramp of the armored horses made the ground tremble. Banners flung out long silken folds in the morning wind; lances swayed like a bristling forest, dipped and sank, their pennons fluttering about them.

Ten men-at-arms, grim, taciturn veterans who could hold their tongues, guarded the royal pavilion. One squire stood in the tent, peering out through a slit in the doorway. But for the handful in the secret, no one else in the vast host knew that it was not Conan who rode on the great stallion at the head of the army.

The Aquilonian host had assumed the customary formation: the strongest part was the center, composed entirely of heavily armed knights; the wings were made up of smaller bodies of horsemen, mounted men-at-arms, mostly, supported by pikemen and archers. The latter were Bossonians from the western marches, strongly built men of medium stature, in leathern jackets and iron head-pieces.

The Nemedian army came on in similar formation, and the two hosts moved toward the river, the wings in advance of the centers. In the center of the Aquilonian host the great lion banner streamed its billowing black folds over the steel-clad figure on the black stallion.

But on his dais in the royal pavilion Conan groaned in anguish of spirit, and cursed with strange heathen oaths.

"The hosts move together," quoth the squire, watching from the door. "Hear the trumpets peal! Ha! The rising sun strikes fire from lance-heads and helmets until I am dazzled. It turns the river crimson – aye, it will be truly crimson before this day is done!

"The foe have reached the river. Now arrows fly between the hosts like stinging clouds that hide the sun. Ha! Well loosed, bowmen! The Bossonians have the better of it! Hark to them shout!"

Faintly in the ears of the king, above the din of trumpets and clanging steel, came the deep fierce shout of the Bossonians as they drew and loosed in perfect unison.

"Their archers seek to hold ours in play while their knights ride into the river," said the squire. "The banks are not steep; they slope to the water's edge. The knights come on, they crash through the willows. By Mitra, the clothyard shafts find every crevice of their harness! Horses and men go down, struggling and thrashing in the water. It is not deep, nor is the current swift, but men are drowning there, dragged under by their armor, and trampled by the frantic horses. Now the knights of Aquilonia advance. They ride into the water and engage the knights of Nemedia. The water swirls about their horses' bellies and the clang of sword against sword is deafening."

"Crom!" burst in agony from Conan's lips. Life was coursing sluggishly back into his veins, but still he could not lift his mighty frame from the dais.

"The wings close in," said the squire. "Pikemen and swordsmen fight hand to hand in the stream, and behind them the bowmen ply their shafts.

"By Mitra, the Nemedian arbalesters are sorely harried, and the Bossonians arch their arrows to drop amid the rear ranks. Their center gains not a foot, and their wings are pushed back up from the stream again."

"Crom, Ymir, and Mitra!" raged Conan. "Gods and devils, could I but reach the fighting, if but to die at the first blow!"

Outside through the long hot day the battle stormed and thundered. The valley shook to charge and counter-charge, to the whistling of shafts, and the crash of rending shields and splintering lances. But the hosts of Aquilonia held fast. Once they were forced back from the bank, but a counter-charge, with the black banner flowing over the black stallion, regained the lost ground. And like an iron rampart they held the right bank of the stream, and at last the squire gave Conan the news that the Nemedians were falling back from the river.

"Their wings are in confusion!" he cried. "Their knights reel back from the sword-play. But what is this? Your banner is in motion – the center sweeps into the stream! By Mitra, Valannus is leading the host across the river!"

"Fool!" groaned Conan. "It may be a trick. He should hold his position; by dawn Prospero will be here with the Poitanian levies."

"The knights ride into a hail of arrows!" cried the squire. "But they do not falter! They sweep on – they have crossed! They charge up the slope! Pallantides has hurled the wings across the river to their support! It is all he can do. The lion banner dips and staggers above the mêlée.

"The knights of Nemedia make a stand. They are broken! They fall back! Their left wing is in full flight, and our pikemen cut them down as they run! I see Valannus, riding and smiting like a madman. He is carried beyond himself by the fighting-lust. Men no longer look to Pallantides. They follow Valannus, deeming him Conan, as he rides with closed vizor.

"But look! There is method in his madness! He swings wide of the Nemedian front, with five thousand knights, the pick of the army. The main host of the Nemedians is in confusion – and look! Their flank is protected by the cliffs, but there is a defile left unguarded! It is like a great cleft in the wall that opens again behind the Nemedian lines. By Mitra, Valannus sees and seizes the opportunity! He has driven their wing before him, and he leads his knights toward that defile. They swing wide of the main battle; they cut through a line of spearmen, they charge into the defile!"

"An ambush!" cried Conan, striving to struggle upright.

"No!" shouted the squire exultantly. "The whole Nemedian host is in full sight! They have forgotten the defile! They never expected to be pushed back that far. Oh, fool, fool, Tarascus, to make such a blunder! Ah, I see lances and pennons pouring from the farther mouth of the defile, beyond the Nemedian lines. They will smite those ranks from the rear and crumple them. *Mitra, what is this?"*

He staggered as the walls of the tent swayed drunkenly. Afar over the thunder of the fight rose a deep bellowing roar, indescribably ominous.

"The cliffs reel!" shrieked the squire. "Ah, gods, what is this? The river foams out of its channel, and the peaks are crumbling! The ground shakes and horses and riders in armor are overthrown! The cliffs! The cliffs are falling!"

With his words there came a grinding rumble and a thunderous concussion, and the ground trembled. Over the roar of the battle sounded screams of mad terror.

"The cliffs have crumbled!" cried the livid squire. "They have thundered down into the defile and crushed every living creature in it! I saw the lion banner wave an instant amid the dust and falling stones, and then it vanished! Ha, the Nemedians shout with triumph! Well may they shout, for the fall of the cliffs has wiped out five thousand of our bravest knights – hark!"

To Conan's ears came a vast torrent of sound, rising and rising in frenzy: *"The king is dead! The king is dead! Flee! Flee! The king is dead!"*

"Liars!" panted Conan. "Dogs! Knaves! Cowards! Oh, Crom, if I could but stand – but crawl to the river with my sword in my teeth! How, boy, do they flee?"

"Aye!" sobbed the squire. "They spur for the river; they are broken, hurled on like spume before a storm. I see Pallantides striving to stem the torrent – he is down, and the horses trample him! They rush into the river, knights, bowmen, pikemen, all mixed and mingled in one mad torrent of destruction. The Nemedians are on their heels, cutting them down like corn."

"But they will make a stand on this side of the river!" cried the king. With an effort that brought the sweat dripping from his temples, he heaved himself up on his elbows.

"Nay!" cried the squire. "They cannot! They are broken! Routed! Oh gods, that I should live to see this day!"

Then he remembered his duty and shouted to the men-at-arms who stood stolidly watching the flight of their comrades. "Get a horse, swiftly, and help me lift the king upon it. We dare not bide here."

But before they could do his bidding, the first drift of the storm was upon them. Knights and spearmen and archers fled among the tents, stumbling over ropes and baggage, and mingled with them were Nemedian riders, who smote right and left at all alien figures. Tent-ropes were cut, fire sprang up in a hundred places, and the plundering had already begun. The grim guardsmen about Conan's tent died where they stood, smiting and thrusting, and over their mangled corpses beat the hoofs of the conquerors.

But the squire had drawn the flap close, and in the confused madness of the slaughter none realized that the pavilion held an occupant. So the flight and the pursuit swept past, and roared away up the valley, and the squire looked out presently to see a cluster of men approaching the royal tent with evident purpose.

"Here comes the king of Nemedia with four companions and his squire," quoth he. "He will accept your surrender, my fair lord – "

"Surrender the devil's heart!" gritted the king.

He had forced himself up to a sitting posture. He swung his legs painfully off the dais, and staggered upright, reeling drunkenly. The squire ran to assist him, but Conan pushed him away.

"Give me that bow!" he gritted, indicating a longbow and quiver that hung from a tent-pole.

"But Your Majesty!" cried the squire in great perturbation. "The battle is lost! It were the part of majesty to yield with the dignity becoming one of royal blood!"

"I have no royal blood," ground Conan. "I am a barbarian and the son of a blacksmith."

Wrenching away the bow and an arrow he staggered toward the opening of the pavilion. So formidable was his appearance, naked but for short leather breeks and sleeveless shirt, open to reveal his great, hairy chest, with his huge limbs and his blue eyes blazing under his tangled black mane, that the squire shrank back, more afraid of his king than of the whole Nemedian host.

Reeling on wide-braced legs Conan drunkenly tore the door-flap open and staggered out under the canopy. The king of Nemedia and his companions had dismounted, and they halted short, staring in wonder at the apparition confronting them.

"Here I am, you jackals!" roared the Cimmerian. "I am the king! Death to you, dog-brothers!"

He jerked the arrow to its head and loosed, and the shaft feathered itself in the breast of the knight who stood beside Tarascus. Conan hurled the bow at the king of Nemedia.

"Curse my shaky hand! Come in and take me if you dare!"

Reeling backward on unsteady legs, he fell with his shoulders against a tent-pole, and propped upright, he lifted his great sword with both hands.

"By Mitra, it *is* the king!" swore Tarascus. He cast a swift look about him, and laughed. "That other was a jackal in his harness! In, dogs, and take his head!"

The three soldiers – men-at-arms wearing the emblem of the royal guards – rushed at the king, and one felled the squire with a blow of a mace. The other two fared less well. As the first rushed in, lifting his sword, Conan met him with a sweeping stroke that severed mail-links like cloth, and sheared the Nemedian's arm and shoulder clean from his body. His corpse, pitching backward, fell across his companion's legs. The man stumbled, and before he could recover, the great sword was through him.

Conan wrenched out his steel with a racking gasp, and staggered back against the tent-pole. His great limbs trembled, his chest heaved, and sweat poured down his face and neck. But his eyes flamed with exultant savagery and he panted: "Why do you stand afar off, dog of Belverus? I can't reach you; come in and die!"

Tarascus hesitated, glanced at the remaining man-at-arms, and his squire, a gaunt, saturnine man in black mail, and took a step forward. He was far inferior in size and strength to the giant Cimmerian, but he was in full armor, and was famed in all the western nations as a swordsman. But his squire caught his arm.

"Nay, Your Majesty, do not throw away your life. I will summon archers to shoot this barbarian, as we shoot lions."

Neither of them had noticed that a chariot had approached while the fight was going on, and now came to a halt before them. But Conan saw, looking over their shoulders, and a queer chill sensation crawled along his spine. There was something vaguely unnatural about the appearance of the black horses that drew the vehicle, but it was the occupant of the chariot that arrested the king's attention.

He was a tall man, superbly built, clad in a long unadorned silk robe. He wore a Shemitish head-dress, and its lower folds hid his features, except for the dark, magnetic eyes. The hands that grasped the reins, pulling the rearing horses back on their haunches, were white but strong. Conan glared at the stranger, all his primitive instincts roused. He sensed an aura of menace and power that exuded from this veiled figure, a menace as definite as the windless waving of tall grass that marks the path of the serpent.

"Hail, Xaltotun!" exclaimed Tarascus. "Here is the king of Aquilonia! He did not die in the landslide as we thought."

"I know," answered the other, without bothering to say how he knew. "What is your present intention?"

"I will summon the archers to slay him," answered the Nemedian. "As long as he lives he will be dangerous to us."

"Yet even a dog has uses," answered Xaltotun. "Take him alive."

Conan laughed raspingly. "Come in and try!" he challenged. "But for my treacherous legs I'd hew you out of that chariot like a woodman hewing a tree. But you'll never take me alive, damn you!"

"He speaks the truth, I fear," said Tarascus. "The man is a barbarian, with the senseless ferocity of a wounded tiger. Let me summon the archers."

"Watch me and learn wisdom," advised Xaltotun.

His hand dipped into his robe and came out with something shining – a glistening sphere. This he threw suddenly at Conan. The Cimmerian contemptuously struck it aside with his sword – at the instant of contact there was a sharp explosion, a flare of white, blinding flame, and Conan pitched senseless to the ground.

"He is dead?" Tarascus's tone was more assertion than inquiry.

"No. He is but senseless. He will recover his senses in a few hours. Bid your men bind his arms and legs and lift him into my chariot."

With a gesture Tarascus did so, and they heaved the senseless king into the chariot, grunting with their burden. Xaltotun threw a velvet cloak over his body, completely covering him from any who might peer in. He gathered the reins in his hands.

"I'm for Belverus," he said. "Tell Amalric that I will be with him if he needs me. But with Conan out of the way, and his army broken, lance and sword should suffice for the rest of the conquest. Prospero cannot be bringing more than ten thousand men to the field, and will doubtless fall back to Tarantia when he hears the news of the battle. Say nothing to Amalric or Valerius or anyone about our capture. Let them think Conan died in the fall of the cliffs."

He looked at the man-at-arms for a long space, until the guardsman moved restlessly, nervous under the scrutiny.

"What is that about your waist?" Xaltotun demanded.

"Why, my girdle, may it please you, my lord!" stuttered the amazed guardsman.

"You lie!" Xaltotun's laugh was merciless as a sword-edge. "It is a poisonous serpent! What a fool you are, to wear a reptile about your waist!"

With distended eyes the man looked down; and to his utter horror he saw the buckle of his girdle rear up at him. It *was* a snake's head! He saw the evil eyes and the dripping fangs, heard the hiss and felt the loathsome contact of the thing about his body. He screamed hideously and struck at it with his naked hand, felt its fangs flesh themselves in that hand – and then he stiffened and fell heavily. Tarascus looked down at him without expression. He saw only the leathern girdle and the buckle, the pointed tongue of which was stuck in the guardsman's palm. Xaltotun turned his hypnotic gaze on Tarascus's squire, and the man turned ashen and began to tremble, but the king interposed: "Nay, we can trust him."

The sorcerer tautened the reins and swung the horses around.

"See that this piece of work remains secret. If I am needed, let Altaro, Orastes' servant, summon me as I have taught him. I will be in your palace at Belverus."

Tarascus lifted his hand in salutation, but his expression was not pleasant to see as he looked after the departing mesmerist.

"Why should he spare the Cimmerian?" whispered the frightened squire.

"That I am wondering myself," grunted Tarascus.

Behind the rumbling chariot the dull roar of battle and pursuit faded in the distance; the setting sun rimmed the cliffs with scarlet flame, and the chariot moved into the vast blue shadows floating up out of the east.

IV

"From What Hell Have You Crawled?"

Of that long ride in the chariot of Xaltotun, Conan knew nothing. He lay like a dead man while the bronze wheels clashed over the stones of mountain roads and swished through the deep grass of fertile valleys, and finally dropping down from the rugged heights, rumbled rhythmically along the broad white road that winds through the rich meadowlands to the walls of Belverus.

Just before dawn some faint reviving of life touched him. He heard a mumble of voices, the groan of ponderous hinges. Through a slit in the cloak that covered him he saw, faintly in the lurid glare of torches, the great black arch of a gateway, and the bearded faces of men-at-arms, the torches striking fire from their spear-heads and helmets.

"How went the battle, my fair lord?" spoke an eager voice, in the Nemedian tongue.

"Well indeed," was the curt reply. "The king of Aquilonia lies slain and his host is broken."

A babble of excited voices rose, drowned the next instant by the whirling wheels of the chariot on the flags. Sparks flashed from under the revolving rims as Xaltotun lashed his steeds through the arch. But Conan heard one of the guardsmen mutter: "From beyond the border to Belverus between sunset and dawn! And the horses scarcely sweating! By Mitra, they – " Then silence drank the voices, and there was only the clatter of hoofs and wheels along the shadowy street.

What he had heard registered itself on Conan's brain but suggested nothing to him. He was like a mindless automaton that hears and sees, but does not understand. Sights and sounds flowed meaninglessly about him. He lapsed again into a deep lethargy, and was only dimly aware when the chariot halted in a deep, high-walled court, and he was lifted from it by many hands and borne up a winding stone stair, and down a long dim corridor. Whispers, stealthy footsteps, unrelated sounds surged or rustled about him, irrelevant and far away.

Yet his ultimate awakening was abrupt and crystal-clear. He possessed full knowledge of the battle in the mountains and its sequences, and he had a good idea of where he was.

He lay on a velvet couch, clad as he was the day before, but with his limbs loaded with chains not even he could break. The room in which he lay was furnished with somber magnificence, the walls covered with black velvet tapestries, the floor with heavy purple carpets. There was no sign of door or window, and one curiously carven gold lamp, swinging from the fretted ceiling, shed a lurid light over all.

In that light the figure seated in a silver, throne-like chair before him seemed unreal and fantastic, with an illusiveness of outline that was heightened by a filmy silken robe. But the features were distinct – unnaturally so in that uncertain light. It was almost as if a weird nimbus played about the man's head, casting the bearded face into bold relief, so that it was the only definite and distinct reality in that mystic, ghostly chamber.

It was a magnificent face, with strongly chiseled features of classical beauty. There was, indeed, something disquieting about the calm tranquility of its aspect, a suggestion of more than human knowledge, of a profound certitude beyond human assurance. Also an uneasy sensation of familiarity twitched at the back of Conan's consciousness. He had never seen this man's face before, he well knew; yet those features reminded him of something or someone. It was like encountering in the flesh some dream-image that had haunted one in nightmares.

"Who are you?" demanded the king belligerently, struggling to a sitting position in spite of his chains.

"Men call me Xaltotun," was the reply, in a strong, golden voice.

"What place is this?" the Cimmerian next demanded.

"A chamber in the palace of King Tarascus, in Belverus."

Conan was not surprized. Belverus, the capital, was at the same time the largest Nemedian city so near the border.

"And where's Tarascus?"

"With the army."

"Well," growled Conan, "if you mean to murder me, why don't you do it and get it over with?"

"I did not save you from the king's archers to murder you in Belverus," answered Xaltotun.

"What the devil did you do to me?" demanded Conan.

"I blasted your consciousness," answered Xaltotun. "How, you would not understand. Call it black magic, if you will."

Conan had already reached that conclusion, and was mulling over something else.

"I think I understand why you spared my life," he rumbled. "Amalric wants to keep me as a check on Valerius, in case the impossible happens and he becomes king of Aquilonia. It's well known that the baron of Tor is behind this move to seat Valerius on my throne. And if I know Amalric, he doesn't intend that Valerius shall be anything more than a figurehead, as Tarascus is now."

"Amalric knows nothing of your capture," answered Xaltotun. "Neither does Valerius. Both think you died at Valkia."

Conan's eyes narrowed as he stared at the man in silence.

"I sensed a brain behind all this," he muttered, "but I thought it was Amalric's. Are Amalric, Tarascus and Valerius all but puppets dancing on your string? Who are you?"

"What does it matter? If I told you, you would not believe me. What if I told you I might set you back on the throne of Aquilonia?"

Conan's eyes burned on him like a wolf.

"What's your price?"

"Obedience to me."

"Go to hell with your offer!" snarled Conan. "I'm no figurehead. I won my crown with my sword. Besides, it's beyond your power to buy and sell the throne of Aquilonia at your will. The kingdom's not conquered; one battle doesn't decide a war."

"You war against more than swords," answered Xaltotun. "Was it a mortal's sword that felled you in your tent before the fight? Nay, it was a child of the dark, a waif of outer space, whose fingers were afire with the frozen coldness of the black gulfs, which froze the blood in your veins and the marrow of your thews. Coldness so cold it burned your flesh like white-hot iron!

"Was it chance that led the man who wore your harness to lead his knights into the defile? – chance that brought the cliffs crashing down upon them?"

Conan glared at him unspeaking, feeling a chill along his spine. Wizards and sorcerers abounded in his barbaric mythology, and any fool could tell that this was no common man. Conan sensed an inexplicable something about him that set him apart – an alien aura of Time and Space, a sense of tremendous and sinister antiquity. But his stubborn spirit refused to flinch.

"The fall of the cliffs was chance," he muttered truculently. "The charge into the defile was what any man would have done."

"Not so. You would not have led a charge into it. You would have suspected a trap. You would never have crossed the river in the first place, until you were sure the Nemedian rout was real. Hypnotic suggestions would not have invaded your mind, even in the madness of battle, to make you mad, and rush blindly into the trap laid for you, as it did the lesser man who masqueraded as you."

"Then if this was all planned," Conan grunted skeptically, "all a plot to trap my host, why did not the 'child of darkness' kill me in my tent?"

"Because I wished to take you alive. It took no wizardry to predict that Pallantides would send another man out in your harness. I wanted you alive and unhurt. You may fit into my scheme of things. There is a vital power about you greater than the craft and cunning of my allies. You are a bad enemy, but might make a fine vassal."

Conan spat savagely at the word, and Xaltotun, ignoring his fury, took a crystal globe from a near-by table and placed it before him. He did not support it in any way, nor place it on anything, but it hung motionless in midair, as solidly as if it rested on an iron pedestal. Conan snorted at this bit of necromancy, but he was nevertheless impressed.

"Would you know of what goes on in Aquilonia?" he asked.

Conan did not reply, but the sudden rigidity of his form betrayed his interest.

Xaltotun stared into the cloudy depths, and spoke: "It is now the evening of the day after the battle of Valkia. Last night the main body of the army camped by Valkia, while squadrons of knights harried the fleeing Aquilonians. At dawn the host broke camp and pushed westward through the mountains. Prospero, with ten thousand Poitanians, was miles from the battlefield when he met the fleeing survivors in the early dawn. He had pushed on all night, hoping to reach the field before the battle joined. Unable to rally the remnants of the broken host, he fell back toward Tarantia. Riding hard, replacing his wearied horses with steeds seized from the countryside, he approaches Tarantia.

"I see his weary knights, their armor gray with dust, their pennons drooping as they push their tired horses through the plain. I see, also, the streets of Tarantia. The city is in turmoil. Somehow word has reached the people of the defeat and the death of King Conan. The mob is mad with fear, crying out that the king is dead, and there is none to lead them against the Nemedians. Giant shadows rush on Aquilonia from the east, and the sky is black with vultures."

Conan cursed deeply.

"What are these but words? The raggedest beggar in the street might prophesy as much. If you say you saw all that in the glass ball, then you're a liar as well as a knave, of which last there's no doubt! Prospero will hold Tarantia, and the barons will rally to him. Count Trocero of Poitain commands the kingdom in my absence, and he'll drive these Nemedian dogs howling back to their kennels. What are fifty thousand Nemedians? Aquilonia will swallow them up. They'll never see Belverus again. It's not Aquilonia which was conquered at Valkia; it was only Conan."

"Aquilonia is doomed," answered Xaltotun, unmoved. "Lance and ax and torch shall conquer her; or if they fail, powers from the dark of ages shall march against her. As the cliffs fell at Valkia, so shall walled cities and mountains fall, if the need arise, and rivers roar from their channels to drown whole provinces.

"Better if steel and bowstring prevail without further aid from the *arts*, for the constant use of mighty spells sometimes sets forces in motion that might rock the universe."

"From what hell have you crawled, you nighted dog?" muttered Conan, staring at the man. The Cimmerian involuntarily shivered; he sensed something incredibly ancient, incredibly evil.

Xaltotun lifted his head, as if listening to whispers across the void. He seemed to have forgotten his prisoner. Then he shook his head impatiently, and glanced impersonally at Conan.

"What? Why, if I told you, you would not believe me. But I am wearied of conversation with you; it is less fatiguing to destroy a walled city than it is to frame my thoughts in words a brainless barbarian can understand."

"If my hands were free," opined Conan, "I'd soon make a brainless corpse out of you."

"I do not doubt it, if I were fool enough to give you the opportunity," answered Xaltotun, clapping his hands.

His manner had changed; there was impatience in his tone, and a certain nervousness in his manner, though Conan did not think this attitude was in any way connected with himself.

"Consider what I have told you, barbarian," said Xaltotun. "You will have plenty of leisure. I have not yet decided what I shall do with you. It depends on circumstances yet unborn. But let this be impressed upon you: that if I decide to use you in my game, it will be better to submit without resistance than to suffer my wrath."

Conan spat a curse at him, just as hangings that masked a door swung apart and four giant negroes entered. Each was clad only in a silken breech-clout supported by a girdle, from which hung a great key.

Xaltotun gestured impatiently toward the king and turned away, as if dismissing the matter entirely from his mind. His fingers twitched queerly. From a carven green jade box he took a handful of shimmering black dust, and placed it in a brazier which stood on a golden tripod at his elbow. The crystal globe, which he seemed to have forgotten, fell suddenly to the floor, as if its invisible support had been removed.

Then the blacks had lifted Conan – for so loaded with chains was he that he could not walk – and carried him from the chamber. A glance back, before the heavy, gold-bound teak door was closed, showed him Xaltotun leaning back in his throne-like chair, his arms folded, while a thin wisp of smoke curled up from the brazier. Conan's scalp prickled. In Stygia, that ancient and evil kingdom that lay far to the south, he had seen such black dust before. It was the pollen of the black lotus, which creates death-like sleep and monstrous dreams; and he knew that only the grisly wizards of the Black Ring, which is the nadir of evil, voluntarily seek the scarlet nightmares of the black lotus, to revive their necromantic powers.

The Black Ring was a fable and a lie to most folk of the western world, but Conan knew of its ghastly reality, and its grim votaries who practise their abominable sorceries amid the black vaults of Stygia and the nighted domes of accursed Sabatea.

He glanced back at the cryptic, gold-bound door, shuddering at what it hid.

Whether it was day or night the king could not tell. The palace of King Tarascus seemed a shadowy, nighted place, that shunned natural illumination. The spirit of darkness and shadow hovered over it, and that spirit, Conan felt, was embodied in the stranger Xaltotun. The negroes carried the king along a winding corridor so dimly lighted that they moved through it like black ghosts bearing a dead man, and down a stone stair that wound endlessly. A torch in the hand of one cast the great deformed shadows streaming along the wall; it was like the descent into hell of a corpse borne by dusky demons.

At last they reached the foot of the stair, and then they traversed a long straight corridor, with a blank wall on one hand pierced by an occasional arched doorway with a stair leading up behind it, and on the other hand another wall showing heavy barred doors at regular intervals of a few feet.

Halting before one of these doors, one of the blacks produced the key that hung at his girdle, and turned it in the lock. Then, pushing open the grille, they entered with their captive. They were in a small dungeon with heavy stone walls, floor and ceiling, and in the opposite wall there was another grilled door. What lay beyond that door Conan could not tell, but he did not believe it was another corridor. The glimmering light of the torch, flickering through the bars, hinted at shadowy spaciousness and echoing depths.

In one corner of the dungeon, near the door through which they had entered, a cluster of rusty chains hung from a great iron ring set in the stone. In these chains a skeleton dangled. Conan glared at it with some curiosity, noticing the state of the bare bones, most of which were splintered and broken; the skull, which had fallen from the vertebræ, was crushed as if by some savage blow of tremendous force.

Stolidly one of the blacks, not the one who had opened the door, removed the chains from the ring, using his key on the massive lock, and dragged the mass of rusty metal and shattered bones over to one side. Then they fastened Conan's chains to that ring, and the third black turned *his* key in the lock of the farther door, grunting when he had assured himself that it was properly fastened.

Then they regarded Conan cryptically, slit-eyed ebony giants, the torch striking highlights from their glossy skin.

He who held the key to the nearer door was moved to remark, gutturally: "This your palace now, white dog-king! None but master and we know. All palace sleep. We keep secret. You live and die here, maybe. Like him!" He contemptuously kicked the shattered skull and sent it clattering across the stone floor.

Conan did not deign to reply to the taunt, and the black, galled perhaps by his prisoner's silence, muttered a curse, stooped and spat full in the king's face. It was an unfortunate move for the black. Conan was seated on the floor, the chains about his waist; ankles and wrists locked to the ring in the wall. He could neither rise, nor move more than a yard out from the wall. But there was considerable slack in the chains that shackled his wrists, and before the bullet-shaped head could be withdrawn out of reach, the king gathered this slack in his mighty hand and smote the black on the head. The man fell like a butchered ox, and his comrades stared to see him lying with his scalp laid open, and blood oozing from his nose and ears.

But they attempted no reprisal, nor did they accept Conan's urgent invitation to approach within reach of the bloody chain in his hand. Presently, grunting in their ape-like speech, they lifted the senseless black and bore him out like a sack of wheat, arms and legs dangling. They used his key to lock the door behind them, but did not remove it from the gold chain that fastened it to his girdle. They took the torch with them, and as they moved up the corridor the darkness slunk behind them like an animate thing. Their soft padding footsteps died away, with the glimmer of their torch, and darkness and silence remained unchallenged.

V
The Haunter of the Pits

Conan lay still, enduring the weight of his chains and the despair of his position with the stoicism of the wilds that had bred him. He did not move, because the jangle of his chains, when he shifted his body, sounded startlingly loud in the darkness and stillness, and it was his instinct, born of a thousand wilderness-bred ancestors, not to betray his position in his helplessness. This did not result from a logical reasoning process; he did not lie quiet because he reasoned that the darkness hid lurking dangers that might discover him in his helplessness. Xaltotun had assured him that he was not to be harmed, and Conan believed that it was in the man's interest to preserve him, at least for the time being. But the instincts of the wild were there, that had caused him in his childhood to lie hidden and silent while wild beasts prowled about his covert.

Even his keen eyes could not pierce the solid darkness. Yet after a while, after a period of time he had no way of estimating, a faint glow became apparent, a sort of slanting gray beam, by which Conan could see, vaguely, the bars of the door at his elbow, and even make out the skeleton of the other grille. This puzzled him, until at last he realized the explanation. He was far below ground, in the pits below the palace; yet for some reason a shaft had been constructed from somewhere above. Outside, the moon had risen to a point where its light slanted dimly down the shaft.

He reflected that in this manner he could tell the passing of the days and nights. Perhaps the sun, too, would shine down that shaft, though on the other hand it might be closed by day. Perhaps it was a subtle method of torture, allowing a prisoner but a glimpse of daylight or moonlight.

His gaze fell on the broken bones in the farther corner, glimmering dimly. He did not tax his brain with futile speculation as to who the wretch had been and for what reason he had been doomed, but he wondered at the shattered condition of the bones. They had not been broken on a rack. Then, as he looked, another unsavory detail made itself evident. The shin-bones were split lengthwise, and there was but one explanation; they had been broken in that manner in order to obtain the marrow. Yet what creature but man breaks bones for their marrow? Perhaps those remnants were mute evidence of a horrible, cannibalistic feast, of some wretch driven to madness by starvation. Conan wondered if his own bones would be found at some future date, hanging in their rusty chains. He fought down the unreasoning panic of a trapped wolf.

The Cimmerian did not curse, scream, weep or rave as a civilized man might have done. But the pain and turmoil in his bosom were none the less fierce. His great limbs quivered with the intensity of his emotions. Somewhere, far to the westward, the Nemedian host was slashing and burning its way through the heart of his kingdom. The small host of the Poitanians could not stand before them. Prospero might be able to hold Tarantia for weeks, or months; but eventually, if not relieved, he must surrender to greater numbers. Surely the barons would rally to him against the invaders. But in the meanwhile he, Conan, must lie helpless in a darkened cell, while others led his spears and fought for his kingdom. The king ground his powerful teeth in red rage.

Then he stiffened as outside the farther door he heard a stealthy step. Straining his eyes he made out a bent, indistinct figure outside the grille. There was a rasp of metal against metal, and he heard the clink of tumblers, as if a key had been turned in the lock. Then the figure moved silently out of his range of vision. Some guard, he supposed, trying the lock. After a while he heard the sound repeated faintly somewhere farther on, and that was followed by the soft opening of a door, and then a swift scurry of softly shod feet retreated in the distance. Then silence fell again.

Conan listened for what seemed a long time, but which could not have been, for the moon still shone down the hidden shaft, but he heard no further sound. He shifted his position at last, and his chains clanked. Then he heard another, lighter footfall – a soft step outside the nearer door, the door through which he had entered the cell. An instant later a slender figure was etched dimly in the gray light.

"King Conan!" a soft voice intoned urgently. "Oh, my lord, are you there?"

"Where else?" he answered guardedly, twisting his head about to stare at the apparition.

It was a girl who stood grasping the bars with her slender fingers. The dim glow behind her outlined her supple figure through the wisp of silk twisted about her loins, and shone vaguely on jeweled breast-plates. Her dark eyes gleamed in the shadows, her white limbs glistened softly, like alabaster. Her hair was a mass of dark foam, at the burnished luster of which the dim light only hinted.

"The keys to your shackles and to the farther door!" she whispered, and a slim white hand came through the bars and dropped three objects with a clink to the flags beside him.

"What game is this?" he demanded. "You speak in the Nemedian tongue, and I have no friends in Nemedia. What deviltry is your master up to now? Has he sent you here to mock me?"

"It is no mockery!" The girl was trembling violently. Her bracelets and breast-plates clinked against the bars she grasped. "I swear by Mitra! I stole the keys from the black jailers. They are the keepers of the pits, and each bears a key which will open only one set of locks. I made them drunk. The one whose head you broke was carried away to a leech, and I could not get his key. But the others I stole. Oh, please do not loiter! Beyond these dungeons lie the pits which are the doors to hell."

Somewhat impressed, Conan tried the keys dubiously, expecting to meet only failure and a burst of mocking laughter. But he was galvanized to discover that one, indeed, loosed him of his shackles, fitting not only the lock that held them to the ring, but the locks on his limbs as well. A few seconds later he stood upright, exulting fiercely in his comparative freedom. A quick stride carried him to the grille, and his fingers closed about a bar and the slender wrist that was pressed against it, imprisoning the owner, who lifted her face bravely to his fierce gaze.

"Who are you, girl?" he demanded. "Why do you do this?"

"I am only Zenobia," she murmured, with a catch of breathlessness, as if in fright; "only a girl of the king's seraglio."

"Unless this is some cursed trick," muttered Conan, "I cannot see why you bring me these keys."

She bowed her dark head, and then lifted it and looked full into his suspicious eyes. Tears sparkled like jewels on her long dark lashes.

"I am only a girl of the king's seraglio," she said, with a certain proud humility. "He has never glanced at me, and probably never will. I am less than one of the dogs that gnaw the bones in his banquet hall.

"But I am no painted toy; I am of flesh and blood. I breathe, hate, fear, rejoice and love. And I have loved you, King Conan, ever since I saw you riding at the head of your knights along the streets of Belverus when you visited King Nimed, years ago. My heart tugged at its strings to leap from my bosom and fall in the dust of the street under your horse's hoofs."

Color flooded her countenance as she spoke, but her dark eyes did not waver. Conan did not at once reply; wild and passionate and untamed he was, yet any but the most brutish of men must be touched with a certain awe or wonder at the baring of a woman's naked soul.

She bent her head then, and pressed her red lips to the fingers that imprisoned her slim wrist. Then she flung up her head as if in sudden recollection of their position, and terror flared in her dark eyes.

"Haste!" she whispered urgently. "It is past midnight. You must be gone."

"But won't they skin you alive for stealing these keys?"

"They'll never know. If the black men remember in the morning who gave them the wine, they will not dare admit the keys were stolen from them while they were drunk. The key that I could not obtain is the one that unlocks this door. You must make your way to freedom through the pits. What awful perils lurk beyond that door I cannot even guess. But greater danger lurks for you if you remain in this cell.

"King Tarascus has returned – "

"What? Tarascus?"

"Aye! He has returned, in great secrecy, and not long ago he descended into the pits and then came out again, pale and shaking, like a man who has dared a great hazard. I heard him whisper to his squire, Arideus, that despite Xaltotun you should die."

"What of Xaltotun?" murmured Conan.

He felt her shudder.

"Do not speak of him!" she whispered. "Demons are often summoned by the sound of their names. The slaves say that he lies in his chamber, behind a bolted door, dreaming the dreams of the black lotus. I believe that even Tarascus secretly fears him, or he would slay you openly. But he has been in the pits tonight, and what he did here, only Mitra knows."

"I wonder if that could have been Tarascus who fumbled at my cell door awhile ago?" muttered Conan.

"Here is a dagger!" she whispered, pressing something through the bars. His eager fingers closed on an object familiar to their touch. "Go quickly through yonder door, turn to the left and make your way along the cells until you come to a stone stair. On your life do not stray from the line of the cells! Climb the stair and open the door at the top; one of the keys will fit it. If it be the will of Mitra, I will await you there." Then she was gone, with a patter of light slippered feet.

Conan shrugged his shoulders, and turned toward the farther grille. This might be some diabolical trap planned by Tarascus, but plunging headlong into a snare was less abhorrent to Conan's temperament than sitting meekly to await his doom. He inspected the weapon the girl had given him, and smiled grimly. Whatever else she might be, she was proven by that dagger to be a person of practical intelligence. It was no slender stiletto, selected because of a jeweled hilt or gold guard, fitted only for dainty murder in milady's boudoir; it was a forthright poniard, a warrior's weapon, broad-bladed, fifteen inches in length, tapering to a diamond-sharp point.

He grunted with satisfaction. The feel of the hilt cheered him and gave him a glow of confidence. Whatever webs of conspiracy were drawn about him, whatever trickery and treachery ensnared him, this knife was real. The great muscles of his right arm swelled in anticipation of murderous blows.

He tried the farther door, fumbling with the keys as he did so. It was not locked. Yet he remembered the black man locking it. That furtive, bent figure, then, had been no jailer seeing that the bolts were in place. He had unlocked the door, instead. There was a sinister suggestion about that unlocked door. But Conan did not hesitate. He pushed open the grille and stepped from the dungeon into the outer darkness.

As he had thought, the door did not open into another corridor. The flagged floor stretched away under his feet, and the line of cells ran away to right and left behind him, but he could not make out the other limits of the place into which he had come. He could see neither the roof nor any other wall. The moonlight filtered into that vastness only through the grilles of the cells, and was almost lost in the darkness. Less keen eyes than his could scarcely have discerned the dim gray patches that floated before each cell door.

Turning to the left, he moved swiftly and noiselessly along the line of dungeons, his bare feet making no sound on the flags. He glanced briefly into each dungeon as he passed it. They were all empty, but locked. In some he caught the glimmer of naked white bones. These pits were a relic of a grimmer age, constructed long ago when Belverus was a fortress rather than a city. But evidently their more recent use had been more extensive than the world guessed.

Ahead of him, presently, he saw the dim outline of a stair sloping sharply upward, and knew it must be the stair he sought. Then he whirled suddenly, crouching in the deep shadows at its foot.

Somewhere behind him something was moving – something bulky and stealthy that padded on feet which were not human feet. He was looking down the long row of cells, before each one of which lay a square of dim gray light that was little more than a patch of less dense darkness. But he saw something moving along these squares. What it was he could not tell, but it was heavy and huge, and yet it moved with more than human ease and swiftness. He glimpsed it as it moved across the squares of gray, then lost it as it merged in the expanses of shadow between. It was uncanny, in its stealthy advance, appearing and disappearing like a blur of the vision.

He heard the bars rattle as it tried each door in turn. Now it had reached the cell he had so recently quitted, and the door swung open as it tugged. He saw a great bulky shape limned faintly and briefly in the gray doorway, and then the thing had vanished into the dungeon. Sweat beaded Conan's face and hands. Now he knew why Tarascus had come so subtly to his door, and later had fled so swiftly. The king had unlocked his door, and, somewhere in these hellish pits, had opened a cell or cage that held some grim monstrosity.

Now the thing was emerging from the cell and was again advancing up the corridor, its misshapen head close to the ground. It paid no more heed to the locked doors. It was smelling out his trail. He saw it more plainly now; the gray light limned a giant anthropomorphic body, but vaster of bulk and girth than any man. It went on two legs, though it stooped forward, and it was grayish and shaggy, its thick coat shot with silver. Its head was a grisly travesty of the human, its long arms hung nearly to the ground.

Conan knew it at last – understood the meaning of those crushed and broken bones in the dungeon, and recognized the haunter of the pits. It was a gray ape, one of the grisly man-eaters from the forests that wave on the mountainous eastern shores of the Sea of Vilayet. Half mythical and altogether horrible, these apes were the goblins of Hyborian legendry, and were in reality ogres of the natural world, cannibals and murderers of the nighted forests.

He knew it scented his presence, for it was coming swiftly now, rolling its barrel-like body rapidly along on its short, mighty, bowed legs. He cast a quick glance up the long stair, but knew that the thing would be on his back before he could mount to the distant door. He chose to meet it face to face.

Conan stepped out into the nearest square of moonlight, so as to have all the advantage of illumination that he could; for the beast, he knew, could see better than himself in the dark. Instantly the brute saw him; its great yellow tusks gleamed in the shadows, but it made no sound. Creatures of night and the silence, the gray apes of Vilayet were voiceless. But in its dim, hideous features, which were a bestial travesty of a human face, showed ghastly exultation.

Conan stood poised, watching the oncoming monster without a quiver. He knew he must stake his life on one thrust; there would be no chance for another; nor would there be time to strike and spring away. The first blow must kill, and kill instantly, if he hoped to survive that awful grapple. He swept his gaze over the short, squat throat, the hairy swagbelly, and the mighty breast, swelling in giant arches like twin shields. It must be the heart; better to risk the blade being deflected by the heavy ribs than to strike in where a stroke was not instantly fatal. With full realization of the odds, Conan matched his speed of eye and hand and his muscular power against the brute might and ferocity of the man-eater. He must meet the brute breast to breast, strike a death-blow, and then trust to the ruggedness of his frame to survive the instant of manhandling that was certain to be his.

As the ape came rolling in on him, swinging wide its terrible arms, he plunged in between them and struck with all his desperate power. He felt the blade sink to the hilt in the hairy breast, and instantly, releasing it, he ducked his head and bunched his whole body into one compact mass of knotted muscles, and as he did so he grasped the closing arms and drove his knee fiercely into the monster's belly, bracing himself against that crushing grapple.

For one dizzy instant he felt as if he were being dismembered in the grip of an earthquake; then suddenly he was free, sprawling on the floor, and the monster was gasping out its life beneath him, its red eyes turned upward, the hilt of the poniard quivering in its breast. His desperate stab had gone home.

Conan was panting as if after long conflict, trembling in every limb. Some of his joints felt as if they had been dislocated, and blood dripped from scratches on his skin where the monster's talons had ripped; his muscles and tendons had been savagely wrenched and twisted. If the beast had lived a second longer, it would surely have dismembered him. But the Cimmerian's mighty strength had resisted, for the fleeting instant it had endured, the dying convulsion of the ape that would have torn a lesser man limb from limb.

VI

The Thrust of a Knife

Conan stooped and tore the knife from the monster's breast. Then he went swiftly up the stair. What other shapes of fear the darkness held he could not guess, but he had no desire to encounter any more. This touch-and-go sort of battling was too strenuous even for the giant Cimmerian. The moonlight was fading from the floor, the darkness closing in, and something like panic pursued him up the stair. He breathed a gusty sigh of relief when he reached the head, and felt the third key turn in the lock. He opened the door slightly, and craned his neck to peer through, half expecting an attack from some human or bestial enemy.

He looked into a bare stone corridor, dimly lighted, and a slender, supple figure stood before the door.

"Your Majesty!" It was a low, vibrant cry, half in relief and half in fear. The girl sprang to his side, then hesitated as if abashed.

"You bleed," she said. "You have been hurt!"

He brushed aside the implication with an impatient hand.

"Scratches that wouldn't hurt a baby. Your skewer came in handy, though. But for it Tarascus's monkey would be cracking my shin-bones for the marrow right now. But what now?"

"Follow me," she whispered. "I will lead you outside the city wall. I have a horse concealed there."

She turned to lead the way down the corridor, but he laid a heavy hand on her naked shoulder.

"Walk beside me," he instructed her softly, passing his massive arm about her lithe waist. "You've played me fair so far, and I'm inclined to believe in you; but I've lived this long only because I've trusted no one too far, man or woman. So! Now if you play me false you won't live to enjoy the jest."

She did not flinch at sight of the reddened poniard or the contact of his hard muscles about her supple body.

"Cut me down without mercy if I play you false," she answered. "The very feel of your arm about me, even in menace, is as the fulfillment of a dream."

The vaulted corridor ended at a door, which she opened. Outside lay another black man, a giant in turban and silk loin-cloth, with a curved sword lying on the flags near his hand. He did not move.

"I drugged his wine," she whispered, swerving to avoid the recumbent figure. "He is the last, and outer, guard of the pits. None ever escaped from them before, and none has ever wished to seek them; so only these black men guard them. Only these of all the servants knew it was King Conan that Xaltotun brought a prisoner in his chariot. I was watching, sleepless, from an upper casement that opened into the court, while the other girls slept; for I knew that a battle was being fought, or had been fought, in the west, and I feared for you....

"I saw the blacks carry you up the stair, and I recognized you in the torchlight. I slipped into this wing of the palace tonight, in time to see them carry you to the pits. I had not dared come here before nightfall. You must have lain in drugged senselessness all day in Xaltotun's chamber.

"Oh, let us be wary! Strange things are afoot in the palace tonight. The slaves said that Xaltotun slept as he often sleeps, drugged by the lotus of Stygia, but Tarascus is in the palace. He entered secretly, through the postern, wrapped in his cloak which was dusty as with long travel, and attended only by his squire, the lean silent Arideus. I cannot understand, but I am afraid."

They came out at the foot of a narrow, winding stair, and mounting it, passed through a narrow panel which she slid aside. When they had passed through, she slipped it back in place, and it became merely a portion of the ornate wall. They were in a more spacious corridor, carpeted and tapestried, over which hanging lamps shed a golden glow.

Conan listened intently, but he heard no sound throughout the palace. He did not know in what part of the palace he was, or in which direction lay the chamber of Xaltotun. The girl was trembling as she drew him along the corridor, to halt presently beside an alcove masked with satin tapestry. Drawing this aside, she motioned for him to step into the niche, and whispered: "Wait here! Beyond that door at the end of the corridor we are likely to meet slaves or eunuchs at any time of the day or night. I will go and see if the way is clear, before we essay it."

Instantly his hair-trigger suspicions were aroused.

"Are you leading me into a trap?"

Tears sprang into her dark eyes. She sank to her knees and seized his muscular hand.

"Oh, my king, do not mistrust me now!" Her voice shook with desperate urgency. "If you doubt and hesitate, we are lost! Why should I bring you up out of the pits to betray you now?"

"All right," he muttered. "I'll trust you; though, by Crom, the habits of a lifetime are not easily put aside. Yet I wouldn't harm you now, if you brought all the swordsmen in Nemedia upon me. But for you Tarascus's cursed ape would have come upon me in chains and unarmed. Do as you wish, girl."

Kissing his hands, she sprang lithely up and ran down the corridor, to vanish through a heavy double door.

He glanced after her, wondering if he was a fool to trust her; then he shrugged his mighty shoulders and pulled the satin hangings together, masking his refuge. It was not strange that a passionate young beauty should be risking her life to aid him; such things had happened often enough in his life. Many women had looked on him with favor, in the days of his wanderings, and in the time of his kingship.

Yet he did not remain motionless in the alcove, waiting for her return. Following his instincts, he explored the niche for another exit, and presently found one – the opening of a narrow passage, masked by the tapestries, that ran to an ornately carved door, barely visible in the dim light that filtered in from the outer corridor. And as he stared into it, somewhere beyond that carven door he heard the sound of another door opening and shutting, and then a low mumble of voices. The familiar sound of one of those voices caused a sinister expression to cross his dark face. Without hesitation he glided down the passage, and crouched like a stalking panther beside the door. It was not locked, and manipulating it delicately, he pushed it open a crack, with a reckless disregard for possible consequences that only he could have explained or defended.

It was masked on the other side by tapestries, but through a thin slit in the velvet he looked into a chamber lit by a candle on an ebony table. There were two men in that chamber. One was a scarred, sinister-looking ruffian in leather breeks and ragged cloak; the other was Tarascus, king of Nemedia.

Tarascus seemed ill at ease. He was slightly pale, and he kept starting and glancing about him, as if expecting and fearing to hear some sound or footstep.

"Go swiftly and at once," he was saying. "*He* is deep in drugged slumber, but I know not when he may awaken."

"Strange to hear words of fear issuing from the lips of Tarascus," rumbled the other in a harsh, deep voice.

The king frowned.

"I fear no common man, as you well know. But when I saw the cliffs fall at Valkia I knew that this devil we had resurrected was no charlatan. I fear his powers, because I do not know the full extent of them. But I know that somehow they are connected with this accursed thing which I have stolen from him. It brought him back to life; so it must be the source of his sorcery.

"He had it hidden well; but following my secret order a slave spied on him and saw him place it in a golden chest, and saw where he hid the chest. Even so, I would not have dared steal it had Xaltotun himself not been sunk in lotus slumber.

"I believe it is the secret of his power. With it Orastes brought him back to life. With it he will make us all slaves, if we are not wary. So take it and cast it into the sea as I have bidden you. And be sure you are so far from land that neither tide nor storm can wash it up on the beach. You have been paid."

"So I have," grunted the ruffian. "And I owe more than gold to you, king; I owe you a debt of gratitude. Even thieves can be grateful."

"Whatever debt you may feel you owe me," answered Tarascus, "will be paid when you have hurled this thing into the sea."

"I'll ride for Zingara and take ship from Kordava," promised the other. "I dare not show my head in Argos, because of the matter of a murder or so – "

"I care not, so it is done. Here it is; a horse awaits you in the court. Go, and go swiftly!"

Something passed between them, something that flamed like living fire. Conan had only a brief glimpse of it; and then the ruffian pulled a slouch hat over his eyes, drew his cloak about his shoulder, and hurried from the chamber. And as the door closed behind him, Conan moved with the devastating fury of unchained blood-lust. He had held himself in check as long as he could. The sight of his enemy so near him set his wild blood seething and swept away all caution and restraint.

Tarascus was turning toward an inner door when Conan tore aside the hangings and leaped like a blood-mad panther into the room. Tarascus wheeled, but even before he could recognize his attacker, Conan's poniard ripped into him.

But the blow was not mortal, as Conan knew the instant he struck. His foot had caught in a fold of the curtains and tripped him as he leaped. The point fleshed itself in Tarascus's shoulder and plowed down along his ribs, and the king of Nemedia screamed.

The impact of the blow and Conan's lunging body hurled him back against the table and it toppled and the candle went out. They were both carried to the floor by the violence of Conan's rush, and the foot of the tapestry hampered them both in its folds. Conan was stabbing blindly in the dark, Tarascus screaming in a frenzy of panicky terror. As if fear lent him superhuman energy, Tarascus tore free and blundered away in the darkness, shrieking: "Help! Guards! Arideus! Orastes! *Orastes!*"

Conan rose, kicking himself free of the tangling tapestries and the broken table, cursing with the bitterness of his blood-thirsty disappointment. He was confused, and ignorant of the plan of the palace. The yells of Tarascus were still resounding in the distance, and a wild outcry was bursting forth in answer. The Nemedian had escaped him in the darkness, and Conan did not know which way he had gone. The Cimmerian's rash stroke for vengeance had failed, and there remained only the task of saving his own hide if he could.

Swearing luridly, Conan ran back down the passage and into the alcove, glaring out into the lighted corridor, just as Zenobia came running up it, her dark eyes dilated with terror.

"Oh, what has happened?" she cried. "The palace is roused! I swear I have not betrayed you – "

"No, it was I who stirred up this hornet's nest," he grunted. "I tried to pay off a score. What's the shortest way out of this?"

She caught his wrist and ran fleetly down the corridor. But before they reached the heavy door at the other end, muffled shouts arose from behind it and the portals began to shake under an assault from the other side. Zenobia wrung her hands and whimpered.

"We are cut off! I locked that door as I returned through it. But they will burst it in a moment. The way to the postern gate lies through it."

Conan wheeled. Up the corridor, though still out of sight, he heard a rising clamor that told him his foes were behind as well as before him.

"Quick! Into this door!" the girl cried desperately, running across the corridor and throwing open the door of a chamber.

Conan followed her through, and then threw the gold catch behind them. They stood in an ornately furnished chamber, empty but for themselves, and she drew him to a gold-barred window, through which he saw trees and shrubbery.

"You are strong," she panted. "If you can tear these bars away, you may yet escape. The garden is full of guards, but the shrubs are thick, and you may avoid them. The southern wall is also the outer wall of the city. Once over that, you have a chance to get away. A horse is hidden for you in a thicket beside the road that runs westward, a few hundred paces to the south of the fountain of Thrallos. You know where it is?"

"Aye! But what of you? I had meant to take you with me."

A flood of joy lighted her beautiful face.

"Then my cup of happiness is brimming! But I will not hamper your escape. Burdened with me you would fail. Nay, do not fear for me. They will never suspect that I aided you willingly. Go! What you have just said will glorify my life throughout the long years."

He caught her up in his iron arms, crushed her slim, vibrant figure to him and

kissed her fiercely on eyes, cheeks, throat and lips, until she lay panting in his embrace; gusty and tempestuous as a storm-wind, even his love-making was violent.

"I'll go," he muttered. "But by Crom, I'll come for you some day!"

Wheeling, he gripped the gold bars and tore them from their sockets with one tremendous wrench; threw a leg over the sill and went down swiftly, clinging to the ornaments on the wall. He hit the ground running and melted like a shadow into the maze of towering rose-bushes and spreading trees. The one look he cast back over his shoulder showed him Zenobia leaning over the window-sill, her arms stretched after him in mute farewell and renunciation.

Guards were running through the garden, all converging toward the palace, where the clamor momentarily grew louder – tall men, in burnished cuirasses and crested helmets of polished bronze. The starlight struck glints from their gleaming armor, among the trees, betraying their every movement; but the sound of their coming ran far before them. To Conan, wilderness-bred, their rush through the shrubbery was like the blundering stampede of cattle. Some of them passed within a few feet of where he lay flat in a thick cluster of bushes, and never guessed his presence. With the palace as their goal, they were oblivious to all else about them. When they had gone shouting on, he rose and fled through the garden with no more noise than a panther would have made.

So quickly he came to the southern wall, and mounted the steps that led to the parapet. The wall was made to keep people out, not in. No sentry patrolling the battlements was in sight. Crouching by an embrasure he glanced back at the great palace rearing above the cypresses behind him. Lights blazed from every window, and he could see figures flitting back and forth across them like puppets on invisible strings. He grinned hardly, shook his fist in a gesture of farewell and menace, and let himself over the outer rim of the parapet.

A low tree, a few yards below the parapet, received Conan's weight, as he dropped noiselessly into the branches. An instant later he was racing through the shadows with the swinging hillman's stride that eats up long miles.

Gardens and pleasure villas surrounded the walls of Belverus. Drowsy slaves, sleeping by their watchman's pikes, did not see the swift and furtive figure that scaled walls, crossed alleys made by the arching branches of trees, and threaded a noiseless way through orchards and vineyards. Watch-dogs woke and lifted their deep-booming clamor at a gliding shadow, half scented, half sensed, and then it was gone.

In a chamber of the palace Tarascus writhed and cursed on a blood-spattered couch, under the deft, quick fingers of Orastes. The palace was thronged with wide-eyed, trembling servitors, but the chamber where the king lay was empty save for himself and the renegade priest.

"Are you sure he still sleeps?" Tarascus demanded again, setting his teeth against the bite of the herb juices with which Orastes was bandaging the long, ragged gash in his shoulder and ribs. "Ishtar, Mitra and Set! That burns like the molten pitch of hell!"

"Which you would be experiencing even now, but for your good fortune," remarked Orastes. "Whoever wielded that knife struck to kill. Yes, I have told you that Xaltotun still sleeps. Why are you so urgent upon that point? What has he to do with this?"

"You know nothing of what has passed in the palace tonight?" Tarascus searched the priest's countenance with burning intensity.

"Nothing. As you know, I have been employed in translating manuscripts for Xaltotun, for some months now, transcribing esoteric volumes written in the younger languages into script he can read. He was well versed in all the tongues and scripts of his day, but he has not yet learned all the newer languages, and to save time he has me translate these works for him, to learn if any new knowledge has been discovered since his time. I did not know that he had returned last night until he sent for me and told me of the battle. Then I returned to my studies, nor did I know that you had returned until the clamor in the palace brought me out of my cell."

"Then you do not know that Xaltotun brought the king of Aquilonia a captive to this palace?"

Orastes shook his head, without particular surprize.

"Xaltotun merely said that Conan would oppose us no more. I supposed that he had fallen, but did not ask the details."

"Xaltotun saved his life when I would have slain him," snarled Tarascus. "I saw his purpose instantly. He would hold Conan captive to use as a club against us – against Amalric, against Valerius, and against myself. So long as Conan lives he is a threat, a unifying factor for Aquilonia, that might be used to compel us into courses we would not otherwise follow. I mistrust this undead Pythonian. Of late I have begun to fear him.

"I followed him, some hours after he had departed eastward. I wished to learn what he intended doing with Conan. I found that he had imprisoned him in the pits. I intended to see that the barbarian died, in spite of Xaltotun. And I accomplished – "

A cautious knock sounded at the door.

"That's Arideus," grunted Tarascus. "Let him in."

The saturnine squire entered, his eyes blazing with suppressed excitement.

"How, Arideus?" exclaimed Tarascus. "Have you found the man who attacked me?"

"You did not see him, my lord?" asked Arideus, as one who would assure himself of a fact he already knows to exist. "You did not recognize him?"

"No. It happened so quick, and the candle was out – all I could think of was that it was some devil loosed on me by Xaltotun's magic – "

"The Pythonian sleeps in his barred and bolted room. But I have been in the pits." Arideus twitched his lean shoulders excitedly.

"Well, speak, man!" exclaimed Tarascus impatiently. "What did you find there?"

"An empty dungeon," whispered the squire. "The corpse of the great ape!"

"What?" Tarascus started upright, and blood gushed from his opened wound.

"Aye! The man-eater is dead – stabbed through the heart – and Conan is gone!"

Tarascus was gray of face as he mechanically allowed Orastes to force him prostrate again and the priest renewed work upon his mangled flesh.

"Conan!" he repeated. "Not a crushed corpse – escaped! Mitra! He is no man, but a devil himself! I thought Xaltotun was behind this wound. I see now. Gods and devils! It was Conan who stabbed me! Arideus!"

"Aye, your Majesty!"

"Search every nook in the palace. He may be skulking through the dark corridors now like a hungry tiger. Let no niche escape your scrutiny, and beware. It is not a civilized man you hunt, but a blood-mad barbarian whose strength and ferocity are those of a wild beast. Scour the palace-grounds and the city. Throw a cordon about the walls. If you find he has escaped from the city, as he may well do, take a troop of horsemen and follow him. Once past the walls it will be like hunting a wolf through the hills. But haste, and you may yet catch him."

"This is a matter which requires more than ordinary human wits," said Orastes. "Perhaps we should seek Xaltotun's advice."

"No!" exclaimed Tarascus violently. "Let the troopers pursue Conan and slay him. Xaltotun can hold no grudge against us if we kill a prisoner to prevent his escape."

"Well," said Orastes, "I am no Acheronian, but I am versed in some of the arts, and the control of certain spirits which have cloaked themselves in material substance. Perhaps I can aid you in this matter."

The fountain of Thrallos stood in a clustered ring of oaks beside the road a mile from the walls of the city. Its musical tinkle reached Conan's ears through the silence of the starlight. He drank deep of its icy stream, and then hurried southward toward a small, dense thicket he saw there. Rounding it, he saw a great white horse tied among the bushes. Heaving a deep gusty sigh he reached it with one stride – a mocking laugh brought him about, glaring.

A dully glinting, mail-clad figure moved out of the shadows into the starlight. This was no plumed and burnished palace guardsman. It was a tall man in morion and gray chain-mail – one of the Adventurers, a class of warriors peculiar to Nemedia; men who had not attained to the wealth and position of knighthood, or had fallen from that estate; hard-bitten fighters, dedicating their lives to war and adventure. They constituted a class of their own, sometimes commanding troops, but themselves accountable to no man but the king. Conan knew that he could have been discovered by no more dangerous a foeman.

A quick glance among the shadows convinced him that the man was alone, and he expanded his great chest slightly, digging his toes into the turf, as his thews coiled tensely.

"I was riding for Belverus on Amalric's business," said the Adventurer, advancing warily. The starlight was a long sheen on the great two-handed sword he bore naked in his hand. "A horse whinnied to mine from the thicket. I investigated and thought it strange a steed should be tethered here. I waited – and lo, I have caught a rare prize!"

The Adventurers lived by their swords.

"I know you," muttered the Nemedian. "You are Conan, king of Aquilonia. I thought I saw you die in the valley of the Valkia, but – "

Conan sprang as a dying tiger springs. Practised fighter though the Adventurer was, he did not realize the desperate quickness that lurks in barbaric sinews. He was caught off guard, his heavy sword half lifted. Before he could either strike or parry, the king's poniard sheathed itself in his throat, above the gorget, slanting downward into his heart. With a choked gurgle he reeled and went down, and Conan ruthlessly tore his blade free as his victim fell. The white horse snorted violently and shied at the sight and scent of blood on the sward.

Glaring down at his lifeless enemy, dripping poniard in hand, sweat glistening on his broad breast, Conan poised like a statue, listening intently. In the woods about there was no sound, save for the sleepy cheep of awakened birds. But in the city, a mile away, he heard the strident blare of a trumpet.

Hastily he bent over the fallen man. A few seconds' search convinced him that whatever message the man might have borne was intended to be conveyed by word of mouth. But he did not pause in his task. It was not many hours until dawn. A few minutes later the white horse was galloping westward along the white road, and the rider wore the gray mail of a Nemedian Adventurer.

VII

The Rending of the Veil

Conan knew his only chance of escape lay in speed. He did not even consider hiding somewhere near Belverus until the chase passed on; he was certain that the uncanny ally of Tarascus would be able to ferret him out. Besides, he was not one to skulk and hide; an open fight or an open chase, either suited his temperament better. He had a long start, he knew. He would lead them a grinding race for the border.

Zenobia had chosen well in selecting the white horse. His speed, toughness and endurance were obvious. The girl knew weapons and horses, and, Conan reflected with some satisfaction, she knew men. He rode westward at a gait that ate up the miles.

It was a sleeping land through which he rode, past grove-sheltered villages and white-walled villas amid spacious fields and orchards that grew sparser as he fared westward. As the villages thinned, the land grew more rugged, and the keeps that frowned from eminences told of centuries of border war. But none rode down from those castles to challenge or halt him. The lords of the keeps were following the banner of Amalric; the pennons that were wont to wave over these towers were now floating over the Aquilonian plains.

When the last huddled village fell behind him, Conan left the road, which was beginning to bend toward the northwest, toward the distant passes. To keep to the road would mean to pass by border towers, still garrisoned with armed men who would not allow him to pass unquestioned. He knew there would be no patrols riding the border marches on either side, as in ordinary times, but there were those towers, and with dawn there would probably be cavalcades of returning soldiers with wounded men in ox-carts.

This road from Belverus was the only road that crossed the border for fifty miles from north to south. It followed a series of passes through the hills, and on either hand lay a wide expanse of wild, sparsely inhabited mountains. He maintained his due westerly direction, intending to cross the border deep in the wilds of the hills that lay to the south of the passes. It was a shorter route, more arduous, but safer for a hunted fugitive. One man on a horse could traverse country an army would find impassable.

But at dawn he had not reached the hills; they were a long, low, blue rampart stretching along the horizon ahead of him. Here there were neither farms nor villages, no white-walled villas looming among clustering trees. The dawn wind stirred the tall stiff grass, and there was nothing but the long rolling swells of brown earth, covered with dry grass, and in the distance the gaunt walls of a stronghold on a low hill. Too many Aquilonian raiders had crossed the mountains in not too-distant days for the countryside to be thickly settled as it was farther to the east.

Dawn ran like a prairie fire across the grasslands, and high overhead sounded a weird crying as a straggling wedge of wild geese winged swiftly southward. In a grassy swale Conan halted and unsaddled his mount. Its sides were heaving, its coat plastered with sweat. He had pushed it unmercifully through the hours before dawn.

While it munched the brittle grass and rolled, he lay at the crest of the low slope, staring eastward. Far away to the northward he could see the road he had left, streaming like a white ribbon over a distant rise. No black dots moved along that glistening ribbon. There was no sign about the castle in the distance to indicate that the keepers had noticed the lone wayfarer.

An hour later the land still stretched bare. The only sign of life was a glint of steel on the far-off battlements, a raven in the sky that wheeled backward and forth, dipping and rising as if seeking something. Conan saddled and rode westward at a more leisurely gait.

As he topped the farther crest of the slope, a raucous screaming burst out over his head, and looking up, he saw the raven flapping high above him, cawing incessantly. As he rode on, it followed him, maintaining its position and making the morning hideous with its strident cries, heedless of his efforts to drive it away.

This kept up for hours, until Conan's teeth were on edge, and he felt that he would give half his kingdom to be allowed to wring that black neck.

"Devils of hell!" he roared in futile rage, shaking his mailed fist at the frantic bird. "Why do you harry me with your squawking? Begone, you black spawn of perdition, and peck for wheat in the farmers' fields!"

He was ascending the first pitch of the hills, and he seemed to hear an echo of the bird's clamor far behind him. Turning in his saddle, he presently made out another black dot hanging in the blue. Beyond that again he caught the glint of the afternoon sun on steel. That could mean only one thing: armed men. And they were not riding along the beaten road, which was out of his sight beyond the horizon. They were following him.

His face grew grim and he shivered slightly as he stared at the raven that wheeled high above him.

"So it is more than the whim of a brainless beast?" he muttered. "Those riders cannot see you, spawn of hell; but the other bird can see you, and they can see him. You follow me, he follows you, and they follow him. Are you only a craftily trained feathered creature, or some devil in the form of a bird? Did Xaltotun set you on my trail? Are *you* Xaltotun?"

Only a strident screech answered him, a screech vibrating with harsh mockery.

Conan wasted no more breath on his dusky betrayer. Grimly he settled to the long grind of the hills. He dared not push the horse too hard; the rest he had allowed it had not been enough to freshen it. He was still far ahead of his pursuers, but they would cut down that lead steadily. It was almost a certainty that their horses were fresher than his, for they had undoubtedly changed mounts at that castle he had passed.

The going grew rougher, the scenery more rugged, steep grassy slopes pitching up to densely timbered mountainsides. Here, he knew, he might elude his hunters, but for that hellish bird that squalled incessantly above him. He could no longer see them in this broken country, but he was certain that they still followed him, guided unerringly by their feathered allies. That black shape became like a demoniac incubus, hounding him through measureless hells. The stones he hurled with a curse went wide or fell harmless, though in his youth he had felled hawks on the wing.

The horse was tiring fast. Conan recognized the grim finality of his position. He sensed an inexorable driving fate behind all this. He could not escape. He was as much a captive as he had been in the pits of Belverus. But he was no son of the Orient to yield passively to what seemed inevitable. If he could not escape, he would at least take some of his foes into eternity with him. He turned into a wide thicket of larches that masked a slope, looking for a place to turn at bay.

Then ahead of him there rang a strange, shrill scream, human yet weirdly timbred. An instant later he had pushed through a screen of branches, and saw the source of that eldritch cry. In a small glade below him four soldiers in Nemedian chain-mail were binding a noose about the neck of a gaunt old woman in peasant garb. A heap of fagots, bound with cord on the ground near by, showed what her occupation had been when surprized by these stragglers.

Conan felt slow fury swell his heart as he looked silently down and saw the ruffians dragging her toward a tree whose low-spreading branches were obviously intended to act as a gibbet. He had crossed the frontier an hour ago. He was standing on his own soil, watching the murder of one of his own subjects. The old woman was struggling with surprizing strength and energy, and as he watched, she lifted her head and voiced again the strange, weird, far-carrying call he had heard before. It was echoed as if in mockery by the raven flapping above the trees. The soldiers laughed roughly, and one struck her in the mouth.

Conan swung from his weary steed and dropped down the face of the rocks, landing with a clang of mail on the grass. The four men wheeled at the sound and drew their swords, gaping at the mailed giant who faced them, sword in hand.

Conan laughed harshly. His eyes were bleak as flint.

"Dogs!" he said without passion and without mercy. "Do Nemedian jackals set themselves up as executioners and hang my subjects at will? First you must take the head of their king. Here I stand, awaiting your lordly pleasure!"

The soldiers stared at him uncertainly as he strode toward them.

"Who is this madman?" growled a bearded ruffian. "He wears Nemedian mail, but speaks with an Aquilonian accent."

"No matter," quoth another. "Cut him down, and then we'll hang the old hag."

And so saying he ran at Conan, lifting his sword. But before he could strike, the king's great blade lashed down, splitting helmet and skull. The man fell before him, but the others were hardy rogues. They gave tongue like wolves and surged about the lone figure in the gray mail, and the clamor and din of steel drowned the cries of the circling raven.

Conan did not shout. His eyes coals of blue fire and his lips smiling bleakly, he lashed right and left with his two-handed sword. For all his size he was quick as a cat on his feet, and he was constantly in motion, presenting a moving target so that thrusts and swings cut empty air oftener than not. Yet when he struck he was perfectly balanced, and his blows fell with devastating power. Three of the four were down, dying in their own blood, and the fourth was bleeding from half a dozen wounds, stumbling in headlong retreat as he parried frantically, when Conan's spur caught in the surcoat of one of the fallen men.

The king stumbled, and before he could catch himself the Nemedian, with the frenzy of desperation, rushed him so savagely that Conan staggered and fell sprawling over the corpse. The Nemedian croaked in triumph and sprang forward, lifting his great sword with both hands over his right shoulder, as he braced his legs wide for the stroke – and then, over the prostrate king, something huge and hairy shot like a thunderbolt full on the soldier's breast, and his yelp of triumph changed to a shriek of death.

Conan, scrambling up, saw the man lying dead with his throat torn out, and a great gray wolf stood over him, head sunk as it smelt the blood that formed a pool on the grass.

The king turned as the old woman spoke to him. She stood straight and tall before him, and in spite of her ragged garb, her features, clear-cut and aquiline, and her keen black eyes, were not those of a common peasant woman. She called to the wolf and it trotted to her side like a great dog and rubbed its giant shoulder against her knee, while it gazed at Conan with great green lambent eyes. Absently she laid her hand upon its mighty neck, and so the two stood regarding the king of Aquilonia. He found their steady gaze disquieting, though there was no hostility in it.

"Men say King Conan died beneath the stones and dirt when the cliffs crumbled by Valkia," she said in a deep, strong, resonant voice.

"So they say," he growled. He was in no mood for controversy, and he thought of those armored riders who were pushing nearer every moment. The raven above him cawed stridently, and he cast an involuntary glare upward, grinding his teeth in a spasm of nervous irritation.

Up on the ledge the white horse stood with drooping head. The old woman looked at it, and then at the raven; and then she lifted a strange weird cry as she had before. As if recognizing the call, the raven wheeled, suddenly mute, and raced eastward. But before it had got out of sight, the shadow of mighty wings fell across it. An eagle soared up from the tangle of trees, and rising above it, swooped and struck the black messenger to the earth. The strident voice of betrayal was stilled for ever.

"Crom!" muttered Conan, staring at the old woman. "Are you a magician, too?"

"I am Zelata," she said. "The people of the valleys call me a witch. Was that child of the night guiding armed men on your trail?"

"Aye." She did not seem to think the answer fantastic. "They cannot be far behind me."

"Lead your horse and follow me, King Conan," she said briefly.

Without comment he mounted the rocks and brought his horse down to the glade by a circuitous path. As he came he saw the eagle reappear, dropping lazily down from the sky, and rest an instant on Zelata's shoulder, spreading its great wings lightly so as not to crush her with its weight.

Without a word she led the way, the great wolf trotting at her side, the eagle soaring above her. Through deep thickets and along tortuous ledges poised over deep ravines she led him, and finally along a narrow precipice-edged path to a curious dwelling of stone, half hut, half cavern, beneath a cliff hidden among the gorges and crags. The eagle flew to the pinnacle of this cliff, and perched there like a motionless sentinel.

Still silent, Zelata stabled the horse in a near-by cave, with leaves and grass piled high for provender, and a tiny spring bubbling in the dim recesses.

In the hut she seated the king on a rude, hide-covered bench, and she herself sat upon a low stool before the tiny fireplace, while she made a fire of tamarisk chunks and prepared a frugal meal. The great wolf drowsed beside her, facing the fire, his huge head sunk on his paws, his ears twitching in his dreams.

"You do not fear to sit in the hut of a witch?" she asked, breaking her silence at last.

An impatient shrug of his gray-mailed shoulders was her guest's only reply. She gave into his hands a wooden dish heaped with dried fruits, cheese and barley bread, and a great pot of the heady upland beer, brewed from barley grown in the high valleys.

"I have found the brooding silence of the glens more pleasing than the babble of city streets," she said. "The children of the wild are kinder than the children of men." Her hand briefly stroked the ruff of the sleeping wolf. "My children were afar from me today, or I had not needed your sword, my king. They were coming at my call."

"What grudge had those Nemedian dogs against you?" Conan demanded.

"Skulkers from the invading army straggle all over the countryside, from the frontier to Tarantia," she answered. "The foolish villagers in the valleys told them that I had a store of gold hidden away, so as to divert their attentions from their villages. They demanded treasure from me, and my answers angered them. But neither skulkers nor the men who pursue you, nor any raven will find you here."

He shook his head, eating ravenously.

"I'm for Tarantia."

She shook her head.

"You thrust your head into the dragon's jaws. Best seek refuge abroad. The heart is gone from your kingdom."

"What do you mean?" he demanded. "Battles have been lost before, yet wars won. A kingdom is not lost by a single defeat."

"And you will go to Tarantia?"

"Aye. Prospero will be holding it against Amalric."

"Are you sure?"

"Hell's devils, woman!" he exclaimed wrathfully. "What else?"

She shook her head. "I feel that it is otherwise. Let us see. Not lightly is the veil rent; yet I will rend it a little, and show you your capital city."

Conan did not see what she cast upon the fire, but the wolf whimpered in his dreams, and a green smoke gathered and billowed up into the hut. And as he watched, the walls and ceiling of the hut seemed to widen, to grow remote and vanish, merging with infinite immensities; the smoke rolled about him, blotting out everything. And in it forms moved and faded, and stood out in startling clarity.

He stared at the familiar towers and streets of Tarantia, where a mob seethed and screamed, and at the same time he was somehow able to see the banners of

Nemedia moving inexorably westward through the smoke and flame of a pillaged land. In the great square of Tarantia the frantic throng milled and yammered, screaming that the king was dead, that the barons were girding themselves to divide the land between them, and that the rule of a king, even of Valerius, was better than anarchy. Prospero, shining in his armor, rode among them, trying to pacify them, bidding them trust Count Trocero, urging them to man the wall and aid his knights in defending the city. They turned on him, shrieking with fear and unreasoning rage, howling that he was Trocero's butcher, a more evil foe than Amalric himself. Offal and stones were hurled at his knights.

A slight blurring of the picture, that might have denoted a passing of time, and then Conan saw Prospero and his knights filing out of the gates and spurring southward. Behind him the city was in an uproar.

"Fools!" muttered Conan thickly. "Fools! Why could they not trust Prospero? Zelata, if you are making game of me, with some trickery – "

"This has passed," answered Zelata imperturbably, though somberly. "It was the evening of the day that has passed when Prospero rode out of Tarantia, with the hosts of Amalric almost within sight. From the walls men saw the flame of their pillaging. So I read it in the smoke. At sunset the Nemedians rode into Tarantia, unopposed. Look! Even now, in the royal hall of Tarantia – "

Abruptly Conan was looking into the great coronation hall. Valerius stood on the regal dais, clad in ermine robes, and Amalric, still in his dusty, blood-stained armor, placed a rich and gleaming circlet on his yellow locks – the crown of Aquilonia! The people cheered; long lines of steel-clad Nemedian warriors looked grimly on, and nobles long in disfavor at Conan's court strutted and swaggered with the emblem of Valerius on their sleeves.

"Crom!" It was an explosive imprecation from Conan's lips as he started up, his great fists clenched into hammers, his veins on his temples knotting, his features convulsed. "A Nemedian placing the crown of Aquilonia on that renegade – in the royal hall of Tarantia!"

As if dispelled by his violence, the smoke faded, and he saw Zelata's black eyes gleaming at him through the mist.

"You have seen – the people of your capital have forfeited the freedom you won for them by sweat and blood; they have sold themselves to the slavers and the butchers. They have shown that they do not trust their destiny. Can you rely upon them for the winning back of your kingdom?"

"They thought I was dead," he grunted, recovering some of his poise. "I have no son. Men can't be governed by a memory. What if the Nemedians have taken Tarantia? There still remain the provinces, the barons, and the people of the countrysides. Valerius has won an empty glory."

"You are stubborn, as befits a fighter. I cannot show you the future, I cannot show you all the past. Nay, *I* show you nothing. I merely make you see windows opened in the veil by powers unguessed. Would you look into the past for a clue of the present?"

"Aye." He seated himself abruptly.

Again the green smoke rose and billowed. Again images unfolded before him, this time alien and seemingly irrelevant. He saw great towering black walls, pedestals half hidden in the shadows upholding images of hideous, half-bestial gods. Men moved in the shadows, dark, wiry men, clad in red, silken loin-cloths. They were bearing a green jade sarcophagus along a gigantic black corridor. But before he could tell much about what he saw, the scene shifted. He saw a cavern, dim, shadowy and haunted with a strange intangible horror. On an altar of black stone stood a curious golden vessel, shaped like the shell of a scallop. Into this cavern came some of the same dark, wiry men who had borne the mummy-case. They seized the golden vessel, and then the shadows swirled around them and what happened he could not say. But he saw a glimmer in a whorl of darkness, like a ball of living fire. Then the smoke was only smoke, drifting up from the fire of tamarisk chunks, thinning and fading.

"But what does this portend?" he demanded, bewildered. "What I saw in Tarantia I can understand. But what means this glimpse of Zamorian thieves sneaking through a subterranean temple of Set, in Stygia? And that cavern – I've never seen or heard of anything like it, in all my wanderings. If you can show me that much, these shreds of vision which mean nothing, disjointed, why can you not show me all that is to occur?"

Zelata stirred the fire without replying.

"These things are governed by immutable laws," she said at last. "I cannot make you understand; I do not altogether understand myself, though I have sought wisdom in the silences of the high places for more years than I can remember. I cannot save you, though I would if I might. Man must, at last, work out his own salvation. Yet perhaps wisdom may come to me in dreams, and in the morn I may be able to give you the clue to the enigma."

"What enigma?" he demanded.

"The mystery that confronts you, whereby you have lost a kingdom," she answered. And then she spread a sheepskin upon the floor before the hearth. "Sleep," she said briefly.

Without a word he stretched himself upon it, and sank into restless but deep sleep through which phantoms moved silently and monstrous shapeless shadows crept. Once, limned against a purple sunless horizon, he saw the mighty walls and towers of a great city such as rose nowhere on the waking earth he knew. Its colossal pylons and purple minarets lifted toward the stars, and over it, floating like a giant mirage, hovered the bearded countenance of the man Xaltotun.

Conan woke in the chill whiteness of early dawn, to see Zelata crouched beside the tiny fire. He had not awakened once in the night, and the sound of the great wolf leaving or entering should have roused him. Yet the wolf was there, beside the hearth, with its shaggy coat wet with dew, and with more than dew. Blood glistened wetly amid the thick fell, and there was a cut upon his shoulder.

Zelata nodded, without looking around, as if reading the thoughts of her royal guest.

"He has hunted before dawn, and red was the hunting. I think the man who hunted a king will hunt no more, neither man nor beast."

Conan stared at the great beast with strange fascination as he moved to take the food Zelata offered him.

"When I come to my throne again I won't forget," he said briefly. "You've befriended me – by Crom, I can't remember when I've lain down and slept at the mercy of man or woman as I did last night. But what of the riddle you would read me this morn?"

A long silence ensued, in which the crackle of the tamarisks was loud on the hearth.

"Find the heart of your kingdom," she said at last. "There lies your defeat and your power. You fight more than mortal man. You will not press the throne again unless you find the heart of your kingdom."

"Do you mean the city of Tarantia?" he asked.

She shook her head. "I am but an oracle, through whose lips the gods speak. My lips are sealed by them lest I speak too much. You must find the heart of your kingdom. I can say no more. My lips are opened and sealed by the gods."

Dawn was still white on the peaks when Conan rode westward. A glance back showed him Zelata standing in the door of her hut, inscrutable as ever, the great wolf beside her.

A gray sky arched overhead, and a moaning wind was chill with a promise of winter. Brown leaves fluttered slowly down from the bare branches, sifting upon his mailed shoulders.

All day he pushed through the hills, avoiding roads and villages. Toward nightfall he began to drop down from the heights, tier by tier, and saw the broad plains of Aquilonia spread out beneath him.

Villages and farms lay close to the foot of the hills on the western side of the mountains, for, for half a century, most of the raiding across the frontier had been done by the Aquilonians. But now only embers and ashes showed where farm huts and villas had stood.

In the gathering darkness Conan rode slowly on. There was little fear of discovery, which he dreaded from friend as well as from foe. The Nemedians had remembered old scores on their westward drive, and Valerius had made no attempt to restrain his allies. He did not count on winning the love of the common people. A vast swath of desolation had been cut through the country from the foothills westward. Conan cursed as he rode over blackened expanses that had been rich fields, and saw the gaunt gable-ends of burned houses jutting against the sky. He moved through an empty and deserted land, like a ghost out of a forgotten and outworn past.

The speed with which the army had traversed the land showed what little resistance it had encountered. Yet had Conan been leading his Aquilonians the invading army would have been forced to buy every foot they gained with their blood. The bitter realization permeated his soul; he was not the representative of a dynasty. He was only a lone adventurer. Even the drop of dynastic blood Valerius boasted had more hold on the minds of men than the memory of Conan and the freedom and power he had given the kingdom.

No pursuers followed him down out of the hills. He watched for wandering or returning Nemedian troops, but met none. Skulkers gave him a wide path, supposing him to be one of the conquerors, what of his harness. Groves and rivers were far more plentiful on the western side of the mountains, and coverts for concealment were not lacking.

So he moved across the pillaged land, halting only to rest his horse, eating frugally of the food Zelata had given him, until, on a dawn when he lay hidden on a river bank where willows and oaks grew thickly, he glimpsed, afar, across the rolling plains dotted with rich groves, the blue and golden towers of Tarantia.

He was no longer in a deserted land, but one teeming with varied life. His progress thenceforth was slow and cautious, through thick woods and unfrequented byways. It was dusk when he reached the plantation of Servius Galannus.

VIII
Dying Embers

The countryside about Tarantia had escaped the fearful ravaging of the more easterly provinces. There were evidences of the march of a conquering army in broken hedges, plundered fields and looted granaries, but torch and steel had not been loosed wholesale.

There was but one grim splotch on the landscape – a charred expanse of ashes and blackened stone, where, Conan knew, had once stood the stately villa of one of his staunchest supporters.

The king dared not openly approach the Galannus farm, which lay only a few miles from the city. In the twilight he rode through an extensive woodland, until he sighted a keeper's lodge through the trees. Dismounting and tying his horse, he approached the thick, arched door with the intention of sending the keeper after Servius. He did not know what enemies the manor house might be sheltering. He had seen no troops, but they might be quartered all over the countryside. But as he drew near, he saw the door open and a compact figure in silk hose and richly embroidered doublet stride forth and turn up a path that wound away through the woods.

"Servius!"

At the low call the master of the plantation wheeled with a startled exclamation. His hand flew to the short hunting-sword at his hip, and he recoiled from the tall gray steel figure standing in the dusk before him.

"Who are you?" he demanded. "What is your – *Mitra!*"

His breath hissed inward and his ruddy face paled. "Avaunt!" he ejaculated. "Why have you come back from the gray lands of death to terrify me? I was always your true liegeman in your lifetime – "

"As I still expect you to be," answered Conan. "Stop trembling, man; I'm flesh and blood."

Sweating with uncertainty Servius approached and stared into the face of the mail-clad giant, and then, convinced of the reality of what he saw, he dropped to one knee and doffed his plumed cap.

"Your Majesty! Truly, this is a miracle passing belief! The great bell in the citadel has tolled your dirge, days agone. Men said you died at Valkia, crushed under a million tons of earth and broken granite."

"It was another in my harness," grunted Conan. "But let us talk later. If there is such a thing as a joint of beef on your board – "

"Forgive me, my lord!" cried Servius, springing to his feet. "The dust of travel is gray on your mail, and I keep you standing here without rest or sup! Mitra! I see well enough now that you are alive, but I swear, when I turned and saw you standing all gray and dim in the twilight, the marrow of my knees turned to water. It is an ill thing to meet a man you thought dead in the woodland at dusk."

"Bid the keeper see to my steed which is tied behind yonder oak," requested Conan, and Servius nodded, drawing the king up the path. The patrician, recovering from his supernatural fright, had become extremely nervous.

"I will send a servant from the manor," he said. "The keeper is in his lodge – but I dare not trust even my servants in these days. It is better that only I know of your presence."

Approaching the great house that glimmered dimly through the trees, he turned aside into a little-used path that ran between close-set oaks whose intertwining branches formed a vault overhead, shutting out the dim light of the gathering dusk. Servius hurried on through the darkness without speaking, and with something resembling panic in his manner, and presently led Conan through a small side-door into a narrow, dimly illuminated corridor. They traversed this in haste and silence, and Servius brought the king into a spacious chamber with a high, oak-beamed ceiling and richly paneled walls. Logs flamed in the wide fireplace, for there was a frosty edge to the air, and a great meat pasty in a stone platter stood smoking on a broad mahogany board. Servius locked the massive door and extinguished the candles that stood in a silver candlestick on the table, leaving the chamber illuminated only by the fire on the hearth.

"Your pardon, your Majesty," he apologized. "These are perilous times; spies lurk everywhere. It were better that none be able to peer through the windows and recognize you. This pasty, however, is just from the oven, as I intended supping on my return from talk with my keeper. If your Majesty would deign – "

"The light is sufficient," grunted Conan, seating himself with scant ceremony, and drawing his poniard.

He dug ravenously into the luscious dish, and washed it down with great gulps of wine from grapes grown in Servius's vineyards. He seemed oblivious to any sense of peril, but Servius shifted uneasily on his settle by the fire, nervously fingering the heavy gold chain about his neck. He glanced continually at the diamond-panes of the casement, gleaming dimly in the firelight, and cocked his ear toward the door, as if half expecting to hear the pad of furtive feet in the corridor without.

Finishing his meal, Conan rose and seated himself on another settle before the fire.

"I won't jeopardize you long by my presence, Servius," he said abruptly. "Dawn will find me far from your plantation."

"My lord – " Servius lifted his hands in expostulation, but Conan waved his protests aside.

"I know your loyalty and your courage. Both are above reproach. But if Valerius has usurped my throne, it would be death for you to shelter me, if you were discovered."

"I am not strong enough to defy him openly," admitted Servius. "The fifty men-at-arms I could lead to battle would be but a handful of straws. You saw the ruins of Emilius Scavonus's plantation?"

Conan nodded, frowning darkly.

"He was the strongest patrician in this province, as you know. He refused to give his allegiance to Valerius. The Nemedians burned him in the ruins of his own villa. After that the rest of us saw the futility of resistance, especially as the people of Tarantia refused to fight. We submitted and Valerius spared our lives, though he levied a tax upon us that will ruin many. But what could we do? We thought you were dead. Many of the barons had been slain, others taken prisoner. The army was shattered and scattered. You have no heir to take the crown. There was no one to lead us – "

"Was there not Count Trocero of Poitain?" demanded Conan harshly.

Servius spread his hands helplessly.

"It is true that his general Prospero was in the field with a small army. Retreating before Amalric, he urged men to rally to his banner. But with your Majesty dead, men remembered old wars and civil brawls, and how Trocero and his Poitanians once rode through these provinces even as Amalric was riding now, with torch and sword. The barons were jealous of Trocero. Some men – spies of Valerius perhaps – shouted that the Count of Poitain intended seizing the crown for himself. Old sectional hates flared up again. If we had had one man with dynastic blood in his veins we would have crowned and followed him against Nemedia. But we had none.

"The barons who followed you loyally would not follow one of their own number, each holding himself as good as his neighbor, each fearing the ambitions of the others. You were the cord that held the fagots together. When the cord was cut, the fagots fell apart. If you had had a son, the barons would have rallied loyally to him. But there was no point for their patriotism to focus upon.

"The merchants and commoners, dreading anarchy and a return of feudal days when each baron was his own law, cried out that any king was better than none, even Valerius, who was at least of the blood of the old dynasty. There was no one to oppose him when he rode up at the head of his steel-clad hosts, with the scarlet dragon of Nemedia floating over him, and rang his lance against the gates of Tarantia.

"Nay, the people threw open the gates and knelt in the dust before him. They had refused to aid Prospero in holding the city. They said they had rather be ruled by Valerius than by Trocero. They said – truthfully – that the barons would not rally to Trocero, but that many would accept Valerius. They said that by yielding to Valerius they would escape the devastation of civil war, and the fury of the Nemedians. Prospero rode southward with his ten thousand knights, and the horsemen of the Nemedians entered the city a few hours later. They did not follow him. They remained to see that Valerius was crowned in Tarantia."

"Then the old witch's smoke showed the truth," muttered Conan, feeling a queer chill along his spine. "Amalric crowned Valerius?"

"Aye, in the coronation hall, with the blood of slaughter scarcely dried on his hands."

"And do the people thrive under his benevolent rule?" asked Conan with angry irony.

"He lives like a foreign prince in the midst of a conquered land," answered Servius bitterly. "His court is filled with Nemedians, the palace troops are of the same breed, and a large garrison of them occupy the citadel. Aye, the hour of the Dragon has come at last.

"Nemedians swagger like lords through the streets. Women are outraged and merchants plundered daily, and Valerius either can, or will, make no attempt to curb them. Nay, he is but their puppet, their figurehead. Men of sense knew he would be, and the people are beginning to find it out.

"Amalric has ridden forth with a strong army to reduce the outlying provinces where some of the barons have defied him. But there is no unity among them. Their jealousy of each other is stronger than their fear of Amalric. He will crush them one by one. Many castles and cities, realizing that, have sent in their submission. Those who resist fare miserably. The Nemedians are glutting their long hatred. And their ranks are swelled by Aquilonians whom fear, gold, or necessity of occupation are forcing into their armies. It is a natural consequence."

Conan nodded somberly, staring at the red reflections of the firelight on the richly carved oaken panels.

"Aquilonia has a king instead of the anarchy they feared," said Servius at last. "Valerius does not protect his subjects against his allies. Hundreds who could not pay the ransom imposed upon them have been sold to the Kothic slave-traders."

Conan's head jerked up and a lethal flame lit his blue eyes. He swore gustily, his mighty hands knotting into iron hammers.

"Aye, white men sell white men and white women, as it was in the feudal days. In the palaces of Shem and of Turan they will live out the lives of slaves. Valerius is king, but the unity for which the people looked, even though of the sword, is not complete.

"Gunderland in the north and Poitain in the south are yet unconquered, and there are unsubdued provinces in the west, where the border barons have the backing of the Bossonian bowmen. Yet these outlying provinces are no real menace to Valerius. They must remain on the defensive, and will be lucky if they are able to keep their independence. Here Valerius and his foreign knights are supreme."

"Let him make the best of it then," said Conan grimly. "His time is short. The people will rise when they learn that I'm alive. We'll take Tarantia back before Amalric can return with his army. Then we'll sweep these dogs from the kingdom."

Servius was silent. The crackle of the fire was loud in the stillness.

"Well," exclaimed Conan impatiently, "why do you sit with your head bent, staring at the hearth? Do you doubt what I have said?"

Servius avoided the king's eye.

"What mortal man can do, you will do, your Majesty," he answered. "I have ridden behind you in battle, and I know that no mortal being can stand before your sword."

"What, then?"

Servius drew his fur-trimmed jupon closer about him, and shivered in spite of the flame.

"Men say your fall was occasioned by sorcery," he said presently.

"What then?"

"What mortal can fight against sorcery? Who is this veiled man who communes at midnight with Valerius and his allies, as men say, who appears and disappears so mysteriously? Men say in whispers that he is a great magician who died thousands of years ago, but has returned from death's gray lands to overthrow the king of Aquilonia and restore the dynasty of which Valerius is heir."

"What matter?" exclaimed Conan angrily. "I escaped from the devil-haunted pits of Belverus, and from diabolism in the mountains. If the people rise – "

Servius shook his head.

"Your staunchest supporters in the eastern and central provinces are dead, fled or imprisoned. Gunderland is far to the north, Poitain far to the south. The Bossonians have retired to their marches far to the west. It would take weeks to gather and concentrate these forces, and before that could be done, each levy would be attacked separately by Amalric and destroyed."

"But an uprising in the central provinces would tip the scales for us!" exclaimed Conan. "We could seize Tarantia and hold it against Amalric until the Gundermen and Poitanians could get here."

Servius hesitated, and his voice sank to a whisper.

"Men say you died accursed. Men say this veiled stranger cast a spell upon you to slay you and break your army. The great bell has tolled your dirge. Men believe you to be dead. And the central provinces would not rise, even if they knew you lived. They would not dare. Sorcery defeated you at Valkia. Sorcery brought the news to Tarantia, for that very night men were shouting of it in the streets.

"A Nemedian priest loosed black magic again in the streets of Tarantia to slay men who still were loyal to your memory. I myself saw it. Armed men dropped like flies and died in the streets in a manner no man could understand. And the lean priest laughed and said: 'I am only Altaro, only an acolyte of Orastes, who is but an acolyte of him who wears the veil; not mine is the power; the power but works through me.'"

"Well," said Conan harshly, "is it not better to die honorably than to live in infamy? Is death worse than oppression, slavery and ultimate destruction?"

"When the fear of sorcery is in, reason is out," replied Servius. "The fear of the central provinces is too great to allow them to rise for you. The outlying provinces would fight for you – but the same sorcery that smote your army at Valkia would smite you again. The Nemedians hold the broadest, richest and most thickly populated sections of Aquilonia, and they cannot be defeated by the forces which might still be at your command. You would be sacrificing your loyal subjects uselessly. In sorrow I say it, but it is true: King Conan, you are a king without a kingdom."

Conan stared into the fire without replying. A smoldering log crashed down among the flames with a bursting shower of sparks. It might have been the crashing ruin of his kingdom.

Again Conan felt the presence of a grim reality behind the veil of material illusion. He sensed again the inexorable drive of a ruthless fate. A feeling of furious panic tugged at his soul, a sense of being trapped, and a red rage that burned to destroy and kill.

"Where are the officials of my court?" he demanded at last.

"Pallantides was sorely wounded at Valkia, was ransomed by his family, and now lies in his castle in Attalus. He will be fortunate if he ever rides again. Publius, the chancellor, has fled the kingdom in disguise, no man knows whither. The council has been disbanded. Some were imprisoned, some banished. Many of your loyal subjects have been put to death. Tonight, for instance, the Countess Albiona dies under the headsman's ax."

Conan started and stared at Servius with such anger smoldering in his blue eyes that the patrician shrank back.

"Why?"

"Because she would not become the mistress of Valerius. Her lands are forfeit, her henchmen sold into slavery, and at midnight, in the Iron Tower, her head must fall. Be advised, my king – to me you will ever be my king – and flee before you are discovered. In these days none is safe. Spies and informers creep among us, betraying the slightest deed or word of discontent as treason and rebellion. If you make yourself known to your subjects it will only end in your capture and death.

"My horses and all the men that I can trust are at your disposal. Before dawn we can be far from Tarantia, and well on our way toward the border. If I cannot aid you to recover your kingdom, I can at least follow you into exile."

Conan shook his head. Servius glanced uneasily at him as he sat staring into the fire, his chin propped on his mighty fist. The firelight gleamed redly on his steel mail, on his baleful eyes. They burned in the firelight like the eyes of a wolf. Servius was again aware, as in the past, and now more strongly than ever, of something alien about the king. That great frame under the mail mesh was too hard and supple for a civilized man; the elemental fire of the primitive burned in those smoldering eyes. Now the barbaric suggestion about the king was more pronounced, as if in his extremity the outward aspects of civilization were stripped away, to reveal the primordial core. Conan was reverting to his pristine type. He did not act as a civilized man would act under the same conditions, nor did his thoughts run in the same channels. He was unpredictable. It was only a stride from the king of Aquilonia to the skin-clad slayer of the Cimmerian hills.

"I'll ride to Poitain, if it may be," Conan said at last. "But I'll ride alone. And I have one last duty to perform as king of Aquilonia."

"What do you mean, your Majesty?" asked Servius, shaken by a premonition.

"I'm going into Tarantia after Albiona tonight," answered the king. "I've failed all my other loyal subjects, it seems – if they take her head, they can have mine too."

"This is madness!" cried Servius, staggering up and clutching his throat, as if he already felt the noose closing about it.

"There are secrets to the Tower which few know," said Conan. "Anyway, I'd be a dog to leave Albiona to die because of her loyalty to me. I may be a king without a kingdom, but I'm not a man without honor."

"It will ruin us all!" whispered Servius.

"It will ruin no one but me if I fail. You've risked enough. I ride alone tonight. This is all I want you to do: procure me a patch for my eye, a staff for my hand, and garments such as travelers wear."

IX

"It Is the King or His Ghost!"

Many men passed through the great arched gates of Tarantia between sunset and midnight – belated travelers, merchants from afar with heavily laden mules, free workmen from the surrounding farms and vineyards. Now that Valerius was supreme in the central provinces, there was no rigid scrutiny of the folk who flowed in a steady stream through the wide gates. Discipline had been relaxed. The Nemedian soldiers who stood on guard were half drunk, and much too busy watching for handsome peasant girls and rich merchants who could be bullied to notice workmen or dusty travelers, even one tall wayfarer whose worn cloak could not conceal the hard lines of his powerful frame.

This man carried himself with an erect, aggressive bearing that was too natural for him to realize it himself, much less dissemble it. A great patch covered one eye, and his leather coif, drawn low over his brows, shadowed his features. With a long thick staff in his muscular brown hand, he strode leisurely through the arch where the torches flared and guttered, and, ignored by the tipsy guardsmen, emerged upon the wide streets of Tarantia.

Upon these well-lighted thoroughfares the usual throngs went about their business, and shops and stalls stood open, with their wares displayed. One thread ran a constant theme through the pattern. Nemedian soldiers, singly or in clumps, swaggered through the throngs, shouldering their way with studied arrogance. Women scurried from their path, and men stepped aside with darkened brows and clenched fists. The Aquilonians were a proud race, and these were their hereditary enemies.

The knuckles of the tall traveler knotted on his staff, but, like the others, he stepped aside to let the men in armor have the way. Among the motley and varied crowd he did not attract much attention in his drab, dusty garments. But once, as he passed a sword-seller's stall and the light that streamed from its wide door fell full upon him, he thought he felt an intense stare upon him, and turning quickly, saw a man in the brown jerkin of a free workman regarding him fixedly. This man turned away with undue haste, and vanished in the shifting throng. But Conan turned into a narrow by-street and quickened his pace. It might have been mere idle curiosity; but he could take no chances.

The grim Iron Tower stood apart from the citadel, amid a maze of narrow streets and crowding houses where the meaner structures, appropriating a space from which the more fastidious shrank, had invaded a portion of the city ordinarily alien to them. The Tower was in reality a castle, an ancient, formidable pile of heavy stone and black iron, which had itself served as the citadel in an earlier, ruder century.

Not a long distance from it, lost in a tangle of partly deserted tenements and warehouses, stood an ancient watch-tower, so old and forgotten that it did not appear on the maps of the city for a hundred years back. Its original purpose had been forgotten, and nobody, of such as saw it at all, noticed that the apparently ancient lock which kept it from being appropriated as sleeping quarters by beggars and thieves, was in reality comparatively new and extremely powerful, cunningly disguised into an appearance of rusty antiquity. Not half a dozen men in the kingdom had ever known the secret of that tower.

No keyhole showed in the massive, green-crusted lock. But Conan's practised fingers, stealing over it, pressed here and there knobs invisible to the casual eye. The door silently opened inward and he entered solid blackness, pushing the door shut behind him. A light would have showed the tower empty, a bare, cylindrical shaft of massive stone.

Groping in a corner with the sureness of familiarity, he found the projections for which he was feeling on a slab of the stone that composed the floor. Quickly he lifted it, and without hesitation lowered himself into the aperture beneath. His feet felt stone steps leading downward into what he knew was a narrow tunnel that ran straight toward the foundations of the Iron Tower, three streets away.

The bell on the citadel, which tolled only at the midnight hour or for the death of a king, boomed suddenly. In a dimly lighted chamber in the Iron Tower a door opened and a form emerged into a corridor. The interior of the Tower was as forbidding as its external appearance. Its massive stone walls were rough, unadorned. The flags of the floor were worn deep by generations of faltering feet, and the vault of the ceiling was gloomy in the dim light of torches set in niches.

The man who trudged down that grim corridor was in appearance in keeping with his surroundings. He was a tall, powerfully-built man, clad in close-fitting black silk. Over his head was drawn a black hood which fell about his shoulders, having two holes for his eyes. From his shoulders hung a loose black cloak, and over one shoulder he bore a heavy ax, the shape of which was that of neither tool nor weapon.

As he went down the corridor, a figure came hobbling up it, a bent, surly old man, stooping under the weight of his pike and a lantern he bore in one hand.

"You are not as prompt as your predecessor, master headsman," he grumbled. "Midnight has just struck, and masked men have gone to milady's cell. They await you."

"The tones of the bell still echo among the towers," answered the executioner. "If I am not so quick to leap and run at the beck of Aquilonians as was the dog who held this office before me, they shall find my arm no less ready. Get you to your duties, old watchman, and leave me to mine. I think mine is the sweeter trade, by Mitra, for you tramp cold corridors and peer at rusty dungeon doors, while I lop off the fairest head in Tarantia this night."

The watchman limped on down the corridor, still grumbling, and the headsman resumed his leisurely way. A few strides carried him around a turn in the corridor, and he absently noted that at his left a door stood partly open. If he had thought, he would have known that that door had been opened since the watchman passed; but thinking was not his trade. He was passing the unlocked door before he realized that aught was amiss, and then it was too late.

A soft tigerish step and the rustle of a cloak warned him, but before he could turn, a heavy arm hooked about his throat from behind, crushing the cry before it could reach his lips. In the brief instant that was allowed him he realized with a surge of panic the strength of his attacker, against which his own brawny thews were helpless. He sensed without seeing the poised dagger.

"Nemedian dog!" muttered a voice thick with passion in his ear. "You've cut off your last Aquilonian head!"

And that was the last thing he ever heard.

In a dank dungeon, lighted only by a guttering torch, three men stood about a young woman who knelt on the rush-strewn flags staring wildly up at them. She was clad only in a scanty shift; her golden hair fell in lustrous ripples about her white shoulders, and her wrists were bound behind her. Even in the uncertain torchlight, and in spite of her disheveled condition and pallor of fear, her beauty was striking. She knelt mutely, staring with wide eyes up at her tormenters. The men were closely masked and cloaked. Such a deed as this needed masks, even in a conquered land. She knew them all, nevertheless; but what she knew would harm no one – after that night.

"Our merciful sovereign offers you one more chance, Countess," said the tallest of the three, and he spoke Aquilonian without an accent. "He bids me say that if you soften your proud, rebellious spirit, he will still open his arms to you. If not – " he gestured toward a grim wooden block in the center of the cell. It was blackly stained, and showed many deep nicks as if a keen edge, cutting through some yielding substance, had sunk into the wood.

Albiona shuddered and turned pale, shrinking back. Every fiber in her vigorous young body quivered with the urge of life. Valerius was young, too, and handsome. Many women loved him, she told herself, fighting with herself for life. But she could not speak the word that would ransom her soft young body from the block and the dripping ax. She could not reason the matter. She only knew that when she thought of the clasp of Valerius's arms, her flesh crawled with an abhorrence greater than the fear of death. She shook her head helplessly, compelled by an impulsion more irresistible than the instinct to live.

"Then there is no more to be said!" exclaimed one of the others impatiently, and he spoke with a Nemedian accent. "Where is the headsman?"

As if summoned by the word, the dungeon door opened silently, and a great figure stood framed in it, like a black shadow from the underworld.

Albiona voiced a low, involuntary cry at the sight of that grim shape, and the others stared silently for a moment, perhaps themselves daunted with superstitious awe at the silent, hooded figure. Through the coif the eyes blazed like coals of blue fire, and as these eyes rested on each man in turn, he felt a curious chill travel down his spine.

Then the tall Aquilonian roughly seized the girl and dragged her to the block. She screamed uncontrollably and fought hopelessly against him, frantic with terror, but he ruthlessly forced her to her knees, and bent her yellow head down to the bloody block.

"Why do you delay, headsman?" he exclaimed angrily. "Perform your task!"

He was answered by a short, gusty boom of laughter that was indescribably menacing. All in the dungeon froze in their places, staring at the hooded shape – the two cloaked figures, the masked man bending over the girl, the girl herself on her knees, twisting her imprisoned head to look upward.

"What means this unseemly mirth, dog?" demanded the Aquilonian uneasily.

The man in the black garb tore his hood from his head and flung it to the ground; he set his back to the closed door and lifted the headsman's ax.

"Do you know me, dogs?" he rumbled. "Do you know me?"

The breathless silence was broken by a scream.

"The king!" shrieked Albiona, wrenching herself free from the slackened grasp of her captor. "Oh, Mitra, *the king!*"

The three men stood like statues, and then the Aquilonian started and spoke, like a man who doubts his own senses.

"Conan!" he ejaculated. "It *is* the king, or his ghost! What devil's work is this?"

"Devil's work to match devils!" mocked Conan, his lips laughing but hell flaming in his eyes. "Come, fall to, my gentlemen. You have your swords, and I this cleaver. Nay, I think this butcher's tool fits the work at hand, my fair lords!"

"At him!" muttered the Aquilonian, drawing his sword. "It is Conan and we must kill or be killed!"

And like men waking from a trance, the Nemedians drew their blades and rushed on the king.

The headsman's ax was not made for such work, but the king wielded the heavy, clumsy weapon as lightly as a hatchet, and his quickness of foot, as he constantly shifted his position, defeated their purpose of engaging him all three at once.

He caught the sword of the first man on his ax-head and crushed in the wielder's breast with a murderous counter-stroke before he could step back or parry. The remaining Nemedian, missing a savage swipe, had his brains dashed out before he could recover his balance, and an instant later the Aquilonian was backed into a corner, desperately parrying the crashing strokes that rained about him, lacking opportunity even to scream for help.

Suddenly Conan's long left arm shot out and ripped the mask from the man's head, disclosing the pallid features.

"Dog!" grated the king. "I thought I knew you. Traitor! Damned renegade! Even this base steel is too honorable for your foul head. Nay, die as thieves die!"

The ax fell in a devastating arc, and the Aquilonian cried out and went to his knees, grasping the severed stump of his right arm from which blood spouted. It had been shorn away at the elbow, and the ax, unchecked in its descent, had gashed deeply into his side, so that his entrails bulged out.

"Lie there and bleed to death," grunted Conan, casting the ax away disgustedly. "Come, Countess!"

Stooping, he slashed the cords that bound her wrists and lifting her as if she had been a child, strode from the dungeon. She was sobbing hysterically, with her arms thrown about his corded neck in a frenzied embrace.

"Easy all," he muttered. "We're not out of this yet. If we can reach the dungeon where the secret door opens on stairs that lead to the tunnel – devil take it, they've heard that noise, even through these walls."

Down the corridor arms clanged and the tramp and shouting of men echoed under the vaulted roof. A bent figure came hobbling swiftly along, lantern held high, and its light shone full on Conan and the girl. With a curse the Cimmerian sprang toward him, but the old watchman, abandoning both lantern and pike, scuttled away down the corridor, screeching for help at the top of his cracked voice. Deeper shouts answered him.

Conan turned swiftly and ran the other way. He was cut off from the dungeon with the secret lock and the hidden door through which he had entered the Tower, and by which he had hoped to leave, but he knew this grim building well. Before he was king he had been imprisoned in it.

He turned off into a side passage and quickly emerged into another, broader corridor, which ran parallel to the one down which he had come, and which was at the moment deserted. He followed this only a few yards, when he again turned back, down another side passage. This brought him back into the corridor he had left, but at a strategic point. A few feet farther up the corridor there was a heavy bolted door, and before it stood a bearded Nemedian in corselet and helmet, his back to Conan as he peered up the corridor in the direction of the growing tumult and wildly waving lanterns.

Conan did not hesitate. Slipping the girl to the ground, he ran at the guard swiftly and silently, sword in hand. The man turned just as the king reached him, bawled in surprize and fright and lifted his pike; but before he could bring the clumsy weapon into play, Conan brought down his sword on the fellow's helmet with a force that would have felled an ox. Helmet and skull gave way together and the guard crumpled to the floor.

In an instant Conan had drawn the massive bolt that barred the door – too heavy for one ordinary man to have manipulated – and called hastily to Albiona, who ran staggering to him. Catching her up unceremoniously with one arm, he bore her through the door and into the outer darkness.

They had come into a narrow alley, black as pitch, walled by the side of the Tower on one hand, and the sheer stone back of a row of buildings on the other. Conan, hurrying through the darkness as swiftly as he dared, felt the latter wall for doors or windows, but found none.

The great door clanged open behind them, and men poured out, with torches gleaming on breastplates and naked swords. They glared about, bellowing, unable to penetrate the darkness which their torches served to illuminate for only a few feet in any direction, and then rushed down the alley at random – heading in the direction opposite to that taken by Conan and Albiona.

"They'll learn their mistake quick enough," he muttered, increasing his pace. "If we ever find a crack in this infernal wall – damn! The street watch!"

Ahead of them a faint glow became apparent, where the alley opened into a narrow street, and he saw dim figures looming against it with a glimmer of steel. It was indeed the street watch, investigating the noise they had heard echoing down the alley.

"Who goes there?" they shouted, and Conan grit his teeth at the hated Nemedian accent.

"Keep behind me," he ordered the girl. "We've got to cut our way through before the prison guards come back and pin us between them."

And grasping his sword, he ran straight at the oncoming figures. The advantage of surprize was his. He could see them, limned against the distant glow, and they could not see him coming at them out of the black depths of the alley. He was among them before they knew it, smiting with the silent fury of a wounded lion.

His one chance lay in hacking through before they could gather their wits. But there were half a score of them, in full mail, hard-bitten veterans of the border wars, in whom the instinct for battle could take the place of bemused wits. Three of them were down before they realized that it was only one man who was attacking them, but even so their reaction was instantaneous. The clangor of steel rose deafeningly, and sparks flew as Conan's sword crashed on basinet and hauberk. He could see better than they, and in the dim light his swiftly moving figure was an uncertain mark. Flailing swords cut empty air or glanced from his blade, and when he struck, it was with the fury and certainty of a hurricane.

But behind him sounded the shouts of the prison guards, returning up the alley at a run, and still the mailed figures before him barred his way with a bristling wall of steel. In an instant the guards would be on his back – in desperation he redoubled his strokes, flailing like a smith on an anvil, and then was suddenly aware of a diversion. Out of nowhere behind the watchmen rose a score of black figures and there was a sound of blows, murderously driven. Steel glinted in the gloom, and men cried out, struck mortally from behind. In an instant the alley was littered with writhing forms. A dark, cloaked shape sprang toward Conan, who heaved up his sword, catching a gleam of steel in the right hand. But the other was extended to him empty and a voice hissed urgently: "This way, your Majesty! Quickly!"

With a muttered oath of surprize, Conan caught up Albiona in one massive arm, and followed his unknown befriender. He was not inclined to hesitate, with thirty prison guardsmen closing in behind him.

Surrounded by mysterious figures he hurried down the alley, carrying the countess as if she had been a child. He could tell nothing of his rescuers except that they wore dark cloaks and hoods. Doubt and suspicion crossed his mind, but at least they had struck down his enemies, and he saw no better course than to follow them.

As if sensing his doubt, the leader touched his arm lightly and said: "Fear not, King Conan; we are your loyal subjects." The voice was not familiar, but the accent was Aquilonian of the central provinces.

Behind them the guards were yelling as they stumbled over the shambles in the mud, and they came pelting vengefully down the alley, seeing the vague dark mass moving between them and the light of the distant street. But the hooded men turned suddenly toward the seemingly blank wall, and Conan saw a door gape there. He muttered a curse. He had traversed that alley by day, in times past, and had never noticed a door there. But through it they went, and the door closed behind them with the click of a lock. The sound was not reassuring, but his guides were hurrying him on, moving with the precision of familiarity, guiding Conan with a hand at either elbow. It was like traversing a tunnel, and Conan felt Albiona's lithe limbs trembling in his arms. Then somewhere ahead of them an opening was faintly visible, merely a somewhat less black arch in the blackness, and through this they filed.

After that there was a bewildering succession of dim courts and shadowy alleys and winding corridors, all traversed in utter silence, until at last they emerged into a broad lighted chamber, the location of which Conan could not even guess, for their devious route had confused even his primitive sense of direction.

X

A Coin from Acheron

Not all his guides entered the chamber. When the door closed, Conan saw only one man standing before him – a slim figure, masked in a black cloak with a hood. This the man threw back, disclosing a pale oval of a face, with calm, delicately chiseled features.

The king set Albiona on her feet, but she still clung to him and stared apprehensively about her. The chamber was a large one, with marble walls partly covered with black velvet hangings and thick rich carpets on the mosaic floor, laved in the soft golden glow of bronze lamps.

Conan instinctively laid a hand on his hilt. There was blood on his hand, blood clotted about the mouth of his scabbard, for he had sheathed his blade without cleansing it.

"Where are we?" he demanded.

The stranger answered with a low, profound bow in which the suspicious king could detect no trace of irony.

"In the temple of Asura, your Majesty."

Albiona cried out faintly and clung closer to Conan, staring fearfully at the black, arched doors, as if expecting the entry of some grisly shape of darkness.

"Fear not, my lady," said their guide. "There is nothing here to harm you, vulgar superstition to the contrary. If your monarch was sufficiently convinced of the innocence of our religion to protect us from the persecution of the ignorant, then certainly one of his subjects need have no apprehensions."

"Who are you?" demanded Conan.

"I am Hadrathus, priest of Asura. One of my followers recognized you when you entered the city, and brought the word to me."

Conan grunted profanely.

"Do not fear that others discovered your identity," Hadrathus assured him. "Your disguise would have deceived any but a follower of Asura, whose cult it is to seek below the aspect of illusion. You were followed to the watch tower, and some of my people went into the tunnel to aid you if you returned by that route. Others, myself among them, surrounded the tower. And now, King Conan, it is yours to command. Here in the temple of Asura you are still king."

"Why should you risk your lives for me?" asked the king.

"You were our friend when you sat upon your throne," answered Hadrathus. "You protected us when the priests of Mitra sought to scourge us out of the land."

Conan looked about him curiously. He had never before visited the temple of Asura, had not certainly known that there was such a temple in Tarantia. The priests of the religion had a habit of hiding their temples in a remarkable fashion. The worship of Mitra was overwhelmingly predominant in the Hyborian nations, but the cult of Asura persisted, in spite of official ban and popular antagonism. Conan had been told dark tales of hidden temples where incense smoke drifted up incessantly from black altars where kidnaped humans were sacrificed before a great coiled serpent, whose fearsome head swayed for ever in the haunted shadows.

Persecution caused the followers of Asura to hide their temples with cunning art, and to veil their rituals in obscurity; and this secrecy, in turn, evoked more monstrous suspicions and tales of evil.

But Conan's was the broad tolerance of the barbarian, and he had refused to persecute the followers of Asura or to allow the people to do so on no better evidence than was presented against them, rumors and accusations that could not be proven.

"If they are black magicians," he had said, "how will they suffer you to harry them? If they are not, there is no evil in them. Crom's devils! Let men worship what gods they will."

At a respectful invitation from Hadrathus he seated himself on an ivory chair, and motioned Albiona to another, but she preferred to sit on a golden stool at his feet, pressing close against his thigh, as if seeking security in the contact. Like most orthodox followers of Mitra, she had an intuitive horror of the followers and cult of Asura, instilled in her infancy and childhood by wild tales of human sacrifice and anthropomorphic gods shambling through shadowy temples.

Hadrathus stood before them, his uncovered head bowed.

"What is your wish, your Majesty?"

"Food, first," he grunted, and the priest smote a golden gong with a silver wand.

Scarcely had the mellow notes ceased echoing when four hooded figures came through a curtained doorway bearing a great four-legged silver platter of smoking dishes and crystal vessels. This they set before Conan, bowing low, and the king wiped his hands on the damask, and smacked his lips with unconcealed relish.

"Beware, your Majesty!" whispered Albiona. "These folk eat human flesh!"

"I'll stake my kingdom that this is nothing but honest roast beef," answered Conan. "Come, lass, fall to! You must be hungry after the prison fare."

Thus advised, and with the example before her of one whose word was the ultimate law to her, the countess complied, and ate ravenously though daintily, while her liege lord tore into the meat joints and guzzled the wine with as much gusto as if he had not already eaten once that night.

"You priests are shrewd, Hadrathus," he said, with a great beef-bone in his hands and his mouth full of meat. "I'd welcome your service in my campaign to regain my kingdom."

Slowly Hadrathus shook his head, and Conan slammed the beef-bone down on the table in a gust of impatient wrath.

"Crom's devils! What ails the men of Aquilonia? First Servius – now you! Can you do nothing but wag your idiotic heads when I speak of ousting these dogs?"

Hadrathus sighed and answered slowly: "My lord, it is ill to say, and I fain would say otherwise. But the freedom of Aquilonia is at an end. Nay, the freedom of the whole world may be at an end! Age follows age in the history of the world, and now we enter an age of horror and slavery, as it was long ago."

"What do you mean?" demanded the king uneasily.

Hadrathus dropped into a chair and rested his elbows on his thighs, staring at the floor.

"It is not alone the rebellious lords of Aquilonia and the armies of Nemedia which are arrayed against you," answered Hadrathus. "It is sorcery – grisly black magic from the grim youth of the world. An awful shape has risen out of the shades of the Past, and none can stand before it."

"What do you mean?" Conan repeated.

"I speak of Xaltotun of Acheron, who died three thousand years ago, yet walks the earth today."

Conan was silent, while in his mind floated an image – the image of a bearded face of calm inhuman beauty. Again he was haunted by a sense of uneasy familiarity. Acheron – the sound of the word roused instinctive vibrations of memory and associations in his mind.

"Acheron," he repeated. "Xaltotun of Acheron – man, are you mad? Acheron has been a myth for more centuries than I can remember. I've often wondered if it ever existed at all."

"It was a black reality," answered Hadrathus, "an empire of black magicians, steeped in evil now long forgotten. It was finally overthrown by the Hyborian tribes of the west. The wizards of Acheron practised foul necromancy, thaumaturgy of the most evil kind, grisly magic taught them by devils. And of all the sorcerers of that accursed kingdom, none was so great as Xaltotun of Python."

"Then how was he ever overthrown?" asked Conan skeptically.

"By some means a source of cosmic power which he jealously guarded was stolen and turned against him. That source has been returned to him, and he is invincible."

Albiona, hugging the headsman's black cloak about her, stared from the priest to the king, not understanding the conversation. Conan shook his head angrily.

"You are making game of me," he growled. "If Xaltotun has been dead three thousand years, how can this man be he? It's some rogue who's taken the old one's name."

Hadrathus leaned to an ivory table and opened a small gold chest which stood there. From it he took something which glinted dully in the mellow light – a broad gold coin of antique minting.

"You have seen Xaltotun unveiled? Then look upon this. It is a coin which was stamped in ancient Acheron, before its fall. So pervaded with sorcery was that black empire, that even this coin has its uses in making magic."

Conan took it and scowled down at it. There was no mistaking its great antiquity. Conan had handled many coins in the years of his plunderings, and had a good practical knowledge of them. The edges were worn and the inscription almost obliterated. But the countenance stamped on one side was still clear-cut and distinct. And Conan's breath sucked in between his clenched teeth. It was not cool in the chamber, but he felt a prickling of his scalp, an icy contraction of his flesh. The countenance was that of a bearded man, inscrutable, with a calm inhuman beauty.

"By Crom! It's he!" muttered Conan. He understood, now, the sense of familiarity that the sight of the bearded man had roused in him from the first.

He had seen a coin like this once before, long ago in a far land.

With a shake of his shoulders he growled: "The likeness is only a coincidence – or if he's shrewd enough to assume a forgotten wizard's name, he's shrewd enough to assume his likeness." But he spoke without conviction. The sight of that coin had shaken the foundations of his universe. He felt that reality and stability were crumbling into an abyss of illusion and sorcery. A wizard was understandable; but this was diabolism beyond sanity.

"We cannot doubt that it is indeed Xaltotun of Python," said Hadrathus. "He it was who shook down the cliffs at Valkia, by his spells that enthrall the elementals of the earth – he it was who sent the creature of darkness into your tent before dawn."

Conan scowled at him. "How did you know that?"

"The followers of Asura have secret channels of knowledge. That does not matter. But do you realize the futility of sacrificing your subjects in a vain attempt to regain your crown?"

Conan rested his chin on his fist, and stared grimly into nothing. Albiona watched him anxiously, her mind groping bewildered in the mazes of the problem that confronted him.

"Is there no wizard in the world who could make magic to fight Xaltotun's magic?" he asked at last.

Hadrathus shook his head. "If there were, we of Asura would know of him. Men say our cult is a survival of the ancient Stygian serpent-worship. That is a lie. Our ancestors came from Vendhya, beyond the Sea of Vilayet and the blue Himelian mountains. We are sons of the East, not the South, and we have knowledge of all the wizards of the East, who are greater than the wizards of the West. And not one of them but would be a straw in the wind before the black might of Xaltotun."

"But he was conquered once," persisted Conan.

"Aye; a cosmic source was turned against him. But now that source is again in his hands, and he will see that it is not stolen again."

"And what is this damnable source?" demanded Conan irritably.

"It is called the Heart of Ahriman. When Acheron was overthrown, the primitive priest who had stolen it and turned it against Xaltotun hid it in a haunted cavern and built a small temple over the cavern. Thrice thereafter the temple was rebuilt, each time greater and more elaborately than before, but always on the site of the original shrine, though men forgot the reason therefor. Memory of the hidden symbol faded from the minds of common men, and was preserved only in priestly books and esoteric volumes. Whence it came no one knows. Some say it is the veritable heart of a god, others that it is a star that fell from the skies long ago. Until it was stolen, none had looked upon it for three thousand years.

"When the magic of the Mitran priests failed against the magic of Xaltotun's acolyte, Altaro, they remembered the ancient legend of the Heart, and the high priest and an acolyte went down into the dark and terrible crypt below the temple into which no priest had descended for three thousand years. In the ancient iron-bound volumes which speak of the Heart in their cryptic symbolism, it is also told of a creature of darkness left by the ancient priest to guard it.

"Far down in a square chamber with arched doorways leading off into immeasurable blackness, the priest and his acolytes found a black stone altar that glowed dimly with inexplicable radiance.

"On that altar lay a curious gold vessel like a double-valved sea-shell which clung to the stone like a barnacle. But it gaped open and empty. The Heart of Ahriman was gone. While they stared in horror, the keeper of the crypt, the creature of darkness, came upon them and mangled the high priest so that he died. But the acolyte fought off the being – a mindless, soulless waif of the pits brought long ago to guard the Heart – and escaped up the long black narrow stairs carrying the dying priest, who, before he died, gasped out the news to his followers, bade them submit to a power they could not overcome, and commanded secrecy. But the word has been whispered about among the priests, and we of Asura learned of it."

"And Xaltotun draws his power from this symbol?" asked Conan, still skeptical.

"No. His power is drawn from the black gulf. But the Heart of Ahriman came from some far universe of flaming light, and against it the powers of darkness cannot stand, when it is in the hands of an adept. It is like a sword that might smite at him, not a sword with which he can smite. It restores life, and can destroy life. He has stolen it, not to use it against his enemies, but to keep them from using it against him."

"A shell-shaped bowl of gold on a black altar in a deep cavern," Conan muttered, frowning as he sought to capture the illusive image. "That reminds me of something I have heard or seen. But what, in Crom's name, *is* this notable Heart?"

"It is in the form of a great jewel, like a ruby, but pulsing with blinding fire with which no ruby ever burned. It glows like living flame – "

But Conan sprang suddenly up and smote his right fist into his left palm like a thunderclap.

"Crom!" he roared. "What a fool I've been! The Heart of Ahriman! The heart of my kingdom! Find the heart of my kingdom, Zelata said. By Ymir, it was the jewel I saw in the green smoke, the jewel which Tarascus stole from Xaltotun while he lay in the sleep of the black lotus!"

Hadrathus was also on his feet, his calm dropped from him like a garment.

"What are you saying? The Heart stolen from Xaltotun?"

"Aye!" Conan boomed. "Tarascus feared Xaltotun and wanted to cripple his power, which he thought resided in the Heart. Maybe he thought the wizard would die if the Heart was lost. By Crom – ahhh!" With a savage grimace of disappointment and disgust he dropped his clenched hand to his side.

"I forgot. Tarascus gave it to a thief to throw into the sea. By this time the fellow must be almost to Kordava. Before I can follow him he'll take ship and consign the Heart to the bottom of the ocean."

"The sea will not hold it!" exclaimed Hadrathus, quivering with excitement. "Xaltotun would himself have cast it into the ocean long ago, had he not known that the first storm would carry it ashore. But on what unknown beach might it not land!"

"Well," Conan was recovering some of his resilient confidence, "there's no assurance that the thief will throw it away. If I know thieves – and I should, for I was a thief in Zamora in my early youth – he won't throw it away. He'll sell it to some rich trader. By Crom!" He strode back and forth in his growing excitement. "It's worth looking for! Zelata bade me find the heart of my kingdom, and all else she showed me proved to be truth. Can it be that the power to conquer Xaltotun lurks in that crimson bauble?"

"Aye! My head upon it!" cried Hadrathus, his face lightened with fervor, his eyes blazing, his fists clenched. "With it in our hands we can dare the powers of Xaltotun! I swear it! If we can recover it, we have an even chance of recovering your crown and driving the invaders from our portals. It is not the swords of Nemedia that Aquilonia fears, but the black arts of Xaltotun."

Conan looked at him for a space, impressed by the priest's fire.

"It's like a quest in a nightmare," he said at last. "Yet your words echo the thought of Zelata, and all else she said was truth. I'll seek for this jewel."

"It holds the destiny of Aquilonia," said Hadrathus with conviction. "I will send men with you – "

"Nay!" exclaimed the king impatiently, not caring to be hampered by priests on his quest, however skilled in esoteric arts. "This is a task for a fighting-man. I go alone. First to Poitain, where I'll leave Albiona with Trocero. Then to Kordava, and to the sea beyond, if necessary. It may be that, even if the thief intends carrying out Tarascus's order, he'll have some difficulty finding an outbound ship at this time of the year."

"And if you find the Heart," cried Hadrathus, "I will prepare the way for your conquest. Before you return to Aquilonia I will spread the word through secret channels that you live and are returning with a magic stronger than Xaltotun's. I will have men ready to rise on your return. They *will* rise, if they have assurance that they will be protected from the black arts of Xaltotun.

"And I will aid you on your journey."

He rose and struck the gong.

"A secret tunnel leads from beneath this temple to a place outside the city wall. You shall go to Poitain on a pilgrim's boat. None will dare molest you."

"As you will." With a definite purpose in mind Conan was afire with impatience and dynamic energy. "Only let it be done swiftly."

In the meantime events were moving not slowly elsewhere in the city. A breathless messenger had burst into the palace where Valerius was amusing himself with his dancing-girls, and throwing himself on his knee, gasped out a garbled story of a bloody prison break and the escape of a lovely captive. He bore also the news that Count Thespius, to whom the execution of Albiona's sentence had been entrusted, was dying and begging for a word with Valerius before he passed.

Hurriedly cloaking himself, Valerius accompanied the man through various winding ways, and came to a chamber where Thespius lay. There was no doubt that the count was dying; bloody froth bubbled from his lips at each shuddering gasp. His severed arm had been bound to stop the flow of blood, but even without that, the gash in his side was mortal.

Alone in the chamber with the dying man, Valerius swore softly.

"By Mitra, I had believed that only one man ever lived who could strike such a blow."

"Valerius!" gasped the dying man. "He lives! Conan lives!"

"What are you saying?" ejaculated the other.

"I swear by Mitra!" gurgled Thespius, gagging on the blood that gushed to his lips. "It was he who carried off Albiona! He is not dead – no phantom come back from hell to haunt us. He is flesh and blood, and more terrible than ever. The alley behind the tower is full of dead men. Beware, Valerius – he has come back – to slay us all – "

A strong shudder shook the blood-smeared figure, and Count Thespius went limp.

Valerius frowned down at the dead man, cast a swift glance about the empty chamber, and stepping swiftly to the door, cast it open suddenly. The messenger and a group of Nemedian guardsmen stood several paces down the corridor. Valerius muttered something that might have indicated satisfaction.

"Have all gates been closed?" he demanded.

"Yes, your Majesty."

"Triple the guards at each. Let no one enter or leave the city without strictest investigation. Set men scouring the streets and searching the quarters. A very valuable prisoner has escaped, with the aid of an Aquilonian rebel. Did any of you recognize the man?"

"No, your Majesty. The old watchman had a glimpse of him, but could only say that he was a giant, clad in the black garb of the executioner, whose naked body we found in an empty cell."

"He is a dangerous man," said Valerius. "Take no chances with him. You all know the Countess Albiona. Search for her, and if you find her, kill her and her companion instantly. Do not try to take them alive."

Returning to his palace chamber, Valerius summoned before him four men of curious and alien aspect. They were tall, gaunt, of yellowish skin, and immobile countenances. They were very similar in appearance, clad alike in long black robes beneath which their sandaled feet were just visible. Their features were shadowed by their hoods. They stood before Valerius with their hands in their wide sleeves, their arms folded. Valerius looked at them without pleasure. In his far journeyings he had encountered many strange races.

"When I found you starving in the Khitan jungles," he said abruptly, "exiles from your kingdom, you swore to serve me. You have served me well enough, in your abominable way. One more service I require, and then I set you free of your oath.

"Conan, the Cimmerian, king of Aquilonia, still lives, in spite of Xaltotun's sorcery – or perhaps because of it. I know not. The dark mind of that resurrected devil is too devious and subtle for a mortal man to fathom. But while Conan lives I am not safe. The people accepted me as the lesser of two evils, when they thought he was dead. Let him reappear and the throne will be rocking under my feet in revolution before I can lift my hand.

"Perhaps my allies mean to use him to replace me, if they decide I have served my purpose. I do not know. I do know that this planet is too small for two kings of Aquilonia. Seek the Cimmerian. Use your uncanny talents to ferret him out wherever he hides or runs. He has many friends in Tarantia. He had aid when he carried off Albiona. It took more than one man, even such a man as Conan, to wreak all that slaughter in the alley outside the tower. But no more. Take your staffs and strike his trail. Where that trail will lead you, I know not. But find him! And when you find him, slay him!"

The four Khitans bowed together, and still unspeaking, turned and padded noiselessly from the chamber.

XI

Swords of the South

Dawn that rose over the distant hills shone on the sails of a small craft that dropped down the river which curves to within a mile of the walls of Tarantia, and loops southward like a great shining serpent. This boat differed from the ordinary craft plying the broad Khorotas – fishermen and merchant barges loaded with rich goods. It was long and slender, with a high, curving prow, and was black as ebony, with white skulls painted along the gunwales. Amidships rose a small cabin, the windows closely masked. Other craft gave the ominously painted boat a wide berth; for it was obviously one of those "pilgrim boats" that carried a lifeless follower of Asura on his last mysterious pilgrimage southward to where, far beyond the Poitanian mountains, a river flowed at last into the blue ocean. In that cabin undoubtedly lay the corpse of the departed worshipper. All men were familiar with the sight of those gloomy craft; and the most fanatical votary of Mitra would not dare touch or interfere with their somber voyages.

Where the ultimate destination lay, men did not know. Some said Stygia; some a nameless island lying beyond the horizon; others said it was in the glamorous and mysterious land of Vendhya where the dead came home at last. But none knew certainly. They only knew that when a follower of Asura died, the corpse went southward down the great river, in a black boat rowed by a giant slave, and neither boat nor corpse nor slave was ever seen again; unless, indeed, certain dark tales were true, and it was always the same slave who rowed the boats southward.

The man who propelled this particular boat was as huge and brown as the others, though closer scrutiny might have revealed the fact that the hue was the result of carefully applied pigments. He was clad in leather loin-clout and sandals, and he handled the long sweep and oars with unusual skill and power. But none approached the grim boat closely, for it was well known that the followers of Asura were accursed, and that these pilgrim boats were loaded with dark magic. So men swung their boats wide and muttered an incantation as the dark craft slid past, and they never dreamed that they were thus assisting in the flight of their king and the Countess Albiona.

It was a strange journey, in that black, slim craft down the great river for nearly two hundred miles to where the Khorotas swings eastward, skirting the Poitanian mountains. Like a dream the ever-changing panorama glided past. During the day Albiona lay patiently in the little cabin, as quietly as the corpse she pretended to be. Only late at night, after the pleasure boats with their fair occupants lounging on silken cushions in the flare of torches held by slaves had left the river, before dawn brought the hurrying fisher-boats, did the girl venture out. Then she held the long sweep, cunningly bound in place by ropes to aid her, while Conan snatched a few hours of sleep. But the king needed little rest. The fire of his desire drove him relentlessly, and his powerful frame was equal to the grinding test. Without halt or pause they drove southward.

So down the river they fled, through nights when the flowing current mirrored the million stars, and through days of golden sunlight, leaving winter behind them as they sped southward. They passed cities in the night, above which throbbed and pulsed the reflection of the myriad lights, lordly river villas and fertile groves. So at last the blue mountains of Poitain rose above them, tier above tier, like ramparts of the gods, and the great river, swerving from those turreted cliffs, swept thunderously through the marching hills with many a rapid and foaming cataract.

Conan scanned the shore-line closely, and finally swung the long sweep and headed inshore at a point where a neck of land jutted into the water, and fir trees grew in a curiously symmetrical ring about a gray, strangely shaped rock.

"How these boats ride those falls we hear roaring ahead of us is more than I can see," he grunted. "Hadrathus said they did – but here's where we halt. He said a man would be waiting for us with horses, but I don't see anyone. How word of our coming could have preceded us I don't know anyway."

He drove inshore and bound the prow to an arching root in the low bank, and then, plunging into the water, washed the brown paint from his skin and emerged dripping, and in his natural color. From the cabin he brought forth a suit of Aquilonian ring-mail which Hadrathus had procured for him, and his sword. These he donned while Albiona put on garments suitable for mountain travel. And when Conan was fully armed, and turned to look toward the shore, he started and his hand went to his sword. For on the shore, under the trees, stood a black-cloaked figure holding the reins of a white palfrey and a bay war-horse.

"Who are you?" demanded the king.

The other bowed low.

"A follower of Asura. A command came. I obeyed."

"How, 'came'?" inquired Conan, but the other merely bowed again.

"I have come to guide you through the mountains to the first Poitanian stronghold."

"I don't need a guide," answered Conan. "I know these hills well. I thank you for the horses, but the countess and I will attract less attention alone than if we were accompanied by an acolyte of Asura."

The man bowed profoundly, and giving the reins into Conan's hands, stepped into the boat. Casting off, he floated down the swift current, toward the distant roar of the unseen rapids. With a baffled shake of his head, Conan lifted the countess into the palfrey's saddle, and then mounted the war-horse and reined toward the summits that castellated the sky.

The rolling country at the foot of the towering mountains was now a borderland, in a state of turmoil, where the barons reverted to feudal practises, and bands of outlaws roamed unhindered. Poitain had not formally declared her separation from Aquilonia, but she was now, to all intents, a self-contained kingdom, ruled by her hereditary count, Trocero. The rolling south country had submitted nominally to Valerius, but he had not attempted to force the passes guarded by strongholds where the crimson leopard banner of Poitain waved defiantly.

The king and his fair companion rode up the long blue slopes in the soft evening. As they mounted higher, the rolling country spread out like a vast purple mantle far beneath them, shot with the shine of rivers and lakes, the yellow glint of broad fields, and the white gleam of distant towers. Ahead of them and far above, they glimpsed the first of the Poitanian holds – a strong fortress dominating a narrow pass, the crimson banner streaming against the clear blue sky.

Before they reached it, a band of knights in burnished armor rode from among the trees, and their leader sternly ordered the travelers to halt. They were tall men, with the dark eyes and raven locks of the south.

"Halt, sir, and state your business, and why you ride toward Poitain."

"Is Poitain in revolt then," asked Conan, watching the other closely, "that a man in Aquilonian harness is halted and questioned like a foreigner?"

"Many rogues ride out of Aquilonia these days," answered the other coldly. "As for revolt, if you mean the repudiation of a usurper, then Poitain is in revolt. We had rather serve the memory of a dead man than the scepter of a living dog."

Conan swept off his helmet, and shaking back his black mane, stared full at the speaker. The Poitanian started violently and went livid.

"Saints of heaven!" he gasped. "It is the king – *alive!*"

The others stared wildly, then a roar of wonder and joy burst from them. They swarmed about Conan, shouting their war-cries and brandishing their swords in their extreme emotion. The acclaim of Poitanian warriors was a thing to terrify a timid man.

"Oh, but Trocero will weep tears of joy to see you, sire!" cried one.

"Aye, and Prospero!" shouted another. "The general has been like one wrapped in a mantle of melancholy, and curses himself night and day that he did not reach the Valkia in time to die beside his king!"

"Now we will strike for empery!" yelled another, whirling his great sword about his head. "Hail, Conan, *king of Poitain!*"

The clangor of bright steel about him and the thunder of their acclaim frightened the birds that rose in gay-hued clouds from the surrounding trees. The hot southern blood was afire, and they desired nothing but for their new-found sovereign to lead them to battle and pillage.

"What is your command, sire?" they cried. "Let one of us ride ahead and bear the news of your coming into Poitain! Banners will wave from every tower, roses will carpet the road before your horse's feet, and all the beauty and chivalry of the south will give you the honor due you – "

Conan shook his head.

"Who could doubt your loyalty? But winds blow over these mountains into the countries of my enemies, and I would rather these didn't know that I lived – yet. Take me to Trocero, and keep my identity a secret."

So what the knights would have made a triumphal procession was more in the nature of a secret flight. They traveled in haste, speaking to no one, except for a whisper to the captain on duty at each pass; and Conan rode among them with his vizor lowered.

The mountains were uninhabited save by outlaws and garrisons of soldiers who guarded the passes. The pleasure-loving Poitanians had no need nor desire to wrest a hard and scanty living from their stern breasts. South of the ranges the rich and beautiful plains of Poitain stretched to the river Alimane; but beyond the river lay the land of Zingara.

Even now, when winter was crisping the leaves beyond the mountains, the tall rich grass waved upon the plains where grazed the horses and cattle for which Poitain was famed. Palm trees and orange groves smiled in the sun, and the gorgeous purple and gold and crimson towers of castles and cities reflected the golden light. It was a land of warmth and plenty, of beautiful women and ferocious warriors. It is not only the hard lands that breed hard men. Poitain was surrounded by covetous neighbors and her sons learned hardihood in incessant wars. To the north the land was guarded by the mountains, but to the south only the Alimane separated the plains of Poitain from the plains of Zingara, and not once but a thousand times had that river run red.

To the east lay Argos and beyond that Ophir, proud kingdoms and avaricious. The knights of Poitain held their lands by the weight and edge of their swords, and little of ease and idleness they knew.

So Conan came presently to the castle of Count Trocero....

Conan sat on a silken divan in a rich chamber whose filmy curtains the warm breeze billowed. Trocero paced the floor like a panther, a lithe, restless man with the waist of a woman and the shoulders of a swordsman, who carried his years lightly.

"Let us proclaim you king of Poitain!" urged the count. "Let those northern pigs wear the yoke to which they have bent their necks. The south is still yours. Dwell here and rule us, amid the flowers and the palms."

But Conan shook his head. "There is no nobler land on earth than Poitain. But it cannot stand alone, bold as are its sons."

"It *did* stand alone for generations," retorted Trocero, with the quick jealous pride of his breed. "We were not always a part of Aquilonia."

"I know. But conditions are not as they were then, when all kingdoms were broken into principalities which warred with each other. The days of dukedoms and free cities are past, the days of empires are upon us. Rulers are dreaming imperial dreams, and only in unity is there strength."

"Then let us unite Zingara with Poitain," argued Trocero. "Half a dozen princes strive against each other, and the country is torn asunder by civil wars. We will conquer it, province by province, and add it to your dominions. Then with the aid of the Zingarans we will conquer Argos and Ophir. *We* will build an empire – "

Again Conan shook his head. "Let others dream imperial dreams. I but wish to hold what is mine. I have no desire to rule an empire welded together by blood and fire. It's one thing to seize a throne with the aid of its subjects and rule them with their consent. It's another to subjugate a foreign realm and rule it by fear. I don't wish to be another Valerius. No, Trocero, I'll rule all Aquilonia and no more, or I'll rule nothing."

"Then lead us over the mountains and we will smite the Nemedians."

Conan's fierce eyes glowed with appreciation.

"No, Trocero. It would be a vain sacrifice. I've told you what I must do to regain my kingdom. I must find the Heart of Ahriman."

"But this is madness!" protested Trocero. "The maunderings of a heretical priest, the mumblings of a mad witch-woman."

"You were not in my tent before Valkia," answered Conan grimly, involuntarily glancing at his right wrist, on which blue marks still showed faintly. "You didn't see the cliffs thunder down to crush the flower of my army. No, Trocero, I've been convinced. Xaltotun's no mortal man, and only with the Heart of Ahriman can I stand against him. So I'm riding to Kordava, alone."

"But that is dangerous," protested Trocero.

"Life is dangerous," rumbled the king. "I won't go as king of Aquilonia, or even as a knight of Poitain, but as a wandering mercenary, as I rode in Zingara in the old days. Oh, I have enemies enough south of the Alimane, in the lands and the waters of the south. Many who won't know me as king of Aquilonia will remember me as Conan of the Barachan pirates, or Amra of the black corsairs. But I have friends, too, and men who'll aid me for their own private reasons." A faintly reminiscent grin touched his lips.

Trocero dropped his hands helplessly and glanced at Albiona, who sat on a near-by divan.

"I understand your doubts, my lord," said she. "But I too saw the coin in the temple of Asura, and look you, Hadrathus said it was dated five hundred years *before* the fall of Acheron. If Xaltotun, then, is the man pictured on the coin, as his Majesty swears he is, that means he was no common wizard, even in his other life, for the years of his life were numbered by centuries, not as the lives of other men are numbered."

Before Trocero could reply, a respectful rap was heard on the door and a voice called: "My lord, we have caught a man skulking about the castle, who says he wishes to speak with your guest. I await your orders."

"A spy from Aquilonia!" hissed Trocero, catching at his dagger, but Conan lifted his voice and called: "Open the door and let me see him."

The door was opened and a man was framed in it, grasped on either hand by stern-looking men-at-arms. He was a slender man, clad in a dark hooded robe.

"Are you a follower of Asura?" asked Conan.

The man nodded, and the stalwart men-at-arms looked shocked and glanced hesitantly at Trocero.

"The word came southward," said the man. "Beyond the Alimane we can not aid you, for our sect goes no farther southward, but stretches eastward with the Khorotas. But this I have learned: the thief who took the Heart of Ahriman from Tarascus never reached Kordava. In the mountains of Poitain he was slain by robbers. The jewel fell into the hands of their chief, who, not knowing its true nature, and being harried after the destruction of his band by Poitanian knights, sold it to the Kothic merchant Zorathus."

"Ha!" Conan was on his feet, galvanized. "And what of Zorathus?"

"Four days ago he crossed the Alimane, headed for Argos, with a small band of armed servants."

"He's a fool to cross Zingara in such times," said Trocero.

"Aye, times are troublous across the river. But Zorathus is a bold man, and reckless in his way. He is in great haste to reach Messantia, where he hopes to find a buyer for the jewel. Perhaps he hopes to sell it finally in Stygia. Perhaps he guesses at its true nature. At any rate, instead of following the long road that winds along the borders of Poitain and so at last comes into Argos far from Messantia, he has struck straight across eastern Zingara, following the shorter and more direct route."

Conan smote the table with his clenched fist so that the great board quivered.

"Then, by Crom, fortune has at last thrown the dice for me! A horse, Trocero, and the harness of a Free Companion! Zorathus has a long start, but not too long for me to overtake him, if I follow him to the end of the world!"

XII

The Fang of the Dragon

At dawn Conan waded his horse across the shallows of the Alimane and struck the wide caravan trail which ran southeastward, and behind him, on the farther bank, Trocero sat his horse silently at the head of his steel-clad knights, with the crimson leopard of Poitain floating its long folds over him in the morning breeze. Silently they sat, those dark-haired men in shining steel, until the figure of their king had vanished in the blue of distance that whitened toward sunrise.

Conan rode a great black stallion, the gift of Trocero. He no longer wore the armor of Aquilonia. His harness proclaimed him a veteran of the Free Companies, who were of all races. His head-piece was a plain morion, dented and battered. The leather and mail-mesh of his hauberk were worn and shiny as if by many campaigns, and the scarlet cloak flowing carelessly from his mailed shoulders was tattered and stained. He looked the part of the hired fighting-man, who had known all vicissitudes of fortune, plunder and wealth one day, an empty purse and a close-drawn belt the next.

And more than looking the part, he felt the part; the awakening of old memories, the resurge of the wild, mad, glorious days of old before his feet were set on the imperial path when he was a wandering mercenary, roistering, brawling, guzzling, adventuring, with no thought for the morrow, and no desire save sparkling ale, red lips, and a keen sword to swing on all the battlefields of the world.

Unconsciously he reverted to the old ways; a new swagger became evident in his bearing, in the way he sat his horse; half-forgotten oaths rose naturally to his lips, and as he rode he hummed old songs that he had roared in chorus with his reckless companions in many a tavern and on many a dusty road or bloody field.

It was an unquiet land through which he rode. The companies of cavalry which usually patrolled the river, alert for raids out of Poitain, were nowhere in evidence. Internal strife had left the borders unguarded. The long white road stretched bare from horizon to horizon. No laden camel trains or rumbling wagons or lowing herds moved along it now; only occasional groups of horsemen in leather and steel, hawk-faced, hard-eyed men, who kept together and rode warily. These swept Conan with their searching gaze but rode on, for the solitary rider's harness promised no plunder, but only hard strokes.

Villages lay in ashes and deserted, the fields and meadows idle. Only the boldest would ride the roads these days, and the native population had been decimated in the civil wars, and by raids from across the river. In more peaceful times the road was thronged with merchants riding from Poitain to Messantia in Argos, or back. But now these found it wiser to follow the road that led east through Poitain, and then turned south down across Argos. It was longer, but safer. Only an extremely reckless man would risk his life and goods on this road through Zingara.

The southern horizon was fringed with flame by night, and in the day straggling pillars of smoke drifted upward; in the cities and plains to the south men were dying, thrones were toppling and castles going up in flames. Conan felt the old tug of the professional fighting-man, to turn his horse and plunge into the fighting, the pillaging and the looting as in the days of old. Why should he toil to regain the rule of a people which had already forgotten him? – why chase a will-o'-the-wisp, why pursue a crown that was lost for ever? Why should he not seek forgetfulness, lose himself in the red tides of war and rapine that had engulfed him so often before? Could he not, indeed, carve out another kingdom for himself? The world was entering an age of iron, an age of war and imperialistic ambition; some strong man might well rise above the ruins of nations as a supreme conqueror. Why should it not be himself? So his familiar devil whispered in his ear, and the phantoms of his lawless and bloody past crowded upon him. But he did not turn aside; he rode onward, following a quest that grew dimmer and dimmer as he advanced, until sometimes it seemed that he pursued a dream that never was.

He pushed the black stallion as hard as he dared, but the long white road lay bare before him, from horizon to horizon. It was a long start Zorathus had, but Conan rode steadily on, knowing that he was traveling faster than the burdened merchants could travel. And so he came to the castle of Count Valbroso, perched like a vulture's eyrie on a bare hill overlooking the road.

Valbroso rode down with his men-at-arms, a lean, dark man with glittering eyes and a predatory beak of a nose. He wore black plate-armor and was followed by thirty spearmen, black-mustached hawks of the border wars, as avaricious and ruthless as himself. Of late the toll of the caravans had been slim, and Valbroso cursed the civil wars that stripped the roads of their fat traffic, even while he blessed them for the free hand they allowed him with his neighbors.

He had not hoped much from the solitary rider he had glimpsed from his tower, but all was grist that came to his mill. With a practised eye he took in Conan's worn mail and dark, scarred face, and his conclusions were the same as those of the riders who had passed the Cimmerian on the road – an empty purse and a ready blade.

"Who are you, knave?" he demanded.

"A mercenary, riding for Argos," answered Conan. "What matter names?"

"You are riding in the wrong direction for a Free Companion," grunted Valbroso. "Southward the fighting is good and also the plundering. Join my company. You won't go hungry. The road remains bare of fat merchants to strip, but I mean to take my rogues and fare southward to sell our swords to whichever side seems strongest."

Conan did not at once reply, knowing that if he refused outright, he might be instantly attacked by Valbroso's men-at-arms. Before he could make up his mind, the Zingaran spoke again:

"You rogues of the Free Companies always know tricks to make men talk. I have a prisoner – the last merchant I caught, by Mitra, and the only one I've seen for a week – and the knave is stubborn. He has an iron box, the secret of which defies us, and I've been unable to persuade him to open it. By Ishtar, I thought I knew all the modes of persuasion there are, but perhaps you, as a veteran Free Companion, know some that I do not. At any rate come with me and see what you may do."

Valbroso's words instantly decided Conan. That sounded a great deal like Zorathus. Conan did not know the merchant, but any man who was stubborn enough to try to traverse the Zingaran road in times like these would very probably be stubborn enough to defy torture.

He fell in beside Valbroso and rode up the straggling road to the top of the hill where the gaunt castle stood. As a man-at-arms he should have ridden behind the count, but force of habit made him careless and Valbroso paid no heed. Years of life on the border had taught the count that the frontier is not the royal court. He was aware of the independence of the mercenaries, behind whose swords many a king had trodden the throne-path.

There was a dry moat, half filled with debris in some places. They clattered across the drawbridge and through the arch of the gate. Behind them the portcullis fell with a sullen clang. They came into a bare courtyard, grown with straggling grass, and with a well in the middle. Shacks for the men-at-arms straggled about the bailey wall, and women, slatternly or decked in gaudy finery, looked from the doors. Fighting-men in rusty mail tossed dice on the flags under the arches. It was more like a bandit's hold than the castle of a nobleman.

Valbroso dismounted and motioned Conan to follow him. They went through a doorway and along a vaulted corridor, where they were met by a scarred, hard-looking man in mail descending a stone staircase – evidently the captain of the guard.

"How, Beloso," quoth Valbroso; "has he spoken?"

"He is stubborn," muttered Beloso, shooting a glance of suspicion at Conan.

Valbroso ripped out an oath and stamped furiously up the winding stair, followed by Conan and the captain. As they mounted, the groans of a man in mortal agony became audible. Valbroso's torture-room was high above the court, instead of in a dungeon below. In that chamber, where a gaunt, hairy beast of a man in leather breeks squatted gnawing a beef-bone voraciously, stood the machines of torture – racks, boots, hooks and all the implements that the human mind devises to tear flesh, break bones and rend and rupture veins and ligaments.

On a rack a man was stretched naked, and a glance told Conan that he was dying. The unnatural elongation of his limbs and body told of unhinged joints and unnamable ruptures. He was a dark man, with an intelligent, aquiline face and quick dark eyes. They were glazed and bloodshot now with pain, and the dew of agony glistened on his face. His lips were drawn back from blackened gums.

"There is the box." Viciously Valbroso kicked a small but heavy iron chest that stood on the floor near by. It was intricately carved, with tiny skulls and writhing dragons curiously intertwined, but Conan saw no catch or hasp that might serve to unlock the lid. The marks of fire, of ax and sledge and chisel showed on it but as scratches.

"This is the dog's treasure box," said Valbroso angrily. "All men of the south know of Zorathus and his iron chest. Mitra knows what is in it. But he will not give up its secret."

Zorathus! It was true, then; the man he sought lay before him. Conan's heart beat suffocatingly as he leaned over the writhing form, though he exhibited no evidence of his painful eagerness.

"Ease those ropes, knave!" he ordered the torturer harshly, and Valbroso and his captain stared. In the forgetfulness of the moment Conan had used his imperial tone, and the brute in leather instinctively obeyed the knife-edge of command in that voice. He eased away gradually, for else the slackening of the ropes had been as great a torment to the torn joints as further stretching.

Catching up a vessel of wine that stood near by, Conan placed the rim to the wretch's lips. Zorathus gulped spasmodically, the liquid slopping over on his heaving breast.

Into the bloodshot eyes came a gleam of recognition, and the froth-smeared lips parted. From them issued a racking whimper in the Kothic tongue.

"Is this death, then? Is the long agony ended? For this is King Conan who died at Valkia, and I am among the dead."

"You're not dead," said Conan. "But you're dying. You'll be tortured no more. I'll see to that. But I can't help you further. Yet before you die, tell me how to open your iron box!"

"My iron box," mumbled Zorathus in delirious disjointed phrases. "The chest forged in unholy fires among the flaming mountains of Khrosha; the metal no chisel can cut. How many treasures has it borne, across the width and the breadth of the world! But no such treasure as it now holds."

"Tell me how to open it," urged Conan. "It can do you no good, and it may aid me."

"Aye, you are Conan," muttered the Kothian. "I have seen you sitting on your throne in the great public hall of Tarantia, with your crown on your head and the scepter in your hand. But you are dead; you died at Valkia. And so I know my own end is at hand."

"What does the dog say?" demanded Valbroso impatiently, not understanding Kothic. "Will he tell us how to open the box?"

As if the voice roused a spark of life in the twisted breast Zorathus rolled his bloodshot eyes toward the speaker.

"Only Valbroso will I tell," he gasped in Zingaran. "Death is upon me. Lean close to me, Valbroso!"

The count did so, his dark face lit with avarice; behind him his saturnine captain, Beloso, crowded closer.

"Press the seven skulls on the rim, one after another," gasped Zorathus. "Press then the head of the dragon that writhes across the lid. Then press the sphere in the dragon's claws. That will release the secret catch."

"Quick, the box!" cried Valbroso with an oath.

Conan lifted it and set it on a dais, and Valbroso shouldered him aside.

"Let me open it!" cried Beloso, starting forward.

Valbroso cursed him back, his greed blazing in his black eyes.

"None but me shall open it!" he cried.

Conan, whose hand had instinctively gone to his hilt, glanced at Zorathus. The man's eyes were glazed and bloodshot, but they were fixed on Valbroso with burning intensity; and was there the shadow of a grim twisted smile on the dying man's lips? Not until the merchant knew he was dying had he given up the secret. Conan turned to watch Valbroso, even as the dying man watched him.

Along the rim of the lid seven skulls were carved among intertwining branches of strange trees. An inlaid dragon writhed its way across the top of the lid, amid ornate arabesques. Valbroso pressed the skulls in fumbling haste, and as he jammed his thumb down on the carved head of the dragon he swore sharply and snatched his hand away, shaking it in irritation.

"A sharp point on the carvings," he snarled. "I've pricked my thumb."

He pressed the gold ball clutched in the dragon's talons, and the lid flew abruptly open. Their eyes were dazzled by a golden flame. It seemed to their dazed minds that the carven box was full of glowing fire that spilled over the rim and dripped through the air in quivering flakes. Beloso cried out and Valbroso sucked in his breath. Conan stood speechless, his brain snared by the blaze.

"Mitra, what a jewel!" Valbroso's hand dived into the chest, came out with a great pulsing crimson sphere that filled the room with a lambent glow. In its glare Valbroso looked like a corpse. And the dying man on the loosened rack laughed wildly and suddenly.

"Fool!" he screamed. "The jewel is yours! I give you death with it! The scratch on your thumb – look at the dragon's head, Valbroso!"

They all wheeled, stared. Something tiny and dully gleaming stood up from the gaping, carved mouth.

"The dragon's fang!" shrieked Zorathus. "Steeped in the venom of the black Stygian scorpion! Fool, fool to open the box of Zorathus with your naked hand! Death! You are a dead man now!"

And with bloody foam on his lips he died.

Valbroso staggered, crying out. "Ah, Mitra, I burn!" he shrieked. "My veins race with liquid fire! My joints are bursting asunder! Death! Death!" And he reeled and crashed headlong. There was an instant of awful convulsions, in which the limbs were twisted into hideous and unnatural positions, and then in that posture the man froze, his glassy eyes staring sightlessly upward, his lips drawn back from blackened gums.

"Dead!" muttered Conan, stooping to pick up the jewel where it rolled on the floor from Valbroso's rigid hand. It lay on the floor like a quivering pool of sunset fire.

"Dead!" muttered Beloso, with madness in his eyes. And then he moved.

Conan was caught off guard, his eyes dazzled, his brain dazed by the blaze of the great gem. He did not realize Beloso's intention until something crashed with terrible force upon his helmet. The glow of the jewel was splashed with redder flame, and he went to his knees under the blow.

He heard a rush of feet, a bellow of ox-like agony. He was stunned but not wholly senseless, and realized that Beloso had caught up the iron box and crashed it down on his head as he stooped. Only his basinet had saved his skull. He staggered up, drawing his sword, trying to shake the dimness out of his eyes. The room swam to his dizzy gaze. But the door was open and fleet footsteps were dwindling down the winding stair. On the floor the brutish torturer was gasping out his life with a great gash under his breast. And the Heart of Ahriman was gone.

Conan reeled out of the chamber, sword in hand, blood streaming down his face from under his burganet. He ran drunkenly down the steps, hearing a clang of steel in the courtyard below, shouts, then the frantic drum of hoofs. Rushing into the bailey he saw the men-at-arms milling about confusedly, while women screeched. The postern gate stood open and a soldier lay across his pike with his head split. Horses, still bridled and saddled, ran neighing about the court, Conan's black stallion among them.

"He's mad!" howled a woman, wringing her hands as she rushed brainlessly about. "He came out of the castle like a mad dog, hewing right and left! Beloso's mad! Where's Lord Valbroso?"

"Which way did he go?" roared Conan.

All turned and stared at the stranger's blood-stained face and naked sword.

"Through the postern!" shrilled a woman, pointing eastward, and another bawled: "Who is this rogue?"

"Beloso has killed Valbroso!" yelled Conan, leaping and seizing the stallion's mane, as the men-at-arms advanced uncertainly on him. A wild outcry burst forth at his news, but their reaction was exactly as he had anticipated. Instead of closing the gates to take him prisoner, or pursuing the fleeing slayer to avenge their lord, they were thrown into even greater confusion by his words. Wolves bound together only by fear of Valbroso, they owed no allegiance to the castle or to each other.

Swords began to clash in the courtyard, and women screamed. And in the midst of it all, none noticed Conan as he shot through the postern gate and thundered down the hill. The wide plain spread before him, and beyond the hill the caravan road divided: one branch ran south, the other east. And on the eastern road he saw another rider, bending low and spurring hard. The plain swam to Conan's gaze, the sunlight was a thick red haze and he reeled in his saddle, grasping the flowing mane with his hand. Blood rained on his mail, but grimly he urged the stallion on.

Behind him smoke began to pour out of the castle on the hill where the count's body lay forgotten and unheeded beside that of his prisoner. The sun was setting; against a lurid red sky the two black figures fled.

The stallion was not fresh, but neither was the horse ridden by Beloso. But the great beast responded mightily, calling on deep reservoirs of reserve vitality. Why the Zingaran fled from one pursuer Conan did not tax his bruised brain to guess. Perhaps unreasoning panic rode Beloso, born of the madness that lurked in that blazing jewel. The sun was gone; the white road was a dim glimmer through a ghostly twilight fading into purple gloom far ahead of him.

The stallion panted, laboring hard. The country was changing, in the gathering dusk. Bare plains gave way to clumps of oaks and alders. Low hills mounted up in the distance. Stars began to blink out. The stallion gasped and reeled in his course. But ahead rose a dense wood that stretched to the hills on the horizon, and between it and himself Conan glimpsed the dim form of the fugitive. He urged on the distressed stallion, for he saw that he was overtaking his prey, yard by yard. Above the pound of the hoofs a strange cry rose from the shadows, but neither pursuer nor pursued gave heed.

As they swept in under the branches that overhung the road, they were almost side by side. A fierce cry rose from Conan's lips as his sword went up; a pale oval of a face was turned toward him, a sword gleamed in a half-seen hand, and Beloso echoed the cry – and then the weary stallion, with a lurch and a groan, missed his footing in the shadows and went heels over head, hurling his dazed rider from the saddle. Conan's throbbing head crashed against a stone, and the stars were blotted out in a thicker night.

How long Conan lay senseless he never knew. His first sensation of returning consciousness was that of being dragged by one arm over rough and stony ground, and through dense underbrush. Then he was thrown carelessly down, and perhaps the jolt brought back his senses.

His helmet was gone, his head ached abominably, he felt a qualm of nausea, and blood was clotted thickly among his black locks. But with the vitality of a wild thing life and consciousness surged back into him, and he became aware of his surroundings.

A broad red moon was shining through the trees, by which he knew that it was long after midnight. He had lain senseless for hours, long enough to have recovered from that terrible blow Beloso had dealt him, as well as the fall which had rendered him senseless. His brain felt clearer than it had felt during that mad ride after the fugitive.

He was not lying beside the white road, he noticed with a start of surprize, as his surroundings began to record themselves on his perceptions. The road was nowhere in sight. He lay on the grassy earth, in a small glade hemmed in by a black wall of tree stems and tangled branches. His face and hands were scratched and lacerated as if he had been dragged through brambles. Shifting his body he looked about him. And then he started violently – something was squatting over him....

At first Conan doubted his consciousness, thought it was but a figment of delirium. Surely it could not be real, that strange, motionless gray being that squatted on its haunches and stared down at him with unblinking soulless eyes.

Conan lay and stared, half expecting it to vanish like a figure of a dream, and then a chill of recollection crept along his spine. Half-forgotten memories surged back, of grisly tales whispered of the shapes that haunted these uninhabited forests at the foot of the hills that mark the Zingaran-Argossean border. *Ghouls*, men called them, eaters of human flesh, spawn of darkness, children of unholy matings of a lost and forgotten race with the demons of the underworld. Somewhere in these primitive forests were the ruins of an ancient, accursed city, men whispered, and among its tombs slunk gray, anthropomorphic shadows – Conan shuddered strongly.

He lay staring at the malformed head that rose dimly above him, and cautiously he extended a hand toward the sword at his hip. With a horrible cry that the man involuntarily echoed, the monster was at his throat.

Conan threw up his right arm, and the dog-like jaws closed on it, driving the mail links into the hard flesh. The misshapen yet man-like hands clutched for his throat, but he evaded them with a heave and roll of his whole body, at the same time drawing his dagger with his left hand.

They tumbled over and over on the grass, smiting and tearing. The muscles coiling under that gray corpse-like skin were stringy and hard as steel wires, exceeding the strength of a man. But Conan's thews were iron too, and his mail saved him from the gnashing fangs and ripping claws long enough for him to drive home his dagger, again and again and again. The horrible vitality of the semi-human monstrosity seemed inexhaustible, and the king's skin crawled at the feel of that slick, clammy flesh. He put all his loathing and savage revulsion behind the plunging blade, and suddenly the monster heaved up convulsively beneath him as the point found its grisly heart, and then lay still.

Conan rose, shaken with nausea. He stood in the center of the glade uncertainly, sword in one hand and dagger in the other. He had not lost his instinctive sense of direction, as far as the points of the compass were concerned, but he did not know in which direction the road lay. He had no way of knowing in which direction the ghoul had dragged him. Conan glared at the silent, black, moon-dappled woods which ringed him, and felt cold moisture bead his flesh. He was without a horse and lost in these haunted woods, and that staring, deformed thing at his feet was a mute evidence of the horrors that lurked in the forest. He stood almost holding his breath in his painful intensity, straining his ears for some crack of twig or rustle of grass.

When a sound did come he started violently. Suddenly out on the night air broke the scream of a terrified horse. His stallion! There were panthers in the wood – or – ghouls ate beasts as well as men.

He broke savagely through the brush in the direction of the sound, whistling shrilly as he ran, his fear drowned in berserk rage. If his horse was killed, there went his last chance of following Beloso and recovering the jewel. Again the stallion screamed with fear and fury, somewhere nearer. There was a sound of lashing heels, and something that was struck heavily and gave way.

Conan burst out into the wide white road without warning, and saw the stallion plunging and rearing in the moonlight, his ears laid back, his eyes and teeth flashing wickedly. He lashed out with his heels at a slinking shadow that ducked and bobbed about him – and then about Conan other shadows moved: gray, furtive shadows that closed in on all sides. A hideous charnel-house scent reeked up in the night air.

With a curse the king hewed right and left with his broadsword, thrust and ripped with his dagger. Dripping fangs flashed in the moonlight, foul paws caught at him, but he hacked his way through to the stallion, caught the rein, leaped into the saddle. His sword rose and fell, a frosty arc in the moon, showering blood as it split misshapen heads, clove shambling bodies. The stallion reared, biting and kicking. They burst through and thundered down the road. On either hand, for a short space, flitted gray abhorrent shadows. Then these fell behind, and Conan, topping a wooded crest, saw a vast expanse of bare slopes sweeping up and away before him.

XIII
"A Ghost out of the Past"

Soon after sunrise Conan crossed the Argossean border. Of Beloso he had seen no trace. Either the captain had made good his escape while the king lay senseless, or had fallen prey to the grim man-eaters of the Zingaran forest. But Conan had seen no signs to indicate the latter possibility. The fact that he had lain unmolested for so long seemed to indicate that the monsters had been engrossed in futile pursuit of the captain. And if the man lived, Conan felt certain that he was riding along the road somewhere ahead of him. Unless he had intended going into Argos he would never have taken the eastward road in the first place.

The helmeted guards at the frontier did not question the Cimmerian. A single wandering mercenary required no passport nor safe-conduct, especially when his unadorned mail showed him to be in the service of no lord. Through the low, grassy hills where streams murmured and oak groves dappled the sward with lights and shadows he rode, following the long road that rose and fell away ahead of him over dales and rises in the blue distance. It was an old, old road, this highway from Poitain to the sea.

Argos was at peace; laden ox-wains rumbled along the road, and men with bare, brown, brawny arms toiled in orchards and fields that smiled away under the branches of the roadside trees. Old men on settles before inns under spreading oak branches called greetings to the wayfarer.

From the men that worked the fields, from the garrulous old men in the inns where he slaked his thirst with great leathern jacks of foaming ale, from the sharp-eyed silk-clad merchants he met upon the road, Conan sought for news of Beloso.

Stories were conflicting, but this much Conan learned: that a lean, wiry Zingaran with the dangerous black eyes and mustaches of the western folk was somewhere on the road ahead of him, and apparently making for Messantia. It was a logical destination; all the sea-ports of Argos were cosmopolitan, in strong contrast with the inland provinces, and Messantia was the most polyglot of all. Craft of all the maritime nations rode in its harbor, and refugees and fugitives from many lands gathered there. Laws were lax; for Messantia thrived on the trade of the sea, and her citizens found it profitable to be somewhat blind in their dealings with seamen. It was not only legitimate trade that flowed into Messantia; smugglers and buccaneers played their part. All this Conan knew well, for had he not, in the days of old when he was a Barachan pirate, sailed by night into the harbor of Messantia to discharge strange cargoes? Most of the pirates of the Barachan Isles – small islands off the southwestern coast of Zingara – were Argossean sailors, and as long as they confined their attentions to the shipping of other nations, the authorities of Argos were not too strict in their interpretation of sea-laws.

But Conan had not limited his activities to those of the Barachans. He had also sailed with the Zingaran buccaneers, and even with those wild black corsairs that swept up from the far south to harry the northern coasts, and this put him beyond the pale of any law. If he were recognized in any of the ports of Argos it would cost him his head. But without hesitation he rode on to Messantia, halting day or night only to rest the stallion and to snatch a few winks of sleep for himself.

He entered the city unquestioned, merging himself with the throngs that poured continually in and out of this great commercial center. No walls surrounded Messantia. The sea and the ships of the sea guarded the great southern trading city.

It was evening when Conan rode leisurely through the streets that marched down to the waterfront. At the ends of these streets he saw the wharves and the masts and sails of ships. He smelled salt water for the first time in years, heard the thrum of cordage and the creak of spars in the breeze that was kicking up whitecaps out beyond the headlands. Again the urge of far wandering tugged at his heart.

But he did not go on to the wharves. He reined aside and rode up a steep flight of wide, worn stone steps, to a broad street where ornate white mansions overlooked the waterfront and the harbor below. Here dwelt the men who had grown rich from the hard-won fat of the seas – a few old sea-captains who had found treasure afar, many traders and merchants who never trod the naked decks nor knew the roar of tempest or sea-fight.

Conan turned in his horse at a certain gold-worked gate, and rode into a court where a fountain tinkled and pigeons fluttered from marble coping to marble flagging. A page in jagged silken jupon and hose came forward inquiringly. The merchants of Messantia dealt with many strange and rough characters but most of these smacked of the sea. It was strange that a mercenary trooper should so freely ride into the court of a lord of commerce.

"The merchant Publio dwells here?" It was more statement than question, and something in the timbre of the voice caused the page to doff his feathered chaperon as he bowed and replied: "Aye, so he does, my captain."

Conan dismounted and the page called a servitor, who came running to receive the stallion's rein.

"Your master is within?" Conan drew off his gauntlets and slapped the dust of the road from cloak and mail.

"Aye, my captain. Whom shall I announce?"

"I'll announce myself," grunted Conan. "I know the way well enough. Bide you here."

And obeying that peremptory command the page stood still, staring after Conan as the latter climbed a short flight of marble steps, and wondering what connection his master might have with this giant fighting-man who had the aspect of a northern barbarian.

Menials at their tasks halted and gaped open-mouthed as Conan crossed a wide, cool balcony overlooking the court and entered a broad corridor through which the sea-breeze swept. Half-way down this he heard a quill scratching, and turned into a broad room whose many wide casements overlooked the harbor.

Publio sat at a carved teakwood desk writing on rich parchment with a golden quill. He was a short man, with a massive head and quick dark eyes. His blue robe was of the finest watered silk, trimmed with cloth-of-gold, and from his thick white throat hung a heavy gold chain.

As the Cimmerian entered, the merchant looked up with a gesture of annoyance. He froze in the midst of his gesture. His mouth opened; he stared as at a ghost out of the past. Unbelief and fear glimmered in his wide eyes.

"Well," said Conan, "have you no word of greeting, Publio?"

Publio moistened his lips.

"Conan!" he whispered incredulously. "Mitra! Conan! *Amra!*"

"Who else?" The Cimmerian unclasped his cloak and threw it with his gauntlets down upon the desk. "How, man?" he exclaimed irritably. "Can't you at least offer me a beaker of wine? My throat's caked with the dust of the highway."

"Aye, wine!" echoed Publio mechanically. Instinctively his hand reached for a gong, then recoiled as from a hot coal, and he shuddered.

While Conan watched him with a flicker of grim amusement in his eyes, the merchant rose and hurriedly shut the door, first craning his neck up and down the corridor to be sure that no slave was loitering about. Then, returning, he took a gold vessel of wine from a near-by table and was about to fill a slender goblet when Conan impatiently took the vessel from him and lifting it with both hands, drank deep and with gusto.

"Aye, it's Conan, right enough," muttered Publio. "Man, are you mad?"

"By Crom, Publio," said Conan, lowering the vessel but retaining it in his hands, "you dwell in different quarters than of old. It takes an Argossean merchant to wring wealth out of a little waterfront shop that stank of rotten fish and cheap wine."

"The old days are past," muttered Publio, drawing his robe about him with a slight involuntary shudder. "I have put off the past like a worn-out cloak."

"Well," retorted Conan, "you can't put *me* off like an old cloak. It isn't much I want of you, but that much I do want. And you can't refuse me. We had too many dealings in the old days. Am I such a fool that I'm not aware that this fine mansion was built on my sweat and blood? How many cargoes from my galleys passed through your shop?"

"All merchants of Messantia have dealt with the sea-rovers at one time or another," mumbled Publio nervously.

"But not with the black corsairs," answered Conan grimly.

"For Mitra's sake, be silent!" ejaculated Publio, sweat starting out on his brow. His fingers jerked at the gilt-worked edge of his robe.

"Well, I only wished to recall it to your mind," answered Conan. "Don't be so fearful. You took plenty of risks in the past, when you were struggling for life and wealth in that lousy little shop down by the wharves, and were hand-and-glove with every buccaneer and smuggler and pirate from here to the Barachan Isles. Prosperity must have softened you."

"I am respectable," began Publio.

"Meaning you're rich as hell," snorted Conan. "Why? Why did you grow wealthy so much quicker than your competitors? Was it because you did a big business in ivory and ostrich feathers, copper and skins and pearls and hammered gold ornaments, and other things from the coast of Kush? And where did you get them so cheaply, while other merchants were paying their weight in silver to the Stygians for them? I'll tell you, in case you've forgotten: you bought them from me, at considerably less than their value, and I took them from the tribes of the Black Coast, and from the ships of the Stygians – I, and the black corsairs."

"In Mitra's name, cease!" begged Publio. "I have not forgotten. But what are you doing here? I am the only man in Argos who knew that the king of Aquilonia was once Conan the buccaneer, in the old days. But word has come southward of the overthrow of Aquilonia and the death of the king."

"My enemies have killed me a hundred times by rumors," grunted Conan. "Yet here I sit and guzzle wine of Kyros." And he suited the action to the word.

Lowering the vessel, which was now nearly empty, he said: "It's but a small thing I ask of you, Publio. I know that you're aware of everything that goes on in Messantia. I want to know if a Zingaran named Beloso, or he might call himself anything, is in this city. He's tall and lean and dark like all his race, and it's likely he'll seek to sell a very rare jewel."

Publio shook his head.

"I have not heard of such a man. But thousands come and go in Messantia. If he is here my agents will discover him."

"Good. Send them to look for him. And in the meantime have my horse cared for, and have food served me here in this room."

Publio assented volubly, and Conan emptied the wine vessel, tossed it carelessly into a corner, and strode to a near-by casement, involuntarily expanding his chest as he breathed deep of the salt air. He was looking down upon the meandering waterfront streets. He swept the ships in the harbor with an appreciative glance, then lifted his head and stared beyond the bay, far into the blue haze of the distance where sea met sky. And his memory sped beyond that horizon, to the golden seas of the south, under flaming suns, where laws were not and life ran hotly. Some vagrant scent of spice or palm woke clear-etched images of strange coasts where mangroves grew and drums thundered, of ships locked in battle and decks running blood, of smoke and flame and the crying of slaughter.... Lost in his thoughts he scarcely noticed when Publio stole from the chamber.

Gathering up his robe, the merchant hurried along the corridors until he came to a certain chamber where a tall, gaunt man with a scar upon his temple wrote continually upon parchment. There was something about this man which made his clerkly occupation seem incongruous. To him Publio spoke abruptly:

"Conan has returned!"

"Conan?" The gaunt man started up and the quill fell from his fingers. "The corsair?"

"Aye!"

The gaunt man went livid. "Is he mad? If he is discovered here we are ruined! They will hang a man who shelters or trades with a corsair as quickly as they'll hang the corsair himself! What if the governor should learn of our past connections with him?"

"He will not learn," answered Publio grimly. "Send your men into the markets and wharfside dives and learn if one Beloso, a Zingaran, is in Messantia. Conan said he had a gem, which he will probably seek to dispose of. The jewel merchants should know of him, if any do. And here is another task for you: pick up a dozen or so desperate villains who can be trusted to do away with a man and hold their tongues afterward. You understand me?"

"I understand." The other nodded slowly and somberly.

"I have not stolen, cheated, lied and fought my way up from the gutter to be undone now by a ghost out of my past," muttered Publio, and the sinister darkness of his countenance at that moment would have surprized the wealthy nobles and ladies who bought their silks and pearls from his many stalls. But when he returned to Conan a short time later, bearing in his own hands a platter of fruit and meats, he presented a placid face to his unwelcome guest.

Conan still stood at the casement, staring down into the harbor at the purple and crimson and vermilion and scarlet sails of galleons and carracks and galleys and dromonds.

"There's a Stygian galley, if I'm not blind," he remarked, pointing to a long, low, slim black ship lying apart from the others, anchored off the low broad sandy beach that curved round to the distant headland. "Is there peace, then, between Stygia and Argos?"

"The same sort that has existed before," answered Publio, setting the platter on the table with a sigh of relief, for it was heavily laden; he knew his guest of old. "Stygian ports are temporarily open to our ships, as ours to theirs. But may no craft of mine meet their cursed galleys out of sight of land! That galley crept into the bay last night. What its masters wish I do not know. So far they have neither bought nor sold. I distrust those dark-skinned devils. Treachery had its birth in that dusky land."

"I've made them howl," said Conan carelessly, turning from the window. "In my galley manned by black corsairs I crept to the very bastions of the sea-washed castles of black-walled Khemi by night, and burned the galleons anchored there. And speaking of treachery, mine host, suppose you taste these viands and sip a bit of this wine, just to show me that your heart is on the right side."

Publio complied so readily that Conan's suspicions were lulled, and without further hesitation he sat down and devoured enough for three men.

And while he ate, men moved through the markets and along the waterfront, searching for a Zingaran who had a jewel to sell or who sought for a ship to carry him to foreign ports. And a tall gaunt man with a scar on his temple sat with his elbows on a wine-stained table in a squalid cellar with a brass lantern hanging from a smoke-blackened beam overhead, and held converse with ten desperate rogues whose sinister countenances and ragged garments proclaimed their profession.

And as the first stars blinked out, they shone on a strange band spurring their mounts along the white road that led to Messantia from the west. They were four men, tall, gaunt, clad in black, hooded robes, and they did not speak. They forced their steeds mercilessly onward, and those steeds were gaunt as themselves, and sweat-stained and weary as if from long travel and far wandering.

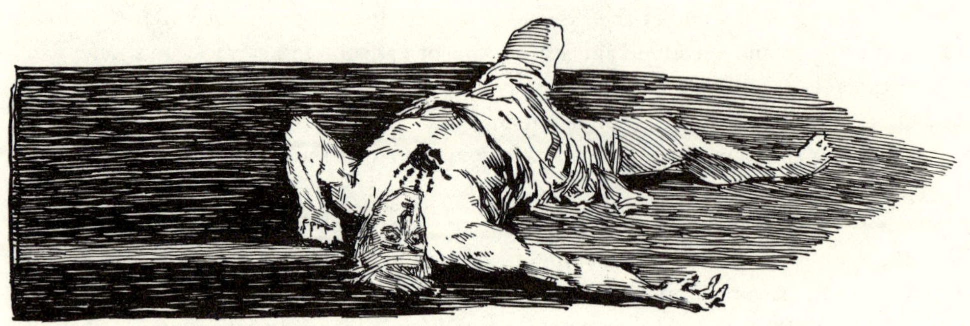

XIV

The Black Hand of Set

Conan woke from a sound sleep as quickly and instantly as a cat. And like a cat he was on his feet with his sword out before the man who had touched him could so much as draw back.

"What word, Publio?" demanded Conan, recognizing his host. The gold lamp burned low, casting a mellow glow over the thick tapestries and the rich coverings of the couch whereon he had been reposing.

Publio, recovering from the start given him by the sudden action of his awakening guest, replied: "The Zingaran has been located. He arrived yesterday, at dawn. Only a few hours ago he sought to sell a huge, strange jewel to a Shemitish merchant, but the Shemite would have naught to do with it. Men say he turned pale beneath his black beard at the sight of it, and closing his stall, fled as from a thing accursed."

"It must be Beloso," muttered Conan, feeling the pulse in his temples pounding with impatient eagerness. "Where is he now?"

"He sleeps in the house of Servio."

"I know that dive of old," grunted Conan. "I'd better hasten before some of these waterfront thieves cut his throat for the jewel."

He took up his cloak and flung it over his shoulders, then donned a helmet Publio had procured for him.

"Have my steed saddled and ready in the court," said he. "I may return in haste. I shall not forget this night's work, Publio."

A few moments later Publio, standing at a small outer door, watched the king's tall figure receding down the shadowy street.

"Farewell to you, corsair," muttered the merchant. "This must be a notable jewel, to be sought by a man who has just lost a kingdom. I wish I had told my knaves to let him secure it before they did their work. But then, something might have gone awry. Let Argos forget Amra, and let my dealings with him be lost in the dust of the past. In the alley behind the house of Servio – that is where Conan will cease to be a peril to me."

Servio's house, a dingy, ill-famed den, was located close to the wharves, facing the waterfront. It was a shambling building of stone and heavy ship-beams, and a long narrow alley wandered up alongside it. Conan made his way along the alley, and as he approached the house he had an uneasy feeling that he was being spied upon. He stared hard into the shadows of the squalid buildings, but saw nothing, though once he caught the faint rasp of cloth or leather against flesh. But that was nothing unusual. Thieves and beggars prowled these alleys all night, and they were not likely to attack him, after one look at his size and harness.

But suddenly a door opened in the wall ahead of him, and he slipped into the shadow of an arch. A figure emerged from the open door and moved along the alley, not furtively, but with a natural noiselessness like that of a jungle beast. Enough starlight filtered into the alley to silhouette the man's profile dimly as he passed the doorway where Conan lurked. The stranger was a Stygian. There was no mistaking that hawk-faced, shaven head, even in the starlight, nor the mantle over the broad shoulders. He passed on down the alley in the direction of the beach, and once Conan thought he must be carrying a lantern among his garments, for he caught a flash of lambent light, just as the man vanished.

But the Cimmerian forgot the stranger as he noticed that the door through which he had emerged still stood open. Conan had intended entering by the main entrance and forcing Servio to show him the room where the Zingaran slept. But if he could get into the house without attracting anyone's attention, so much the better.

A few long strides brought him to the door, and as his hand fell on the lock he stifled an involuntary grunt. His practised fingers, skilled among the thieves of Zamora long ago, told him that the lock had been forced, apparently by some terrific pressure from the outside that had twisted and bent the heavy iron bolts, tearing the very sockets loose from the jambs. How such damage could have been wrought so violently without awakening everyone in the neighborhood Conan could not imagine, but he felt sure that it had been done that night. A broken lock, if discovered, would not go unmended in the house of Servio, in this neighborhood of thieves and cutthroats.

Conan entered stealthily, poniard in hand, wondering how he was to find the chamber of the Zingaran. Groping in total darkness he halted suddenly. He sensed death in that room, as a wild beast senses it – not as peril threatening him, but a dead thing, something freshly slain. In the darkness his foot hit and recoiled from something heavy and yielding. With a sudden premonition he groped along the wall until he found the shelf that supported the brass lamp, with its flint, steel and tinder beside it. A few seconds later a flickering, uncertain light sprang up, and he stared narrowly about him.

A bunk built against the rough stone wall, a bare table and a bench completed the furnishings of the squalid chamber. An inner door stood closed and bolted. And on the hard-beaten dirt floor lay Beloso. On his back he lay, with his head drawn back between his shoulders so that he seemed to stare with his wide glassy eyes at the sooty beams of the cobwebbed ceiling. His lips were drawn back from his teeth in a frozen grin of agony. His sword lay near him, still in its scabbard. His shirt was torn open, and on his brown, muscular breast was the print of a black hand, thumb and four fingers plainly distinct.

Conan glared in silence, feeling the short hairs bristle at the back of his neck.

"Crom!" he muttered. "The black hand of Set!"

He had seen that mark of old, the death-mark of the black priests of Set, the grim cult that ruled in dark Stygia. And suddenly he remembered that curious flash he had seen emanating from the mysterious Stygian who had emerged from this chamber.

"The Heart, by Crom!" he muttered. "He was carrying it under his mantle. He stole it. He burst that door by his magic, and slew Beloso. He was a priest of Set."

A quick investigation confirmed at least part of his suspicions. The jewel was not on the Zingaran's body. An uneasy feeling rose in Conan that this had not happened by chance, or without design; a conviction that the mysterious Stygian galley had come into the harbor of Messantia on a definite mission. How could the priests of Set know that the Heart had come southward? Yet the thought was no more fantastic than the necromancy that could slay an armed man by the touch of an open, empty hand.

A stealthy footfall outside the door brought him round like a great cat. With one motion he extinguished the lamp and drew his sword. His ears told him that men were out there in the darkness, were closing in on the doorway. As his eyes became accustomed to the sudden darkness, he could make out dim figures ringing the entrance. He could not guess their identity, but as always he took the initiative – leaping suddenly forth from the doorway without awaiting the attack.

His unexpected movement took the skulkers by surprize. He sensed and heard men close about him, saw a dim masked figure in the starlight before him; then his sword crunched home, and he was fleeting away down the alley before the slower-thinking and slower-acting attackers could intercept him.

As he ran he heard, somewhere ahead of him, a faint creak of oar-locks, and he forgot the men behind him. A boat was moving out into the bay! Gritting his teeth he increased his speed, but before he reached the beach he heard the rasp and creak of ropes, and the grind of the great sweep in its socket.

Thick clouds, rolling up from the sea, obscured the stars. In thick darkness Conan came upon the strand, straining his eyes out across the black restless water. Something was moving out there – a long, low, black shape that receded in the darkness, gathering momentum as it went. To his ears came the rhythmical clack of long oars. He ground his teeth in helpless fury. It was the Stygian galley and she was racing out to sea, bearing with her the jewel that meant to him the throne of Aquilonia.

With a savage curse he took a step toward the waves that lapped against the sands, catching at his hauberk and intending to rip it off and swim after the vanishing ship. Then the crunch of a heel in the sand brought him about. He had forgotten his pursuers.

Dark figures closed in on him with a rush of feet through the sands. The first went down beneath the Cimmerian's flailing sword, but the others did not falter. Blades whickered dimly about him in the darkness or rasped on his mail. Blood and entrails spilled over his hand and someone screamed as he ripped murderously upward. A muttered voice spurred on the attack, and that voice sounded vaguely familiar. Conan plowed through the clinging, hacking shapes toward the voice. A faint light gleaming momentarily through the drifting clouds showed him a tall gaunt man with a great livid scar on his temple. Conan's sword sheared through his skull as through a ripe melon.

Then an ax, swung blindly in the dark, crashed on the king's basinet, filling his eyes with sparks of fire. He lurched and lunged, felt his sword sink deep and heard a shriek of agony. Then he stumbled over a corpse, and a bludgeon knocked the dented helmet from his head; the next instant the club fell full on his unprotected skull.

The king of Aquilonia crumpled into the wet sands. Over him wolfish figures panted in the gloom.

"Strike off his head," muttered one.

"Let him lie," grunted another. "Help me tie up my wounds before I bleed to death. The tide will wash him into the bay. See, he fell at the water's edge. His skull's split; no man could live after such blows."

"Help me strip him," urged another. "His harness will fetch a few pieces of silver. And haste. Tiberio is dead, and I hear seamen singing as they reel along the strand. Let us be gone."

There followed hurried activity in the darkness, and then the sound of quickly receding footsteps. The tipsy singing of the seamen grew louder.

In his chamber Publio, nervously pacing back and forth before a window that overlooked the shadowed bay, whirled suddenly, his nerves tingling. To the best of his knowledge the door had been bolted from within; but now it stood open and four men filed into the chamber. At the sight of them his flesh crawled. Many strange beings Publio had seen in his lifetime, but none before like these. They were tall and gaunt, black-robed, and their faces were dim yellow ovals in the shadows of their coifs. He could not tell much about their features and was unreasoningly glad that he could not. Each bore a long, curiously mottled staff.

"Who are you?" he demanded, and his voice sounded brittle and hollow. "What do you wish here?"

"Where is Conan, he who was king of Aquilonia?" demanded the tallest of the four in a passionless monotone that made Publio shudder. It was like the hollow tone of a Khitan temple bell.

"I do not know what you mean," stammered the merchant, his customary poise shaken by the uncanny aspect of his visitors. "I know no such man."

"He has been here," returned the other with no change of inflection. "His horse is in the courtyard. Tell us where he is before we do you an injury."

"Gebal!" shouted Publio frantically, recoiling until he crouched against the wall. *"Gebal!"*

The four Khitans watched him without emotion or change of expression.

"If you summon your slave he will die," warned one of them, which only served to terrify Publio more than ever.

"Gebal!" he screamed. "Where are you, curse you? Thieves are murdering your master!"

Swift footsteps padded in the corridor outside, and Gebal burst into the chamber – a Shemite, of medium height and mightily muscled build, his curled blue-black beard bristling, and a short leaf-shaped sword in his hand.

He stared in stupid amazement at the four invaders, unable to understand their presence; dimly remembering that he had drowsed unexplainably on the stair he was guarding and up which they must have come. He had never slept on duty before. But his master was shrieking with a note of hysteria in his voice, and the Shemite drove like a bull at the strangers, his thickly muscled arm drawing back for the disemboweling thrust. But the stroke was never dealt.

A black-sleeved arm shot out, extending the long staff. Its end but touched the Shemite's brawny breast and was instantly withdrawn. The stroke was horribly like the dart and recovery of a serpent's head.

Gebal halted short in his headlong plunge, as if he had encountered a solid barrier. His bull head toppled forward on his breast, the sword slipped from his fingers, and then he *melted* slowly to the floor. It was as if all the bones of his frame had suddenly become flabby. Publio turned sick.

"Do not shout again," advised the tallest Khitan. "Your servants sleep soundly, but if you awaken them they will die, and you with them. Where is Conan?"

"He is gone to the house of Servio, near the waterfront, to search for the Zingaran Beloso," gasped Publio, all his power of resistance gone out of him. The merchant did not lack courage; but these uncanny visitants turned his marrow to water. He started convulsively at a sudden noise of footsteps hurrying up the stair outside, loud in the ominous stillness.

"Your servant?" asked the Khitan.

Publio shook his head mutely, his tongue frozen to his palate. He could not speak.

One of the Khitans caught up a silken cover from a couch and threw it over the corpse. Then they melted behind the tapestry, but before the tallest man disappeared, he murmured: "Talk to this man who comes, and send him away quickly. If you betray us, neither he nor you will live to reach that door. Make no sign to show him that you are not alone." And lifting his staff suggestively, the yellow man faded behind the hangings.

Publio shuddered and choked down a desire to retch. It might have been a trick of the light, but it seemed to him that occasionally those staffs moved slightly of their own accord, as if possessed of an unspeakable life of their own.

He pulled himself together with a mighty effort, and presented a composed aspect to the ragged ruffian who burst into the chamber.

"We have done as you wished, my lord," this man exclaimed. "The barbarian lies dead on the sands at the water's edge."

Publio felt a movement in the arras behind him, and almost burst from fright. The man swept heedlessly on.

"Your secretary, Tiberio, is dead. The barbarian slew him, and four of my companions. We bore their bodies to the rendezvous. There was nothing of value on the barbarian except a few silver coins. Are there any further orders?"

"None!" gasped Publio, white about the lips. "Go!"

The desperado bowed and hurried out, with a vague feeling that Publio was both a man of weak stomach and few words.

The four Khitans came from behind the arras.

"Of whom did this man speak?" the taller demanded.

"Of a wandering stranger who did me an injury," panted Publio.

"You lie," said the Khitan calmly. "He spoke of the king of Aquilonia. I read it in your expression. Sit upon that divan and do not move or speak. I will remain with you while my three companions go search for the body."

So Publio sat and shook with terror of the silent, inscrutable figure which watched him, until the three Khitans filed back into the room, with the news that Conan's body did not lie upon the sands. Publio did not know whether to be glad or sorry.

"We found the spot where the fight was fought," they said. "Blood was on the sand. But the king was gone."

The fourth Khitan drew imaginary symbols upon the carpet with his staff, which glistened scalily in the lamplight.

"Did you read naught from the sands?" he asked.

"Aye," they answered. "The king lives, and he has gone southward in a ship."

The tall Khitan lifted his head and gazed at Publio, so that the merchant broke into a profuse sweat.

"What do you wish of me?" he stuttered.

"A ship," answered the Khitan. "A ship well manned for a long voyage."

"For how long a voyage?" stammered Publio, never thinking of refusing.

"To the ends of the world, perhaps," answered the Khitan, "or to the molten seas of hell that lie beyond the sunrise."

XV
The Return of the Corsair

Conan's first sensation of returning consciousness was that of motion; under him was no solidity, but a ceaseless heaving and plunging. Then he heard wind humming through cords and spars, and knew he was aboard a ship even before his blurred sight cleared. He heard a mutter of voices and then a dash of water deluged him, jerking him sharply into full animation. He heaved up with a sulfurous curse, braced his legs and glared about him, with a burst of coarse guffaws in his ears and the reek of unwashed bodies in his nostrils.

He was standing on the poopdeck of a long galley which was running before the wind that whipped down from the north, her striped sail bellying against the taut sheets. The sun was just rising, in a dazzling blaze of gold and blue and green. To the left of the shore-line was a dim purple shadow. To the right stretched the open ocean. This much Conan saw at a glance that likewise included the ship itself.

It was long and narrow, a typical trading-ship of the southern coasts, high of poop and stern, with cabins at either extremity. Conan looked down into the open waist, whence wafted that sickening abominable odor. He knew it of old. It was the body-scent of the oarsmen, chained to their benches. They were all negroes, forty men to each side, each confined by a chain locked about his waist, with the other end welded to a heavy ring set deep in the solid runway beam that ran between the benches from stem to stern. The life of a slave aboard an Argossean galley was a hell unfathomable. Most of these were Kushites, but some thirty of the blacks who now rested on their idle oars and stared up at the stranger with dull curiosity were from the far southern isles, the homelands of the corsairs. Conan recognized them by their straighter features and hair, their rangier, cleaner-limbed build. And he saw among them men who had followed him of old.

But all this he saw and recognized in one swift, all-embracing glance as he rose, before he turned his attention to the figures about him. Reeling momentarily on braced legs, his fists clenched wrathfully, he glared at the figures clustered about him. The sailor who had drenched him stood grinning, the empty bucket still poised in his hand, and Conan cursed him with venom, instinctively reaching for his hilt. Then he discovered that he was weaponless and naked except for his short leather breeks.

"What lousy tub is this?" he roared. "How did I come aboard here?"

The sailors laughed jeeringly – stocky, bearded Argosseans to a man – and one, whose richer dress and air of command proclaimed him captain, folded his arms and said domineeringly: "We found you lying on the sands. Somebody had rapped you on the pate and taken your clothes. Needing an extra man, we brought you aboard."

"What ship is this?" Conan demanded.

"The *Venturer*, out of Messantia, with a cargo of mirrors, scarlet silk cloaks, shields, gilded helmets and swords to trade to the Shemites for copper and gold ore. I am Demetrio, captain of this vessel and your master henceforward."

"Then I'm headed in the direction I wanted to go, after all," muttered Conan, heedless of that last remark. They were racing southeastward, following the long curve of the Argossean coast. These trading-ships never ventured far from the shore-line. Somewhere ahead of him he knew that low dark Stygian galley was speeding southward.

"Have you sighted a Stygian galley – " began Conan, but the beard of the burly, brutal-faced captain bristled. He was not in the least interested in any question his prisoner might wish to ask, and felt it high time he reduced this independent wastrel to his proper place.

"Get for'ard!" he roared. "I've wasted time enough with you! I've done you the honor of having you brought to the poop to be revived, and answered enough of your infernal questions. Get off this poop! You'll work your way aboard this galley – "

"I'll buy your ship – " began Conan, before he remembered that he was a penniless wanderer.

A roar of rough mirth greeted these words, and the captain turned purple, thinking he sensed ridicule.

"You mutinous swine!" he bellowed, taking a threatening step forward, while his hand closed on the knife at his belt. "Get for'ard before I have you flogged! You'll keep a civil tongue in your jaws, or by Mitra, I'll have you chained among the blacks to tug an oar!"

Conan's volcanic temper, never long at best, burst into explosion. Not in years, even before he was king, had a man spoken to him thus and lived.

"Don't lift your voice to me, you tar-breeched dog!" he roared in a voice as gusty as the sea-wind, while the sailors gaped dumfounded. "Draw that toy and I'll feed you to the fishes!"

"Who do you think you are?" gasped the captain.

"I'll show you!" roared the maddened Cimmerian, and he wheeled and bounded toward the rail, where weapons hung in their brackets.

The captain drew his knife and ran at him bellowing, but before he could strike, Conan gripped his wrist with a wrench that tore the arm clean out of the socket. The captain bellowed like an ox in agony, and then rolled clear across the deck as he was hurled contemptuously from his attacker. Conan ripped a heavy ax from the rail and wheeled cat-like to meet the rush of the sailors. They ran in, giving tongue like hounds, clumsy-footed and awkward in comparison to the pantherish Cimmerian. Before they could reach him with their knives he sprang among them, striking right and left too quickly for the eye to follow, and blood and brains spattered as two corpses struck the deck.

Knives flailed the air wildly as Conan broke through the stumbling, gasping mob and bounded to the narrow bridge that spanned the waist from poop to forecastle, just out of reach of the slaves below. Behind him the handful of sailors on the poop were floundering after him, daunted by the destruction of their fellows, and the rest of the crew – some thirty in all – came running across the bridge toward him, with weapons in their hands.

Conan bounded out on the bridge and stood poised above the upturned black faces, ax lifted, black mane blown in the wind.

"Who am I?" he yelled. "Look, you dogs! Look, Ajonga, Yasunga, Laranga! *Who am I?*"

And from the waist rose a shout that swelled to a mighty roar: "Amra! It is Amra! The Lion has returned!"

The sailors who caught and understood the burden of that awesome shout paled and shrank back, staring in sudden fear at the wild figure on the bridge. Was this in truth that blood-thirsty ogre of the southern seas who had so mysteriously vanished years ago, but who still lived in gory legends? The blacks were frothing crazy now, shaking and tearing at their chains and shrieking the name of Amra like an invocation. Kushites who had never seen Conan before took up the yell. The slaves in the pen under the after-cabin began to batter at the walls, shrieking like the damned.

Demetrio, hitching himself along the deck on one hand and his knees, livid with the agony of his dislocated arm, screamed: "In and kill him, dogs, before the slaves break loose!"

Fired to desperation by that word, the most dread to all galleymen, the sailors charged on to the bridge from both ends. But with a lion-like bound Conan left the bridge and hit like a cat on his feet on the runway between the benches.

"Death to the masters!" he thundered, and his ax rose and fell crashingly full on a shackle-chain, severing it like match-wood. In an instant a shrieking slave was free, splintering his oar for a bludgeon. Men were racing frantically along the bridge above, and all hell and bedlam broke loose on the *Venturer*. Conan's ax rose and fell without pause, and with every stroke a frothing, screaming black giant broke free, mad with hate and the fury of freedom and vengeance.

Sailors leaping down into the waist to grapple or smite at the naked white giant hewing like one possessed at the shackles, found themselves dragged down by hands of slaves yet unfreed, while others, their broken chains whipping and snapping about their limbs, came up out of the waist like a blind, black torrent, screaming like fiends, smiting with broken oars and pieces of iron, tearing and rending with talons and teeth. In the midst of the mêlée the slaves in the pen broke down the walls and came surging up on the decks, and with fifty blacks freed of their benches Conan abandoned his iron-hewing and bounded up on the bridge to add his notched ax to the bludgeons of his partizans.

Then it was massacre. The Argosseans were strong, sturdy, fearless like all their race, trained in the brutal school of the sea. But they could not stand against these maddened giants, led by the tigerish barbarian. Blows and abuse and hellish suffering were avenged in one red gust of fury that raged like a typhoon from one end of the ship to the other, and when it had blown itself out, but one white man lived aboard the *Venturer*, and that was the blood-stained giant about whom the chanting blacks thronged to cast themselves prostrate on the bloody deck and beat their heads against the boards in an ecstasy of hero-worship.

Conan, his mighty chest heaving and glistening with sweat, the red ax gripped in his blood-smeared hand, glared about him as the first chief of men might have glared in some primordial dawn, and shook back his black mane. In that moment he was not king of Aquilonia; he was again lord of the black corsairs, who had hacked his way to lordship through flame and blood.

"Amra! Amra!" chanted the delirious blacks, those who were left to chant. "The Lion has returned! Now will the Stygians howl like dogs in the night, and the black dogs of Kush will howl! Now will villages burst in flames and ships founder! *Aie*, there will be wailing of women and the thunder of the spears!"

"Cease this yammering, dogs!" Conan roared in a voice that drowned the clap of the sail in the wind. "Ten of you go below and free the oarsmen who are yet chained. The rest of you man the sweeps and bend to oars and halyards. Crom's devils, don't you see we've drifted inshore during the fight? Do you want to run aground and be retaken by the Argosseans? Throw these carcasses overboard. Jump to it, you rogues, or I'll notch your hides for you!"

With shouts and laughter and wild singing they leaped to do his commands. The corpses, white and black, were hurled overboard, where triangular fins were already cutting the water.

Conan stood on the poop, frowning down at the black men who watched him expectantly. His heavy brown arms were folded, his black hair, grown long in his wanderings, blew in the wind. A wilder and more barbaric figure never trod the bridge of a ship, and in this ferocious corsair few of the courtiers of Aquilonia would have recognized their king.

"There's food in the hold!" he roared. "Weapons in plenty for you, for this ship carried blades and harness to the Shemites who dwell along the coast. There are enough of us to work ship, aye, and to fight! You rowed in chains for the Argossean dogs: will you row as free men for Amra?"

"Aye!" they roared. "We are thy children! Lead us where you will!"

"Then fall to and clean out that waist," he commanded. "Free men don't labor in such filth. Three of you come with me to break out food from the after-cabin. By Crom, I'll pad out your ribs before this cruise is done!"

Another yell of approbation answered him, as the half-starved blacks scurried to do his bidding. The sail bellied as the wind swept over the waves with renewed force, and the white crests danced along the sweep of the wind. Conan planted his feet to the heave of the deck, breathed deep and spread his mighty arms. King of Aquilonia he might no longer be; king of the blue ocean he was still.

XVI
Black-Walled Khemi

The *Venturer* swept southward like a living thing, her oars pulled now by free and willing hands. She had been transformed from a peaceful trader into a war-galley, insofar as the transformation was possible. Men sat at the benches now with swords at their sides and gilded helmets on their kinky heads. Shields were hung along the rails, and sheafs of spears, bows and arrows adorned the mast. Even the elements seemed to work for Conan now; the broad purple sail bellied to a stiff breeze that held day by day, needing little aid from the oars.

But though Conan kept a man on the masthead day and night, they did not sight a long, low, black galley fleeing southward ahead of them. Day by day the blue waters rolled empty to their view, broken only by fishing-craft which fled like frightened birds before them, at sight of the shields hung along the rail. The season for trading was practically over for the year, and they sighted no other ships.

When the lookout did sight a sail, it was to the north, not the south. Far on the skyline behind them appeared a racing-galley, with full spread of purple sail. The blacks urged Conan to turn and plunder it, but he shook his head. Somewhere south of him a slim black galley was racing toward the ports of Stygia. That night, before darkness shut down, the lookout's last glimpse showed him the racing-galley on the horizon, and at dawn it was still hanging on their tail, afar off, tiny in the distance. Conan wondered if it was following him, though he could think of no logical reason for such a supposition. But he paid little heed. Each day that carried him farther southward filled him with fiercer impatience. Doubts never assailed him. As he believed in the rise and set of the sun he believed that a priest of Set had stolen the Heart of Ahriman. And where would a priest of Set carry it but to Stygia? The blacks sensed his eagerness, and toiled as they had never toiled under the lash, though ignorant of his goal. They anticipated a red career of pillage and plunder and were content. The men of the southern isles knew no other trade; and the Kushites of the crew joined whole-heartedly in the prospect of looting their own people, with the callousness of their race. Blood-ties meant little; a victorious chieftain and personal gain everything.

Soon the character of the coastline changed. No longer they sailed past steep cliffs with blue hills marching behind them. Now the shore was the edge of broad meadowlands which barely rose above the water's edge and swept away and away into the hazy distance. Here were few harbors and fewer ports, but the green plain was dotted with the cities of the Shemites; green sea, lapping the rim of the green plains, and the zikkurats of the cities gleaming whitely in the sun, some small in the distance.

Through the grazing-lands moved the herds of cattle, and squat, broad riders with cylindrical helmets and curled blue-black beards, with bows in their hands. This was the shore of the lands of Shem, where there was no law save as each city-state could enforce its own. Far to the eastward, Conan knew, the meadowlands gave way to desert, where there were no cities and the nomadic tribes roamed unhindered.

Still as they plied southward, past the changeless panorama of city-dotted meadowland, at last the scenery again began to alter. Clumps of tamarind appeared, the palm groves grew denser. The shore-line became more broken, a marching rampart of green fronds and trees, and behind them rose bare, sandy hills. Streams poured into the sea, and along their moist banks vegetation grew thick and of vast variety.

So at last they passed the mouth of a broad river that mingled its flow with the ocean, and saw the great black walls and towers of Khemi rise against the southern horizon.

The river was the Styx, the real border of Stygia. Khemi was Stygia's greatest port, and at that time her most important city. The king dwelt at more ancient Luxur, but in Khemi reigned the priest-craft; though men said the center of their dark religion lay far inland, in a mysterious, deserted city near the bank of the Styx. This river, springing from some nameless source far in the unknown lands south of Stygia, ran northward for a thousand miles before it turned and flowed westward for some hundreds of miles, to empty at last into the ocean.

The *Venturer*, showing no lights, stole past the port in the night, and before dawn discovered her, anchored in a small bay a few miles south of the city. It was surrounded by marsh, a green tangle of mangroves, palms and lianas, swarming with crocodiles and serpents. Discovery was extremely unlikely. Conan knew the place of old; he had hidden there before, in his corsair days.

As they slid silently past the city whose great black bastions rose on the jutting prongs of land which locked the harbor, torches gleamed and smoldered luridly, and to their ears came the low thunder of drums. The port was not crowded with ships, as were the harbors of Argos. The Stygians did not base their glory and power upon ships and fleets. Trading-vessels and war-galleys, indeed, they had, but not in proportion to their inland strength. Many of their craft plied up and down the great river, rather than along the sea-coasts.

The Stygians were an ancient race, a dark, inscrutable people, powerful and merciless. Long ago their rule had stretched far north of the Styx, beyond the meadowlands of Shem, and into the fertile uplands now inhabited by the peoples of Koth and Ophir and Argos. Their borders had marched with those of ancient Acheron. But Acheron had fallen, and the barbaric ancestors of the Hyborians had swept southward in wolfskins and horned helmets, driving the ancient rulers of the land before them. The Stygians had not forgotten.

All day the *Venturer* lay at anchor in the tiny bay, walled in with green branches and tangled vines through which flitted gay-plumed, harsh-voiced birds, and among which glided bright-scaled, silent reptiles. Toward sundown a small boat crept out and down along the shore, seeking and finding that which Conan desired – a Stygian fisherman in his shallow, flat-prowed boat.

They brought him to the deck of the *Venturer* – a tall, dark, rangily built man, ashy with fear of his captors, who were ogres of that coast. He was naked except for his silken breeks, for, like the Hyrkanians, even the commoners and slaves of Stygia wore silk; and in his boat was a wide mantle such as these fishermen flung about their shoulders against the chill of the night.

He fell to his knees before Conan, expecting torture and death.

"Stand on your legs, man, and quit trembling," said the Cimmerian impatiently, who found it difficult to understand abject terror. "You won't be harmed. Tell me but this: has a galley, a black racing-galley returning from Argos, put into Khemi within the last few days?"

"Aye, my lord," answered the fisherman. "Only yesterday at dawn the priest Thutothmes returned from a voyage far to the north. Men say he has been to Messantia."

"What did he bring from Messantia?"

"Alas, my lord, I know not."

"Why did he go to Messantia?" demanded Conan.

"Nay, my lord, I am but a common man. Who am I to know the minds of the priests of Set? I can only speak what I have seen and what I have heard men whisper along the wharves. Men say that news of great import came southward, though of what none knows; and it is well known that the lord Thutothmes put off in his black galley in great haste. Now he is returned, but what he did in Argos, or what cargo he brought back, none knows, not even the seamen who manned his galley. Men say that he has opposed Thoth-Amon, who is the master of all priests of Set, and dwells in Luxur, and that Thutothmes seeks hidden power to overthrow the Great One. But who am I to say? When priests war with one another a common man can but lie on his belly and hope neither treads upon him."

Conan snarled in nervous exasperation at this servile philosophy, and turned to his men. "I'm going alone into Khemi to find this thief Thutothmes. Keep this man prisoner, but see that you do him no hurt. Crom's devils, stop your yowling! Do you think we can sail into the harbor and take the city by storm? I must go alone."

Silencing the clamor of protests, he doffed his own garments and donned the prisoner's silk breeches and sandals, and the band from the man's hair, but scorned the short fisherman's knife. The common men of Stygia were not allowed to wear swords, and the mantle was not voluminous enough to hide the Cimmerian's long blade, but Conan buckled to his hip a Ghanata knife, a weapon borne by the fierce desert men who dwelt to the south of the Stygians, a broad, heavy, slightly curved blade of fine steel, edged like a razor and long enough to dismember a man.

Then, leaving the Stygian guarded by the corsairs, Conan climbed into the fisher's boat.

"Wait for me until dawn," he said. "If I haven't come then, I'll never come, so hasten southward to your own homes."

As he clambered over the rail, they set up a doleful wail at his going, until he thrust his head back into sight to curse them into silence. Then, dropping into the boat, he grasped the oars and sent the tiny craft shooting over the waves more swiftly than its owner had ever propelled it.

XVII

"He Has Slain the Sacred Son of Set!"

The harbor of Khemi lay between two great jutting points of land that ran into the ocean. He rounded the southern point, where the great black castles rose like a man-made hill, and entered the harbor just at dusk, when there was still enough light for the watchers to recognize the fisherman's boat and mantle, but not enough to permit recognition of betraying details. Unchallenged he threaded his way among the great black war galleys lying silent and unlighted at anchor, and drew up to a flight of wide stone steps which mounted up from the water's edge. There he made his boat fast to an iron ring set in the stone, as numerous similar craft were tied. There was nothing strange in a fisherman leaving his boat there. None but a fisherman could find a use for such a craft, and they did not steal from one another.

No one cast him more than a casual glance as he mounted the long steps, unobtrusively avoiding the torches that flared at intervals above the lapping black water. He seemed but an ordinary, empty-handed fisherman, returning after a fruitless day along the coast. If one had observed him closely, it might have seemed that his step was somewhat too springy and sure, his carriage somewhat too erect and confident for a lowly fisherman. But he passed quickly, keeping in the shadows, and the commoners of Stygia were no more given to analysis than were the commoners of the less exotic races.

In build he was not unlike the warrior castes of the Stygians, who were a tall, muscular race. Bronzed by the sun, he was nearly as dark as many of them. His black hair, square-cut and confined by a copper band, increased the resemblance. The characteristics which set him apart from them were the subtle difference in his walk, and his alien features and blue eyes.

But the mantle was a good disguise, and he kept as much in the shadows as possible, turning away his head when a native passed him too closely.

But it was a desperate game, and he knew he could not long keep up the deception. Khemi was not like the sea-ports of the Hyborians, where types of every race swarmed. The only aliens here were negro and Shemite slaves; and he resembled neither even as much as he resembled the Stygians themselves. Strangers were not welcome in the cities of Stygia; tolerated only when they came as ambassadors or licensed traders. But even then the latter were not allowed ashore after dark. And now there were no Hyborian ships in the harbor at all. A strange restlessness ran through the city, a stirring of ancient ambitions, a whispering none could define except those who whispered. This Conan felt rather than knew, his whetted primitive instincts sensing unrest about him.

If he were discovered his fate would be ghastly. They would slay him merely for being a stranger; if he were recognized as Amra, the corsair chief who had swept their coasts with steel and flame – an involuntary shudder twitched Conan's broad shoulders. Human foes he did not fear, nor any death by steel or fire. But this was a black land of sorcery and nameless horror. Set the Old Serpent, men said, banished long ago from the Hyborian races, yet lurked in the shadows of the cryptic temples, and awful and mysterious were the deeds done in the nighted shrines.

He had drawn away from the waterfront streets with their broad steps leading down to the water, and was entering the long shadowy streets of the main part of the city. There was no such scene as was offered by any Hyborian city – no blaze of lamps and cressets, with gay-clad people laughing and strolling along the pavements, and shops and stalls wide open and displaying their wares.

Here the stalls were closed at dusk. The only lights along the streets were torches, flaring smokily at wide intervals. People walking the streets were comparatively few; they went hurriedly and unspeaking, and their numbers decreased with the lateness of the hour. Conan found the scene gloomy and unreal; the silence of the people, their furtive haste, the great black stone walls that rose on each side of the streets. There was a grim massiveness about Stygian architecture that was overpowering and oppressive.

Few lights showed anywhere except in the upper parts of the buildings. Conan knew that most of the people lay on the flat roofs, among the palms of artificial gardens under the stars. There was a murmur of weird music from somewhere. Occasionally a bronze chariot rumbled along the flags, and there was a brief glimpse of a tall, hawk-faced noble, with a silk cloak wrapped about him, and a gold band with a rearing serpent-head emblem confining his black mane; of the ebon, naked charioteer bracing his knotty legs against the straining of the fierce Stygian horses.

But the people who yet traversed the streets on foot were commoners, slaves, tradesmen, harlots, toilers, and they became fewer as he progressed. He was making toward the temple of Set, where he knew he would be likely to find the priest he sought. He believed he would know Thutothmes if he saw him, though his one glance had been in the semi-darkness of the Messantian alley. That the man he had seen there had been the priest he was certain. Only occultists high in the mazes of the hideous Black Ring possessed the power of the black hand that dealt death by its touch; and only such a man would dare defy Thoth-Amon, whom the western world knew only as a figure of terror and myth.

The street broadened, and Conan was aware that he was getting into the part of the city dedicated to the temples. The great structures reared their black bulks against the dim stars, grim, indescribably menacing in the flare of the few torches. And suddenly he heard a low scream from a woman on the other side of the street and somewhat ahead of him – a naked courtezan wearing the tall plumed head-dress of her class. She was shrinking back against the wall, staring across at something he could not yet see. At her cry the few people on the street halted suddenly as if frozen. At the same instant Conan was aware of a sinister slithering ahead of him. Then about the dark corner of the building he was approaching poked a hideous, wedge-shaped head, and after it flowed coil after coil of rippling, darkly glistening trunk.

The Cimmerian recoiled, remembering tales he had heard – serpents were sacred to Set, god of Stygia, who men said was himself a serpent. Monsters such as this were kept in the temples of Set, and when they hungered, were allowed to crawl forth into the streets to take what prey they wished. Their ghastly feasts were considered a sacrifice to the scaly god.

The Stygians within Conan's sight fell to their knees, men and women, and passively awaited their fate. One the great serpent would select, would lap in scaly coils, crush to a red pulp and swallow as a rat-snake swallows a mouse. The others would live. That was the will of the gods.

But it was not Conan's will. The python glided toward him, its attention probably attracted by the fact that he was the only human in sight still standing erect. Gripping his great knife under his mantle, Conan hoped the slimy brute would pass him by. But it halted before him and reared up horrifically in the flickering torchlight, its forked tongue flickering in and out, its cold eyes glittering with the ancient cruelty of the serpent-folk. Its neck arched, but before it could dart, Conan whipped his knife from under his mantle and struck like a flicker of lightning. The broad blade split that wedge-shaped head and sheared deep into the thick neck.

Conan wrenched his knife free and sprang clear as the great body knotted and looped and whipped terrifically in its death throes. In the moment that he stood staring in morbid fascination, the only sound was the thud and swish of the snake's tail against the stones.

Then from the shocked votaries burst a terrible cry: "Blasphemer! He has slain the sacred son of Set! Slay him! Slay! Slay!"

Stones whizzed about him and the crazed Stygians rushed at him, shrieking hysterically, while from all sides others emerged from their houses and took up the cry. With a curse Conan wheeled and darted into the black mouth of an alley. He heard the patter of bare feet on the flags behind him as he ran more by feel than by sight, and the walls resounded to the vengeful yells of the pursuers. Then his left hand found a break in the wall, and he turned sharply into another, narrower alley. On both sides rose sheer black stone walls. High above him he could see a thin line of stars. These giant walls, he knew, were the walls of temples. He heard, behind him, the pack sweep past the dark mouth in full cry. Their shouts grew distant, faded away. They had missed the smaller alley and run straight on in the blackness. He too kept straight ahead, though the thought of encountering another of Set's "sons" in the darkness brought a shudder from him.

Then somewhere ahead of him he caught a moving glow, like that of a crawling glow-worm. He halted, flattened himself against the wall and gripped his knife. He knew what it was: a man approaching with a torch. Now it was so close he could make out the dark hand that gripped it, and the dim oval of a dark face. A few more steps and the man would certainly see him. He sank into a tigerish crouch – the torch halted. A door was briefly etched in the glow, while the torch-bearer fumbled with it. Then it opened, the tall figure vanished through it, and darkness closed again on the alley. There was a sinister suggestion of furtiveness about that slinking figure, entering the alley-door in darkness; a priest, perhaps, returning from some dark errand.

But Conan groped toward the door. If one man came up that alley with a torch, others might come at any time. To retreat the way he had come might mean to run full into the mob from which he was fleeing. At any moment they might return, find the narrower alley and come howling down it. He felt hemmed in by those sheer, unscalable walls, desirous of escape, even if escape meant invading some unknown building.

The heavy bronze door was not locked. It opened under his fingers and he peered through the crack. He was looking into a great square chamber of massive black stone. A torch smoldered in a niche in the wall. The chamber was empty. He glided through the lacquered door and closed it behind him.

His sandaled feet made no sound as he crossed the black marble floor. A teak door stood partly open, and gliding through this, knife in hand, he came out into a great, dim, shadowy place whose lofty ceiling was only a hint of darkness high above him, toward which the black walls swept upward. On all sides black-arched doorways opened into the great still hall. It was lit by curious bronze lamps that gave a dim weird light. On the other side of the great hall a broad black marble stairway, without a railing, marched upward to lose itself in gloom, and above him on all sides dim galleries hung like black stone ledges.

Conan shivered; he was in a temple of some Stygian god, if not Set himself, then someone only less grim. And the shrine did not lack an occupant. In the midst of the great hall stood a black stone altar, massive, somber, without carvings or ornament, and upon it coiled one of the great sacred serpents, its iridescent scales shimmering in the lamplight. It did not move, and Conan remembered stories that the priests kept these creatures drugged part of the time. The Cimmerian took an uncertain step out from the door, then shrank back suddenly, not into the room he had just quitted, but into a velvet-curtained recess. He had heard a soft step somewhere near by.

From one of the black arches emerged a tall, powerful figure in sandals and silken loin-cloth, with a wide mantle trailing from his shoulders. But face and head were hidden by a monstrous mask, a half-bestial, half-human countenance, from the crest of which floated a mass of ostrich plumes.

In certain ceremonies the Stygian priests went masked. Conan hoped the man would not discover him, but some instinct warned the Stygian. He turned abruptly from his destination, which apparently was the stair, and stepped straight to the recess. As he jerked aside the velvet hanging, a hand darted from the shadows, crushed the cry in his throat and jerked him headlong into the alcove, and the knife impaled him.

Conan's next move was the obvious one suggested by logic. He lifted off the grinning mask and drew it over his own head. The fisherman's mantle he flung over the body of the priest, which he concealed behind the hangings, and drew the priestly mantle about his own brawny shoulders. Fate had given him a disguise. All Khemi might well be searching now for the blasphemer who dared defend himself against a sacred snake; but who would dream of looking for him under the mask of a priest?

He strode boldly from the alcove and headed for one of the arched doorways at random; but he had not taken a dozen strides when he wheeled again, all his senses edged for peril.

A band of masked figures filed down the stair, appareled exactly as he was. He hesitated, caught in the open, and stood still, trusting to his disguise, though cold sweat gathered on his forehead and the backs of his hands. No word was spoken. Like phantoms they descended into the great hall and moved past him toward a black arch. The leader carried an ebon staff which supported a grinning white skull, and Conan knew it was one of the ritualistic processions so inexplicable to a foreigner, but which played a strong – and often sinister – part in the Stygian religion. The last figure turned his head slightly toward the motionless Cimmerian, as if expecting him to follow. Not to do what was obviously expected of him would rouse instant suspicion. Conan fell in behind the last man and suited his gait to their measured pace.

They traversed a long, dark, vaulted corridor in which, Conan noticed uneasily, the skull on the staff glowed phosphorescently. He felt a surge of unreasoning, wild animal panic that urged him to rip out his knife and slash right and left at these uncanny figures, to flee madly from this grim, dark temple. But he held himself in check, fighting down the dim monstrous intuitions that rose in the back of his mind and peopled the gloom with shadowy shapes of horror; and presently he barely stifled a sigh of relief as they filed through a great double-valved door which was three times higher than a man, and emerged into the starlight.

Conan wondered if he dared fade into some dark alley; but hesitated, uncertain, and down the long dark street they padded silently, while such folk as they met turned their heads away and fled from them. The procession kept far out from the walls; to turn and bolt into any of the alleys they passed would be too conspicuous. While he mentally fumed and cursed, they came to a low-arched gateway in the southern wall, and through this they filed. Ahead of them and about them lay clusters of low, flat-topped mud houses, and palm-groves, shadowy in the starlight. Now if ever, thought Conan, was his time to escape his silent companions.

But the moment the gate was left behind them those companions were no longer silent. They began to mutter excitedly among themselves. The measured, ritualistic gait was abandoned, the staff with its skull was tucked unceremoniously under the leader's arm, and the whole group broke ranks and hurried onward. And Conan hurried with them. For in the low murmur of speech he had caught a word that galvanized him. The word was: "*Thutothmes!*"

XVIII

"I Am the Woman Who Never Died"

Conan stared with burning interest at his masked companions. One of them was Thutothmes, or else the destination of the band was a rendezvous with the man he sought. And he knew what that destination was, when beyond the palms he glimpsed a black triangular bulk looming against the shadowy sky.

They passed through the belt of huts and groves, and if any man saw them he was careful not to show himself. The huts were dark. Behind them the black towers of Khemi rose gloomily against the stars that were mirrored in the waters of the harbor; ahead of them the desert stretched away in dim darkness; somewhere a jackal yapped. The quick-passing sandals of the silent neophytes made no noise in the sand. They might have been ghosts, moving toward that colossal pyramid that rose out of the murk of the desert. There was no sound over all the sleeping land.

Conan's heart beat quicker as he gazed at the grim black wedge that stood etched against the stars, and his impatience to close with Thutothmes in whatever conflict the meeting might mean was not unmixed with a fear of the unknown. No man could approach one of those somber piles of black stone without apprehension. The very name was a symbol of repellent horror among the northern nations, and legends hinted that the Stygians did not build them; that they were in the land at whatever immeasurably ancient date the dark-skinned people came into the land of the great river.

As they approached the pyramid he glimpsed a dim glow near the base which presently resolved itself into a doorway, on either side of which brooded stone lions with the heads of women, cryptic, inscrutable, nightmares crystallized in stone. The leader of the band made straight for the doorway, in the deep well of which Conan saw a shadowy figure.

The leader paused an instant beside this dim figure, and then vanished into the dark interior, and one by one the others followed. As each masked priest passed through the gloomy portal he was halted briefly by the mysterious guardian and something passed between them, some word or gesture Conan could not make out. Seeing this, the Cimmerian purposely lagged behind, and stooping, pretended to be fumbling with the fastening of his sandal. Not until the last of the masked figures had disappeared did he straighten and approach the portal.

He was uneasily wondering if the guardian of the temple were human, remembering some tales he had heard. But his doubts were set at rest. A dim bronze cresset glowing just within the door lighted a long narrow corridor that ran away into blackness, and a man standing silent in the mouth of it, wrapped in a wide black cloak. No one else was in sight. Obviously the masked priests had disappeared down the corridor.

Over the cloak that was drawn about his lower features, the Stygian's piercing eyes regarded Conan sharply. With his left hand he made a curious gesture. On a venture Conan imitated it. But evidently another gesture was expected; the Stygian's right hand came from under his cloak with a gleam of steel and his murderous stab would have pierced the heart of an ordinary man.

But he was dealing with one whose thews were nerved to the quickness of a jungle cat. Even as the dagger flashed in the dim light, Conan caught the dusky wrist and smashed his clenched right fist against the Stygian's jaw. The man's head went back against the stone wall with a dull crunch that told of a fractured skull.

Standing for an instant above him, Conan listened intently. The cresset burned low, casting vague shadows about the door. Nothing stirred in the blackness beyond, though far away and below him, as it seemed, he caught the faint, muffled note of a gong.

He stooped and dragged the body behind the great bronze door which stood wide, opened inward, and then the Cimmerian went warily but swiftly down the corridor, toward what doom he did not even try to guess.

He had not gone far when he halted, baffled. The corridor split in two branches, and he had no way of knowing which the masked priests had taken. At a venture he chose the left. The floor slanted slightly downward and was worn smooth as by many feet. Here and there a dim cresset cast a faint nightmarish twilight. Conan wondered uneasily for what purpose these colossal piles had been reared, in what forgotten age. This was an ancient, ancient land. No man knew how many ages the black temples of Stygia had looked against the stars.

Narrow black arches opened occasionally to right and left, but he kept to the main corridor, although a conviction that he had taken the wrong branch was growing in him. Even with their start of him, he should have overtaken the priests by this time. He was growing nervous. The silence was like a tangible thing, and yet he had a feeling that he was not alone. More than once, passing a nighted arch he seemed to feel the glare of unseen eyes fixed upon him. He paused, half minded to turn back to where the corridor had first branched. He wheeled abruptly, knife lifted, every nerve tingling.

A girl stood at the mouth of a smaller tunnel, staring fixedly at him. Her ivory skin showed her to be Stygian of some ancient noble family, and like all such women she was tall, lithe, voluptuously figured, her hair a great pile of black foam, among which gleamed a sparkling ruby. But for her velvet sandals and broad jewel-crusted girdle about her supple waist she was quite nude.

"What do you here?" she demanded.

To answer would betray his alien origin. He remained motionless, a grim, somber figure in the hideous mask with the plumes floating over him. His alert gaze sought the shadows behind her and found them empty. But there might be hordes of fighting-men within her call.

She advanced toward him, apparently without apprehension though with suspicion.

"You are not a priest," she said. "You are a fighting-man. Even with that mask that is plain. There is as much difference between you and a priest as there is between a man and a woman. By Set!" she exclaimed, halting suddenly, her eyes flaring wide. "I do not believe you are even a Stygian!"

With a movement too quick for the eye to follow, his hand closed about her round throat, lightly as a caress.

"Not a sound out of you!" he muttered.

Her smooth ivory flesh was cold as marble, yet there was no fear in the wide, dark, marvelous eyes which regarded him.

"Do not fear," she answered calmly. "I will not betray you. But are you mad to come, a stranger and a foreigner, to the forbidden temple of Set?"

"I'm looking for the priest Thutothmes," he answered. "Is he in this temple?"

"Why do you seek him?" she parried.

"He has something of mine which was stolen."

"I will lead you to him," she volunteered, so promptly that his suspicions were instantly roused.

"Don't play with me, girl," he growled.

"I do not play with you. I have no love for Thutothmes."

He hesitated, then made up his mind; after all, he was as much in her power as she was in his.

"Walk beside me," he commanded, shifting his grasp from her throat to her wrist. "But walk with care. If you make a suspicious move – "

She led him down the slanting corridor, down and down, until there were no more cressets, and he groped his way in darkness, aware less by sight than by feel and sense of the woman at his side. Once when he spoke to her, she turned her head toward him and he was startled to see her eyes glowing like golden fire in the dark. Dim doubts and vague monstrous suspicions haunted his mind, but he followed her, through a labyrinthine maze of black corridors that confused even his primitive sense of direction. He mentally cursed himself for a fool, allowing himself to be led into that black abode of mystery; but it was too late to turn back now. Again he felt life and movement in the darkness about him, sensed peril and hunger burning impatiently in the blackness. Unless his ears deceived him he caught a faint sliding noise that ceased and receded at a muttered command from the girl.

She led him at last into a chamber lighted by a curious seven-branched candelabrum in which black candles burned weirdly. He knew they were far below the earth. The chamber was square, with walls and ceiling of polished black marble and furnished after the manner of the ancient Stygians; there was a couch of ebony, covered with black velvet, and on a black stone dais lay a carven mummy-case.

Conan stood waiting expectantly, staring at the various black arches which opened into the chamber. But the girl made no move to go farther. Stretching herself on the couch with feline suppleness, she intertwined her fingers behind her sleek head and regarded him from under long, drooping lashes.

"Well?" he demanded impatiently. "What are you doing? Where's Thutothmes?"

"There is no haste," she answered lazily. "What is an hour – or a day, or a year, or a century, for that matter? Take off your mask. Let me see your features."

With a grunt of annoyance Conan dragged off the bulky headpiece, and the girl nodded as if in approval as she scanned his dark scarred face and blazing eyes.

"There is strength in you – great strength; you could strangle a bullock."

He moved restlessly, his suspicion growing. With his hand on his hilt he peered into the gloomy arches.

"If you've brought me into a trap," he said, "you won't live to enjoy your handiwork. Are you going to get off that couch and do as you promised, or do I have to – "

His voice trailed away. He was staring at the mummy-case, on which the countenance of the occupant was carved in ivory with the startling vividness of a forgotten art. There was a disquieting familiarity about that carven mask, and with something of a shock he realized what it was; there was a startling resemblance between it and the face of the girl lolling on the ebon couch. She might have been the model from which it was carved, but he knew the portrait was at least centuries old. Archaic hieroglyphics were scrawled across the lacquered lid, and, seeking back into his mind for tag-ends of learning, picked up here and there as incidentals of an adventurous life, he spelled them out, and said aloud: "Akivasha!"

"You have heard of Princess Akivasha?" inquired the girl on the couch.

"Who hasn't?" he grunted. The name of that ancient, evil, beautiful princess still lived the world over in song and legend, though ten thousand years had rolled their cycles since the daughter of Tuthamon had reveled in purple feasts amid the black halls of ancient Luxur.

"Her only sin was that she loved life and all the meanings of life," said the Stygian girl. "To win life she courted death. She could not bear to think of growing old and shriveled and worn, and dying at last as hags die. She wooed Darkness like a lover and his gift was life – life that, not being life as mortals know it, can never grow old and fade. She went into the shadows to cheat age and death – "

Conan glared at her with eyes that were suddenly burning slits. And he wheeled and tore the lid from the sarcophagus. It was empty. Behind him the girl was laughing and the sound froze the blood in his veins. He whirled back to her, the short hairs on his neck bristling.

"*You* are Akivasha!" he grated.

She laughed and shook back her burnished locks, spread her arms sensuously.

"I am Akivasha! I am the woman who never died, who never grew old! Who fools say was lifted from the earth by the gods, in the full bloom of her youth and beauty, to queen it for ever in some celestial clime! Nay, it is in the shadows that mortals find immortality! Ten thousand years ago I died to live for ever! Give me your lips, strong man!"

Rising lithely she came to him, rose on tiptoe and flung her arms about his massive neck. Scowling down into her upturned, beautiful countenance he was aware of a fearful fascination and an icy fear.

"Love me!" she whispered, her head thrown back, eyes closed and lips parted. "Give me of your blood to renew my youth and perpetuate my everlasting life! I will make you, too, immortal! I will teach you the wisdom of all the ages, all the secrets that have lasted out the eons in the blackness beneath these dark temples. I will make you king of that shadowy horde which revel among the tombs of the ancients when night veils the desert and bats flit across the moon. I am weary of priests and magicians, and captive girls dragged screaming through the portals of death. I desire a man. Love me, barbarian!"

She pressed her dark head down against his mighty breast, and he felt a sharp pang at the base of his throat. With a curse he tore her away and flung her sprawling across the couch.

"Damned vampire!" Blood was trickling from a tiny wound in his throat.

She reared up on the couch like a serpent poised to strike, all the golden fires of hell blazing in her wide eyes. Her lips drew back, revealing white pointed teeth.

"Fool!" she shrieked. "Do you think to escape me? You will live and die in

darkness! I have brought you far below the temple. You can never find your way out alone. You can never cut your way through those which guard the tunnels. But for my protection the sons of Set would long ago have taken you into their bellies. Fool, I shall yet drink your blood!"

"Keep away from me or I'll slash you asunder," he grunted, his flesh crawling with revulsion. "You may be immortal, but steel will dismember you."

As he backed toward the arch through which he had entered, the light went out suddenly. All the candles were extinguished at once, though he did not know how; for Akivasha had not touched them. But the vampire's laugh rose mockingly behind him, poison-sweet as the viols of hell, and he sweated as he groped in the darkness for the arch in a near-panic. His fingers encountered an opening and he plunged through it. Whether it was the arch through which he had entered he did not know, nor did he very much care. His one thought was to get out of the haunted chamber which had housed that beautiful, hideous, undead fiend for so many centuries.

His wanderings through those black, winding tunnels were a sweating nightmare. Behind him and about him he heard faint slitherings and glidings, and once the echo of that sweet, hellish laughter he had heard in the chamber of Akivasha. He slashed ferociously at sounds and movements he heard or imagined he heard in the darkness near him, and once his sword cut through some yielding tenuous substance that might have been cobwebs. He had a desperate feeling that he was being played with, lured deeper and deeper into ultimate night, before being set upon by demoniac talon and fang.

And through his fear ran the sickening revulsion of his discovery. The legend of Akivasha was so old, and among the evil tales told of her ran a thread of beauty and idealism, of everlasting youth. To so many dreamers and poets and lovers she was not alone the evil princess of Stygian legend, but the symbol of eternal youth and beauty, shining for ever in some far realm of the gods. And this was the hideous reality. This foul perversion was the truth of that everlasting life. Through his physical revulsion ran the sense of a shattered dream of man's idolatry, its glittering gold proved slime and cosmic filth. A wave of futility swept over him, a dim fear of the falseness of all men's dreams and idolatries.

And now he knew that his ears were not playing him tricks. He was being followed, and his pursuers were closing in on him. In the darkness sounded shufflings and slidings that were never made by human feet; no, nor by the feet of any normal animal. The underworld had its bestial life too, perhaps. They were behind him. He turned to face them, though he could see nothing, and slowly backed away. Then the sounds ceased, even before he turned his head and saw, somewhere down the long corridor, a glow of light.

XIX
In the Hall of the Dead

Conan moved cautiously in the direction of the light he had seen, his ear cocked over his shoulder, but there was no further sound of pursuit, though he *felt* the darkness pregnant with sentient life.

The glow was not stationary; it moved, bobbing grotesquely along. Then he saw the source. The tunnel he was traversing crossed another, wider corridor some distance ahead of him. And along this latter tunnel filed a bizarre procession – four tall, gaunt men in black, hooded robes, leaning on staffs. The leader held a torch above his head – a torch that burned with a curious steady glow. Like phantoms they passed across his limited range of vision and vanished, with only a fading glow to tell of their passing. Their appearance was indescribably eldritch. They were not Stygians, not like anything Conan had ever seen. He doubted if they were even humans. They were like black ghosts, stalking ghoulishly along the haunted tunnels.

But his position could be no more desperate than it was. Before the inhuman feet behind him could resume their slithering advance at the fading of the distant illumination, Conan was running down the corridor. He plunged into the other tunnel and saw, far down it, small in the distance, the weird procession moving in the glowing sphere. He stole noiselessly after them, then shrank suddenly back against the wall as he saw them halt and cluster together as if conferring on some matter. They turned as if to retrace their steps, and he slipped into the nearest archway. Groping in the darkness to which he had become so accustomed that he could all but see through it, he discovered that the tunnel did not run straight, but meandered, and he fell back beyond the first turn, so that the light of the strangers should not fall on him as they passed.

But as he stood there, he was aware of a low hum of sound from somewhere behind him, like the murmur of human voices. Moving down the corridor in that direction, he confirmed his first suspicion. Abandoning his original intention of following the ghoulish travelers to whatever destination might be theirs, he set out in the direction of the voices.

Presently he saw a glint of light ahead of him, and turning into the corridor from which it issued, saw a broad arch filled with a dim glow at the other end. On his left a narrow stone stair went upward, and instinctive caution prompted him to turn and mount that stair. The voices he heard were coming from beyond that flame-filled arch.

The sounds fell away beneath him as he climbed, and presently he came out through a low arched door into a vast open space glowing with a weird radiance.

He was standing on a shadowy gallery from which he looked down into a broad dim-lit hall of colossal proportions. It was a hall of the dead, which few ever see but the silent priests of Stygia. Along the black walls rose tier above tier of carven, painted sarcophagi. Each stood in a niche in the dusky stone, and the tiers mounted up and up to be lost in the gloom above. Thousands of carven masks stared impassively down upon the group in the midst of the hall, rendered futile and insignificant by that vast array of the dead.

Of this group ten were priests, and though they had discarded their masks Conan knew they were the priests he had accompanied to the pyramid. They stood before a tall, hawk-faced man beside a black altar on which lay a mummy in rotting swathings. And the altar seemed to stand in the heart of a living fire which pulsed and shimmered, dripping flakes of quivering golden flame on the black stones about it. This dazzling glow emanated from a great red jewel which lay upon the altar, and in the reflection of which the faces of the priests looked ashy and corpse-like. As he looked, Conan felt the pressure of all the weary leagues and the weary nights and days of his long quest, and he trembled with the mad urge to rush among those silent priests, clear his way with mighty blows of naked steel, and grasp the red gem with passion-taut fingers. But he gripped himself with iron control, and crouched down in the shadow of the stone balustrade. A glance showed him that a stair led down into the hall from the gallery, hugging the wall and half hidden in the shadows. He glared into the dimness of the vast place, seeking other priests or votaries, but saw only the group about the altar.

In that great emptiness the voice of the man beside the altar sounded hollow and ghostly:

". . . And so the word came southward. The night wind whispered it, the ravens croaked of it as they flew, and the grim bats told it to the owls and the serpents that lurk in hoary ruins. Werewolf and vampire knew, and the ebon-bodied demons that

prowl by night. The sleeping Night of the World stirred and shook its heavy mane, and there began a throbbing of drums in deep darkness, and the echoes of far weird cries frightened men who walked by dusk. For the Heart of Ahriman had come again into the world to fulfill its cryptic destiny.

"Ask me not how I, Thutothmes of Khemi and the Night, heard the word before Thoth-Amon who calls himself prince of all wizards. There are secrets not meet for such ears even as yours, and Thoth-Amon is not the only lord of the Black Ring.

"I knew, and I went to meet the Heart which came southward. It was like a magnet which drew me, unerringly. From death to death it came, riding on a river of human blood. Blood feeds it, blood draws it. Its power is greatest when there is blood on the hands that grasp it, when it is wrested by slaughter from its holder. Wherever it gleams, blood is spilt and kingdoms totter, and the forces of nature are put in turmoil.

"And here I stand, the master of the Heart, and have summoned you to come secretly, who are faithful to me, to share in the black kingdom that shall be. Tonight you shall witness the breaking of Thoth-Amon's chains which enslave us, and the birth of empire.

"Who am I, even I, Thutothmes, to know what powers lurk and dream in those crimson deeps? It holds secrets forgotten for three thousand years. But I shall learn. These shall tell me!"

He waved his hand toward the silent shapes that lined the hall.

"See how they sleep, staring through their carven masks! Kings, queens, generals, priests, wizards, the dynasties and the nobility of Stygia for ten thousand years! The touch of the Heart will awaken them from their long slumber. Long, long the Heart throbbed and pulsed in ancient Stygia. Here was its home in the centuries before it journeyed to Acheron. The ancients knew its full powers, and they will tell me when by its magic I restore them to life to labor for me.

"I will rouse them, will waken them, will learn their forgotten wisdom, the knowledge locked in those withered skulls. By the lore of the dead we shall enslave the living! Aye, kings and generals and wizards of eld shall be our helpers and our slaves. Who shall stand before us?

"Look! This dried, shriveled thing on the altar was once Thothmekri, a high priest of Set, who died three thousand years ago. He was an adept of the Black Ring. He knew of the Heart. He will tell us of its powers."

Lifting the great jewel, the speaker laid it on the withered breast of the mummy, and lifted his hand as he began an incantation. But the incantation was never finished. With his hand lifted and his lips parted he froze, glaring past his acolytes, and they wheeled to stare in the direction in which he was looking.

Through the black arch of a door four gaunt, black-robed shapes had filed into the great hall. Their faces were dim yellow ovals in the shadow of their hoods.

"Who are you?" ejaculated Thutothmes in a voice as pregnant with danger as the hiss of a cobra. "Are you mad, to invade the holy shrine of Set?"

The tallest of the strangers spoke, and his voice was toneless as a Khitan temple bell.

"We follow Conan of Aquilonia."

"He is not here," answered Thutothmes, shaking back his mantle from his right hand with a curious menacing gesture, like a panther unsheathing his talons.

"You lie. He is in this temple. We tracked him from a corpse behind the bronze door of the outer portal through a maze of corridors. We were following his devious trail when we became aware of this conclave. We go now to take it up again. But first give us the Heart of Ahriman."

"Death is the portion of madmen," murmured Thutothmes, moving nearer the speaker. His priests closed in on cat-like feet, but the strangers did not appear to heed.

"Who can look upon it without desire?" said the Khitan. "In Khitai we have heard of it. It will give us power over the people which cast us out. Glory and wonder dream in its crimson deeps. Give it to us, before we slay you."

A fierce cry rang out as a priest leaped with a flicker of steel. Before he could strike, a scaly staff licked out and touched his breast, and he fell as a dead man falls. In an instant the mummies were staring down on a scene of blood and horror. Curved knives flashed and crimsoned, snaky staffs licked in and out, and whenever they touched a man, that man screamed and died.

At the first stroke Conan had bounded up and was racing down the stairs. He caught only glimpses of that brief, fiendish fight – saw men swaying, locked in battle and streaming blood; saw one Khitan, fairly hacked to pieces, yet still on his feet and dealing death, when Thutothmes smote him on the breast with his open empty hand, and he dropped dead, though naked steel had not been enough to destroy his uncanny vitality.

By the time Conan's hurtling feet left the stair, the fight was all but over. Three of the Khitans were down, slashed and cut to ribbons and disemboweled, but of the Stygians only Thutothmes remained on his feet.

He rushed at the remaining Khitan, his empty hand lifted like a weapon, and that hand was black as that of a negro. But before he could strike, the staff in the tall Khitan's hand licked out, seeming to elongate itself as the yellow man thrust. The point touched the bosom of Thutothmes and he staggered; again and yet again the staff licked out, and Thutothmes reeled and fell dead, his features blotted out in a rush of blackness that made the whole of him the same hue as his enchanted hand.

The Khitan turned toward the jewel that burned on the breast of the mummy, but Conan was before him.

In a tense stillness the two faced each other, amid that shambles, with the carven mummies staring down upon them.

"Far have I followed you, oh king of Aquilonia," said the Khitan calmly. "Down the long river, and over the mountains, across Poitain and Zingara and through the hills of Argos and down the coast. Not easily did we pick up your trail from Tarantia, for the priests of Asura are crafty. We lost it in Zingara, but we found your helmet in the forest below the border hills, where you had fought with the ghouls of the forests. Almost we lost the trail again tonight among these labyrinths."

Conan reflected that he had been fortunate in returning from the vampire's chamber by another route than that by which he had been led to it. Otherwise he would have run full into these yellow fiends instead of sighting them from afar as they smelled out his spoor like human bloodhounds, with whatever uncanny gift was theirs.

The Khitan shook his head slightly, as if reading his mind.

"That is meaningless; the long trail ends here."

"Why have you hounded me?" demanded Conan, poised to move in any direction with the celerity of a hair-trigger.

"It was a debt to pay," answered the Khitan. "To you who are about to die I will not withhold knowledge. We were vassals of the king of Aquilonia, Valerius. Long we served him, but of that service we are free now – my brothers by death, and I by the fulfilment of obligation. I shall return to Aquilonia with two hearts; for myself the Heart of Ahriman; for Valerius the heart of Conan. A kiss of the staff that was cut from the living Tree of Death – "

The staff licked out like the dart of a viper, but the slash of Conan's knife was quicker. The staff fell in writhing halves, there was another flicker of the keen steel like a jet of lightning, and the head of the Khitan rolled to the floor.

Conan wheeled and extended his hand toward the jewel – then he shrank back, his hair bristling, his blood congealing icily.

For no longer a withered brown thing lay on the altar. The jewel shimmered on the full, arching breast of a naked, living man who lay among the moldering bandages. Living? Conan could not decide. The eyes were like dark murky glass under which shone inhuman somber fires.

Slowly the man rose, taking the jewel in his hand. He towered beside the altar, dusky, naked, with a face like a carven image. Mutely he extended his hand toward Conan, with the jewel throbbing like a living heart within it. Conan took it, with an eery sensation of receiving gifts from the hand of the dead. He somehow realized that the proper incantations had not been made – the conjurement had not been completed – life had not been fully restored to this corpse.

"Who are you?" demanded the Cimmerian.

The answer came in a toneless monotone, like the dripping of water from stalactites in subterranean caverns. "I was Thothmekri; I am dead."

"Well, lead me out of this accursed temple, will you?" Conan requested, his flesh crawling.

With measured, mechanical steps the dead man moved toward a black arch. Conan followed him. A glance back showed him once again the vast, shadowy hall with its tiers of sarcophagi, the dead men sprawled about the altar; the head of the Khitan he had slain stared sightless up at the sweeping shadows.

The glow of the jewel illuminated the black tunnels like an ensorceled lamp, dripping golden fire. Once Conan caught a glimpse of ivory flesh in the shadows, believed he saw the vampire that was Akivasha shrinking back from the glow of the jewel; and with her, other less human shapes scuttled or shambled into the darkness.

The dead man strode straight on, looking neither to right nor left, his pace as changeless as the tramp of doom. Cold sweat gathered thick on Conan's flesh. Icy doubts assailed him. How could he know that this terrible figure out of the past was leading him to freedom? But he knew that, left to himself, he could never untangle this bewitched maze of corridors and tunnels. He followed his awful guide through blackness that loomed before and behind them and was filled with skulking shapes of horror and lunacy that cringed from the blinding glow of the Heart.

Then the bronze doorway was before him, and Conan felt the night wind blowing across the desert, and saw the stars, and the starlit desert across which streamed the great black shadow of the pyramid. Thothmekri pointed silently into the desert, and then turned and stalked soundlessly back in the darkness. Conan stared after that silent figure that receded into the blackness on soundless, inexorable feet as one that moves to a known and inevitable doom, or returns to everlasting sleep.

With a curse the Cimmerian leaped from the doorway and fled into the desert as if pursued by demons. He did not look back toward the pyramid, or toward the black towers of Khemi looming dimly across the sands. He headed southward toward the coast, and he ran as a man runs in ungovernable panic. The violent exertion shook his brain free of black cobwebs; the clean desert wind blew the nightmares from his soul and his revulsion changed to a wild tide of exultation before the desert gave way to a tangle of swampy growth through which he saw the black water lying before him, and the *Venturer* at anchor.

He plunged through the undergrowth, hip-deep in the marshes; dived headlong into the deep water, heedless of sharks or crocodiles, and swam to the galley and was clambering up the chain on to the deck, dripping and exultant, before the watch saw him.

"Awake, you dogs!" roared Conan, knocking aside the spear the startled lookout thrust at his breast. "Heave up the anchor! Lay to the doors! Give that fisherman a helmet full of gold and put him ashore! Dawn will soon be breaking, and before sunrise we must be racing for the nearest port of Zingara!"

He whirled about his head the great jewel, which threw off splashes of light that spotted the deck with golden fire.

XXI

Out of the Dust Shall Acheron Arise

Winter had passed from Aquilonia. Leaves sprang out on the limbs of trees, and the fresh grass smiled to the touch of the warm southern breezes. But many a field lay idle and empty, many a charred heap of ashes marked the spot where proud villas or prosperous towns had stood. Wolves prowled openly along the grass-grown highways, and bands of gaunt, masterless men slunk through the forests. Only in Tarantia was feasting and wealth and pageantry.

Valerius ruled like one touched with madness. Even many of the barons who had welcomed his return cried out at last against him. His tax-gatherers crushed rich and poor alike; the wealth of a looted kingdom poured into Tarantia, which became less like the capital of a realm than the garrison of conquerors in a conquered land. Its merchants waxed rich, but it was a precarious prosperity; for none knew when he might be accused of treason on a trumped-up charge, and his property confiscated, himself cast into prison or brought to the bloody block.

Valerius made no attempt to conciliate his subjects. He maintained himself by means of the Nemedian soldiery and by desperate mercenaries. He knew himself to be a puppet of Amalric. He knew that he ruled only on the sufferance of the Nemedian. He knew that he could never hope to unite Aquilonia under his rule and cast off the yoke of his masters, for the outland provinces would resist him to the last drop of blood. And for that matter the Nemedians would cast him from his throne if he made any attempt to consolidate his kingdom. He was caught in his own vise. The gall of defeated pride corroded his soul, and he threw himself into a reign of debauchery, as one who lives from day to day, without thought or care for tomorrow.

Yet there was subtlety in his madness, so deep that not even Amalric guessed it. Perhaps the wild, chaotic years of wandering as an exile had bred in him a bitterness beyond common conception. Perhaps his loathing of his present position increased this bitterness to a kind of madness. At any event he lived with one desire: to cause the ruin of all who associated with him.

He knew that his rule would be over the instant he had served Amalric's purpose; he knew, too, that so long as he continued to oppress his native kingdom the Nemedian would suffer him to reign, for Amalric wished to crush Aquilonia into ultimate submission, to destroy its last shred of independence, and then at last to seize it himself, rebuild it after his own fashion with his vast wealth, and use its men and natural resources to wrest the crown of Nemedia from Tarascus. For the throne of an emperor was Amalric's ultimate ambition, and Valerius knew it. Valerius did not know whether Tarascus suspected this, but he knew that the king of Nemedia approved of his ruthless course. Tarascus hated Aquilonia, with a hate born of old wars. He desired only the destruction of the western kingdom.

And Valerius intended to ruin the country so utterly that not even Amalric's wealth could ever rebuild it. He hated the baron quite as much as he hated the Aquilonians, and hoped only to live to see the day when Aquilonia lay in utter ruin, and Tarascus and Amalric were locked in hopeless civil war that would as completely destroy Nemedia.

He believed that the conquest of the still defiant provinces of Gunderland and Poitain and the Bossonian marches would mark his end as king. He would then have served Amalric's purpose, and could be discarded. So he delayed the conquest of these provinces, confining his activities to objectless raids and forays, meeting Amalric's urges for action with all sorts of plausible objections and postponements.

His life was a series of feasts and wild debauches. He filled his palace with the fairest girls of the kingdom, willing or unwilling. He blasphemed the gods and sprawled drunken on the floor of the banquet hall wearing the golden crown, and staining his royal purple robes with the wine he spilled. In gusts of blood-lust he festooned the gallows in the market square with dangling corpses, glutted the axes of the headsmen and sent his Nemedian horsemen thundering through the land pillaging and burning. Driven to madness, the land was in a constant upheaval of frantic revolt, savagely suppressed. Valerius plundered and raped and looted and destroyed until even Amalric protested, warning him that he would beggar the kingdom beyond repair, not knowing that such was his fixed determination.

But while in both Aquilonia and Nemedia men talked of the madness of the king, in Nemedia men talked much of Xaltotun, the masked one. Yet few saw him on the streets of Belverus. Men said he spent much time in the hills, in curious conclaves with surviving remnants of an old race: dark, silent folk who claimed descent from an ancient kingdom. Men whispered of drums beating far up in the dreaming hills, of fires glowing in the darkness, and strange chantings borne on the winds, chantings and rituals forgotten centuries ago except as meaningless formulas mumbled beside mountain hearths in villages whose inhabitants differed strangely from the people of the valleys.

The reason for these conclaves none knew, unless it was Orastes, who frequently accompanied the Pythonian, and on whose countenance a haggard shadow was growing.

But in the full flood of spring a sudden whisper passed over the sinking kingdom that woke the land to eager life. It came like a murmurous wind drifting up from the south, waking men sunk in the apathy of despair. Yet how it first came none could truly say. Some spoke of a strange, grim old woman who came down from the mountains with her hair flowing in the wind, and a great gray wolf following her like a dog. Others whispered of the priests of Asura who stole like furtive phantoms from Gunderland to the marches of Poitain, and to the forest villages of the Bossonians.

However the word came, revolt ran like a flame along the borders. Outlying Nemedian garrisons were stormed and put to the sword, foraging parties were cut to pieces; the west was up in arms, and there was a different air about the rising, a fierce resolution and inspired wrath rather than the frantic despair that had motivated the preceding revolts. It was not only the common people; barons were fortifying their castles and hurling defiance at the governors of the provinces. Bands of Bossonians were seen moving along the edges of the marches: stocky, resolute men in brigandines and steel caps, with longbows in their hands. From the inert stagnation of dissolution and ruin the realm was suddenly alive, vibrant and dangerous. So Amalric sent in haste for Tarascus, who came with an army.

In the royal palace in Tarantia the two kings and Amalric discussed the rising. They had not sent for Xaltotun, immersed in his cryptic studies in the Nemedian hills. Not since that bloody day in the valley of the Valkia had they called upon him for aid of his magic, and he had drawn apart, communing but little with them, apparently indifferent to their intrigues.

Nor had they sent for Orastes, but he came, and he was white as spume blown before the storm. He stood in the gold-domed chamber where the kings held conclave and they beheld in amazement his haggard stare, the fear they had never guessed the mind of Orastes could hold.

"You are weary, Orastes," said Amalric. "Sit upon this divan and I will have a slave fetch you wine. You have ridden hard – "

Orastes waved aside the invitation.

"I have killed three horses on the road from Belverus. I cannot drink wine, I cannot rest, until I have said what I have to say."

He paced back and forth as if some inner fire would not let him stand motionless, and halting before his wondering companions:

"When we employed the Heart of Ahriman to bring a dead man back to life," Orastes said abruptly, "we did not weigh the consequences of tampering in the black dust of the past. The fault is mine, and the sin. We thought only of our ambitions, forgetting what ambitions this man might himself have. And we have loosed a demon upon the earth, a fiend inexplicable to common humanity. I have plumbed deep in evil, but there is a limit to which I, or any man of my race and age, can go. My ancestors were clean men, without any demoniacal taint; it is only I who have sunk into the pits, and I can sin only to the extent of my personal individuality. But behind Xaltotun lie a thousand centuries of black magic and diabolism, an ancient tradition of evil. He is beyond our conception not only because he is a wizard himself, but also because he is the son of a race of wizards.

"I have seen things that have blasted my soul. In the heart of the slumbering hills I have watched Xaltotun commune with the souls of the damned, and invoke the ancient demons of forgotten Acheron. I have seen the accursed descendants of that accursed empire worship him and hail him as their arch-priest. I have seen what he plots – and I tell you it is no less than the restoration of the ancient, black, grisly kingdom of Acheron!"

"What do you mean?" demanded Amalric. "Acheron is dust. There are not enough survivals to make an empire. Not even Xaltotun can reshape the dust of three thousand years."

"You know little of his black powers," answered Orastes grimly. "I have seen the very hills take on an alien and ancient aspect under the spell of his incantations. I have glimpsed, like shadows behind the realities, the dim shapes and outlines of valleys, forests, mountains and lakes that are not as they are today, but as they were in that dim yesterday – have even sensed, rather than glimpsed, the purple towers of forgotten Python shimmering like figures of mist in the dusk.

"And in the last conclave to which I accompanied him, understanding of his sorcery came to me at last, while the drums beat and the beast-like worshippers howled with their heads in the dust. I tell you he would restore Acheron by his magic, by the sorcery of a gigantic blood-sacrifice such as the world has never seen. He would enslave the world, and with a deluge of blood *wash away the present and restore the past!*"

"You are mad!" exclaimed Tarascus.

"Mad?" Orastes turned a haggard stare upon him. "Can any man see what I have seen and remain wholly sane? Yet I speak the truth. He plots the return of Acheron, with its towers and wizards and kings and horrors, as it was in the long ago. The descendants of Acheron will serve him as a nucleus upon which to build, but it is the blood and the bodies of the people of the world today that will furnish the mortar and the stones for the rebuilding. I cannot tell you how. My own brain reels when I try to understand. *But I have seen!* Acheron will be Acheron again, and even the hills, the forests and the rivers will resume their ancient aspect. Why not? If I, with my tiny store of knowledge, could bring to life a man dead three thousand years, why cannot the greatest wizard of the world bring back to life a kingdom dead three thousand years? Out of the dust shall Acheron arise at his bidding."

"How can we thwart him?" asked Tarascus, impressed.

"There is but one way," answered Orastes. "We must steal the Heart of Ahriman!"

"But I – " began Tarascus involuntarily, then closed his mouth quickly.

None had noticed him, and Orastes was continuing.

"It is a power that can be used against him. With it in my hands I might defy him. But how shall we steal it? He has it hidden in some secret place, from which not even a Zamorian thief might filch it. I cannot learn its hiding-place. If he would only sleep again the sleep of the black lotus – but the last time he slept thus was after the battle of the Valkia, when he was weary because of the great magic he had performed, and – "

The door was locked and bolted, but it swung silently open and Xaltotun stood before them, calm, tranquil, stroking his patriarchal beard; but the lambent lights of hell flickered in his eyes.

"I have taught you too much," he said calmly, pointing a finger like an index of doom at Orastes. And before any could move, he had cast a handful of dust on the floor near the feet of the priest, who stood like a man turned to marble. It flamed, smoldered; a blue serpentine of smoke rose and swayed upward about Orastes in a slender spiral. And when it had risen above his shoulders it curled about his neck with a whipping suddenness like the stroke of a snake. Orastes' scream was choked to a gurgle. His hands flew to his neck, his eyes were distended, his tongue protruded. The smoke was like a blue rope about his neck; then it faded and was gone, and Orastes slumped to the floor a dead man.

Xaltotun smote his hands together and two men entered, men often observed accompanying him – small, repulsively dark, with red, oblique eyes and pointed, rat-like teeth. They did not speak. Lifting the corpse, they bore it away.

Dismissing the matter with a wave of his hand, Xaltotun seated himself at the ivory table about which sat the pale kings.

"Why are you in conclave?" he demanded.

"The Aquilonians have risen in the west," answered Amalric, recovering from the grisly jolt the death of Orastes had given him. "The fools believe that Conan is alive, and coming at the head of a Poitanian army to reclaim his kingdom. If he had reappeared immediately after Valkia, or if a rumor had been circulated that he lived, the central provinces would not have risen under him, they feared your powers so. But they have become so desperate under Valerius's misrule that they are ready to follow any man who can unite them against us, and prefer sudden death to torture and continual misery.

"Of course the tale has lingered stubbornly in the land that Conan was not really slain at Valkia, but not until recently have the masses accepted it. But Pallantides is back from exile in Ophir, swearing that the king was ill in his tent that day, and that a man-at-arms wore his harness, and a squire who but recently recovered from the stroke of a mace received at Valkia confirms his tale – or pretends to.

"An old woman with a pet wolf has wandered up and down the land, proclaiming that King Conan yet lives, and will return some day to reclaim the crown. And of late the cursed priests of Asura sing the same song. They claim that word has come to them by some mysterious means that Conan is returning to reconquer his domain. I cannot catch either her or them. This is, of course, a trick of Trocero's. My spies tell me there is indisputable evidence that the Poitanians are gathering to invade Aquilonia. I believe that Trocero will bring forward some pretender who he will claim is King Conan."

Tarascus laughed, but there was no conviction in his laughter. He surreptitiously felt of a scar beneath his jupon, and remembered ravens that cawed on the trail of a fugitive; remembered the body of his squire, Arideus, brought back from the border mountains horribly mangled, by a great gray wolf, his terrified soldiers said. But he also remembered a red jewel stolen from a golden chest while a wizard slept, and he said nothing.

And Valerius remembered a dying nobleman who gasped out a tale of fear, and he remembered four Khitans who disappeared into the mazes of the south and never returned. But he held his tongue, for hatred and suspicion of his allies ate at him like a worm, and he desired nothing so much as to see both rebels and Nemedians go down locked in the death grip.

But Amalric exclaimed: "It is absurd to dream that Conan lives!"

For answer Xaltotun cast a roll of parchment on the table.

Amalric caught it up, glared at it. From his lips burst a furious, incoherent cry. He read:

To Xaltotun, grand fakir of Nemedia: Dog of Acheron, I am returning to my kingdom, and I mean to hang your hide on a bramble.

CONAN.

"A forgery!" exclaimed Amalric.

Xaltotun shook his head.

"It is genuine. I have compared it with the signature on the royal documents on record in the libraries of the court. None could imitate that bold scrawl."

"Then if Conan lives," muttered Amalric, "this uprising will not be like the others, for he is the only man living who can unite the Aquilonians. But," he protested, "this is not like Conan. Why should he put us on our guard with his boasting? One would think that he would strike without warning, after the fashion of the barbarians."

"We are already warned," pointed out Xaltotun. "Our spies have told us of preparations for war in Poitain. He could not cross the mountains without our knowledge; so he sends me his defiance in characteristic manner."

"Why to you?" demanded Valerius. "Why not to me, or to Tarascus?"

Xaltotun turned his inscrutable gaze upon the king.

"Conan is wiser than you," he said at last. "He already knows what you kings have yet to learn – that it is not Tarascus, nor Valerius, no, nor Amalric, but Xaltotun who is the real master of the western nations."

They did not reply; they sat staring at him, assailed by a numbing realization of the truth of his assertion.

"There is no road for me but the imperial highway," said Xaltotun. "But first we must crush Conan. I do not know how he escaped me at Belverus, for knowledge of what happened while I lay in the slumber of the black lotus is denied me. But he is in the south, gathering an army. It is his last, desperate blow, made possible only by the desperation of the people who have suffered under Valerius. Let them rise; I hold them all in the palm of my hand. We will wait until he moves against us, and then we will crush him once and for all.

"Then we shall crush Poitain and Gunderland and the stupid Bossonians. After them Ophir, Argos, Zingara, Koth – all the nations of the world we shall weld into one vast empire. You shall rule as my satraps, and as my captains shall be greater than kings are now. I am unconquerable, for the Heart of Ahriman is hidden where no man can ever wield it against me again."

Tarascus averted his gaze, lest Xaltotun read his thoughts. He knew the wizard had not looked into the golden chest with its carven serpents that had seemed to sleep, since he laid the Heart therein. Strange as it seemed, Xaltotun did not know that the Heart had been stolen; the strange jewel was beyond or outside the ring of his dark wisdom; his uncanny talents did not warn him that the chest was empty. Tarascus did not believe that Xaltotun knew the full extent of Orastes' revelations, for the Pythonian had not mentioned the restoration of Acheron, but only the building of a new, earthly empire. Tarascus did not believe that Xaltotun was yet quite sure of his power; if they needed his aid in their ambitions, no less he needed theirs. Magic depended, to a certain extent after all, on sword strokes and lance thrusts. The king read meaning in Amalric's furtive glance; let the wizard use his arts to help them defeat their most dangerous enemy. Time enough then to turn against him. There might yet be a way to cheat this dark power they had raised.

XXII
Drums of Peril

Confirmation of the war came when the army of Poitain, ten thousand strong, marched through the southern passes with waving banners and shimmer of steel. And at their head, the spies swore, rode a giant figure in black armor, with the royal lion of Aquilonia worked in gold upon the breast of his rich silken surcoat. Conan lived! The king lived! There was no doubt of it in men's minds now, whether friend or foe.

With the news of the invasion from the south there also came word, brought by hard-riding couriers, that a host of Gundermen was moving southward, reinforced by the barons of the northwest and the northern Bossonians. Tarascus marched with thirty-one thousand men to Galparan, on the river Shirki, which the Gundermen must cross to strike at the towns still held by the Nemedians. The Shirki was a swift, turbulent river rushing southwestward through rocky gorges and canyons, and there were few places where an army could cross at that time of the year, when the stream was almost bank-full with the melting of the snows. All the country east of the Shirki was in the hands of the Nemedians, and it was logical to assume that the Gundermen would attempt to cross either at Galparan, or at Tanasul, which lay to the south of Galparan. Reinforcements were daily expected from Nemedia, until word came that the king of Ophir was making hostile demonstrations on Nemedia's southern border, and to spare any more troops would be to expose Nemedia to the risk of an invasion from the south.

Amalric and Valerius moved out from Tarantia with twenty-five thousand men, leaving as large a garrison as they dared to discourage revolts in the cities during their absence. They wished to meet and crush Conan before he could be joined by the rebellious forces of the kingdom.

The king and his Poitanians had crossed the mountains, but there had been no actual clash of arms, no attack on towns or fortresses. Conan had appeared and disappeared. Apparently he had turned westward through the wild, thinly settled hill country, and entered the Bossonian marches, gathering recruits as he went. Amalric and Valerius with their host, Nemedians, Aquilonian renegades, and ferocious mercenaries, moved through the land in baffled wrath, looking for a foe which did not appear.

Amalric found it impossible to obtain more than vague general tidings about Conan's movements. Scouting-parties had a way of riding out and never returning, and it was not uncommon to find a spy crucified to an oak. The countryside was up and striking as peasants and country-folk strike – savagely, murderously and secretly. All that Amalric knew certainly was that a large force of Gundermen and northern Bossonians was somewhere to the north of him, beyond the Shirki, and that Conan with a smaller force of Poitanians and southern Bossonians was somewhere to the southwest of him.

He began to grow fearful that if he and Valerius advanced farther into the wild country, Conan might elude them entirely, march around them and invade the central provinces behind them. Amalric fell back from the Shirki valley and camped in a plain a day's ride from Tanasul. There he waited. Tarascus maintained his position at Galparan, for he feared that Conan's maneuvers were intended to draw him southward, and so let the Gundermen into the kingdom at the northern crossing.

To Amalric's camp came Xaltotun in his chariot drawn by the uncanny horses that never tired, and he entered Amalric's tent where the baron conferred with Valerius over a map spread on an ivory camp table.

This map Xaltotun crumpled and flung aside.

"What your scouts cannot learn for you," quoth he, "my spies tell me, though their information is strangely blurred and imperfect, as if unseen forces were working against me.

"Conan is advancing along the Shirki river with ten thousand Poitanians, three thousand southern Bossonians, and barons of the west and south with their retainers to the number of five thousand. An army of thirty thousand Gundermen and northern Bossonians is pushing southward to join him. They have established contact by means of secret communications used by the cursed priests of Asura, who seem to be opposing me, and whom I will feed to a serpent when the battle is over – I swear it by Set!

"Both armies are headed for the crossing at Tanasul, but I do not believe that the Gundermen will cross the river. I believe that Conan will cross, instead, and join them."

"Why should Conan cross the river?" demanded Amalric.

"Because it is to his advantage to delay the battle. The longer he waits, the stronger he will become, the more precarious our position. The hills on the other side of the river swarm with people passionately loyal to his cause – broken men, refugees, fugitives from Valerius's cruelty. From all over the kingdom men are hurrying to join his army, singly and by companies. Daily, parties from our armies are ambushed and cut to pieces by the country-folk. Revolt grows in the central provinces, and will soon burst into open rebellion. The garrisons we left there are not sufficient, and we can hope for no reinforcements from Nemedia for the time being. I see the hand of Pallantides in this brawling on the Ophirean frontier. He has kin in Ophir.

"If we do not catch and crush Conan quickly the provinces will be in blaze of revolt behind us. We shall have to fall back to Tarantia to defend what we have taken; and we may have to fight our way through a country in rebellion, with Conan's whole force at our heels, and then stand siege in the city itself, with enemies within as well as without. No, we cannot wait. We must crush Conan before his army grows too great, before the central provinces rise. With his head hanging above the gate at Tarantia you will see how quickly the rebellion will fall apart."

"Why do you not put a spell on his army to slay them all?" asked Valerius, half in mockery.

Xaltotun stared at the Aquilonian as if he read the full extent of the mocking madness that lurked in those wayward eyes.

"Do not worry," he said at last. "My arts shall crush Conan finally like a lizard under the heel. But even sorcery is aided by pikes and swords."

"If he crosses the river and takes up his position in the Goralian hills he may be hard to dislodge," said Amalric. "But if we catch him in the valley on this side of the river we can wipe him out. How far is Conan from Tanasul?"

"At the rate he is marching he should reach the crossing sometime tomorrow night. His men are rugged and he is pushing them hard. He should arrive there at least a day before the Gundermen."

"Good!" Amalric smote the table with his clenched fist. "I can reach Tanasul before he can. I'll send a rider to Tarascus, bidding him follow me to Tanasul. By the time he arrives I will have cut Conan off from the crossing and destroyed him. Then our combined force can cross the river and deal with the Gundermen."

Xaltotun shook his head impatiently.

"A good enough plan if you were dealing with anyone but Conan. But your twenty-five thousand men are not enough to destroy his eighteen thousand before the Gundermen come up. They will fight with the desperation of wounded panthers. And suppose the Gundermen come up while the hosts are locked in battle? You will be caught between two fires and destroyed before Tarascus can arrive. He will reach Tanasul too late to aid you."

"What then?" demanded Amalric.

"Move with your whole strength against Conan," answered the man from Acheron. "Send a rider bidding Tarascus join us here. We will wait his coming. Then we will march together to Tanasul."

"But while we wait," protested Amalric, "Conan will cross the river and join the Gundermen."

"Conan will not cross the river," answered Xaltotun.

Amalric's head jerked up and he stared into the cryptic dark eyes.

"What do you mean?"

"Suppose there were torrential rains far to the north, at the head of the Shirki? Suppose the river came down in such flood as to render the crossing at Tanasul impassable? Could we not then bring up our entire force at our leisure, catch Conan on this side of the river and crush him, and then, when the flood subsided, which I think it would do the next day, could we not cross the river and destroy the Gundermen? Thus we could use our full strength against each of these smaller forces in turn."

Valerius laughed as he always laughed at the prospect of the ruin of either friend or foe, and drew a restless hand jerkily through his unruly yellow locks. Amalric stared at the man from Acheron with mingled fear and admiration.

"If we caught Conan in Shirki valley with the hill ridges to his right and the river in flood to his left," he admitted, "with our whole force we could annihilate him. Do you think – are you sure – do you believe such rains will fall?"

"I go to my tent," answered Xaltotun, rising. "Necromancy is not accomplished by the waving of a wand. Send a rider to Tarascus. And let none approach my tent."

That last command was unnecessary. No man in that host could have been bribed to approach that mysterious black silken pavilion, the door-flaps of which were always closely drawn. None but Xaltotun ever entered it, yet voices were often heard issuing from it; its walls billowed sometimes without a wind, and weird music came from it. Sometimes, deep in midnight, its silken walls were lit red by flames flickering within, limning misshapen silhouettes that passed to and fro.

Lying in his own tent that night, Amalric heard the steady rumble of a drum in Xaltotun's tent; through the darkness it boomed steadily, and occasionally the Nemedian could have sworn that a deep, croaking voice mingled with the pulse of the drum. And he shuddered, for he knew that voice was not the voice of Xaltotun. The drum rustled and muttered on like deep thunder, heard afar off, and before dawn Amalric, glancing from his tent, caught the red flicker of lightning afar on the northern horizon. In all other parts of the sky the great stars blazed whitely. But the distant lightning flickered incessantly, like the crimson glint of firelight on a tiny, turning blade.

At sunset of the next day Tarascus came up with his host, dusty and weary from hard marching, the footmen straggling hours behind the horsemen. They camped in the plain near Amalric's camp, and at dawn the combined army moved westward.

Ahead of him roved a swarm of scouts, and Amalric waited impatiently for them to return and tell of the Poitanians trapped beside a furious flood. But when the scouts met the column it was with the news that Conan had crossed the river!

"What?" exclaimed Amalric. "Did he cross before the flood?"

"There was no flood," answered the scouts, puzzled. "Late last night he came up to Tanasul and flung his army across."

"No flood?" exclaimed Xaltotun, taken aback for the first time in Amalric's knowledge. "Impossible! There were mighty rains upon the headwaters of the Shirki last night and the night before that!"

"That may be, your lordship," answered the scout. "It is true the water was muddy, and the people of Tanasul said that the river rose perhaps a foot yesterday; but that was not enough to prevent Conan's crossing."

Xaltotun's sorcery had failed! The thought hammered in Amalric's brain. His horror of this strange man out of the past had grown steadily since that night in Belverus when he had seen a brown, shriveled mummy swell and grow into a living man. And the death of Orastes had changed lurking horror into active fear. In his heart was a grisly conviction that the man – or devil – was invincible. Yet now he had undeniable proof of his failure.

Yet even the greatest of necromancers might fail occasionally, thought the baron. At any rate, he dared not oppose the man from Acheron yet. Orastes was dead, writhing in Mitra only knew what nameless hell, and Amalric knew his sword would scarcely prevail where the black wisdom of the renegade priest had failed. What grisly abomination Xaltotun plotted lay in the unpredictable future. Conan and his host were a present menace against which Xaltotun's wizardry might well be needed before the play was all played.

They came to Tanasul, a small fortified village at the spot where a reef of rocks made a natural bridge across the river, passable always except in times of greatest flood. Scouts brought in the news that Conan had taken up his position in the Goralian hills, which began to rise a few miles beyond the river. And just before sundown the Gundermen had arrived in his camp.

Amalric looked at Xaltotun, inscrutable and alien in the light of the flaring torches. Night had fallen.

"What now? Your magic has failed. Conan confronts us with an army nearly as strong as our own, and he has the advantage of position. We have a choice of two evils: to camp here and await his attack, or to fall back toward Tarantia and await reinforcements."

"We are ruined if we wait," answered Xaltotun. "Cross the river and camp on the plain. We will attack at dawn."

"But his position is too strong!" exclaimed Amalric.

"Fool!" A gust of passion broke the veneer of the wizard's calm. "Have you forgotten Valkia? Because some obscure elemental principle prevented the flood do you deem me helpless? I had intended that your spears should exterminate our enemies; but do not fear: it is my arts shall crush their host. Conan is in a trap. He will never see another sun set. Cross the river!"

They crossed by the flare of torches. The hoofs of the horses clinked on the rocky bridge, splashed through the shallows. The glint of the torches on shields and breast-plates was reflected redly in the black water. The rock bridge was broad on which they crossed, but even so it was past midnight before the host was camped in the plain beyond. Above them they could see fires winking redly in the distance. Conan had turned at bay in the Goralian hills, which had more than once before served as the last stand of an Aquilonian king.

Amalric left his pavilion and strode restlessly through the camp. A weird glow flickered in Xaltotun's tent, and from time to time a demoniacal cry slashed the silence, and there was a low sinister muttering of a drum that rustled rather than rumbled.

Amalric, his instincts whetted by the night and the circumstances, felt that Xaltotun was opposed by more than physical force. Doubts of the wizard's power assailed him. He glanced at the fires high above him, and his face set in grim lines. He and his army were deep in the midst of a hostile country. Up there among those hills lurked thousands of wolfish figures out of whose hearts and souls all emotion and hope had been scourged except a frenzied hate for their conquerors, a mad lust for vengeance. Defeat meant annihilation, retreat through a land swarming with blood-mad enemies. And on the morrow he must hurl his host against the grimmest fighter in the western nations, and his desperate horde. If Xaltotun failed them now –

Half a dozen men-at-arms strode out of the shadows. The firelight glinted on their breast-plates and helmet crests. Among them they half led, half dragged a gaunt figure in tattered rags.

Saluting, they spoke: "My lord, this man came to the outposts and said he desired word with King Valerius. He is an Aquilonian."

He looked more like a wolf – a wolf the traps had scarred. Old sores that only fetters make showed on his wrists and ankles. A great brand, the mark of hot iron, disfigured his face. His eyes glared through the tangle of his matted hair as he half crouched before the baron.

"Who are you, you filthy dog?" demanded the Nemedian.

"Call me Tiberias," answered the man, and his teeth clicked in an involuntary spasm. "I have come to tell you how to trap Conan."

"A traitor, eh?" rumbled the baron.

"Men say you have gold," mouthed the man, shivering under his rags. "Give some to me! Give me gold and I will show you how to defeat the king!" His eyes glazed widely, his outstretched, upturned hands were spread like quivering claws.

Amalric shrugged his shoulders in distaste. But no tool was too base for his use.

"If you speak the truth you shall have more gold than you can carry," he said. "If you are a liar and a spy I will have you crucified head-down. Bring him along."

In the tent of Valerius, the baron pointed to the man who crouched shivering before them, huddling his rags about him.

"He says he knows a way to aid us on the morrow. We will need aid, if Xaltotun's plan is no better than it has proved so far. Speak on, dog."

The man's body writhed in strange convulsions. Words came in a stumbling rush:

"Conan camps at the head of the Valley of Lions. It is shaped like a fan, with steep hills on either side. If you attack him tomorrow you will have to march straight up the valley. You cannot climb the hills on either side. But if King Valerius will deign to accept my service, I will guide him through the hills and show him how he can come upon King Conan from behind. But if it is to be done at all, we must start soon. It is many hours' riding, for one must go miles to the west, then miles to the north, then turn eastward and so come into the Valley of Lions from behind, as the Gundermen came."

Amalric hesitated, tugging his chin. In these chaotic times it was not rare to find men willing to sell their souls for a few gold pieces.

"If you lead me astray you will die," said Valerius. "You are aware of that, are you not?"

The man shivered, but his wide eyes did not waver.

"If I betray you, slay me!"

"Conan will not dare divide his force," mused Amalric. "He will need all his men to repel our attack. He cannot spare any to lay ambushes in the hills. Besides, this fellow knows his hide depends on his leading you as he promised. Would a dog like him sacrifice himself? Nonsense! No, Valerius, I believe the man is honest."

"Or a greater thief than most, for he would sell his liberator," laughed Valerius. "Very well. I will follow the dog. How many men can you spare me?"

"Five thousand should be enough," answered Amalric. "A surprize attack on their rear will throw them into confusion, and that will be enough. I shall expect your attack about noon."

"You will know when I strike," answered Valerius.

As Amalric returned to his pavilion he noted with gratification that Xaltotun was still in his tent, to judge from the blood-freezing cries that shuddered forth into the night air from time to time. When presently he heard the clink of steel and the jingle of bridles in the outer darkness, he smiled grimly. Valerius had about served his purpose. The baron knew that Conan was like a wounded lion that rends and tears even in his death-throes. When Valerius struck from the rear, the desperate strokes of the Cimmerian might well wipe his rival out of existence before he himself succumbed. So much the better. Amalric felt he could well dispense with Valerius, once he had paved the way for a Nemedian victory.

The five thousand horsemen who accompanied Valerius were hard-bitten Aquilonian renegades for the most part. In the still starlight they moved out of the sleeping camp, following the westward trend of the great black masses that rose against the stars ahead of them. Valerius rode at their head, and beside him rode Tiberias, a leather thong about his wrist gripped by a man-at-arms who rode on the other side of him. Others kept close behind with drawn swords.

"Play us false and you die instantly," Valerius pointed out. "I do not know every sheep-path in these hills, but I know enough about the general configuration of the country to know the directions we must take to come in behind the Valley of Lions. See that you do not lead us astray."

The man ducked his head and his teeth chattered as he volubly assured his captor of his loyalty, staring up stupidly at the banner that floated over him, the golden serpent of the old dynasty.

Skirting the extremities of the hills that locked the Valley of Lions, they swung wide to the west. An hour's ride and they turned north, forging through wild and rugged hills, following dim trails and tortuous paths. Sunrise found them some miles northwest of Conan's position, and here the guide turned eastward and led them through a maze of labyrinths and crags. Valerius nodded, judging their position by various peaks thrusting up above the others. He had kept his bearings in a general way, and he knew they were still headed in the right direction.

But now, without warning, a gray fleecy mass came billowing down from the north, veiling the slopes, spreading out through the valleys. It blotted out the sun; the world became a blind gray void in which visibility was limited to a matter of yards. Advance became a stumbling, groping muddle. Valerius cursed. He could no longer see the peaks that had served him as guide-posts. He must depend wholly upon the traitorous guide. The golden serpent drooped in the windless air.

Presently Tiberias seemed himself confused; he halted, stared about uncertainly.

"Are you lost, dog?" demanded Valerius harshly.

"Listen!"

Somewhere ahead of them a faint vibration began, the rhythmic rumble of a drum.

"Conan's drum!" exclaimed the Aquilonian.

"If we are close enough to hear the drum," said Valerius, "why do we not hear the shouts and the clang of arms? Surely battle has joined."

"The gorges and the winds play strange tricks," answered Tiberias, his teeth chattering with the ague that is frequently the lot of men who have spent much time in damp underground dungeons. "Listen!"

Faintly to their ears came a low muffled roar.

"They are fighting down in the valley!" cried Tiberias. "The drum is beating on the heights. Let us hasten!"

He rode straight on toward the sound of the distant drum as one who knows his ground at last. Valerius followed, cursing the fog. Then it occurred to him that it would mask his advance. Conan could not see him coming. He would be at the Cimmerian's back before the noonday sun dispelled the mists.

Just now he could not tell what lay on either hand, whether cliffs, thickets or gorges. The drum throbbed unceasingly, growing louder as they advanced, but they heard no more of the battle. Valerius had no idea toward what point of the compass they were headed. He started as he saw gray rock walls looming through the smoky drifts on either hand, and realized that they were riding through a narrow defile. But the guide showed no sign of nervousness, and Valerius hove a sigh of relief when the walls widened out and became invisible in the fog. They were through the defile; if an ambush had been planned, it would have been made in that pass.

But now Tiberias halted again. The drum was rumbling louder, and Valerius could not determine from what direction the sound was coming. Now it seemed ahead of him, now behind, now on one hand or the other. Valerius glared about him impatiently, sitting on his war-horse with wisps of mist curling about him and the moisture gleaming on his armor. Behind him the long lines of steel-clad riders faded away and away like phantoms into the mist.

"Why do you tarry, dog?" he demanded.

The man seemed to be listening to the ghostly drum. Slowly he straightened in his saddle, turned his head and faced Valerius, and the smile on his lips was terrible to see.

"The fog is thinning, Valerius," he said in a new voice, pointing a bony finger. "Look!"

The drum was silent. The fog was fading away. First the crests of cliffs came in sight above the gray clouds, tall and spectral. Lower and lower crawled the mists, shrinking, fading. Valerius started up in his stirrups with a cry that the horsemen echoed behind him. On all sides of them the cliffs towered. They were not in a wide, open valley as he had supposed. They were in a blind gorge walled by sheer cliffs hundreds of feet high. The only entrance or exit was that narrow defile through which they had ridden.

"Dog!" Valerius struck Tiberias full in the mouth with his clenched mailed hand. "What devil's trick is this?"

Tiberias spat out a mouthful of blood and shook with fearful laughter.

"A trick that shall rid the world of a beast! Look, dog!"

Again Valerius cried out, more in fury than in fear.

The defile was blocked by a wild and terrible band of men who stood silent as images – ragged, shock-headed men with spears in their hands – hundreds of them. And up on the cliffs appeared other faces – thousands of faces – wild, gaunt, ferocious faces, marked by fire and steel and starvation.

"A trick of Conan's!" raged Valerius.

"Conan knows nothing of it," laughed Tiberias. "It was the plot of broken men, of men you ruined and turned to beasts. Amalric was right. Conan has not divided his army. We are the rabble who followed him, the wolves who skulked in these hills, the homeless men, the hopeless men. This was our plan, and the priests of Asura aided us with the mist. Look at them, Valerius! Each bears the mark of your hand, on his body or on his heart!

"Look at me! You do not know me, do you, what of this scar your hangman burned upon me? Once you knew me. Once I was lord of Amilius, the man whose sons you murdered, whose daughter your mercenaries ravished and slew. You said I would not sacrifice myself to trap you? Almighty gods, if I had a thousand lives I would give them all to buy your doom!

"And I have bought it! Look on the men you broke, dead man who once played the king! Their hour has come! This gorge is your tomb. Try to climb the cliffs: they are steep, they are high. Try to fight your way back through the defile: spears will block your path, boulders will crush you from above! Dog! I will be waiting for you in hell!"

Throwing back his head he laughed until the rocks rang. Valerius leaned from his saddle and slashed down with his great sword, severing shoulder-bone and breast. Tiberias sank to the earth, still laughing ghastlily through a gurgle of gushing blood.

The drums had begun again, encircling the gorge with guttural thunder; boulders came crashing down; above the screams of dying men shrilled the arrows in blinding clouds from the cliffs.

XXIII
The Road to Acheron

Dawn was just whitening the east when Amalric drew up his hosts in the mouth of the Valley of Lions. This valley was flanked by low, rolling but steep hills, and the floor pitched upward in a series of irregular natural terraces. On the uppermost of these terraces Conan's army held its position, awaiting the attack. The host that had joined him, marching down from Gunderland, had not been composed exclusively of spearmen. With them had come seven thousand Bossonian archers, and four thousand barons and their retainers of the north and west, swelling the ranks of his cavalry.

The pikemen were drawn up in a compact wedge-shaped formation at the narrow head of the valley. There were nineteen thousand of them, mostly Gundermen, though some four thousand were Aquilonians of the other provinces. They were flanked on either hand by five thousand Bossonian archers. Behind the ranks of the pikemen the knights sat their steeds motionless, lances raised: ten thousand knights of Poitain, nine thousand Aquilonians, barons and their retainers.

It was a strong position. His flanks could not be turned, for that would mean climbing the steep, wooded hills in the teeth of the arrows and swords of the Bossonians. His camp lay directly behind him, in a narrow, steep-walled valley which was indeed merely a continuation of the Valley of Lions, pitching up at a higher level. He did not fear a surprize from the rear, because the hills behind him were full of refugees and broken men whose loyalty to him was beyond question.

But if his position was hard to shake, it was equally hard to escape from. It was a trap as well as a fortress for the defenders, a desperate last stand of men who did not expect to survive unless they were victorious. The only line of retreat possible was through the narrow valley at their rear.

Xaltotun mounted a hill on the left side of the valley, near the wide mouth. This hill rose higher than the others, and was known as the King's Altar, for a reason long forgotten. Only Xaltotun knew, and his memory dated back three thousand years.

He was not alone. His two familiars, silent, hairy, furtive and dark, were with him, and they bore a young Aquilonian girl, bound hand and foot. They laid her on an ancient stone, which was curiously like an altar, and which crowned the summit of the hill. For long centuries it had stood there, worn by the elements until many doubted that it was anything but a curiously shapen natural rock. But what it was, and why it stood there, Xaltotun remembered from of old. The familiars went away, with their bent backs like silent gnomes, and Xaltotun stood alone beside the stone altar, his dark beard blown in the wind, overlooking the valley.

He could see clear back to the winding Shirki, and up into the hills beyond the head of the valley. He could see the gleaming wedge of steel drawn up at the head of the terraces, the burganets of the archers glinting among the rocks and bushes, the silent knights motionless on their steeds, their pennons flowing above their helmets, their lances rising in a bristling thicket.

Looking in the other direction he could see the long serried lines of the Nemedians moving in ranks of shining steel into the mouth of the valley. Behind them the gay pavilions of the lords and knights and the drab tents of the common soldiers stretched back almost to the river.

Like a river of molten steel the Nemedian host flowed into the valley, the great scarlet dragon rippling over it. First marched the bowmen, in even ranks, arbalests half raised, bolts nocked, fingers on triggers. After them came the pikemen, and behind them the real strength of the army – the mounted knights, their banners unfurled to the wind, their lances lifted, walking their great steeds forward as if they rode to a banquet.

And higher up on the slopes the smaller Aquilonian host stood grimly silent.

There were thirty thousand Nemedian knights, and, as in most Hyborian nations, it was the chivalry which was the sword of the army. The footmen were used only to clear the way for a charge of the armored knights. There were twenty-one thousand of these, pikemen and archers.

The bowmen began loosing as they advanced, without breaking ranks, launching their quarrels with a whir and tang. But the bolts fell short or rattled harmlessly from the overlapping shields of the Gundermen. And before the arbalesters could come within killing range, the arching shafts of the Bossonians were wreaking havoc in their ranks.

A little of this, a futile attempt at exchanging fire, and the Nemedian bowmen began falling back in disorder. Their armor was light, their weapons no match for the Bossonian longbows. The western archers were sheltered by bushes and rocks. Moreover, the Nemedian footmen lacked something of the morale of the horsemen, knowing as they did that they were being used merely to clear the way for the knights.

The crossbowmen fell back, and between their opening lines the pikemen advanced. These were largely mercenaries, and their masters had no compunction about sacrificing them. They were intended to mask the advance of the knights until the latter were within smiting distance. So while the arbalesters plied their bolts from either flank at long range, the pikemen marched into the teeth of the blast from above, and behind them the knights came on.

When the pikemen began to falter beneath the savage hail of death that whistled down the slopes among them, a trumpet blew, their companies divided to right and left, and through them the mailed knights thundered.

They ran full into a cloud of stinging death. The clothyard shafts found every crevice in their armor and the housings of the steeds. Horses scrambling up the grassy terraces reared and plunged backward, bearing their riders with them. Steel-clad forms littered the slopes. The charge wavered and ebbed back.

Back down in the valley Amalric reformed his ranks. Tarascus was fighting with drawn sword under the scarlet dragon, but it was the baron of Tor who commanded that day. Amalric swore as he glanced at the forest of lance-tips visible above and beyond the head-pieces of the Gundermen. He had hoped his retirement would draw the knights out in a charge down the slopes after him, to be raked from either flank by his bowmen and swamped by the numbers of his horsemen. But they had not moved. Camp-servants brought skins of water from the river. Knights doffed their helmets and drenched their sweating heads. The wounded on the slopes screamed vainly for water. In the upper valley, springs supplied the defenders. They did not thirst that long, hot spring day.

On the King's Altar, beside the ancient, carven stone, Xaltotun watched the steel tide ebb and flow. On came the knights, with waving plumes and dipping lances. Through a whistling cloud of arrows they plowed to break like a thundering wave on the bristling wall of spears and shields. Axes rose and fell above the plumed helmets, spears thrust upward, bringing down horses and riders. The pride of the Gundermen was no less fierce than that of the knights. They were not spear-fodder, to be sacrificed for the glory of better men. They were the finest infantry in the world, with a tradition that made their morale unshakable. The kings of Aquilonia had long learned the worth of unbreakable infantry. They held their formation unshaken; over their gleaming ranks flowed the great lion banner, and at the tip of the wedge a giant figure in black armor roared and smote like a hurricane, with a dripping ax that split steel and bone alike.

The Nemedians fought as gallantly as their traditions of high courage demanded. But they could not break the iron wedge, and from the wooded knolls on either hand arrows raked their close-packed ranks mercilessly. Their own bowmen were useless, their pikemen unable to climb the heights and come to grips with the Bossonians. Slowly, stubbornly, sullenly, the grim knights fell back, counting their empty saddles. Above them the Gundermen made no outcry of triumph. They closed their ranks, locking up the gaps made by the fallen. Sweat ran into their eyes from under their steel caps. They gripped their spears and waited, their fierce hearts swelling with pride that a king should fight on foot with them. Behind them the Aquilonian knights had not moved. They sat their steeds, grimly immobile.

A knight spurred a sweating horse up the hill called the King's Altar, and glared at Xaltotun with bitter eyes.

"Amalric bids me say that it is time to use your magic, wizard," he said. "We are dying like flies down there in the valley. We cannot break their ranks."

Xaltotun seemed to expand, to grow tall and awesome and terrible.

"Return to Amalric," he said. "Tell him to reform his ranks for a charge, but to await my signal. Before that signal is given he will see a sight that he will remember until he lies dying!"

The knight saluted as if compelled against his will, and thundered down the hill at breakneck pace.

Xaltotun stood beside the dark altar-stone and stared across the valley, at the dead and wounded men on the terraces, at the grim, blood-stained band at the head of the slopes, at the dusty, steel-clad ranks reforming in the vale below. He glanced up at the sky, and he glanced down at the slim white figure on the dark stone. And lifting a dagger inlaid with archaic hieroglyphs, he intoned an immemorial invocation:

"Set, god of darkness, scaly lord of the shadows, by the blood of a virgin and the sevenfold symbol I call to your sons below the black earth! Children of the deeps, below the red earth, under the black earth, awaken and shake your awful manes! Let the hills rock and the stones topple upon my enemies! Let the sky grow dark above them, the earth unstable beneath their feet! Let a wind from the deep black earth curl up beneath their feet, and blacken and shrivel them – "

He halted short, dagger lifted. In the tense silence the roar of the hosts rose beneath him, borne on the wind.

On the other side of the altar stood a man in a black hooded robe, whose coif shadowed pale delicate features and dark eyes calm and meditative.

"Dog of Asura!" whispered Xaltotun, and his voice was like the hiss of an angered serpent. "Are you mad, that you seek your doom? Ho, Baal! Chiron!"

"Call again, dog of Acheron!" said the other, and laughed. "Summon them loudly. They will not hear, unless your shouts reverberate in hell."

From a thicket on the edge of the crest came a somber old woman in peasant garb, her hair flowing over her shoulders, a great gray wolf following at her heels.

"Witch, priest and wolf," muttered Xaltotun grimly, and laughed. "Fools, to pit your charlatan's mummery against my arts! With a wave of my hand I brush you from my path!"

"Your arts are straws in the wind, dog of Python," answered the Asurian. "Have you wondered why the Shirki did not come down in flood and trap Conan on the other bank? When I saw the lightning in the night I guessed your plan, and my spells dispersed the clouds you had summoned before they could empty their torrents. You did not even know that your rain-making wizardry had failed."

"You lie!" cried Xaltotun, but the confidence in his voice was shaken. "I have felt the impact of a powerful sorcery against mine – but no man on earth could undo the rain-magic, once made, unless he possessed the very heart of sorcery."

"But the flood you plotted did not come to pass," answered the priest. "Look at your allies in the valley, Pythonian! You have led them to the slaughter! They are caught in the fangs of the trap, and you cannot aid them. Look!"

He pointed. Out of the narrow gorge of the upper valley, behind the Poitanians, a horseman came flying, whirling something about his head that flashed in the sun. Recklessly he hurtled down the slopes, through the ranks of the Gundermen, who sent up a deep-throated roar and clashed their spears and shields like thunder in the hills. On the terraces between the hosts the sweat-soaked horse reared and plunged, and his wild rider yelled and brandished the thing in his hands like one demented. It was the torn remnant of a scarlet banner, and the sun struck dazzlingly on the golden scales of a serpent that writhed thereon.

"Valerius is dead!" cried Hadrathus ringingly. "A fog and a drum lured him to his doom! I gathered that fog, dog of Python, and I dispersed it! I, with my magic which is greater than your magic!"

"What matters it?" roared Xaltotun, a terrible sight, his eyes blazing, his features convulsed. "Valerius was a fool. I do not need him. I can crush Conan without human aid!"

"Why have you delayed?" mocked Hadrathus. "Why have you allowed so many of your allies to fall pierced by arrows and spitted on spears?"

"Because blood aids great sorcery!" thundered Xaltotun, in a voice that made the rocks quiver. A lurid nimbus played about his awful head. "Because no wizard wastes his strength thoughtlessly. Because I would conserve my powers for the great days to be, rather than employ them in a hill-country brawl. But now, by Set, I shall loose them to the uttermost! Watch, dog of Asura, false priest of an outworn god, and see a sight that shall blast your reason for evermore!"

Hadrathus threw back his head and laughed, and hell was in his laughter.

"Look, black devil of Python!"

His hand came from under his robe holding something that flamed and burned in the sun, changing the light to a pulsing golden glow in which the flesh of Xaltotun looked like the flesh of a corpse.

Xaltotun cried out as if he had been stabbed.

"The Heart! The Heart of Ahriman!"

"Aye! The one power that is greater than your power!"

Xaltotun seemed to shrivel, to grow old. Suddenly his beard was shot with snow, his locks flecked with gray.

"The Heart!" he mumbled. "You stole it! Dog! Thief!"

"Not I! It has been on a long journey far to the southward. But now it is in my hands, and your black arts cannot stand against it. As it resurrected you, so shall it hurl you back into the night whence it drew you. You shall go down the dark road to Acheron, which is the road of silence and the night. The dark empire, unreborn, shall remain a legend and a black memory. Conan shall reign again. And the Heart of Ahriman shall go back into the cavern below the temple of Mitra, to burn as a symbol of the power of Aquilonia for a thousand years!"

Xaltotun screamed inhumanly and rushed around the altar, dagger lifted; but from somewhere – out of the sky, perhaps, or the great jewel that blazed in the hand of Hadrathus – shot a jetting beam of blinding blue light. Full against the breast of Xaltotun it flashed, and the hills re-echoed the concussion. The wizard of Acheron went down as though struck by a thunderbolt, and before he touched the ground he was fearfully altered. Beside the altar-stone lay no fresh-slain corpse, but a shriveled mummy, a brown, dry, unrecognizable carcass sprawling among moldering swathings.

Somberly old Zelata looked down.

"He was not a living man," she said. "The Heart lent him a false aspect of life, that deceived even himself. I never saw him as other than a mummy."

Hadrathus bent to unbind the swooning girl on the altar, when from among the trees appeared a strange apparition – Xaltotun's chariot drawn by the weird horses. Silently they advanced to the altar and halted, with the chariot wheel almost touching the brown withered thing on the grass. Hadrathus lifted the body of the wizard and placed it in the chariot. And without hesitation the uncanny steeds turned and moved off southward, down the hill. And Hadrathus and Zelata and the gray wolf watched them go – down the long road to Acheron which is beyond the ken of men.

Down in the valley Amalric had stiffened in his saddle when he saw that wild horseman curvetting and caracoling on the slopes while he brandished that blood-stained serpent-banner. Then some instinct jerked his head about, toward the hill known as the King's Altar. And his lips parted. Every man in the valley saw it – an arching shaft of dazzling light that towered up from the summit of the hill, showering golden fire. High above the hosts it burst in a blinding blaze that momentarily paled the sun.

"That's not Xaltotun's signal!" roared the baron.

"No!" shouted Tarascus. "It's a signal to the Aquilonians! Look!"

Above them the immobile ranks were moving at last, and a deep-throated roar thundered across the vale.

"Xaltotun has failed us!" bellowed Amalric furiously. "Valerius has failed us! We have been led into a trap! Mitra's curse on Xaltotun who led us here! Sound the retreat!"

"Too late!" yelled Tarascus. *"Look!"*

Up on the slopes the forest of lances dipped, leveled. The ranks of the Gundermen rolled back to right and left like a parting curtain. And with a thunder like the rising roar of a hurricane, the knights of Aquilonia crashed down the slopes.

The impetus of that charge was irresistible. Bolts driven by the demoralized arbalesters glanced from their shields, their bent helmets. Their plumes and pennons streaming out behind them, their lances lowered, they swept over the wavering lines of pikemen and roared down the slopes like a wave.

Amalric yelled an order to charge, and the Nemedians with desperate courage spurred their horses at the slopes. They still outnumbered the attackers.

But they were weary men on tired horses, charging uphill. The onrushing knights had not struck a blow that day. Their horses were fresh. They were coming downhill and they came like a thunderbolt. And like a thunderbolt they smote the struggling ranks of the Nemedians – smote them, split them apart, ripped them asunder and dashed the remnants headlong down the slopes.

After them on foot came the Gundermen, blood-mad, and the Bossonians were swarming down the hills, loosing as they ran at every foe that still moved.

Down the slopes washed the tide of battle, the dazed Nemedians swept on the crest of the wave. Their archers had thrown down their arbalests and were fleeing. Such pikemen as had survived the blasting charge of the knights were cut to pieces by the ruthless Gundermen.

In a wild confusion the battle swept through the wide mouth of the valley and into the plain beyond. All over the plain swarmed the warriors, fleeing and pursuing, broken into single combat and clumps of smiting, hacking knights on rearing, wheeling horses. But the Nemedians were smashed, broken, unable to re-form or make a stand. By the hundreds they broke away, spurring for the river. Many reached it, rushed across and rode eastward. The countryside was up behind them; the people hunted them like wolves. Few ever reached Tarantia.

The final break did not come until the fall of Amalric. The baron, striving in vain to rally his men, rode straight at the clump of knights that followed the giant in black armor whose surcoat bore the royal lion, and over whose head floated the golden lion banner with the scarlet leopard of Poitain beside it. A tall warrior in gleaming armor couched his lance and charged to meet the lord of Tor. They met like a thunderclap. The Nemedian's lance, striking his foe's helmet, snapped bolts and rivets and tore off the casque, revealing the features of Pallantides. But the Aquilonian's lance-head crashed through shield and breast-plate to transfix the baron's heart.

A roar went up as Amalric was hurled from his saddle, snapping the lance that impaled him, and the Nemedians gave way as a barrier bursts under the surging impact of a tidal wave. They rode for the river in a blind stampede that swept the plain like a whirlwind. The hour of the Dragon had passed.

Tarascus did not flee. Amalric was dead, the color-bearer slain, and the royal Nemedian banner trampled in the blood and dust. Most of his knights were fleeing and the Aquilonians were riding them down; Tarascus knew the day was lost, but with a handful of faithful followers he raged through the mêlée, conscious of but one desire – to meet Conan, the Cimmerian. And at last he met him.

Formations had been destroyed utterly, close-knit bands broken asunder and swept apart. The crest of Trocero gleamed in one part of the plain, those of Prospero and Pallantides in others. Conan was alone. The house-troops of Tarascus had fallen one by one. The two kings met man to man.

Even as they rode at each other, the horse of Tarascus sobbed and sank under him. Conan leaped from his own steed and ran at him, as the king of Nemedia disengaged himself and rose. Steel flashed blindingly in the sun, clashed loudly, and blue sparks flew; then a clang of armor as Tarascus measured his full length on the earth beneath a thunderous stroke of Conan's broadsword.

The Cimmerian placed a mail-shod foot on his enemy's breast, and lifted his sword. His helmet was gone; he shook back his black mane and his blue eyes blazed with their old fire.

"Do you yield?"

"Will you give me quarter?" demanded the Nemedian.

"Aye. Better than you'd have given me, you dog. Life for you and all your men who throw down their arms. Though I ought to split your head for an infernal thief," the Cimmerian added.

Tarascus twisted his neck and glared over the plain. The remnants of the Nemedian host were flying across the stone bridge with swarms of victorious Aquilonians at their heels, smiting with the fury of glutted vengeance. Bossonians and Gundermen were swarming through the camp of their enemies, tearing the tents to pieces in search of plunder, seizing prisoners, ripping open the baggage and upsetting the wagons.

Tarascus cursed fervently, and then shrugged his shoulders, as well as he could, under the circumstances.

"Very well. I have no choice. What are your demands?"

"Surrender to me all your present holdings in Aquilonia. Order your garrisons to march out of the castles and towns they hold, without their arms, and get your infernal armies out of Aquilonia as quickly as possible. In addition you shall return all Aquilonians sold as slaves, and pay an indemnity to be designated later, when the damage your occupation of the country has caused has been properly estimated. You will remain as hostage until these terms have been carried out."

"Very well," surrendered Tarascus. "I will surrender all the castles and towns now held by my garrisons without resistance, and all the other things shall be done. What ransom for my body?"

Conan laughed and removed his foot from his foe's steel-clad breast, grasped his shoulder and heaved him to his feet. He started to speak, then turned to see Hadrathus approaching him. The priest was as calm and self-possessed as ever, picking his way between rows of dead men and horses.

Conan wiped the sweat-smeared dust from his face with a blood-stained hand. He had fought all through the day, first on foot with the pikemen, then in the saddle, leading the charge. His surcoat was gone, his armor splashed with blood and battered with strokes of sword, mace and ax. He loomed gigantically against a background of blood and slaughter, like some grim pagan hero of mythology.

"Well done, Hadrathus!" quoth he gustily. "By Crom, I am glad to see your signal! My knights were almost mad with impatience and eating their hearts out to be at sword-strokes. I could not have held them much longer. What of the wizard?"

"He has gone down the dim road to Acheron," answered Hadrathus. "And I – I am for Tarantia. My work is done here, and I have a task to perform at the temple of Mitra. All our work is done here. On this field we have saved Aquilonia – and more than Aquilonia. Your ride to your capital will be a triumphal procession through a kingdom mad with joy. All Aquilonia will be cheering the return of their king. And so, until we meet again in the great royal hall – farewell!"

Conan stood silently watching the priest as he went. From various parts of the field knights were hurrying toward him. He saw Pallantides, Trocero, Prospero. Servius Galannus, their armor splashed with crimson. The thunder of battle was giving way to a roar of triumph and acclaim. All eyes, hot with strife and shining with exultation, were turned toward the great black figure of the king; mailed arms brandished red-stained swords. A confused torrent of sound rose, deep and thunderous as the sea-surf: *"Hail, Conan, king of Aquilonia!"*

Tarascus spoke.

"You have not yet named my ransom."

Conan laughed and slapped his sword home in its scabbard. He flexed his mighty arms, and ran his blood-stained fingers through his thick black locks, as if feeling there his re-won crown.

"There is a girl in your seraglio named Zenobia."

"Why, yes, so there is."

"Very well." The king smiled as at an exceedingly pleasant memory. "She shall be your ransom, and naught else. I will come to Belverus for her as I promised. She was a slave in Nemedia, but I will make her queen of Aquilonia!"

A Witch Shall Be Born

A Witch Shall Be Born

I
The Blood-Red Crescent

Taramis, Queen of Khauran, awakened from a dream-haunted slumber to a silence that seemed more like the stillness of nighted catacombs than the normal quiet of a sleeping palace. She lay staring into the darkness, wondering why the candles in their golden candelabra had gone out. A flecking of stars marked a gold-barred casement that lent no illumination to the interior of the chamber. But as Taramis lay there, she became aware of a spot of radiance glowing in the darkness before her. She watched, puzzled. It grew and its intensity deepened as it expanded, a widening disk of lurid light hovering against the dark velvet hangings of the opposite wall. Taramis caught her breath, starting up to a sitting position. A dark object was visible in that circle of light – *a human head.*

In a sudden panic the queen opened her lips to cry out for her maids, then she checked herself. The glow was more lurid, the head more vividly limned. It was a woman's head, small, delicately molded, superbly poised, with a high-piled mass of lustrous black hair. The face grew distinct as she stared – and it was the sight of this face which froze the cry in Taramis's throat. The features were her own! She might have been looking into a mirror which subtly altered her reflection, lending it a tigerish gleam of eye, a vindictive curl of lip.

"Ishtar!" gasped Taramis. "I am bewitched!"

Appallingly, the apparition spoke, and its voice was like honeyed venom.

"Bewitched? No, sweet sister! Here is no sorcery."

"Sister?" stammered the bewildered girl. "I have no sister."

"You never had a sister?" came the sweet, poisonously mocking voice. "Never a twin sister whose flesh was as soft as yours to caress or hurt?"

"Why, once I had a sister," answered Taramis, still convinced that she was in the grip of some sort of nightmare. "But she died."

The beautiful face in the disk was convulsed with the aspect of a fury; so hellish became its expression that Taramis, cowering back, half expected to see snaky locks writhe hissing about the ivory brow.

"You lie!" The accusation was spat from between the snarling red lips. "She did not die! Fool! Oh, enough of this mummery! Look – and let your sight be blasted!"

Light ran suddenly along the hangings like flaming serpents, and incredibly the candles in the golden sticks flared up again. Taramis crouched on her velvet couch, her lithe legs flexed beneath her, staring wide-eyed at the pantherish figure which posed mockingly before her. It was as if she gazed upon another Taramis, identical with herself in every contour of feature and limb, yet animated by an alien and evil personality. The face of this stranger waif reflected the opposite of every characteristic the countenance of the queen denoted. Lust and mystery sparkled in her scintillant eyes, cruelty lurked in the curl of her full red lips. Each movement of her supple body was subtly suggestive. Her coiffure imitated that of the queen, on her feet were gilded sandals such as Taramis wore in her boudoir. The sleeveless, low-necked silk tunic, girdled at the waist with a cloth-of-gold cincture, was a duplicate of the queen's night-garment.

"Who are you?" gasped Taramis, an icy chill she could not explain creeping along her spine. "Explain your presence before I call my ladies-in-waiting to summon the guard!"

"Scream until the roof-beams crack," callously answered the stranger. "Your sluts will not wake till dawn, though the palace spring into flames about them. Your guardsmen will not hear your squeals; they have been sent out of this wing of the palace."

"What!" exclaimed Taramis, stiffening with outraged majesty. "Who dared give my guardsmen such a command?"

"I did, sweet sister," sneered the other girl. "A little while ago, before I entered. They thought it was their darling adored queen. Ha! How beautifully I acted the part! With what imperious dignity, softened by womanly sweetness, did I address the great louts who knelt in their armor and plumed helmets!"

Taramis felt as if a stifling net of bewilderment were being drawn about her.

"Who are you?" she cried desperately. "What madness is this? Why do you come here?"

"Who am I?" There was the spite of a she-cobra's hiss in the soft response. The girl stepped to the edge of the couch, grasped the queen's white shoulders with fierce fingers, and bent to glare full into the startled eyes of Taramis. And under the spell of that hypnotic glare, the queen forgot to resent the unprecedented outrage of violent hands laid on regal flesh.

"Fool!" gritted the girl between her teeth. "Can you ask? Can you wonder? I am Salome!"

"Salome!" Taramis breathed the word, and the hairs prickled on her scalp as she realized the incredible, numbing truth of the statement. "I thought you died within the hour of your birth," she said feebly.

"So thought many," answered the woman who called herself Salome. "They carried me into the desert to die, damn them! I, a mewing, puling babe whose life was so young it was scarcely the flicker of a candle. And do you know why they bore me forth to die?"

"I – I have heard the story – " faltered Taramis.

Salome laughed fiercely, and slapped her bosom. The low-necked tunic left the upper parts of her firm breasts bare, and between them there shone a curious mark – a crescent, red as blood.

"The mark of the witch!" cried Taramis, recoiling.

"Aye!" Salome's laughter was dagger-edged with hate. "The curse of the kings of Khauran! Aye, they tell the tale in the market-places, with wagging beards and rolling eyes, the pious fools! They tell how the first queen of our line had traffic with a fiend of darkness and bore him a daughter who lives in foul legendry to this day. And thereafter in each century a girl baby was born into the Askhaurian dynasty, with a scarlet half-moon between her breasts, that signified her destiny.

"'Every century a witch shall be born.' So ran the ancient curse. And so it has come to pass. Some were slain at birth, as they sought to slay me. Some walked the earth as witches, proud daughters of Khauran, with the moon of hell burning upon their ivory bosoms. Each was named Salome. I too am Salome. It was always Salome, the witch. It will always be Salome, the witch, even when the mountains of ice have roared down from the pole and ground the civilizations to ruin, and a new world has risen from the ashes and dust – even then there shall be Salomes to walk the earth, to trap men's hearts by their sorcery, to dance before the kings of the world, and see the heads of the wise men fall at their pleasure!"

"But – but you – " stammered Taramis.

"I?" The scintillant eyes burned like dark fires of mystery. "They carried me into the desert far from the city, and laid me naked on the hot sand, under the flaming sun. And then they rode away and left me for the jackals and the vultures and the desert wolves.

"But the life in me was stronger than the life in common folk, for it partakes of the essence of the forces that seethe in the black gulfs beyond mortal ken. The hours passed, and the sun slashed down like the molten flames of hell, but I did not die – aye, something of that torment I remember, faintly and far-away, as one remembers a dim, formless dream. Then there were camels, and yellow-skinned men who wore silk robes and spoke in a weird tongue. Strayed from the caravan road, they passed close by, and their leader saw me, and recognized the scarlet crescent on my bosom. He took me up and gave me life.

"He was a magician from far Khitai, returning to his native kingdom after a journey to Stygia. He took me with him to purple-towered Paikang, its minarets rising amid the vine-festooned jungles of bamboo, and there I grew to womanhood under his teaching. Age had steeped him deep in black wisdom, not weakened his powers of evil. Many things he taught me – " She paused, smiling enigmatically, with wicked mystery gleaming in her dark eyes. Then she tossed her head.

"He drove me from him at last, saying that I was but a common witch in spite of his teachings, and not fit to command the mighty sorcery he would have taught me. He would have made me queen of the world and ruled the nations through me, he said, but I was only a harlot of darkness. But what of it? I could never endure to seclude myself in a golden tower, and spend the long hours staring into a crystal globe, mumbling over incantations written on serpent's skin in the blood of virgins, poring over musty volumes in forgotten languages.

"He said I was but an earthly sprite, knowing naught of the deeper gulfs of cosmic sorcery. Well, this world contains all I desire – power, and pomp, and glittering pageantry, handsome men and soft women for my paramours and my slaves. He had told me who I was, of the curse and my heritage. I have returned to take that to which I have as much right as you. Now it is mine by right of possession."

"What do you mean?" Taramis sprang up and faced her sister, stung out of her bewilderment and fright. "Do you imagine that by drugging a few of my maids and tricking a few of my guardsmen you have established a claim to the throne of Khauran? Do not forget that *I* am queen of Khauran! I shall give you a place of honor, as my sister, but – "

Salome laughed hatefully.

"How generous of you, dear, sweet sister! But before you begin putting me in my place – perhaps you will tell me whose soldiers camp in the plain outside the city walls?"

"They are the Shemitish mercenaries of Constantius, the Kothic *voivode* of the Free Companies."

"And what do they in Khauran?" cooed Salome. Taramis felt that she was being subtly mocked, but she answered with an assumption of dignity which she scarcely felt.

"Constantius asked permission to pass along the borders of Khauran on his way to Turan. He himself is hostage for their good behavior as long as they are within my domains."

"And Constantius," pursued Salome. "Did he not ask your hand today?"

Taramis shot her a clouded glance of suspicion.

"How did you know that?"

An insolent shrug of the slim naked shoulders was the only reply.

"You refused, dear sister?"

"Certainly I refused!" exclaimed Taramis angrily. "Do you, an Askhaurian princess yourself, suppose that the queen of Khauran could treat such a proposal with anything but disdain? Wed a bloody-handed adventurer, a man exiled from his own kingdom because of his crimes, and the leader of organized plunderers and hired murderers?

"I should never have allowed him to bring his black-bearded slayers into Khauran. But he is virtually a prisoner in the south tower, guarded by my soldiers. Tomorrow I shall bid him order his troops to leave the kingdom. He himself shall be kept captive until they are over the border. Meantime, my soldiers man the walls of the city, and I have warned him that he will answer for any outrages perpetrated on the villagers or shepherds by his mercenaries."

"He is confined in the south tower?" asked Salome.

"That is what I said. Why do you ask?"

For answer Salome clapped her hands, and lifting her voice, with a gurgle of cruel mirth in it, called: "The queen grants you an audience, Falcon!"

A gold-arabesqued door opened and a tall figure entered the chamber, at the sight of which Taramis cried out in amazement and anger.

"Constantius! You dare enter my chamber!"

"As you see, your majesty!" He bent his dark, hawk-like head in mock humility.

Constantius, whom men called the Falcon, was tall, broad-shouldered, slim-waisted, lithe and strong as pliant steel. He was handsome in an aquiline, ruthless sort of way. His face was burnt dark by the sun and his hair, which grew far back from his high, narrow forehead, was black as a raven. His dark eyes were penetrating and alert, the hardness of his thin lips not softened by his thin black moustache. His boots were of Kordavan leather, his hose and doublet of plain, dark silk, tarnished with the wear of the camps and the stains of armor rust.

Twisting his moustache he let his gaze travel up and down the shrinking queen with an effrontery that made her wince.

"By Ishtar, Taramis," he said silkily, "I find you more alluring in your night-tunic than in your queenly robes. Truly, this is an auspicious night!"

Fear grew in the queen's dark eyes. She was no fool; she knew that Constantius would never dare this outrage unless he was sure of himself.

"You are mad," she said. "If I am in your power in this chamber, you are no less in the power of my subjects who will rend you to pieces if you touch me. Go at once, if you would live."

Both laughed mockingly, and Salome made an impatient gesture.

"Enough of this farce; let us on to the next act in the comedy. Listen, dear sister: it was I who sent Constantius here. When I decided to take the throne of Khauran, I cast about for a man to aid me, and chose the Falcon, because of his utter lack of all characteristics men call good."

"I am overwhelmed, princess," murmured Constantius sardonically, with a profound bow.

"I sent him to Khauran, and, once his men were camped in the plain outside, and he was in the palace, I entered the city by that small gate in the west wall – the fools guarding it thought it was you returning from some nocturnal adventure –"

"You slut!" Taramis's cheeks flamed and her resentment got the better of her regal reserve. She valued her reputation of virtue.

Salome smiled hardly.

"They were properly surprized and shocked, but admitted me without question. I entered the palace the same way, and gave the order to the surprized guards that sent them marching away, as well as the men who guarded Constantius in the south tower. Then I came here, attending to the ladies-in-waiting on the way."

Taramis's fingers clenched and she paled, as she sensed the sinister shape of a monstrous plot behind all this.

"Well, what next?" she asked in a shaky voice.

"Listen!" Salome inclined her head. Faintly through the casement there came the clank of marching men in armor; gruff voices shouted in an alien tongue, and cries of alarm mingled with the shouts.

"The people awaken and grow fearful," said Constantius sardonically. "You had better go and reassure them, Salome!"

"Call me Taramis," answered Salome. "We must become accustomed to it."

"What have you done?" cried Taramis. "What have you done?"

"I have gone to the gates and ordered the soldiers to open them," answered Salome. "They were astounded, but they obeyed. That is the Falcon's army you hear, marching into the city."

"You devil!" cried Taramis. "You have betrayed my people, in my guise! You have made me seem a traitor! Oh, I shall go to them –"

With a cruel laugh Salome caught her wrist and jerked her back. The magnificent suppleness of the queen was helpless against the vindictive strength that steeled Salome's slender limbs.

"You know how to reach the dungeons from the palace, Constantius?" said the witch-girl. "Good. Take this spit-fire and lock her into the strongest cell. The gaolers are all sound in drugged sleep. I saw to that. Send a man to cut their throats before they can awaken. None must ever know what has transpired tonight. Thenceforward I am Taramis, and Taramis is a nameless prisoner in an unknown dungeon."

Constantius smiled with a glint of strong white teeth under his thin moustache.

"Very good; but you would not deny me a little – ah – amusement first?"

"Not I! Tame the scornful hussy as you will." With a wicked laugh Salome flung her sister into the Kothian's arms, and turned away through the door that opened into the outer corridor.

Fright widened Taramis's lovely eyes, her supple figure rigid and straining against Constantius's embrace. She forgot the men marching in the streets, forgot the outrage to her queenship, in the face of the menace to her womanhood. She forgot all sensations but terror and shame as she faced the complete cynicism of Constantius's burning, mocking eyes, felt his hard arms crushing her writhing body.

Salome, hurrying along the corridor outside, smiled spitefully as a scream of despair and poignant agony rang shuddering through the palace.

II
The Tree of Death

The young soldier's hose and shirt were smeared with dried blood, wet with sweat and grey with dust. Blood oozed from the deep gash in his thigh, from the cuts on his breast and shoulder. Perspiration glistened on his livid face and his fingers were knotted in the cover of the divan on which he lay. Yet his words reflected mental suffering that outweighed physical pain.

"She must be mad!" he repeated again and again, like one still stunned by some monstrous and incredible happening. "It's like a nightmare! Taramis, whom all Khauran loves, betraying her people to that devil from Koth! Oh, Ishtar, why was I not slain? Better die than live to see our queen turn traitor and harlot!"

"Lie still, Valerius," begged the girl who was washing and bandaging his wounds with trembling hands. "Oh, please lie still, darling! You will make your wounds worse. I dared not summon a leech –"

"No," muttered the wounded youth. "Constantius's blue-bearded devils will be searching the quarters for wounded Khaurani; they'll hang every man who has wounds to show he fought against them. Oh, Taramis, how could you betray the people who worshipped you?" In his fierce agony he writhed, weeping in rage and shame, and the terrified girl caught him in her arms, straining his tossing head against her bosom, imploring him to be quiet.

"Better death than the black shame that has come upon Khauran this day," he groaned. "Did you see it, Ivga?"

"No, Valerius." Her soft, nimble fingers were again at work, gently cleansing and closing the gaping edges of his raw wounds. "I was awakened by the noise of fighting in the streets – I looked out a casement and saw the Shemites cutting down the people – then presently I heard you calling me faintly from the alley door."

"I had reached the limits of my strength," he muttered. "I fell in the alley and could not rise. I knew they'd find me soon if I lay there – I killed three of the blue-bearded beasts, by Ishtar! They'll never swagger through Khauran's streets, by the gods! The fiends are tearing their hearts in hell!"

The trembling girl crooned soothingly to him, as to a wounded child, and closed his panting lips with her own cool sweet mouth. But the fire that raged in his soul would not allow him to lie silent.

"I was not on the wall when the Shemites entered," he burst out. "I was asleep in the barracks, with the others not on duty. It was just before dawn when our captain entered, and his face was pale under his helmet. 'The Shemites are in the city,' he said. 'The queen came to the southern gate and gave orders that they should be admitted. She made the men come down from the walls, where they've been on guard since Constantius entered the kingdom. I don't understand it, and neither does anyone else, but I heard her give the order, and we obeyed as we always do. We are ordered to assemble in the square before the palace. Form ranks outside the barracks and march – leave your arms and armor here. Ishtar knows what this means, but it is the queen's order.'

"Well, when we came to the square the Shemites were drawn up on foot opposite the palace, ten thousand of the blue-bearded devils, fully armed, and people's heads were thrust out of every window and door on the square. The streets leading into the square were thronged by bewildered folk. Taramis was standing on the steps of the palace, alone except for Constantius, who stood stroking his moustache like a great lean cat who has just devoured a sparrow. But fifty Shemites with bows in their hands were ranged below them.

"That's where the queen's guard should have been, but they were drawn up at the foot of the palace stair, as puzzled as we, though they had come fully armed, in spite of the queen's order.

"Taramis spoke to us then, and told us that she had reconsidered the proposal made her by Constantius – why, only yesterday she threw it in his teeth in open court! – and that she had decided to make him her royal consort. She did not explain why she had brought the Shemites into the city so treacherously. But she said that, as Constantius had control of a body of professional fighting men, the army of Khauran would no longer be needed, and therefore she disbanded it, and ordered us to go quietly to our homes.

"Why, obedience to our queen is second nature to us, but we were struck dumb and found no word to answer. We broke ranks almost before we knew what we were doing, like men in a daze.

"But when the palace guard was ordered to likewise disarm and disband, the captain of the guard, Conan, interrupted. Men said he was off duty the night before, and drunk. But he was wide awake now. He shouted to the guardsmen to stand as they were until they received an order from him – and such is his dominance of his men, that they obeyed in spite of the queen. He strode up to the palace steps and glared at Taramis – and then he roared: 'This is not the queen! This isn't Taramis! It's some devil in masquerade!'

"Then hell was to pay! I don't know just what happened. I think a Shemite struck Conan, and Conan killed him. The next instant the square was a battle-ground. The Shemites fell on the guardsmen, and their spears and arrows struck down many soldiers who had already disbanded.

"Some of us grabbed up such weapons as we could and fought back. We hardly knew what we were fighting for, but it was against Constantius and his devils, I swear it. Not against Taramis, I swear it! Constantius shouted to cut the traitors down. We were not traitors!" Despair and bewilderment shook his voice. The girl murmured pityingly, not understanding it all, but aching in sympathy with her lover's suffering.

"The people did not know which side to take. It was a madhouse of confusion and bewilderment. We who fought didn't have a chance, in no formation, without armor and only half-armed. The guards were fully armed and drawn up in a square, but there were only five hundred of them. They took a heavy toll before they were cut down, but there could be only one conclusion to such a battle. And while her people were being slaughtered before her, Taramis stood on the palace steps, with Constantius's arm about her waist, and laughed like a heartless, beautiful fiend! Gods, it's all mad – mad!

"I never saw a man fight like Conan fought. He put his back to the courtyard wall and before they overpowered him the dead men were strewn in heaps thigh-deep about him. But at last they dragged him down, a hundred against one. When I saw him fall I dragged myself away feeling as if the world had burst under my very fingers. I heard Constantius call to his dogs to take the captain alive – stroking his moustache, with that hateful smile on his cursed lips!"

That smile was on the lips of Constantius at that very moment. He sat his horse among a cluster of his men – thick-bodied Shemites with curled blue-black beards and hooked noses; the low-swinging sun struck glints from their peaked helmets and the silvered scales of their corselets. Nearly a mile behind, the walls and towers of Khauran rose sheer out of the meadowlands.

By the side of the caravan road a heavy cross had been planted, and on this grim tree a man hung, nailed there by iron spikes through his hands and feet. Naked but for a loin-cloth, the man was almost a giant in stature, and his muscles stood out in thick corded ridges on limbs and body, which the sun had long ago burned brown. The perspiration of agony beaded his face and his mighty breast, but from under the tangled black mane that fell over his low, broad forehead, his blue eyes blazed with an unquenched fire. Blood oozed sluggishly from the lacerations in his hands and feet.

Constantius saluted him mockingly.

"I am sorry, captain," he said, "that I can not remain to ease your last hours, but I have duties to perform in yonder city – I must not keep our delicious queen waiting!" He laughed softly. "So I leave you to your own devices – and those beauties!" He pointed meaningly at the black shadows which swept incessantly back and forth, high above.

"Were it not for them, I imagine that a powerful brute like yourself should live on the cross for days. Do not cherish any illusions of rescue because I am leaving you unguarded. I have had it proclaimed that any one seeking to take your body, living or dead, from the cross, will be flayed alive together with all the members of his family, in the public square. I am so firmly established in Khauran that my order is as good as a regiment of guardsmen. I am leaving no guard, because the vultures will not approach as long as anyone is near, and I do not wish them to feel any constraint! That is also why I brought you so far from the city. These desert vultures approach the walls no closer than this spot.

"And so, brave captain, farewell! I will remember you when, in an hour, Taramis lies in my arms."

Blood started afresh from the pierced palms as the victim's mallet-like fists clenched convulsively on the spike-heads. Knots and bunches of muscle started out on the massive arms, and Conan bent his head forward and spat savagely at Constantius's. The *voivode* laughed coolly, wiped the saliva from his gorget and reined his horse about.

"Remember me when the vultures are tearing at your living flesh," he called mockingly. "The desert scavengers are a particularly voracious breed. I have seen men hang for hours on a cross, eyeless, earless, and scalpless, before the sharp beaks had eaten their way into his vitals."

Without a backward glance he rode toward the city, a supple, erect figure, gleaming in his burnished armor, his stolid bearded henchmen jogging beside him. A faint rising of dust from the worn trail marked their passing.

The man hanging on the cross was the one touch of sentient life in a landscape that seemed desolate and deserted in the late evening. Khauran, less than a mile away, might have been on the other side of the world, and existing in another age. Shaking the sweat out of his eyes, Conan stared blankly at the familiar terrain. On either hand of the city and beyond it, stretched the fertile meadowlands, with cattle browsing in the distance where fields and vineyards checkered the plain. The western and northern horizons were dotted with villages, miniature in the distance. A lesser distance to the southeast a silvery gleam marked the course of a river, and beyond that river sandy desert began abruptly to stretch away and away beyond the horizon. Conan stared at that expanse of empty waste shimmering tawnily in the late sunlight as a trapped hawk stares at the open sky. A revulsion shook him when he glanced at the gleaming towers of Khauran. The city had betrayed him – trapped him into circumstances that left him hanging to a wooden cross like a hare nailed to a tree. If he could but descend from this tree of torment and lose himself in that empty waste –turn his back for ever on the crooked streets and walled lairs where men plotted to betray humanity.

A red lust for vengeance swept away the thought. Curses ebbed fitfully from the man's lips. All his universe contracted, focused, became incorporated in the four iron spikes that held him from life and freedom. His great muscles quivered, knotting like iron cables. With the sweat starting out on his greying skin, he sought to gain leverage, to tear the nails from the wood. It was useless. They had been driven deep. Then he tried to tear his hands off the spikes, and it was not the knifing, abysmal agony that finally caused him to cease his effort, but the futility of it. The spike-heads were broad and heavy; he could not drag them through the wounds. A surge of helplessness shook the giant, for the first time in his life. He hung motionless, his head resting on his breast, shutting his eyes against the aching glare of the sun.

A beat of wings caused him to look up, just as a feathered shadow shot down out of the sky. A keen beak, stabbing at his eyes, cut his cheek, and he jerked his head aside, shutting his eyes involuntarily. He shouted, a croaking, desperate shout of menace, and the vultures swerved away and retreated, frightened by the sound. They resumed their wary circling above his head. Blood trickled over Conan's mouth, and he licked his lips involuntarily, spat at the salty taste.

Thirst assailed him savagely. He had drunk deeply of wine the night before, and no water had touched his lips since before the battle in the square, that dawn. And killing was thirsty salt-sweaty work. He glared at the distant river as a man in hell glares through the opened grille. He thought of gushing freshets of white water he had breasted, laved to the shoulders in liquid jade. He remembered great horns of foaming ale, jacks of sparkling wine gulped carelessly or spilled on the tavern floor. He bit his lip to keep from bellowing in intolerable anguish as a tortured animal bellows.

The sun sank, a lurid ball in a fiery sea of blood. Against a crimson rampart that banded the horizon the towers of the city floated unreal as a dream. The very sky was tinged with blood to his misted glare. He licked his blackened lips and stared with blood-shot eyes at the distant river. It too seemed crimson like blood, and the shadows crawling up from the east seemed black as ebony.

In his dulled ears sounded the louder beat of wings. Lifting his head he watched the shadows wheeling above him with the burning glare of a wolf. He knew that his shouts would frighten them away no longer. One dipped – dipped – lower and lower. Conan drew his head back as far as he could, waiting, watching with the terrible patience of the wilderness and its children. The vulture swept in with a

swift roar of wings. Its beak flashed down, ripping the skin on Conan's chin as he jerked aside his head; then before the bird could flash away, Conan's head lunged forward on his mighty neck muscles and his teeth, snapping like those of a wolf, locked on the bare, wattled neck.

Instantly the vulture exploded into squawking flapping hysteria. Its thrashing wings blinded the man, and its talons ripped his chest. But grimly he hung on, the muscles starting out in lumps on his jaws. And the scavenger's neck bones crunched between those powerful teeth. With a spasmodic flutter the bird hung limp. Conan let go, spat blood from his mouth. The other vultures, terrified by the fate of their companion, were in full flight to a distant tree where they perched like black demons in conclave.

Ferocious triumph surged through Conan's numbed brain. Life beat strongly and savagely through his veins. He could still deal death; he still lived. Every twinge of sensation, even of agony, was a negation of death.

"By Mitra!" Either a voice spoke, or he suffered from hallucination. "In all my life I have never seen such a thing!"

Shaking the sweat and blood from his eyes, Conan saw four horsemen sitting their steeds in the twilight and staring up at him. Three were lean, white-robed hawks, Zuagir tribesmen without a doubt, nomads from beyond the river. The other was dressed like them in a white, girdled *khalat* and a flowing head-dress which, banded about the temples with a triple circlet of braided camel-hair, fell to his shoulders. But he was not a Shemite. The dusk was not so thick, nor Conan's hawk-like sight so clouded that he could not perceive the man's facial characteristics.

He was as tall as Conan, though not so heavy-limbed. His shoulders were broad and his supple figure was hard as steel and whalebone. A short black beard did not altogether mask the aggressive jut of his lean jaw, and grey eyes cold and piercing as a sword gleamed from the shadow of the *kafieh*. Quieting his restless steed with a quick sure hand, this man spoke: "By Mitra, I should know this man!"

"Aye!" It was the guttural accents of a Zuagir. "It is the Cimmerian who was captain of the queen's guard!"

"She must be casting off all her old favorites," muttered the rider. "Who'd have ever thought it of Queen Taramis? I'd rather have had a long, bloody war. It would have given us desert folk a chance to plunder. As it is we've come this close to the walls and found only this nag" – he glanced at a fine gelding led by one of the nomads – "and this dying dog."

Conan lifted his bloody head.

"If I could come down from this beam I'd make a dying dog out of you, you Zaporoskan thief!" he rasped through blackened lips.

"Mitra, the knave knows me!" exclaimed the other. "How, knave, do you know me?"

"There's only one of your breed in these parts," muttered Conan. "You are Olgerd Vladislav, the outlaw chief."

"Aye! And once a *hetman* of the *kozaki* of the Zaporoskan River, as you have guessed. Would you like to live?"

"Only a fool would ask that question," panted Conan.

"I am a hard man," said Olgerd, "and toughness is the only quality I respect in a man. I shall judge if you are a man, or only a dog after all, fit only to lie here and die."

"If we cut him down we may be seen from the walls," objected one of the nomads.

Olgerd shook his head.

"The dusk is too deep. Here, take this axe, Djebal, and cut down the cross at the base."

"If it falls forward it will crush him," objected Djebal. "I can cut it so it will fall backward, but then the shock of the fall may crack his skull and tear loose all his entrails."

"If he's worthy to ride with me he'll survive it," answered Olgerd imperturbably. "If not, then he doesn't deserve to live. Cut!"

The first impact of the battle-axe against the wood and its accompanying vibrations sent lances of agony through Conan's swollen feet and hands. Again and again the blade fell and each stroke reverberated on his bruised brain, setting his tortured nerves aquiver. But he set his teeth and made no sound. The axe cut through, the cross reeled on its splintered base and toppled backward. Conan made his whole body a solid knot of iron-hard muscle, jammed his head back hard against the wood and held it rigid there. The beam struck the ground heavily and rebounded slightly. The impact tore his wounds and dazed him for an instant. He fought the rushing tide of blackness, sick and dizzy, but realized that the iron muscles that sheathed his vitals had saved him from permanent injury.

And he had made no sound, though blood oozed from his nostrils and his belly-muscles quivered with nausea. With a grunt of approval Djebal bent over him with a pair of pinchers used to draw horse-shoe nails, and gripped the head of the spike in Conan's right hand, tearing the skin to get a grip on the deeply embedded head. The pinchers were small for that work. Djebal sweated and tugged, swearing and wrestling with the stubborn iron, working it back and forth – in swollen flesh as well as in wood. Blood started, oozing over the Cimmerian's fingers. He lay so still he might have been dead, except for the spasmodic rise and fall of his great chest. The spike gave way, and Djebal held up the blood-stained thing with a grunt of satisfaction, then flung it away and bent over the other.

The process was repeated, and then Djebal turned his attention to Conan's skewered feet. But the Cimmerian, struggling up to a sitting posture, wrenched the pinchers from his fingers and sent him staggering backward with a violent shove. Conan's hands were swollen to almost twice their normal size. His fingers felt like misshapen thumbs, and closing his hands was an agony that brought blood streaming from under his grinding teeth. But somehow, clutching the pinchers clumsily with both hands, he managed to wrench out first one spike and then the other. They were not driven so deeply in the wood as the others had been.

He rose stiffly and stood upright on his swollen, lacerated feet, swaying drunkenly, the icy sweat dripping from his face and body. Cramps assailed him and he clamped his jaws against the desire to retch.

Olgerd, watching him impersonally, motioned him toward the stolen horse. Conan stumbled toward it and every step was a stabbing, throbbing hell that flecked his lips with bloody foam. One misshapen, groping hand fell clumsily on the saddle bow, a bloody foot somehow found the stirrup. Setting his teeth he swung up, and he almost fainted in mid-air; but he came down in the saddle – and as he did so, Olgerd struck the horse sharply with his whip. The startled beast reared, and the man in the saddle swayed and slumped like a sack of sand, almost unseated. Conan had wrapped a rein about each hand, holding it in place with a clamping thumb. Drunkenly he exerted the strength of his knotted biceps, wrenching the horse down; it screamed, its jaw almost dislocated.

One of the Shemites lifted a water-flask questioningly.

Olgerd shook his head.

"Let him wait until we get to camp. It's only ten miles. If he's fit to live in the desert he'll live that long without a drink."

The group rode like swift ghosts toward the river; among them Conan swayed like a drunken man in the saddle, blood-shot eyes glazed, foam drying on his blackened lips.

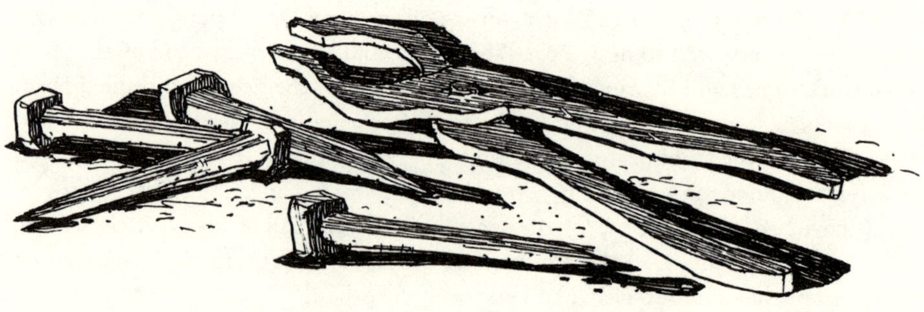

III

A Letter to Nemedia

The savant Astreas, travelling in the east in his never-tiring search for knowledge, wrote a letter to his friend and fellow-philosopher Alcemides, in his native Nemedia, which constitutes the entire knowledge of the western nations concerning the events of that period in the east, always a hazy, half-mythical region in the minds of the western folk.

Astreas wrote, in part: "– You can scarcely conceive, my dear old friend, of the conditions now existing in this tiny kingdom since Queen Taramis admitted Constantius and his mercenaries, an event which I briefly described in my last, hurried letter. Seven months have passed since then, during which time it seems as though the devil himself had been loosed in this unfortunate realm. Taramis seems to have gone quite mad; whereas formerly she was famed for her virtue, justice and tranquillity, she is now notorious for qualities precisely opposite to those just enumerated. Her private life is a scandal – or perhaps 'private' is not the correct term, since the queen makes no attempt to conceal the debauchery of her court. She constantly indulges in the most infamous revelries, in which the unfortunate ladies of the court are forced to join, young married women as well as virgins.

"She herself has not bothered to marry her paramour, Constantius, who sits on the throne beside her and reigns as her royal consort, and his officers follow his example, and do not hesitate to debauch any woman they desire, regardless of her rank or station. The wretched kingdom groans under exorbitant taxation, the farms are stripped to the bone, and the merchants go in rags which are all that is left them by the tax-gatherers. Nay, they are lucky if they escape with a whole skin.

"I sense your incredulity, good Alcemides; you will fear that I exaggerate conditions in Khauran. Such conditions would be unthinkable in any of the western countries, admittedly. But you must realize the vast difference that exists between west and east, especially this part of the east. In the first place, Khauran is a kingdom of no great size, one of the many principalities which at one time formed the eastern part of the empire of Koth, and which later regained the independence which was theirs at a still earlier age. This part of the world is made up of these tiny realms, diminutive in comparison with the great kingdoms of the west, or the great sultanates of the farther east, but important in their control of the caravan routes, and in the wealth concentrated in them.

"Khauran is the most southeasterly of these principalities, bordering on the very deserts of eastern Shem. The city of Khauran is the only city of any magnitude in the realm, and stands within sight of the river which separates the grasslands from the sandy desert, like a watch-tower to guard the fertile meadows behind it. The land is so rich that it yields three and four crops a year, and the plains north and west of the city are dotted with villages. To one accustomed to the great plantations and stock-farms of the west, it is strange to see these tiny fields and vineyards; yet wealth in grain and fruit pours from them as from a horn of plenty. The villagers are agriculturists – nothing else. Of a mixed, aboriginal race, they are unwarlike, unable to protect themselves, and forbidden the possession of arms. Dependent wholly upon the soldiers of the city for protection, they are helpless under the present conditions. So the savage revolt of the rural sections which would be a certainty in any western nation, is here impossible.

"They toil supinely under the iron hand of Constantius, and his black-bearded Shemites ride incessantly through the fields, with whips in their hands, like the slave-drivers of the black serfs who toil in the plantations of southern Zingara.

"Nor do the people of the city fare any better. Their wealth is stripped from them, their fairest daughters taken to glut the insatiable lust of Constantius and his mercenaries. These men are utterly without mercy or compassion, possessed of all the characteristics our armies learned to abhor in our wars against the Shemitish allies of Argos – inhuman cruelty, lust, and wild beast ferocity. The people of the city are Khauran's ruling caste, predominantly Hyborian, and valorous and warlike. But the treachery of their queen delivered them into the hands of their oppressors. The Shemites are the only armed force in Khauran, and the most hellish punishment is inflicted on any Khaurani found possessing weapons. A systematic persecution to destroy the young Khaurani men able to bear arms has been savagely pursued. Many have ruthlessly been slaughtered, others sold as slaves to the Turanians. Thousands have fled the kingdom and either entered the service of other rulers, or become outlaws, lurking in numerous bands along the borders.

"At present there is some possibility of invasion from the desert, which is inhabited by tribes of Shemitish nomads. The mercenaries of Constantius are men from the Shemitish cities of the west, Pelishtim, Anakim, Akkharim, and are ardently hated by the Zuagirs and other wandering tribes. As you know, good Alcemides, the countries of these barbarians are divided into the western meadowlands which stretch to the distant ocean, and in which rise the cities of the town-dwellers, and the eastern deserts, where the lean nomads hold sway; there is incessant warfare between the dwellers of the cities and the dwellers of the desert.

"The Zuagirs have fought with and raided Khauran for centuries, without success, but they resent its conquest by their western kin. It is rumored that their natural antagonism is being fomented by the man who was formerly the captain of the queen's guard, and who, somehow escaping the hate of Constantius, who actually had him upon the cross, fled to the nomads. He is called Conan, and is himself a barbarian, one of those gloomy Cimmerians whose ferocity our soldiers have more than once learned to their bitter cost. It is rumored that he has become the right-hand man of Olgerd Vladislav, the *kozak* adventurer who wandered down from the northern steppes and made himself chief of a band of Zuagirs. There are also rumors that this band has increased vastly in the last few months, and that Olgerd, incited no doubt by this Cimmerian, is even considering a raid on Khauran.

"It can not be anything more than a raid, as the Zuagirs are without siege-machines, or the knowledge of investing a city, and it has been proven repeatedly in the past that the nomads in their loose formation, or rather lack of formation, are no match in hand-to-hand fighting for the well-disciplined, fully-armed warriors of the Shemitish cities. The natives of Khauran would perhaps welcome this conquest, since the nomads could deal with them no more harshly than their present masters, and even total extermination would be preferable to the suffering they have to endure. But they are so cowed and helpless that they could give no aid to the invaders.

"Their plight is most wretched. Taramis, apparently possessed of a demon, stops at nothing. She has abolished the worship of Ishtar, and turned the temple into a shrine of idolatry. She has destroyed the ivory image of the goddess which these eastern Hyborians worship (and which, inferior as it is to the true religion of Mitra which we western nations recognize, is still superior to the devil-worship of the Shemites) and filled the temple of Ishtar with obscene images of every imaginable sort – gods and goddesses of the night, portrayed in all the salacious and perverse poses and with all the revolting characteristics that a degenerate brain could conceive. Many of these images are to be identified as foul deities of the Shemites, the Turanians, the Vendhyans, and the Khitans, but others are reminiscent of a hideous and half-remembered antiquity, vile shapes forgotten except in the most obscure legends. Where the queen gained the knowledge of them I dare not even hazard a guess.

"She has instituted human sacrifice, and since her mating with Constantius, no less than five hundred men, women and children have been immolated. Some of these have died on the altar she has set up in the temple, herself wielding the sacrificial dagger, but most have met a more horrible doom.

"Taramis has placed some sort of monster in a crypt in the temple. What it is, whence it came, none knows. But shortly after she had crushed the desperate revolt of her soldiers against Constantius, she spent a night alone in the desecrated temple, alone except for a dozen bound captives, and the shuddering people saw thick, foul-smelling smoke curling up from the dome, heard all night the frenetic chanting of the queen, and the agonized cries of her tortured captives; and toward dawn another voice mingled with these sounds – a strident, inhuman croaking that froze the blood of all who heard. In the full dawn Taramis reeled drunkenly from the temple, her eyes blazing with demoniac triumph. The captives were never seen again, nor the croaking voice heard. But there is a room in the temple into which none ever goes but the queen, driving a human sacrifice before her. And this victim is never seen again. All know that in that grim chamber lurks some monster from the black night of ages, which devours the shrieking humans Taramis delivers up to it.

"I can no longer think of her as a mortal woman, but as a rabid she-fiend, crouching in her blood-fouled lair amongst the bones and fragments of her victims, with taloned, crimsoned fingers. That the gods allow her to pursue her awful course unchecked almost shakes my faith in divine justice.

"When I compare her present conduct with her deportment when first I came to Khauran, seven months ago, I am confused with bewilderment, and almost inclined to the belief held by many of the people – that a demon has possessed the body of Taramis. A young soldier, Valerius, had another belief. He believed that a witch had assumed a form identical to that of Khauran's adored ruler. He believed that Taramis had been spirited away in the night, and confined in some dungeon, and that this being ruling in her place was but a female sorcerer. He swore that he would find the real queen, if she still lived, but I greatly fear that he himself has fallen victim to the cruelty of Constantius. He was implicated in the revolt of the palace guards, escaped and remained in hiding for some time, stubbornly refusing to seek safety abroad, and it was during this time that I encountered him and he told me his beliefs.

"But he has disappeared, as so many have, whose fate one dares not conjecture, and I fear he has been apprehended by the spies of Constantius.

"But I must conclude this letter and slip it out of the city by means of a swift carrier-pigeon, which will carry it to the post whence I purchased it, on the borders of Koth. By rider and camel-train it will eventually come to you. I must haste, before dawn. It is late, and the stars gleam whitely on the gardened roofs of

Khauran. A shuddering silence envelops the city, in which I hear the throb of a sullen drum from the distant temple. I doubt not that Taramis is there, concocting more deviltry."

But the savant was incorrect in his conjecture concerning the whereabouts of the woman he called Taramis. The girl whom the world knew as queen of Khauran stood in a dungeon, lighted only by a flickering torch which played on her features, etching the diabolical cruelty of her beautiful countenance.

On the bare stone floor before her crouched a figure whose nakedness was scarcely covered by tattered rags.

This figure Salome touched contemptuously with the upturned toe of her gilded sandal, and smiled vindictively as her victim shrank away.

"You do not love my caresses, sweet sister?"

Taramis was still beautiful, in spite of her rags and the imprisonment and abuse of seven weary months. She did not reply to her sister's taunts, but bent her head as one grown accustomed to mockery.

This resignation did not please Salome. She bit her red lip, and stood tapping the toe of her shoe against the flags as she frowned down at the passive figure. Salome was clad in the barbaric splendor of a woman of Shushan. Jewels glittered in the torchlight on her gilded sandals, on her gold breast-plates and the slender chains that held them in place. Gold anklets clashed as she moved, jeweled bracelets weighted her bare arms. Her tall coiffure was that of a Shemitish woman, and jade pendants hung from gold hoops in her ears, flashing and sparkling with each impatient movement of her haughty head. A gem-crusted girdle supported a silk skirt so transparent that it was in the nature of a cynical mockery of the convention that requires that nakedness be concealed.

Suspended from her shoulders and trailing down her back hung a darkly scarlet cloak, and this was thrown carelessly over the crook of one arm and the bundle that arm supported.

Salome stooped suddenly and with her free hand grasped her sister's disheveled hair and forced back the girl's head to stare into her eyes. Taramis met that tigerish glare without flinching.

"You are not so ready with your tears as formerly, sweet sister," muttered the witch-girl.

"You shall wring no more tears from me," answered Taramis. "Too often you have revelled in the spectacle of the queen of Khauran sobbing for mercy on her knees. I know that you have spared me only to torment me; that is why you have limited your tortures to such torments as neither slay nor permanently disfigure. But I fear you no longer; you have strained out the last vestige of hope, fright and shame from me. Slay me and be done with it, for I have shed my last tear for your enjoyment, you she-devil from hell!"

"You flatter yourself, my dear sister," purred Salome. "So far it is only your handsome body that I have caused to suffer, only your pride and self-esteem that I have crushed. You forget that, unlike myself, you are capable of mental torment. I have observed this when I have regaled you with narratives concerning the comedies I have enacted with some of your stupid subjects. But this time I have brought more vivid proof of these farces. Did you know that Krallides, your faithful councillor, had come skulking back from Turan and been captured?"

Taramis turned pale.

"What – what have you done to him?"

For answer Salome drew the mysterious bundle from under her cloak. She shook off the silken swathings and held it up – the head of a young man, the features frozen in a convulsion as if death had come in the midst of inhuman agony.

Taramis cried out as if a blade had pierced her heart.

"Oh, Ishtar! Krallides!"

"Aye! He was seeking to stir up the people against me, poor fool. Telling them that Conan spoke the truth when he said I was not Taramis. How would the people rise against the Falcon's Shemites? With sticks and pebbles? Bah! Dogs are eating his headless body in the market-place, and this foul carrion shall be cast into the sewer to rot.

"How, sister!" She paused, smiling down at her victim. "Have you discovered that you still have unshed tears? Good! I reserved the mental torment for the last. Hereafter I shall show you many such sights as – this!"

Standing there in the torchlight with the severed head in her hand she did not look like anything ever borne by a human woman, in spite of her awful beauty. Taramis did not look up. She lay face down on the slimy floor, her slim body shaken in sobs of agony, beating her clenched hands against the stones. Salome sauntered toward the door, her anklets clashing sullenly at each step, her ear-pendants winking in the torch glare.

A few moments later she emerged from a door under a sullen arch that let into a court which in turn opened upon a winding alley. A man standing there turned toward her – a giant Shemite, with somber eyes and shoulders like a bull, his great black beard falling over his mighty, silver-mailed breast.

"She wept?" His rumble was like that of a bull, deep, low-pitched and stormy. He was the general of the mercenaries, one of the few even of Constantius's associates who knew the secret of the queens of Khauran.

"Aye, Khumbanigash. There are whole sections of her sensibilities that I have not touched. When one sense is dulled by continual laceration, I will discover a newer, more poignant pang. Here, dog!" A trembling, shambling figure in rags, filth and matted hair approached, one of the beggars that slept in the alleys and open courts. There were many beggars now in Khauran. Salome tossed the head to him.

"Here, deaf one; cast that in the nearest sewer. Make the sign with your hands, Khumbanigash. He can not hear."

The general complied, and the tousled head bobbed, as the man turned painfully away.

"Why do you keep up this farce?" rumbled Khumbanigash. "You are so firmly established on the throne that nothing can unseat you. What if the Khaurani fools learn the truth? They can do nothing. Proclaim yourself in your true identity! Show them their beloved ex-queen – and cut off her head in the public square!"

"Not yet, good Khumbanigash –"

The arched door slammed on the hard accents of Salome, the stormy reverberations of Khumbanigash. The mute beggar crouched in the courtyard, and there was none to see that the hands which held the severed head were quivering strongly – brown, sinewy hands, strangely incongruous with the bent body and filthy tatters.

"I knew it!" It was a fierce, vibrant whisper, scarcely audible. "She lives! Oh, Krallides, your martyrdom was not in vain! They have her locked in that dungeon! Oh, Ishtar, if you love true men, aid me now!"

IV

Wolves of the Desert

Olgerd Vladislav filled his jeweled goblet with crimson wine from a golden jug and thrust the vessel across the ebony table to Conan the Cimmerian. Olgerd's apparel would have satisfied the vanity of any Zaporoskan *hetman.*

His *khalat* was of white silk, with pearls sewn on the bosom. Girdled at the waist with a Bakhauriot belt, its skirts were drawn back to reveal his wide silken breeches, tucked into short boots of soft green leather, adorned with gold thread. On his head was a green silk turban, wound about a spired helmet chased with gold. His only weapon was a broad curved Cherkess knife in an ivory sheath girdled high on his left hip, *kozak* fashion. Throwing himself back in his gilded chair with its carven eagles, Olgerd spread his booted legs before him, with a gusty exhalation of satisfaction, and gulped down the sparkling wine noisily.

To his splendor the huge Cimmerian opposite him offered a strong contrast, with his square-cut black mane, brown scarred countenance and burning blue eyes. He was clad in black mesh-mail, and the only glitter about him was the broad gold buckle of the belt which supported his sword in its worn leather scabbard.

They were alone in the silk-walled tent, which was hung with gilt-worked tapestries and littered with rich carpets and velvet cushions, the loot of the caravans. From outside came a low, incessant murmur, the sound that always accompanies a great throng of men, in camp or otherwise. An occasional gust of desert wind rattled the palm-leaves.

"Today in the shadow, tomorrow in the sun," quoth Olgerd, loosening his crimson girdle a trifle and reaching again for the wine-jug. "That's the way of life. Once I was a *hetman* on the Zaporoska; now I'm a desert chief. Seven months ago you were hanging on a cross outside Khauran. Now you're lieutenant to the most powerful raider between Turan and the western meadows. You should be thankful to me!"

"For recognizing my usefulness?" Conan laughed and lifted the jug. "When you allow the elevation of a man, one can be sure that you'll profit by his advancement. I've earned everything I've won, with my blood and sweat." He glanced at the scars on the insides of his palms. There were scars, too, on his body, scars that had not been there seven months ago.

"You fight like a regiment of devils," conceded Olgerd. "But don't get to thinking that you've had anything to do with the recruits who've swarmed in to join us. It was our success at raiding, guided by my wit, that brought them in. These nomads are always looking for a successful leader to follow, and they have more faith in a foreigner than in one of their own race.

"There's no limit to what we may accomplish! We have eleven thousand men now. In another year we may have three times that number. We've contented ourselves, so far, with raids on the Turanian outposts and the city-states to the west. With thirty or forty thousand men we'll raid no longer. We'll invade and conquer and establish ourselves as rulers. I'll be emperor of all Shem yet, and you'll be my vizier, as long as you carry out my orders unquestioningly. In the meantime, I think we'll ride eastward and storm that Turanian outpost at Vezek, where the caravans pay toll."

Conan shook his head. "I think not."

Olgerd glared, his quick temper irritated.

"What do you mean, *you* think not? *I* do the thinking for this army!"

"There are enough men in this band now for my purpose," answered the Cimmerian. "I'm sick of waiting. I have a score to settle."

"Oh!" Olgerd scowled, and gulped wine, then grinned. "Still thinking of that cross, eh? Well, I like a good hater. But that can wait."

"You told me once you'd aid me in taking Khauran," said Conan.

"Yes, but that was before I began to see the full possibilities of our power," answered Olgerd. "I was only thinking of the loot in the city. I don't want to waste our strength unprofitably. Khauran is too strong a nut for us to crack now. Maybe in a year –"

"Within the week," answered Conan, and the *kozak* stared at the certainty in his voice.

"Listen," said Olgerd, "even if I were willing to throw away men on such a hare-brained attempt – what could you expect? Do you think these wolves could besiege and take a city like Khauran?"

"There'll be no siege," answered the Cimmerian. "I know how to draw Constantius out into the plain."

"And what then?" cried Olgerd with an oath. "In the arrow-play our horsemen would have the worst of it, for the armor of the *asshuri* is the better, and when it came to sword-strokes their close-marshalled ranks of trained swordsmen would cleave through our loose lines and scatter our men like chaff before the wind."

"Not if there were three thousand desperate Hyborian horsemen fighting in a solid wedge such as I could teach them," answered Conan.

"And where would you secure three thousand Hyborians?" asked Olgerd with vast sarcasm. "Will you conjure them out of the air?"

"I *have* them," answered the Cimmerian imperturbably. "Three thousand men of Khauran camp at the oasis of Akrel awaiting my orders."

"*What?*" Olgerd glared like a startled wolf.

"Aye. Men who had fled from the tyranny of Constantius. Most of them have been living the lives of outlaws in the deserts east of Khauran, and are gaunt and hard and desperate as man-eating tigers. One of them will be a match for any three squat mercenaries. It takes oppression and hardship to stiffen men's guts and put the fire of hell into their thews. They were broken up into small bands; all they needed was a leader. They believed the word I sent them by my riders, and assembled at the oasis and put themselves at my disposal."

"All this without my knowledge?" A feral light began to gleam in Olgerd's eyes. He hitched at his weapon-girdle.

"It was I they wished to follow, not you."

"And what did you tell these outcasts to gain their allegiance?" There was a dangerous ring in Olgerd's voice.

"I told them that I'd use this horde of desert wolves to help them destroy Constantius and give Khauran back into the hands of its citizens."

"You fool!" whispered Olgerd. "Do you deem yourself chief already?"

The men were on their feet, facing one another across the ebony board, devil-lights dancing in Olgerd's cold grey eyes, a grim smile on the Cimmerian's hard lips.

"I'll have you torn between four palm trees," said the *kozak* calmly.

"Call the men and bid them do it!" challenged Conan. "See if they obey you!"

Baring his teeth in a snarl, Olgerd lifted his hand – then paused. There was something about the confidence in the Cimmerian's dark face that shook him. His eyes began to burn like those of a wolf.

"You scum of the western hills," he muttered. "Have you dared seek to undermine my power?"

"I didn't have to," answered Conan. "You lied when you said I had nothing to do with bringing in the new recruits. I had everything to do with it. They took your orders, but they fought for me. There is not room for two chiefs of the Zuagirs.

They know I am the stronger man. I understand them better than you, and they, me; because I am a barbarian too."

"And what will they say when you ask them to fight for the Khaurani?" asked Olgerd sardonically.

"They'll follow me. I'll promise them a camel-train of gold from the palace. Khauran will be willing to pay that as a guerdon for getting rid of Constantius. After that, I'll lead them against the Turanians as you have planned. They want loot, and they'd as soon fight Constantius for it as anybody."

In Olgerd's eyes grew a recognition of defeat. In his red dreams of empire he had missed what was going on about him. Happenings and events that had seemed meaningless before now flashed into his mind, with their true significance, bringing a realization that Conan spoke no idle boast. The giant black-mailed figure before him was the real chief of the Zuagirs.

"Not if you die!" muttered Olgerd, and his hand flickered toward his hilt. But quick as the stroke of a great cat Conan's arm shot across the table and his fingers locked on Olgerd's forearm. There was a distinct snap of breaking bones, and for a tense instant the scene held: the men facing one another as motionless as images, perspiration starting out on Olgerd's forehead. Conan laughed, never easing his grip on the broken arm.

"Are you fit to live, Olgerd?"

His smile did not alter as the corded muscles rippled in knotting ridges along his forearm and his fingers ground into the *kozak's* quivering flesh. There was the sound of broken bones grating together and Olgerd's face turned the color of ashes; blood oozed from his lip where his teeth sank, but he uttered no sound.

With a laugh Conan released him and drew back, and the *kozak* swayed, caught the table edge with his good hand to steady himself.

"I give you life, Olgerd, as you gave it to me," said Conan tranquilly. "Though it was for your own ends that you took me down from the cross. It was a bitter test you gave me then; you couldn't have endured it; neither could any one, but a western barbarian.

"Take your horse and go. It's tied behind the tent, and food and water are in the saddle-bags. None will see your going, but go quickly. There's no room for a fallen chief on the desert. If the warriors see you, maimed and deposed, they'll never let you leave the camp alive."

Olgerd did not reply. Slowly, without a word, he turned and stalked across the tent, through the flapped opening. Unspeaking he climbed into the saddle of the great white stallion that stood tethered there in the shade of a spreading palm-tree; and unspeaking, with his broken arm thrust in the bosom of his *khalat*, he reined the steed about and rode eastward into the open desert, out of the life of the people of the Zuagir.

Inside the tent Conan emptied the wine-jug and smacked his lips with relish. Tossing the empty vessel into a corner, he braced his belt and strode out through the front opening, halting for a moment to let his gaze sweep over the lines of camel-hair tents that stretched before him, and the white-robed figures that moved among them, arguing, singing, mending bridles or whetting tulwars.

He lifted his voice in a thunder that carried to the farthest confines of the encampment: "Aie, you dogs, sharpen your ears and listen! Gather around here. I have a tale to tell you."

V
The Voice from the Crystal

In a chamber in a tower near the city wall a group of men listened attentively to the words of one of their number. They were young men, but hard and sinewy, with the bearing that comes only to men rendered desperate by adversity. They were clad in mail shirts and worn leather, swords hung at their girdles.

"I knew that Conan spoke the truth when he said it was not Taramis!" the speaker exclaimed. "For months I have haunted the outskirts of the palace, playing the part of a deaf beggar. At last I learned what I had believed – that our queen was a prisoner in the dungeons that adjoin the palace. I watched my opportunity and captured a Shemitish gaoler – knocked him senseless as he left the courtyard late one night – dragged him into a cellar nearby and questioned him. Before he died he told me what I have just told you, and what we have suspected all along – that the woman ruling Khauran is a witch: Salome. Taramis, he said, is imprisoned in the lowest dungeon in the prison.

"This invasion of the Zuagirs gives us the opportunity we sought. What Conan means to do, I can not say. Perhaps he merely wishes vengeance on Constantius. Perhaps he intends sacking the city and destroying it. He is a barbarian and no one can understand their minds.

"But this is what we must do: rescue Taramis while the battle rages! Constantius will march out into the plain to give battle. Even now his men are mounting. He will do this because there is not sufficient food in the city to stand a siege. Conan burst out of the desert so suddenly that there was no time to bring in supplies. And the Cimmerian is equipped for a siege. Scouts have reported that the

Zuagirs have siege engines, built, undoubtedly, according to the instructions of Conan, who learned all the arts of war among the western nations.

"Constantius does not desire a long siege; so he will march with his warriors into the plain, where he expects to scatter Conan's forces at one stroke. He will leave only a few hundred men in the city, and they will be on the walls and in the towers commanding the gates.

"The prison will be left all but unguarded. When we have freed Taramis our next actions will depend upon circumstances. If Conan wins, we must show Taramis to the people and bid them rise – they will! Oh, they will! With their bare hands they are enough to overpower the Shemites left in the city and close the gates, against both the mercenaries and the nomads! Neither must get within the walls! Then we will parley with Conan. He was always loyal to Taramis. If he knows the truth, and she appeals to him, I believe he will spare the city. If, which is more probable, Constantius prevails, and Conan is routed, we must steal out of the city with the queen and seek safety in flight.

"Is all clear?"

They replied with one voice.

"Then let us loosen our blades in our scabbards, commend our souls to Ishtar, and start for the prison, for the mercenaries are already marching through the southern gate."

This was true. The dawnlight glinted on peaked helmets pouring in a steady stream through the broad arch, on the bright housings of the chargers. This would be a battle of horsemen, such as is possible only in the lands of the east. The riders flowed through the gates like a river of steel – somber figures in black and silver mail, with their curled beards and hooked noses, and their inexorable eyes in which glimmered the fatality of their race – the utter lack of doubt or of mercy.

The streets and the walls were lined with throngs of people who watched silently these warriors of an alien race riding forth to defend their native city. There was no sound; dully, expressionless they watched, those gaunt people in shabby garments, their caps in their hands.

In a tower that overlooked the broad street that led to the southern gate, Salome lolled on a velvet couch cynically watching Constantius as he settled his broad sword-belt about his lean hips and drew on his gauntlets. They were alone in the chamber. Outside, the rhythmical clank of harness and shuffle of horses' hoofs welled up through the gold-barred casements.

"Before nightfall," quoth Constantius, giving a twirl to his thin moustache, "you'll have some captives to feed to your temple-devil. Does it not grow weary of soft, city-bred flesh? Perhaps it would relish the harder thews of a desert man."

"Take care you do not fall prey to a fiercer beast than Thaug," warned the girl. "Do not forget who it is that leads these desert animals."

"I am not likely to forget," he answered. "That is one reason why I am advancing to meet him. The dog has fought in the west and knows the art of siege. My scouts had some trouble in approaching his columns – for his outriders have eyes like hawks – but they did get close enough to see the engines he is dragging on ox-cart wheels drawn by camels – catapults, rams, ballistas, mangonels – by Ishtar, he must have had ten thousand men working day and night for a month. Where he got the material for their construction is more than I can understand. Perhaps he has a treaty with the Turanians, and gets supplies from them.

"Anyway, they won't do him any good. I've fought these desert-wolves before – an exchange of arrows for awhile, in which the armor of my warriors protects them – then a charge and my squadrons sweep through the loose swarms of the nomads, wheel and sweep back through, scattering them to the four winds. I'll ride back through the south gate before sunset, with hundreds of naked captives staggering at my horse's tail. We'll hold a fete tonight, in the great square. My soldiers delight in flaying their enemies alive – we will have a whole-sale skinning, and make these weak-kneed townsfolk watch. As for Conan, it will afford me intense pleasure, if we take him alive, to impale him on the palace steps."

"Skin as many as you like," answered Salome indifferently. "I would like a dress made of human hide, carefully tanned. But at least a hundred captives you must give to me – for the altar, and for Thaug."

"It shall be done," answered Constantius, with his gauntleted hand brushing back the thin hair from his high bald forehead, burned dark by the sun. "For victory and the fair honor of Taramis!" he said sardonically, and, taking his vizored helmet under his arm, he lifted a hand in salute, and strode clanking from the chamber. His voice drifted back, harshly lifted in orders to his officers.

Salome leaned back on the couch, yawned, stretched herself like a great supple cat, and called: "Zang!"

A cat-footed priest, with features like yellowed parchment stretched over a skull, entered noiselessly.

Salome turned to an ivory pedestal on which stood two crystal globes, and taking from it the smaller, she handed the glistening sphere to the priest.

"Ride with Constantius," she said. "Give me the news of the battle. Go!"

The skull-faced man bowed low, with understanding, and hiding the globe under his dark mantle, hurried from the chamber.

Outside in the city there was no sound, except the clank of hoofs and after awhile the clang of a closing gate. Salome mounted a wide marble stair that led to the flat, canopied, marble-battlemented roof. She was above all other buildings of the city. The streets were deserted, the great square in front of the palace was empty. In normal times folk shunned the grim temple which rose on the opposite side of that square, but now the town looked like a dead city. Only on the southern wall and the roofs that overlooked it was there any sign of life. There the people massed thickly. They made no demonstration, did not know whether to hope for the victory or defeat of Constantius. Victory meant further misery under his intolerable rule; defeat probably meant the sack of the city and red massacre. No word had come from Conan. They did not know what to expect at his hands. They remembered that he was a barbarian. The silence of those clustered masses was oppressive, almost uncanny.

The squadrons of the mercenaries were moving out into the plain. In the distance, just this side of the river, other dark masses were moving, barely recognizable as men on horses. Objects dotted the further bank; Conan had not brought his siege engines across the river, apparently fearing an attack in the midst of the crossing. But he had crossed with his full force of horsemen. The sun rose and struck glints of fire from the dark multitudes. The squadrons from the city broke into a gallop; a deep roar reached the ears of the people on the wall.

The rolling masses merged, intermingled; at that distance it was a tangled confusion in which no details stood out. Charge and counter-charge were not to be identified. Clouds of dust rose from the plains, under the stamping hoofs, veiling the action. Through these swirling clouds masses of riders loomed, appearing and disappearing, and spears flashed.

Salome shrugged her shoulders and descended the stair. The palace lay silent. All the slaves were on the wall, gazing vainly southward with the citizens.

She entered the chamber where she had talked with Constantius, and approached the pedestal, noting that the crystal globe was clouded, shot with bloody streaks of crimson. She bent over the ball, swearing under her breath.

"Zang!" she called. "Zang!"

Mists swirled in the sphere, resolving themselves into billowing dust-clouds through which black figures rushed unrecognizably; steel glinted like lightning in the murk. Then the face of Zang leaped into startling distinctness; it was as if the wide eyes gazed up at Salome. Blood trickled from a gash in the skull-like head, the skin was grey with sweat-runnelled dust. The lips parted, writhing; to other ears than Salome's it would have seemed that the face in the crystal contorted silently. But to her sound came as plainly from those ashen lips as if the priest had been in the same room with her, instead of miles away, shouting into the smaller crystal. Only the gods of darkness knew what unseen, magic filaments linked together those shimmering spheres.

"Salome!" shrieked the bloody head. *"Salome!"*

"I hear!" she cried. "Speak! How goes the battle?"

"Doom is upon us!" screamed the skull-like apparition. "Khauran is lost! Aie, my horse is down and I can not win clear! Men are falling around me! They are dying like flies, in their silvered mail!"

"Stop yammering and tell me what happened!" she cried harshly.

"We rode at the desert-dogs and they came on to meet us!" yowled the priest. "Arrows flew in clouds between the hosts and the nomads wavered. Constantius ordered the charge. In even ranks we thundered upon them.

"Then the masses of their horde opened to right and left, and through the cleft rushed three thousand Hyborian horsemen whose presence we had not even suspected. Men of Khauran, mad with hate! Big men in full armor on massive horses! In a solid wedge of steel they smote us like a thunderbolt. They split our ranks asunder before we knew what was upon us, and then the desert-men swarmed on us from either flank.

"They have ripped our ranks apart, broken and scattered us! It is a trick of that devil Conan! The siege engines are false – mere frames of palm trunks and painted silk, that fooled our scouts who saw them from afar. A trick to draw us out to our doom! Our warriors flee! Khumbanigash is down – Conan slew him. I do not see Constantius. The Khaurani rage through our milling masses like blood-mad lions, and the desert-men feather us with arrows. I – ahhh!"

There was a flicker as of lightning, or trenchant steel, a burst of bright blood – then abruptly the image vanished, like a bursting bubble, and Salome was staring into an empty crystal ball that mirrored only her own furious features.

She stood perfectly still for a few moments, erect and staring into space. Then she clapped her hands and another skull-like priest entered, as silent and immobile as the first.

"Constantius is beaten," she said swiftly. "We are doomed. Conan will be crashing at our gates within the hour. If he catches me, I have no illusions as to what I can expect. But first I am going to make sure that my cursed sister never ascends the throne again. Follow me! Come what may, we shall give Thaug a feast."

As she descended the stairs and galleries of the palace, she heard a faint rising echo from the distant walls. The people there had begun to realize that the battle was going against Constantius. Through the dust clouds masses of horsemen were visible, racing toward the city.

Palace and prison were connected by a long closed gallery, whose vaulted roof rose on gloomy arches. Hurrying along this, the false queen and her slave passed through a heavy door at the other end that let them into the dim-lit recesses of the prison. They had emerged into a wide, arched corridor at a point near where a stone stair descended into the darkness. Salome recoiled suddenly, swearing. In the gloom of the hall lay a motionless form – a Shemitish gaoler, his short beard tilted toward the roof as his head hung on a half-severed neck. As panting voices from below reached the girl's ears, she shrank back into the black shadow of an arch, pushing the priest behind her, her hand groping in her girdle.

VI
The Vulture's Wings

It was the smoky light of a torch which roused Taramis, queen of Khauran, from the slumber in which she sought forgetfulness. Lifting herself on her hand she raked back her tangled hair and blinked up, expecting to meet the mocking countenance of Salome, malign with new torments. Instead a cry of pity and horror reached her ears.

"Taramis! Oh, my queen!"

The sound was so strange to her ears that she thought she was still dreaming. Behind the torch she could make out figures now, the glint of steel, then five countenances bent toward her, not swarthy and hook-nosed, but lean, aquiline faces, browned by the sun. She crouched in her tatters, staring wildly.

One of the figures sprang forward and fell on one knee before her, arms stretched appealingly toward her.

"Oh, Taramis! Thank Ishtar we have found you! Do you not remember me, Valerius? Once with your own lips you praised me, after the battle of Korveka!"

"Valerius!" she stammered. Suddenly tears welled into her eyes. "Oh, I dream! It is some magic of Salome's, to torment me!"

"No!" The cry rang with exultation. "It is your own true vassals come to rescue you! Yet we must hasten. Constantius fights in the plain against Conan, who has brought the Zuagirs across the river, but three hundred Shemites yet hold the city. We slew the gaoler and took his keys, and have seen no other guards. But we must begone. Come!"

The queen's legs gave way, not from weakness but from the reaction. Valerius lifted her like a child, and with the torch-bearer hurrying before them, they left the dungeon and went up a slimy stone stair. It seemed to mount endlessly, but presently they emerged into a wide corridor and started down it.

They were passing a dark arch when the torch was suddenly struck out, and the bearer cried out in fierce, brief agony. A burst of blue fire glared in the dark corridor, in which the furious face of Salome was limned momentarily, with a beast-like figure crouching beside her – then the eyes of the watchers were blinded by that blaze.

Valerius tried to stagger along the corridor with the queen; dazedly he heard the sound of murderous blows driven deep in flesh, accompanied by gasps of death and a bestial grunting. Then the queen was torn brutally from his arms, and a savage blow on his helmet dashed him to the floor.

Grimly he crawled to his feet, shaking his head in an effort to rid himself of the blue flame which seemed still to dance devilishly before him. When his blinded sight cleared, he found himself alone in the corridor – alone except for the dead. His four companions lay in their blood, heads and bosoms cleft and gashed. Blinded and dazed in that hell-born glare, they had died without an opportunity of defending themselves. The queen was gone.

With a bitter, poignant curse Valerius caught up his sword, tearing his cleft helmet from his head to clatter on the flags; blood ran down his cheek from a cut in his scalp.

Reeling, frantic with indecision, he heard a voice calling his name in desperate urgency: "Valerius! *Valerius!*"

He staggered in the direction of the voice, and rounded a corner just in time to have his arms filled with a soft, supple figure which flung itself frantically at him.

"Ivga! Are you mad!"

"I had to come!" she sobbed. "I followed you – hid in an arch of the outer court. A moment ago I saw *her* emerge with a brute who carried a woman in his arms. I knew it was Taramis, and that you had failed! Oh, you are hurt!"

"A scratch!" He put aside her clinging hands. "Quick, Ivga, tell me which way they went!"

"They fled across the square toward the temple."

He paled. "Ishtar! Oh, the fiend! She means to give Taramis to the devil she worships! Quick, Ivga! Run to the south wall where the people watch the battle! Tell them that their real queen has been found – that the impostor has dragged her to the temple! Go!"

Sobbing, the girl sped away, her light sandals pattering on the cobble-stones, and Valerius raced across the court, plunged into the street, dashed into the square upon which it debouched, and raced for the great structure that rose on the opposite side.

His flying feet spurned the marble as he darted up the broad stair and through the pillared portico. Evidently their prisoner had given them some trouble. Taramis, sensing the doom intended for her, was fighting against it with all the strength of her splendid young body. Once she had broken away from the brutish priest, only to be dragged down again.

The group was half way down the broad nave, at the other end of which stood the grim altar and beyond that the great metal door, obscenely carven, through which many had gone, but from which only Salome had ever emerged. Taramis's breath came in panting gasps; her tattered garment had been torn from her in the struggle. She writhed in the grasp of her apish captor like a white, naked nymph in the arms of a satyr. Salome watched cynically, though impatiently, moving toward the carven door, and from the dusk that lurked along the lofty walls the obscene gods and gargoyles leered down, as if imbued with salacious life.

Choking with fury Valerius rushed down the great hall sword in hand. At a sharp cry from Salome, the skull-faced priest looked up, then released Taramis, drew a heavy knife, already smeared with blood, and ran at the oncoming Khaurani.

But cutting down men blinded by the devil's-flame loosed by Salome was different from fighting a wiry young Hyborian afire with hate and rage.

Up went the dripping knife, but before it could fall Valerius's long keen narrow blade slashed through the air, and the fist that held the knife jumped from its wrist in a shower of blood. Valerius, berserk, slashed again and yet again before the crumpling figure could fall. The blade licked through flesh and bone. The skull-like head fell one way, the half-sundered torso the other.

Valerius whirled on his toes, quick and fierce as a jungle-cat, glaring about for Salome. She must have exhausted her fire-dust in the prison. She was bending over Taramis, grasping her sister's black locks in one hand, in the other lifting a dagger. Then with a fierce cry Valerius's sword was sheathed in her breast with such fury that the point sprang out between her shoulders. With an awful shriek the witch sank down, writhing in convulsions, grasping at the naked blade as it was withdrawn, smoking and dripping. Her eyes were unhuman; with a more than human vitality she clung to the life that ebbed through the wound that split the crimson crescent on her ivory bosom. She grovelled on the floor, clawing and biting at the naked stones in her agony.

Sickened at the sight, Valerius stooped and lifted the half-fainting queen. Turning his back on the twisting figure upon the floor, he ran toward the door, stumbling in his haste. He staggered out upon the portico, halted at the head of the steps. The square thronged with people. Some had come at Ivga's incoherent cries; others had deserted the walls in fear of the onsweeping hordes out of the desert, fleeing unreasoningly toward the center of the city. Dumb resignation had vanished. The throng seethed and milled, yelling and screaming. About the road there sounded somewhere the splintering of stone and timbers.

A band of grim Shemites cleft the crowd – the guards of the northern gates, hurrying toward the south gate to reinforce their comrades there. They reined up short at the sight of the youth on the steps, holding the limp, naked figure in his arms. The heads of the throng turned toward the temple; the crowd gaped, a new bewilderment added to their swirling confusion.

"Here is your queen!" yelled Valerius, straining to make himself understood above the clamor. The people gave back a bewildered roar. They did not understand, and Valerius sought in vain to lift his voice above their bedlam. The Shemites rode toward the temple steps, beating a way through the crowd with their spears.

Then a new, grisly element introduced itself into the frenzy. Out of the gloom of the temple behind Valerius wavered a slim white figure, laced with crimson. The people screamed; there in the arms of Valerius hung the woman they thought their queen; yet there in the temple door staggered another figure, like a reflection of the other. Their brains reeled. Valerius felt his blood congeal as he stared at the swaying witch-girl. His sword had transfixed her, sundered her heart. She should be dead; by all laws of nature she should be dead. Yet there she swayed, on her feet, clinging horribly to life.

"Thaug!" she screamed, reeling in the doorway. *"Thaug!"* As in answer to that frightful invocation there boomed a thunderous croaking from within the temple, the snapping and cracking of wood and metal.

"That is the queen!" roared the captain of the Shemites, lifting his bow. "Shoot down the man and the other woman!"

But the roar of a roused hunting-pack rose from the people; they had guessed the truth at last, understood Valerius's frenzied appeals, knew that the girl who hung limply in his arms was their true queen. With a soul-shaking yell they surged on the Shemites, tearing and smiting with tooth and nail and naked hands, with the desperation of hard-pent fury loosed at last. Above them Salome swayed and tumbled down the marble stair, dead at last.

Arrows flickered about him as Valerius ran back between the pillars of the portico, shielding the body of the queen with his own. Shooting and slashing ruthlessly the mounted Shemites were holding their own with the maddened crowd. Valerius darted to the temple door – with one foot on the threshold he recoiled, crying out in horror and despair.

Out of the gloom at the other end of the great hall a vast dark form heaved up – came rushing toward him in gigantic frog-like hops. He saw the gleam of great unearthly eyes, the shimmer of fangs or talons. He fell back from the door, and then the whir of a shaft past his ear warned him that death was also behind him. He wheeled desperately. Four or five Shemites had cut their way through the throng and were spurring their horses up the steps, their bows lifted to shoot him down. He sprang behind a pillar, on which the arrows splintered. Taramis had fainted. She hung like a dead woman in his arms.

Before the Shemites could loose again, the doorway was blocked by a gigantic shape. With affrighted yells the mercenaries wheeled and began beating a frantic way through the throng, which crushed back in sudden, galvanized horror, trampling one another in their stampede.

But the monster seemed to be watching Valerius and the girl. Squeezing its vast, unstable bulk through the door, it bounded toward him, as he ran down the steps. He felt it looming behind him, a giant shadowy thing, like a travesty of nature cut out of the heart of night, a black shapelessness in which only the staring eyes and gleaming fangs were distinct.

There came a sudden thunder of hoofs; a rout of Shemites, bloody and battered, streamed across the square from the south, ploughing blindly through the packed throng. Behind them swept a horde of horsemen yelling in a familiar tongue, waving red swords – the exiles, returned! With them rode fifty black-bearded desert-riders, and at their head a giant figure in black mail.

"Conan!" shrieked Valerius. *"Conan!"*

The giant yelled a command. Without checking their headlong pace, the desert men lifted their bows, drew and loosed. A cloud of arrows sang across the square, over the seething heads of the multitude, and sank feather-deep in the black monster. It halted, wavered, reared, a black blot against the marble pillars. Again the sharp cloud sang, and yet again, and the horror collapsed and rolled down the steps, as dead as the witch who had summoned it out of the night of ages.

Conan drew rein beside the portico, leaped off. Valerius had laid the queen on the marble, sinking beside her in utter exhaustion. The people surged about, crowding in. The Cimmerian cursed them back, lifted her dark head, pillowed it against his mailed shoulder.

"By Crom, what is this? The real Taramis! Aye, by the gods! But who is that yonder?"

"The demon who wore her shape," panted Valerius.

Conan swore heartily. Ripping a cloak from the shoulders of a soldier, he wrapped it about the naked queen. Her long dark lashes quivered on her cheeks; her eyes opened, stared up unbelievingly into the Cimmerian's scarred face.

"Conan!" Her soft fingers caught at his rugged hands. "Do I dream? *She* told me you were dead –"

"Scarcely!" He grinned hardly. "You do not dream. You are queen of Khauran

again. I broke Constantius, out there by the river. Most of his dogs never lived to reach the walls, for I gave orders that no prisoners be taken – except Constantius. The city-guard closed the gate in our faces, but we burst it in with rams swung from our saddles. I left all my wolves outside, except this fifty. I didn't trust them in here, and these Khaurani lads were enough for the gate-guards."

"It has been a nightmare!" she whimpered. "Oh, my poor people! You must help me try to repay them for all they have suffered, Conan, henceforth councillor as well as captain!"

Conan laughed, but shook his head. Rising, he set the queen upon her feet, and beckoned to a number of his Khaurani horsemen who had not continued the pursuit of the fleeing Shemites. They sprang from their horses, eager to do the bidding of their new-found queen.

"No, lass, that's over with. I'm chief of the Zuagirs now, and must lead them to plunder the Turanians, as I promised. This lad, Valerius, will make you a better captain than I. I wasn't made to dwell among marble walls, anyway. But I must leave you now, and complete what I've begun. Shemites still live in Khauran."

As Valerius started to follow Taramis across the square toward the palace, through a lane opened by the wildly cheering multitude, he felt a soft hand slipped timidly into his sinewy fingers and turned to receive the slender body of Ivga in his arms. He crushed her to him and drank her kisses with the gratitude of a weary fighter who has attained rest at last through tribulation and storm.

But not all men seek rest and peace; some are born with the spirit of the storm in their blood, restless harbingers of violence and bloodshed, knowing no other path.........

The sun was rising. The ancient caravan road was throng with white-robed horsemen, in a wavering line that stretched from the walls of Khauran to a spot far out in the plain. Conan the Cimmerian sat at the head of that column, near the jagged end of a wooden beam that stuck up out of the ground. Near that stump rose a heavy cross, and on that cross a man hung by spikes through his hands and feet.

"Seven months ago, Constantius," said Conan, "it was I who hung there, and you who sat here."

Constantius did not reply; he licked his grey lips and his eyes were glassy with pain and fear. Muscles writhed like cords along his lean body.

"You are more fit to inflict torture than to endure it," said Conan tranquilly. "I hung here on a cross as you are hanging, and I lived, thanks to circumstances and a stamina peculiar to barbarians. But you civilized men are soft; your lives are not nailed to your spines as are ours. Your fortitude consists mainly in inflicting torment, not in enduring it. You will be dead before sundown. And so, Falcon of the desert, I leave you to the companionship of another bird of the desert."

He gestured toward the vultures whose shadows swept across the sands as they wheeled overhead. From the lips of Constantius came an inhuman cry of despair and horror.

Conan lifted his reins and rode toward the river that shone like silver in the morning sun. Behind him the white-clad riders struck into a trot; the gaze of each, as he passed a certain spot, turned impersonally and with the desert man's lack of compassion toward the cross and the gaunt figure that hung there, black against the sunrise. Their horses' hoofs beat out a knell in the dust. Lower and lower swept the wings of the hungry vultures.

THE END

Miscellanea

Untitled Synopsis (The People of the Black Circle)

The king of Vendhya, Bundha Chand, died in his palace in the royal city of Ayodhya. His young sister, Yasmina Devi, could not understand why he should die, since he had neither been poisoned nor wounded. As he died he called to her with a far away voice that seemed to come from beyond wind-blown gulfs, and said that his soul had been trapped by wizards in a stone room on a high mountain in the night where the wind roared among peaks that shouldered the stars. They were drawing his soul into the body of a foul night-weird, and in a moment of lucidity, he begged her to plunge her jewel-hilted golden-guarded dagger into his heart, to send his soul to Asura before the wizards could draw it back to the tower on the mountain crag. While he was dying, temple gongs and conch shells brayed and thundered in the city, and in a room whose latticed balcony overlooked a long street where torches tossed luridly, a man who called himself Kerim Shah, a noble of Iranistan, watched the wailing thousands cryptically, and speaking to a man in a plain camel-hair robe, called Khemsa, asked him why the destruction of the young king could not have been thus accomplished months or years ago. To which Khemsa answered that even magic was governed by the stars. The stars were properly placed for the destruction of Bhunda Chand – the Serpent in the House of the King. He said that a lock of the king's black hair had been obtained and sent by a camel caravan across the Jhumda River, to Peshkhauri which guards the Zhaibar Pass, up the Zhaibar into the hills of Ghulistan. The lock of hair, in a golden case crusted with jewels, had been stolen from a princess of Khosala, who had vainly loved Bhunda Chand, begging from him this small token. With this lock of hair forming a point of contact between himself and them – for discarded portions of the human body have invisible connections with the living body – a cult of wizards called Rakhashas, and by themselves the Black Seers, had performed a sorcery which robbed the young king of life, and almost his soul. Kerim Shah revealed in his conversation, what Khemsa already knew, that he was not a prince from Iranistan, but a Hyrcanian, a chief of Turan, and emissary of Yezdigerd, king of Turan, and the mightiest emperor of the East, reigning on the shores of the Sea of Vilayet. Bhunda Chand had defeated the Turanians in a great battle on the River Jhumda. Yezdigerd, plotting his destruction, had sent Kerim Shah to Vendhya, to try to conquer the Kshatriya warriors by sorcery where force had not succeeded. Meanwhile, in the palace, Yasmini Devi had stabbed her brother to save his soul, and then fallen prostrate on the reed-strown floor, while outside the priests howled and slashed themselves with copper daggers, and the gongs thundered with a strident clamor. Then the scene shifted to Peshkhauri in the shadow of the mountains of Ghulistan. The tribes of

Ghulistan were kin to those of Iranistan, but more untamed. The armies of Turan had marched through their valleys but had not conquered the hill tribes. The chief cities, Hirut, Secunderam, Bhalkhan, were in the hands of the Turanians but Khahabhul, where dwelt the king of Ghulistan, whose rule the tribes seldom acknowledge, was free, and the Turanians made no attempt to tax or otherwise oppress the mountain tribes. The governor of Peshkhauri had captured seven Afghulis, and according to instructions from Ayodhya, had sent word into the mountains that their chief, Conan, a wanderer from the west who had become a notable bandit in the hills, should come and himself bargain for their release. But Conan was wary, for the Kshatriyas had not always kept their bargains with the hill tribes. On a night the governor was in his chamber the wide window of which, open to allow the cool mountain breeze to temper the heat of the plains, was adjacent to a battlement. Through it he could see the blue Himelian night, dotted with great white stars. He was writing a letter on parchment with a golden pen dipped in the juice of crushed lotos, when to him came a masked woman, in filmy gossamer robes which did not conceal the rich silk vest and girdle and trousers beneath; her slippers were cloth-of-gold, and her head-dress, supporting the veil which fell below her breasts, was bound about with a gold-worked cord, adorned with a golden crescent. The governor recognized her as the Devi, and expostulated with her, citing the unrest of the hill tribes and the turbulence of their foreign chief, Conan, who had raided to the very walls of Peshkhauri. This indeed was not within the walls, but in the great fortress outside, near the foothills. She replied that she had learned that her brother's destruction was accomplished by the wizards known as the Black Seers, and since it would be folly to lead a Kshatriya army up into the hills, she intended bringing about her vengeance through a chief of the tribes. She ordered the governor to demand, as a price for the lives of the seven Afghulis, the destruction of the Black Seers. Then she left, but she had not gotten to her apartments when she remembered something else she wished to tell him, and she returned. Perhaps she saw a stallion tied under the outer wall. Meanwhile, the governor had heard some one drop upon the battlement outside from a turret, and the next instant a man sprang through the window, with a yard-long Zhaibar knife in his hand, and bade the governor make no sound. It was Conan, the chief of the Afghulis; he was a tall, strongly and supply built man, clad like a hillman, which attire seemed incongruous, for he was not an Eastern, but a barbaric Cimmerian. He demanded what the governor wished with him, and when told, he was suspicious. At that instant the Devi entered, the governor cried out her name in his alarm, and Conan, realizing who she was, struck the governor down with the hilt of his knife, caught up the Devi, leaped through the window onto the parapet, gained his horse and rode for the mountains, shouting in his wild exultation. The governor ordered out a party of horsemen in full pursuit. Meanwhile, a girl who acted as Khemsa's spy, took him the word. He and Kerim Shah had followed the Devi to Peshkhauri. She urged him to take advantage of his knowledge of the black art – knowledge forbidden him by his masters without their permit – and make himself rich. Her idea was that they should destroy the seven men in prison – for she knew that part of the ransom Conan would demand for the Devi would be their release – and then follow Conan into the mountains and take the girl away from him, and collect the ransom themselves. Her idea in destroying the prisoners was to gain time for themselves. So he went to the prison and destroyed them by his black magic, and he and the girl went into the mountains. In the meantime Kerim Shah had heard of the abduction – though the governor tried to keep it a secret – and he sent a rider to Secunderam to inform the satrap there, and bid him send a force southward strong enough to take the Devi away from the hillmen. He himself went into the hills with some Irakzai tribesmen he had bribed. Meanwhile Conan, who was making for the country of the Afghulis, which lay adjacent to the Zhaibar Pass, lamed his horse and was pressed so closely by the pursuing Kshatriyas that he was forced to take refuge among the Wazulis. The chief of the Wazulis was his friend, but Khemsa, following close, destroyed the chief, and the warriors tried to take the Devi from him. After a savage fight Conan won clear, taking her with him, and encountering Khemsa, resisted his magic and saw him and the girl destroyed by greater magic. The Black Seers were taking notice at last. The girl was taken from him, and carried to their tower. He fell in with Kerim Shah, and the Turanian, hearing that the Black Seers had turned against him, went with his Irakzais and Conan. In storming the tower, all were destroyed except Conan and Kerim Shah. Then they fought for the girl, and Conan won. In the meantime the force had advanced from Secunderam and fallen on the Afghulis, taking them by surprize. A force of Kshatriyas were advancing up a valley, and the Devi won her freedom by bargaining with Conan, and hurling her warriors into the battle to crush and rout the Turanians. Then he returned her safely to her people.

The Story Thus Far...

(The October and November 1934 installments of *The People of the Black Circle* in Weird Tales were headed by a short recap of the preceding chapters. Such paragraphs were usually written by the magazine's staff; those for this particular Conan story were written by Howard himself, for reasons unknown.)

(The People of the Black Circle) Robert E. Howard.

THE STORY THUS FAR.

Yasmina Devi, queen of Vendhya, sought vengeance for her brother, King Bhunda Chand, who had met his death through the sorcery of the Black Seers of Yimsha, magicians who dwelt on a mountain in Ghulistan. She did not know that his death was part of a plot of King Yezdigerd of Turan to conquer Vendhya. Yezdigerd had enlisted the aid of the Black Seers and sent to Vendhya a spy, Kerim Shah, accompanied by Khemsa, an acolyte of the Black Seers, to destroy the royal family.

Yasmina wished to secure the assistance of Conan, a Cimmerian, but chief of the Afghulis of Ghulistan, a wild country of barbarians. At her orders the governor of Peshkhauri, a border city, captured seven Afghuli headmen and threatened to hang them unless Conan put his forces at her disposal. But Conan came to Peshkhauri by night and kidnaped the Devi herself and carried her into the hills, as a hostage for the release of his men.

Gitara, Yasmina's treacherous maid, persuaded Khemsa to rebel against his masters, the Black Seers, and try to capture Yasmina from Conan to wring a huge ransom from Vendhya. Khemsa employed his sorcery to kill the seven Afghuli captives, so they could not be used by the governor to obtain Yasmina's release, and with Gitara, followed Conan and his prisoner into the hills. Kerim Shah, deserted by Khemsa, despatched a message to to the satrap of Secunderam, a Turanian outpost, ordering an army to be sent to Afghulistan to capture the Devi from Conan, and rode into the hills with a band of Irakzai, to meet the oncoming army and guide it.

In the meantime Conan, pursued by the governor's troops, had sought shelter with his friend Yar Afzal, chief of the Wazulis. Khemsa killed Yar Afzal with his magic, and tricked the Wazulis into attacking Conan, meaning to steal the Devi during the fight. But Conan escaped from the village on Yar Afzal's black stallion, carrying Yasmina with him, and Khemsa, approaching through a defile in the hills, was surprized and knocked down by the rush of the horse. The Wazulis, pursuing Conan, attacked Khemsa, who loosed upon them all the horrors of his black magic.

(The People of the Black Circle) Robert E. Howard

THE STORY THUS FAR.
(First Eight Chapters.)

Yasmina Devi, queen of Vendhya, sought vengeance for her brother, who had met his death through the sorcery of the Black Seers of Yimsha, magicians who dwelt on a mountain Ghulistan, a wild barbaric hill country.

To secure the assistance of Conan, chief of the Afghulis of that country, she had the governor of Peshkhauri capture seven Afghuli headmen as hostages. But Conan kidnaped Yasmina and carried her into the mountains. Three others desired to secure possession of Yasmina: Kerim Shah, a spy of Yezdigerd, king of Turan, who plotted the conquest of Vendhya; Khemsa, a former acolyte of the Black Seers, and his sweetheart, Gitara, Yasmina's treacherous maid. These two wished to wring a huge ransom from Vendhya.

Khemsa employed his black magic to kill the seven Afghuli headmen so they could not be used to buy Yasmina's release from Conan, and he and he and Gitara followed Conan into the hills.

Conan, in the meantime, had sought shelter with his friend Yar Afzal, chief of the Wazulis. Khemsa killed Yar Afzal with his magic, and tricked the Wazulis into driving Conan from their village. He then sought to take Yasmina from Conan, but during a fight between the two, the Black Seers themselves arrived on the scene. They destroyed Gitara and Khemsa, and carried Yasmina away with them. Before Khemsa died he gave Conan a Stygian girdle of great magic powers.

Conan, riding toward Afghulistan to gather his followers to rescue Yasmina, met five hundred of them seeking him. They had learned of the death of the seven headmen, and believed he had betrayed them. Escaping from them, he met the spy, Kerim Shah, with a band of Irakzai, riding to meet a Turanian army which was forcing its way through the hills to capture Yasmina, whom they thought a captive among the Afghulis.

Striking a temporary truce, Conan and Kerim Shah rode together toward Yimsha.

In the meantime Yasmina, in the wizard castle, had met the mysterious figure called the Master, who told her she was to be his slave. To terrify her into subjection he forced her to relive all her past reincarnations, and when she awoke, she saw a hooded shape near her in the gloom. It clasped her in its bony arms, and she screamed to see a fleshless skull grinning from the shadow of the hood.

Untitled Synopsis

Amalric, a son of a nobleman of the great house of Valerus, of western Aquilonia, halted at a palm-bordered spring in the desolate vastness of the desert that lies south of Stygia, with two companions, members of the bandit tribe of Ghanata, a negro race mixed with Shemitish blood. The Ghanatas with Amalric were named Gobir, and Saidu. Just at dusk, as they prepared to eat their frugal meal of dried dates, the third member of the tribe rode up – Tilutan, a black giant, famous for his ferocity and swordsmanship. He carried across his saddle-bow an unconscious white girl, whom he had found falling with exhaustion and thirst out on the desert as he hunted for the rare desert antelope. He cast the girl down beside the spring and began reviving her. Gobir and Saidu watched Amalric, expecting him to try to rescue her, but he feigned inidifference, and asked them which would take the girl after Tilutan wearied of her. That started an argument, and he cast down a pair of dice, telling them to gamble for her. As they crouched over the dice, he drew his sword and split Gobir's skull. Instantly Saidu attacked him, and Tilutan threw down the girl and ran at him, drawing his terrible scimitar. Amalric wheeled about, causing Saidu to receive the thrust instead of himself, and hurling the wounded man into Tilutan's arms, grappled with the giant. Tilutan bore Amalric to the earth, and was strangling him, and threw him down, and rose to procure his sword and cut off his head. But as he ran at him, his girdle became unwound and he tripped and fell over it. His sword flew from his hand and Amalric caught it up and slashed his head nearly off. Then he reeled and fell senseless. He came to life again with the girl splashing him with water. He found she spoke a language akin to the Kothic, and they could understand each other. She said her name was Lissa; she was a beautiful youngster, white soft white skin, violet eyes, and dark wavy hair. Her innocence shamed the wild young soldier of fortune, and he forwent his intention of raping her. She supposed that he had fought his companions merely to rescue her, and he did not disillusion her. She said that she was an inhabitant of the city of Gazal, lying not far to the southeast. She had run away from Gazal, on foot, her water supply had given out, and she had fainted just as she was discovered by Tilutan. Amalric put her on a camel, he mounted a horse – the other beasts having broken away and bolted into the desert during the fight – and dawn found them approaching Gazal. Amalric was astounded to find the city a mass of ruins, except for a tower in the southeastern corner. When he spoke of it, Lissa turned pale, and begged him not to talk of it. He found the people were a dreamy, kindly race, without practical sense, much given to poetry and day dreams. There were not many of them, and they were a dying race. They had come into the desert and built the city over an oasis long ago – a cultured, scholarly race, not given to war. They were never attacked by any of the fierce and brutal nomadic tribes, because these people looked on Gazal with superstitious awe, and worshipped the thing that lurked in the southeastern tower. Amalric told Lissa his story – that he had been a soldier in the army of Argos, under the Zingaran Prince Zapayo da Kova, which had sailed in ships down the Kushite coast, landed in southern Stygia, and sought to invade the kingdom from that direction, while the armies of Koth invaded from the north. But Koth had treacherously made peace with Stygia, and the army in the south was trapped. They found their escape to the sea cut off, and tried to fight their way eastward, hoping to gain the lands of the Shemites. But the army was annihilated in the desert. Amalric had fled with his companion, Conan, a giant Cimmerian, but they had been attacked by a band of wild-riding brown-skinned men of strange dress and appearance, and Conan was cut down. Amalric escaped under cover of night, and wandered in the desert, suffering from hunger and thirst, until he fell in with the three vultures of the Ghanata. He spoke of the unreality of the city of Gazal, and Lissa told him of her childish yet passionate desire to break way from the stagnating environment, and see something of the world. She gave herself to him as naturally as a child, and as they lay together on a silk-covered couch in a chamber lighted only by the starlight, they heard awful cries from a building nearby. Amalric would have investigated, but Lissa clung to him, trembling, and told him the secret of the lonely tower. There dwelt a supernatural monster, which occasionally descended into the city and devoured one of the inhabitants. What the thing was, Lissa did not know. But she told of bats flying from the tower at dusk, and returning before dawn, and of piteous cries from victims carried up into the mysterious tower. Amalric was unnerved, and recognized the thing as a mysterious deity worshipped by certain cults among the negro tribes. He urged Lissa to flee with him before dawn – the inhabitants of Gazal had so far lost their initiative that they were helpless, unable to fight or flee – like men hypnotized, which the young Aquilonian believed to be the case. He went to prepare their mounts, and returning, heard Lissa give an awful scream. He rushed into the chamber and found it empty. Sure she had been seized by the monster, he rushed to the tower, ascended a stair, and found himself in an upper chamber in which he found a white man, of strange beauty. Remembering an ancient incantation repeated to him by an old Kushite priest of a rival cult, he repeated it, binding the demon into his human form. A terrific battle then ensued, in which he drove his sword through the being's heart. As it died it screamed horribly for vengeance and was answered by voices from the air. Then it altered in a hideous manner, and Amalric fled in horror. He met Lissa at the foot of the stair. She had been frightened by a glimpse of the creature dragging its human prey through the corridors, and had run away in ungovernable panic and hidden herself. Realizing that her lover had gone to the tower to seek her, she had come to share his fate. He crushed her briefly in his arms, and led her to where he had left their mounts. It was dawn when they rode out of the city, she upon the camel and he upon the horse. Looking back on the sleeping city, in which there were no animals at all, they saw seven horsemen ride out – black robed men on gaunt black horses – following them. Panic assailed them, for they knew those were no human riders. All day they pushed their steeds mercilessly, westward, toward the distant coast. They found no water, and the horse became exhausted just before sundown. All the while the black figures had followed relentlessly, and as dusk fell they began to close in rapidly. Amalric knew they were ghoulish creatures summoned from the abyss by the death cry of the monster in the tower. As darkness gathered, the pursuers were close upon them. A bat-shaped shadow blotted out the moon, and the fugitives could smell the charnel-house reek of their hunters. Suddenly the camel stumbled and fell, and the fiends closed in. Lissa shrieked. Then there came a drum of hoofs, a gusty voice roared, and the fiends were swept away by the headlong charge of a band of horsemen. The leader of these dismounted and bent over the exhausted youth and girl, and as the moon came out, he swore in a familiar voice. It was Conan the Cimmerian. Camp was made and the fugitives given food and drink. The Cimmerian's companions were the wild-looking brown men who had attacked him and Amalric. They were the riders of Tombalku, that semi-mythical desert city whose kings had subjugated the tribes of the southwestern desert and the negro races of the steppes. Conan told them that he had been knocked senseless and carried to the distant city to be exhibited to the kings of Tombalku. There were always two of these kings, though one was generally merely a figure-head. Carried before the kings, he was doomed to die by torture, and he demanded that liquor be given him, and cursed the kings roundly. At that, one of them woke from his drowse with interest. He was a big fat negro, while the other was a lean brown-skinned man, named Zehbeh. The negro stared at Conan, and greeted him by the name of Amra, the Lion. The black man's name was Sakumbe, and he was an adventurer from the West Coast who had been connected with Conan when the latter was a corsair devastating the coast. He had become one of the kings of Tombalku partly because of the support of the negro population, partly because of the machinations of a fanatical priest, Askia, who had risen to power over Zehbeh's priest, Daura. He had Conan instantly freed, and raised to the high position of general of all the horsemen – incidentally having the present incumbent, one Kordofo, poisoned. In Tombalku were various factions – Zehbeh and the brown priests, Kordofo's kin who hated both Zehbeh and Sakumbe, and Sakumbe and his supporters, of whom the most powerful was Conan himself. All this Conan told Amalric, and the next day they rode on toward Tombalku. Conan had been riding to drive from the land the Ghanata thieves. In three days they reached Tombalku, a strange fantastic city set in the sands of the desert, beside an oasis of many springs. It was a city of many tongues. The dominant caste, the founders of the city, were a warlike brown race, descendents of the Aphaki, a Shemitish tribe which pushed into the desert several hundred years before, and mixed with the negro races. The subject tribes included the Tibu, a desert race, of mixed negro and Stygian blood; and the Bagirmi, Mandingo, Dongola, Bornu, and other negro tribes of the grasslands to the south. They arrived in Tombalku in time to witness the horrible execution of Daura, the Aphaki priest, by Askia. The Aphaki were enraged, but helpless against the determined stand of their black subjects to whom they had taught the arts of war. Sakumbe, once a man of remarkable courage, vitality and statescraft, had degenerated into a mountainous mass of fat, caring for nothing except women and wine. Conan played dice with him, got drunk with him, and suggested that they eliminate Zehbeh entirely. The Cimmerian wished to be a king of Tombalku himself. So Askia was persuaded to denounced Zehbeh, and in the bloody civil war that followed, the Aphaki were defeated, and Zehbeh fled the city with his riders. Conan took his seat beside Sakumbe, but strive as he would, he found the negro the real ruler of the city, because of his ascendency over the black races. Meanwhile, Askia had been suspicious of Amalric, and he finally denounced him as the slayer of the god worshipped by the cult of which he was a priest, and demanded that he and the girl be given to the torture. Conan refused, and Sakumbe, completely dominated by the Cimmerian, backed him up. Then Askia turned on Sakumbe and destroyed him by means of an awful magic. Conan, realizing that with Sakumbe slain, the blacks would rend him and his friends, shouted to Amalric, and cut a way through the bewildered warriors. As the companions strove to reach the outer walls, Zehbeh and his Aphaki attacked the city, and in a wild holocaust of blood and flame, Tombalku was almost destroyed, and Conan, Amalric and Lissa escaped.

Untitled Draft

Chapter 1.

Three men squatted beside the water hole, beneath the sunset sky that painted the desert umber and red. One was white, and his name was Amalric; the other two were Ghanatas, their tatters scarcely concealing their wiry black frames. Men called them Gobir and Saidu; they looked like vultures as they crouched beside the water hole.

Near by a camel ground its cud noisely, and a pair of weary horses vainly nuzzled the bare sand. The men munched dried dates cheerlessly, the black men intent only on the working of their jaws, the white man occasionally glancing at the dull red sky, or out across the level monotony where the shadows were gathering and deepening. He was first to see the horseman who rode up and drew rein with a jerk that set the steed rearing.

The rider was a giant whose skin, blacker than that of the other two, as well as his thick lips and flaring nostrils, told of negro blood in vastly predominating abundance. His wide silk pantaloons, gathered in about his bare ankles, were supported by a broad girdle wrapped repeatedly about his huge belly; that girdle also supported a flaring-tipped scimitar few men could wield with one hand. With that scimitar the man was famed where ever the dark-skinned sons of the desert rode. He was Tilutan, the pride of the Ghanata.

Across his saddle bow a limp shape lay, or rather hung. Breath hissed through the teeth of the Ghanatas as they caught the gleam of white limbs. It was a white girl who hung across Tilutan's saddle bow, face down, her loose hair flowing over his stirrup in a rippling black wave. The black grinned with a glint of white teeth, and cast her casually in to the sand, where she lay laxly, unconscious. Instinctively Gobir and Saidu turned toward Amalric, and Tilutan watched him from his saddle. Three black men against one white. The entrance of a white woman into the scene wrought a subtle change in the atmosphere.

Amalric was the only one who was apparently oblivious to the tenseness. He raked back his rebellious yellow locks absently, and glanced indifferently at the girl's limp figure. If there was a momentary gleam in his grey eyes, the others did not catch it.

Tilutan swung down from his saddle, contemptuously tossing the rein to Amalric.

"Tend my horse," he said. "By Jhil, I did not find a desert antelope, but I found this little filly. She was reeling through the sands, and she fell just as I approached. I think she fainted from weariness and thirst. Get away from there, you jackals, and let me give her a drink."

The big black stretched her out beside the water hole, and began laving her face and wrists, and trickling a few drops between her parched lips. She moaned presently and stirred vaguely. Gobir and Saidu crouched with their hands on their knees, staring at her over Tilutan's burly shoulder. Amalric stood a little apart from them, his interest seeming only casual.

"She is coming to," announced Gobir.

Saidu said nothing, but he licked his thick lips involuntarily, animal-like.

Amalric's gaze travelled impersonally over the prostrate form, from the torn sandals to the loose crown of glossy black hair. Her only garment was a silk kirtle, girdled at the waist. It left her arms, neck and part of her bosom bare, and the skirt ended several inches above her knees. On the parts revealed rested the gaze of the Ghanatas with devouring intensity, taking in the soft contours, childish in their white tenderness, yet rounded with budding womanhood.

Amalric shrugged his shoulders.

"After Tilutan, who?" he asked carelessly.

A pair of lean heads turned toward him, blood-shot eyes rolled at the question, then the black men turned and mutually stared at one another. Sudden rivalry crackled electrically between them.

"Don't fight," urged Amalric. "Cast the dice." His hand came from under his worn tunic, and he threw down a pair of dice before them. A claw like hand seized them.

"Aye!" agreed Gobir. "We cast – after Tilutan, the winner!"

Amalric cast a glance toward the giant black, who still bent above his captive, bringing life back into her exhausted body. As he looked, her long lashed lids parted; deep violet eyes stared up into the leering face of the black man, bewilderedly. An explosive exclamation of gratification escaped the thick lips of Tilutan. Wrenching a flask from his girdle, he put it to her mouth. She drank the wine mechanically. Amalric avoided her wandering gaze; one white men and three blacks – either of them his match.

Gobir and Saidu bent above the dice; Saidu cupped them in his palm, breathed on them for luck, shook and threw. Two vulture-like heads bent over the spinning cubes in the dim light. And Amalric drew and struck with the same motion. The edge sliced through a thick neck, severing the wind-pipe, and Gobir fell across the dice, spurting blood, his head hanging by a shred.

Simultaneously Saidu, with the desperate quickness of a desert man, shot to his feet and hacked ferociously at the slayer's head. Amalric barely had time to catch the stroke on his lifted sword. The whistling scimitar beat the straight blade down on the white man's head, staggering him. Amalric released his sword and threw both arms about Saidu, dragging him into close quarters where his scimitar was useless. Under the desert man's rags, the wiry frame was like steel cords.

Tilutan, comprehending the matter instantly, had cast the girl down and risen with a roar. He rushed toward the strugglers like a charging bull his great scimitar flaming in his hand. Amalric saw him coming, and his flesh turned cold. Saidu was jerking and wrenching, handicapped by the scimitar he was still seeking futilely to turn against his antagonist. Their feet twisted and stamped in the sand, their bodies ground against one another. Amalric smashed his sandal heel down on the Ghanata's bare instep, feeling bones give way. Saidu howled and plunged convulsively, and Amalric, aiding his leap with a desperate heave of his own. They lurched drunkenly about, just as Tilutan struck with a rolling drive of his broad shoulders. Amalric felt the steel rasp under part of his arm, and chug deep into Saidu's body. The Ghanata gave an agonized scream, and his convulsive start tore himself free of Amalric's grasp. Tilutan roared a furious oath and wrenching his steel free, hurled the dying man aside, but before he could strike again, Amalric, his skin crawling with the fear of that great curved blade, had grappled with him.

Despair swept over him as he felt the strength of the negro. Tilutan was wiser than Saidu. He dropped the scimitar and with a bellow, caught Amalric's throat with both hands. The great black fingers locked like iron, and Amalric, striving vainly to break their grip, was borne down, with the Ghanata's great weight pinning him to the earth. The smaller man was shaken like a rat in the jaws of a dog. His head was smashed savagely against the sandy earth. As in a red mist he saw the furious face of the negro, the thick lips writhed back in a bestial grin of hate, the teeth glistening. A bestial snarling slavered from the thick black throat.

"You want her, you white dog!" the Ghanata mouthed, insane with rage and lust." Arrrrghhh! I break your back! I tear it out your throat! I – my scimitar! I cut off your head and make her kiss it!"

A final ferocious smash of Amalric's head against the hard packed sand, and Tilutan half lifted him and hurled him down in an excess of bestial passion. Rising, the black ran, stooping like an ape, and caught up his scimitar where it lay like a broad crescent of steel in the sand. Yelling in ferocious exultation, he turned and charged back, brandishing the blade on high. Amalric rose slowly to meet him, dazed, shaken, sick from the manhandling he had received.

Tilutan's girdle had become unwound in the fight, and now the end dangled about his feet. He tripped, stumbled, fell headlong, throwing out his arms to save himself. The scimitar flew from his hand.

Amalric, galvanized, caught up the scimitar, and took a reeling step forward. The desert swam darkly to his gaze. In the dusk before him he saw Tilutan's face suddenly ashy. The wide mouth gaped, the whites of the eyeballs rolled up. The black froze on one knee and a hand, as if incapable of further motion. Then the scimitar fell, cleaving the round shaven head to the chin, where its downward course was checked with a sickening jerk. Amalric had a dim impression of a black face, divided by a widening red line, fading in the thickening shadows, then darkness caught him with a rush.

Something soft and cool was touching Amalric's face with gentle persistence. He groped blindly and his hand closed on something warm, firm and resilient. Then his sight cleared and he looked into a soft oval face, framed in lustrous black hair. As in a trance he gazed unspeaking, hungrily dwelling on each detail of the full red lips, dark violet eyes, and alabaster throat. With a start he realized the vision was speaking in a soft musical voice. The words were strange, yet possessed an illusive familiarity. A small white hand, holding a dripping bunch of silk was passed gently over his throbbing head and his face. He sat up dizzily.

It was night, under the star-splashed skies. The camel still munched its cud, a horse whinnied restlessly. Not far away lay a hulking black figure with its cleft head in a horrible puddle of blood and brains. Amalric looked up at the girl who knelt beside him, talking in her gentle unknown tongue. As the mists cleared from his brain, he began to understand her. Harking back into half forgotten tongues he had learned and spoken in the past, he remembered a language used by a scholarly class in a southern province of Koth.

"Who are you, girl?" he demanded, prisoning a small hand in his own hardened fingers.

"I am Lissa." The name was spoken with almost the suggestion of a lisp. It was like the rippling of a slender stream. "I am glad you are conscious. I feared you were not alive."

"A little more and I wouldn't have been," he muttered, glancing at the grisly sprawl that had been Tilutan. She paled, and refused to follow his gaze. Her hand trembled, and in their nearness, Amalric thought he could feel the quick throb of her heart.

"It was horrible," she faltered. "Like an awful dream. Anger – and blows – and blood – "

"It might have been worse," he growled.

She seemed sensitive to every changing inflection of voice or mood. Her free hand stole timidly to his arm.

"I did not mean to offend you. It was very brave for you to risk your life for a stranger. You are noble as the knights about which I have read."

He cast a quick glance at her. Her wide clear eyes met his, reflecting only the thought she had spoken. He started to speak, then changed his mind and said another thing.

"What are you doing in the desert?"

"I came from Gazal," she answered. "I – I was running away. I could not stand it any longer. But it was hot and lonely and weary, and I saw only sand, sand – and the blazing blue sky. The sands burned my feet, and my sandals were worn out quickly. I was so thirsty, my canteen was soon empty. And then I wished to return to Gazal, but one direction looked like another. I did not know which way to go. I was terribly afraid, and started running in the direction in which I thought Gazal to be. I do not remember much after that; I ran until I could run no further, and I must have lain in the burning sand for awhile. I remember rising and staggering on, and toward the last, I thought I heard some one shouting, and saw a black man on a black horse riding toward me, and then I knew no more, until I awoke and found myself lying with my head in that man's lap, while he gave me wine to drink. Then there was shouting and fighting –" she shuddered. "When it was all over, I crept to where you lay like a dead man, and I tried to bring you to – "

"Why?" he demanded.

She seemed at a loss. "Why," she floundered, "why, you were hurt – and – why, it is what anyone would do. Besides, I realized that you were fighting to protect me from these black men. The people of Gazal have always said that the black people were wicked, and would harm the helpless."

"That's no exclusive characteristic of the blacks," muttered Amalric. "Where is this Gazal?"

"It can not be far," she answered. "I walked a whole day – and then I do not know how far the black man carried me, after he found me. But he must have discovered me about sunset, so he could not have come far."

"In what direction?" he demanded.

"I do not know. I travelled eastward when I left the city."

"City?" he muttered. "A day's travel from this spot? I had thought there was only desert for a thousand miles."

"Gazal is in the desert," she answered. "It is built amidst the palms of an oasis."

Putting her aside, he got to his feet, swearing softly as he fingered his throat, the skin of which was bruised and lacerated. He examined the three blacks in turn, finding no life in either. Then one by one he dragged them a short distance out into the desert. Somewhere the jackals began yelping. Returning to the water hole, where the girl squatted patiently, he cursed to find only the black stallion of Tilutan with the camel. The other horses had broken their tithers and bolted during the fight.

Amalric went to the girl and proffered her a handful of dried dates. She nibbled at them eagerly, while the other sat and watched her, his chin on his fists, an increasing impatience throbbing in his veins.

"Why did you run away?" he asked abruptly. "Are you a slave?"

"We have no slaves in Gazal," she answered. "Oh, I was weary – so weary of the eternal monotony. I wished to see something of the outer world. Tell me, from what land do you come?"

"I was born in the western hills of Aquilonia," he answered.

She clapped her hands like a delighted child.

"I know where it is! I have seen it on the maps. It is the westernmost country of the Hyborians, and its king is Epeus the Sword-wielder!"

Amalric experienced a distinct shock. His head jerked up and he stared at his fair companion.

"Epeus? Why, Epeus has been dead for nine hundred years. The king's name is Vilerus."

"Oh, of course," she said, rather embarrassedly. "I am foolish. Of course, Epeus was king nine centuries ago, as you say. But tell me – tell me all about the world!"

"Why, that's a big order," he answered nonplussed. "You have not traveled?"

"This is the first time I have ever been out of sight of the walls of Gazal," she declared.

His gaze was fixed on the curve of her white bosom. He was not interested in her adventures at the moment, and Gazal might have been Hell for all he cared.

He started to speak, then changing his mind caught her roughly in his arms, his muscles tensed for the struggle he expected. But he encountered no restistance. Her soft yielding body lay across his knees, and she looked up at him somewhat in surprize, but without fear or embarrassment. She might have been a child, submitting to a new kind of play. Something about her direct gaze confused him. If she had screamed, wept, fought, or smiled knowingly, he would have known how to deal with her.

"Who in Mitra's name are you, girl?" he asked roughly. "You are neither touched with the sun, nor playing a game with me. Your speech shows you to be no ignorant country lass, innocent in ignorance. Yet you seem to know nothing of the world and its ways."

"I am a daughter of Gazal," she answered helplessly. "If you saw Gazal perhaps you would understand."

He lifted her and set down in the sand. Rising, he brought a saddle blanket and spread it out for her.

"Sleep, Lissa," he said, his voice harsh with conflicting emotions. "Tomorrow I mean to see Gazal."

At dawn they started westward. Amalric had placed Lissa on the camel, showing her how to maintain her balance. She clung to the seat with both hands, showing no knowledge whatever of camels, which again surprized the young Aquilonian. A girl raised in the desert, she had never before been on a camel, nor, until the preceding night, had she ever ridden or been carried on a horse. Amalric had manufactured a sort of cloak for her, and she wore it without question, not asking whence it came, accepting it as she accepted all things he did for her, gratefully, but blindly, without asking the reason. Amalric did not tell her that the silk that shielded her from the sun had once covered the black hide of her abductor.

As they rode she again begged him to tell her something of the world, like a child asking for a story.

"I know Aquilonia is far from this desert," she said. "Stygia lies between, and the Lands of Shem, and other countries. How is it that you are here, so far from your home land?"

He rode for a space in silence, his hand on the camel's guide-rope.

"Argos and Stygia were at war," he said abruptly. "Koth became embroiled. The Kothians urged a simultaneous invasion of Stygia. Argos raised an army of mercenaries, which went into ships and sailed southward along the coast. At the same time, a Kothic army was to invade Stygia by land. I was one of that mercenary army. We met the Stygian fleet and defeated it, driving it back into Khemi. We should have landed and looted the city, and advanced along the course of the Styx – but our admiral was cautious. Our leader was Prince Zapayo da Kova, a Zingaran. We cruised southward until we reached the jungle-clad coasts of Kush. There we landed, and the ships anchored, while the army pushed eastward, along the Stygian border, burning and pillaging as we went. It was our intention to turn northward at a certain point and strike into the heart of Stygia, to form a juncture with the Kothic host which was supposed to be pushing down from the north. Then word came that we were betrayed. Koth had concluded a separate peace with the Stygians. A Stygian army was pushing southward to intercept us, while another already had cut us off from the coast.

"Prince Zapayo, in desperation, conceived the mad idea of marching eastward, hoping to skirt the Stygian border and eventually reach the eastern Lands of Shem. But the army from the north overtook us. We turned and fought. All day we fought, and drove them back in route to their camp. But the next day the pursuing army came up from the west, and crushed between the hosts, our army ceased to be. We were broken, annihilated, destroyed. There were few left to flee. But when night fell, I broke away with my companion, a Cimmerian named Conan, a brute of a man, with the strength of a bull.

"We rode southward into the desert, because there was no other direction in which we might go. Conan had been in this part of the world before, and he believed we had a chance to survive. Far to the south we found an oasis, but Stygian riders harried us, and we fled again, from oasis to oasis, fleeing, starving, thirsting, until we found ourselves in a barren unknown land of blazing sand and empty sand. We rode until our horses were reeling, and we were half delirious. Then one night we saw fires, and rode up to them, taking a desperate chance that we might make friends with them. As soon as we came within range, a shower of arrows greeted us. Conan's horse was hit, and reared, throwing its rider. His neck must have broken like a twig, for he never moved. I got away in the darkness, somehow, though my horse died under me. I had only a glance of the attackers – tall, lean, brown men, wearing strange barbaric garments.

"I wandered on foot through the desert, and fell in with those three vultures you saw yesterday. They were jackals – Ghanatas, members of a robber tribe, of mixed blood, negro and Mitra knows what else. The only reason they didn't murder me was because I had nothing they wished. For a month I have been wandering and thieving with them, because there was nothing else I could do."

"I do not know it was like that," she murmured faintly. "They said there were wars and cruelty out in the world, but it seemed like a dream and far away. But hearing you speak of treachery and battle seems almost like seeing it."

"Do no enemies ever come against Gazal?" he demanded.

She shook her head. "Men ride wide of Gazal. Sometimes I have seen black dots moving in lines along the horizons, and the old men said it was armies moving to war, but they never come near Gazal."

Amalric felt a dim stirring of uneasiness. This desert, seemingly empty of life, never the less contained some of the fiercest tribes on earth – the Ghanatas, who ranged far to the east; the masked Tibu, whom he believed dwelt further to the south; and somewhere off to the southwest lay the semi-mythical empire of Tombalku, ruled by a wild and barbaric race. It was strange that a city in the midst of this savage land should be left so completely alone that one of its inhabitants did not even know the meaning of war.

When he turned his gaze elsewhere, strange thoughts assailed him. Was the girl touched by the sun? Was she a demon in womanly form come out of the desert to lure him to some cryptic doom? A glance at her clinging childishly to the high peak of the camel saddle was sufficient to dispel these broodings. Then again doubt assailed him. Was he bewitched? Had she cast a spell on him?

Westward they forged steadily, halting only to nibble dates and drink water at midday. Amalric fashioned a frail shelter out of his sword and sheath and the saddle blankets, to shield her from the burning sun. Weary and stiff from the tossing, bucking gait of the camel, she had to be lifted down in his arms. As he felt again the voluptuous sweetness of her soft body, he felt a hot throb of passion sear through him, and he stood momentarily motionless, intoxicated with the nearness of her, before he laid her down in the shade of the make-shift tent.

He felt a touch of almost anger at the clear gaze with which she met his, at the docility with which she yielded her young body to his hands. It was as if she was unaware of things which might harm her; her innocent trust shamed him and pent a helpless wrath within him.

As they ate, he did not taste the dates he munched; his eyes burned on her, avidly drinking in every detail of her lithe young figure. She seemed as unaware of his intentness as a child. When he lifted her to place her again on her camel, and her arms went instinctively about his neck, he shuddered. But he lifted her up on her mount, and they took up the journey once more.

It was just before sundown when Lissa pointed and cried out: "Look! The towers of Gazal!"

On the desert rim he saw them – spires and minarets, rising in a jade-green cluster against the blue sky. But for the girl, he would have thought it the phantom city of a mirage. He glanced at Lissa curiously; she showed no signs of eager joy at her home coming. She sighed, and her slim shoulders seemed to droop.

As they approached the details swam more plainly into view. Sheer from the desert sands rose the wall which enclosed the towers. And Amalric saw that the wall was crumbling in many places. The towers, too, he saw, were much in disrepair. Roofs sagged, broken battlements gaped, spires leaned drunkenly. Panic assailed him; was it a city of the dead to which he rode, guided by a vampire? A quick glance at the girl reassured him. No demon could lurk in that divinely molded exterior. She glanced at him with a strange wistful questioning in her deep eyes, turned irresolutely toward the desert, then, with a deep sigh, set her face toward the city, as if gripped by a subtle and fatalistic despair.

Now through the gaps of the jade green wall, Amalric saw figures moving within the city. No one hailed them as they rode through a broad breach in the wall, and came out into a broad street. Close at hand, limned in the sinking sun, the decay was more apparent. Grass grew rank in the streets, pushing through shattered paving; grass grew rank in the small plazas. Streets and courts likewise were littered with rubbish of masonry and fallen stones.

Domes rose, cracked and discolored. Portals gaped, vacant of doors. Every where ruin had laid his hand. Then Amalric saw one spire untouched; a shining red cylindrical tower which rose in the extreme south eastern corner of the city. It shone among the ruins.

Amalric indicated it.

"Why is that tower less in ruins than the others?" he asked. Lissa turned pale; she trembled, and caught his hand convulsively.

"Do not speak of it!" she whispered. "Do not look toward it – do not even *think* of it!"

Amalric scowled; the nameless implication of her words somehow changed the aspect of the mysterious tower. Now it seemed like a serpent's head rearing among ruin and desolation.

The young Aquilonian looked warily about him. After all, he had no assurance that the people of Gazal would receive him in a friendly manner. He saw people moving leisurely about the streets. They halted and stared at him, and for some reason his flesh crawled. They were men and women with kindly features, and their looks were mild. But their interest seemed so slight – so vague and impersonal. They made no movement to approach him or to speak to him. It might have been the most common thing in the world for an armed horseman to ride into their city from the desert; yet Amalric knew that was not the case, and the casual manner with which the people of Gazal received him, caused a faint uneasiness in his bosom.

Lissa spoke to them, indicating Amalric, whose hand she lifted like an affectionate child. "This is Amalric of Aquilonia, who rescued me from the black people and has brought me home."

A polite murmur of welcome rose from the people, and several of them approached to extend their hands. Amalric thought he had never seen such vague, kindly faces; their eyes were soft and mild, without fear and without wonder. Yet they were not the eyes of stupid oxen; rather, they were the eyes of people wrapped in dreams.

Their stare gave him a feeling of unreality; he hardly knew what was said to him. His mind was occupied by the strangeness of it all; these quiet dreamy people, in their silken tunics and soft sandals, moving with aimless vagueness among the discolored ruins. A lotus paradise of illusion? Somehow the thought of that sinister red tower struck a discordant note.

One of the men, his face smooth and unlined, but his hair silver, was saying: "Aquilonia? There was an invasion – we heard – King Bragorus of Nemedia – how went the war?"

"He was driven back," answered Amalric briefly, resisting a shudder. Nine hundred years had passed since Bragorus led his spearmen across the marches of Aquilonia.

His questioner did not press him further; the people drifted away, and Lissa tugged at his hand. He turned, feasted his eyes upon her; in a realm of illusion and dream, her soft firm body anchored his wandering conjectures. She was no dream; she was real; her body was sweet and tangible as cream and honey.

"Come, let us go to rest and eat."

"What of the people?" he demurred. "Will you not tell them of your experiences?"

"They would not heed, except for a few minutes," she answered. "They would listen a little, and then drift away. They hardly know I have been gone. Come!"

Amalric led the horse and camel into an enclosed court where the grass grew high, and water seeped from a broken fountain into a marble trough. There he tethered them, then he followed Lissa. Taking his hand she led him across the court, into an arched doorway. Night had fallen. In the open space above the court, the stars were clustering, etching the jagged pinnacles. Through a series of dark chambers Lissa went, moving with the sureness of long practise. Amalric groped after her, guided by her little hand in his. He found it no pleasant adventure. The scent of dust and decay hung in the thick darkness. Under his feet sometimes were broken tiles, by the feel of them, sometimes worn carpets. His free hand touched the fretted arches of doorways. Then the stars gleamed through a broken roof, showing him a dim winding hallway, hung with rotting tapestries. They rustled in a faint wind and their noise was like the whispering of witches, causing the hair to stir next his scalp.

Then they came into a chamber dimly lighted by the starshine streaming through open windows, and Lissa released his hand, fumbled an instant and produced a faint light of some sort. It was a glassy knob which glowed with a golden radiance. She set it on a marble table, and indicated that Amalric should recline on a couch thickly littered with silks. Groping into some mysterious recess, she produced a gold vessel of wine, and others containing food unfamiliar to Amalric. There were dates; the others, pallid and insipid to his taste, he did not recognize. The wine was pleasant to the palate, but no more heady than dish water.

Seated on a marble seat opposite him, Lissa nibbled daintily.

"What sort of place is this?" he demanded. "You are like these people – yet strangely unlike."

"They say I am like our ancestors," answered Lissa. "Long ago they came into the desert and built this city over a great oasis which was in reality only a series of springs. The stone they took from the ruins of a much older city – only the red tower – " her voice dropped and she glanced nervously at the star-framed windows – "only the red tower stood there. It was empty – then.

"Our ancestors, who were called Gazali, once dwelt in southern Koth. They were noted for their scholarly wisdom. But they sought to revive the worship of Mitra, which the Kothians had long ago abandoned, and the king drove them from his kingdom. They came southward, many of them, priests, scholars, teachers, scientists, with their Shemitish slaves.

"They reared Gazal in the desert; but the slaves revolted almost as soon as the city was built, and fleeing, mixed with the wild tribes of the desert. They were not illy treated – word came to them in the night – a word which sent them fleeing madly from the city into the desert.

"My people dwelt here, learning to manufacture their food and drink from such material as was at hand. Their learning was a marvel. When the slaves fled, they took with them every camel, horse and donkey in the city. There was no communication with the outer world. There are whole chambers in Gazal filled with maps and books and chronicles, but they are all nine years old at the lest; for it was nine hundred years ago that my people fled from Koth. Since then no man of the outside world has set foot in Gazal. And the people are slowly vanishing. They have become so dreamy and introspective that they have neither human passions nor ambitions. The city falls into ruins and none moves hand to repair it. Horror – " she choked and shuddered; "when horror came upon them, they could neither flee nor fight."

"What do you mean?" he whispered, a cold wind blowing on his spine. The rustling of rotten hangings down nameless black corridors stirred dim fear in his soul.

She shook her head; she rose, came around the marble table, laid hands on his shoulders. Her eyes were wet and they shone with horror and a desperate yearning that caught at his throat. Instinctively his arm went around her lithe form, and he felt her tremble.

"Hold me!" she begged. "I am afraid! Oh, I have dreamed of such a man as you. I am not like my people; they are dead men walking forgotten streets; but I am alive. I am warm and sentient. I hunger and thirst and yearn for life. I can not abide the silent streets and ruined halls and dim people of Gazal, though I have never known anything else. That is why I ran away – I yearned for life – "

She was sobbing uncontrollably in his arms. Her hair streamed over his face; her fragrance made him dizzy. Her firm body strained against his. She was lying across his knees, her arms locked about his neck. Straining her to his breast he crushed her lips with his. Eyes, lips, cheeks, hair, throat, breasts, he showered with hot kisses, until her sobs changed to panting gasps. His passion was not the violence of a ravisher. The passion that slumbered in her woke in one overpowering wave. The glowing gold ball, struck by his groping fingers, tumbled to the floor and was extinguished. Only the starshine gleamed through the windows.

Lying in Amalric's arms on the silk-heaped couch, Lissa opened her heart and whispered her dreams and hopes and aspirations, childish, pathetic, terrible.

"I'll take you away," he muttered. "Tomorrow. You are right. Gazal is a city of the dead; we will seek life and the outer world. It is violent, rough, cruel; but better that than this living death – "

The night was broken by a shuddering cry of agony, horror and despair. Its timbre brought out cold sweat on Amalric's skin. He started upright from the couch, but Lissa clung to him desperately.

"No, no!" she begged in a frantic whisper. "Do not go! Stay!"

"But murder is being done!" he exclaimed, fumbling for his sword. The cries seemed to come from across an outer court. Mingled with them there was an indescribable tearing, rending sound. They rose higher and thinner, unbearable in their hopeless agony, then sank away in a long shuddering sob.

"I have heard men dying on the rack cry out like that!" muttered Amalric, shaking with horror. "What devil's work is this?"

Lissa was trembling violently in a frenzy of terror. He felt the wild pounding of her heart.

"It is the Horror of which I spoke!" she whispered. "The Horror which dwells in the red tower. Long ago it came – some say it dwelt there in the lost years, and returned after the building of Gazal. It devours human beings. Bats fly from the tower. What it is, no one knows, since none have seen it and lived to tell of it. It is a god or a devil. That is why the slaves fled; why the desert people shun Gazal. Many of us have gone into its awful belly. Eventually all will have gone, and it will rule over an empty city, as men say it ruled over the ruins from which Gazal was reared."

"Why have the people stayed to be devoured?" he demanded.

"I do not know," she whimpered; "they dream – "

"Hypnosis," muttered Amalric; "hypnosis coupled with decay. I saw it in their eyes. This devil has them mesmerized. Mitra, what a foul secret!"

Lissa pressed her face against his bosom and clung to him.

"But what are we to do?" he asked uneasily.

"There is nothing to do," she whispered. "Your sword would be helpless. Perhaps *It* will not harm us. It has taken a victim tonight. We must wait like sheep for the butcher."

"I'll be damned if I will!" Amalric exclaimed, galvanized. "We will not wait for morning. We'll go tonight. Make a bundle of food and drink. I'll get the horse and camel and bring them to the court outside. Meet me there!"

Since the unknown monster had already struck, Amalric felt that he was safe in leaving the girl alone for a few minutes. But his flesh crawled as he groped his way down the winding corridor and through the black chambers where the swinging tapestries whispered. He found the beasts huddled nervously together in the court where he had left them. The stallion whinnied anxiously and nuzzled him, as if sensing peril in the breathless night.

He saddled and bridled and hurriedly led them through the narrow opening onto the street. A few minutes later he was standing in the starlit court. And even as he reached it, he was electrified by an awful scream which rang shudderingly upon the air. It came from the chamber where he had left Lissa.

He answered that piteous cry with a wild yell; drawing his sword he rushed across the court, hurled himself through the window. The golden ball was glowing again, carving out black shadows in the shrinking corners. Silks lay scattered on the floor. The marble seat was upset. But the chamber was empty.

A sick weakness overcame Amalric and he staggered against the marble table, the dim light waving dizzily to his sight. Then he was swept by a mad rage. The red tower! There the fiend would bear his victim!

He darted back across the court, sought the streets and raced toward the tower which glowed with an unholy light under the stars. The streets did not run straight. He cut through silent black buildings and crossed courts whose rank grass waved in the night wind.

Ahead of him, clustered about the crimson tower, rose a heap of ruins, where decay had eaten more savagely than at the rest of the city. Apparently none dwelt among them. They reeled and tumbled, a crumbling mass of quaking masonry, with the red tower rearing up among them like a poisonous red flower from charnel house ruin.

To reach the tower he would be forced to traverse the ruins. Recklessly he plunged into the black mass, groping for a door. He found one and entered, thrusting his sword ahead of him. Then he saw such a vista as men sometimes see in fantastic dreams. Far ahead of him stretched a long corridor, visible in a faint unhallowed glow, its black walls hung with strange shuddersome tapestries. Far down it he saw a receding figure – a white, naked, stooped figure, lurching along, dragging something the sight of which filled him with sweating horror. Then the apparition vanished from his sight, and with it vanished the eery glow. Amalric stood in the soundless dark, seeing nothing, hearing nothing; thinking only of a stooped white figure that dragged a limp human down a long black corridor.

As he groped onward, a vague memory stirred in his brain – the memory of a grisly tale mumbled to him over a dying fire in the skull-heaped devil-devil hut of a black witchman – a tale of a god which dwelt in a crimson house in a ruined city and which was worshipped by darksome cults in dank jungles and along sullen dusky rivers. And there stirred, too, in his mind, an incantation whispered in his ear in awed and shuddering tones, while the night had held its breath, the lions had ceased to roar along the river, and the very fronds had ceased their scraping one against the other.

Ollam-onga, whispered a dark wind down the sightless corridor. *Ollam-onga* whispered the dust that ground beneath his stealthy feet. Sweat stood on his skin and the sword shook in his hand. He stole through the house of a god, and fear held him in its bony hand. *The house of the god* – the full horror of the phrase filled his mind. All the ancestral fears and the fears that reached beyond ancestry and primordial race-memory crowded upon him; horror cosmic and unhuman sickened him. His weak humanity crushed him in its realization as he went through the house of darkness that was the house of a god.

About him shimmered a glow so faint it was scarcely discernable; he knew that he was approaching the tower itself. Another instant and he groped his way through an arched door and stumbled upon strangely spaced steps. Up them he went, and as he climbed that blind fury which is mankind's last defense against diabolism and all the hostile forces of the universe, surged in him, and he forgot his fear. Burning with terrible eagerness, he climbed up and up through the thick evil darkness until he came into a chamber lit by a weird glow.

And before him stood a white naked figure. Amalric halted, his tongue cleaving to his palate. It was a naked white man, to all appearances, which stood gazing at him, mighty arms folded on an alabaster breast. The features were classic, cleanly carven, with more than human beauty. But the eyes were balls of luminous fire, such as never looked from any human head. In those eyes Amalric glimpsed the frozen fires of the ultimate hells, touched by awful shadows.

Then before him the form began to grow dim in outline; to waver – with a terrible effort the Aquilonian burst the bonds of silence and spoke a cryptic and awful incantation. And as the frightful words cut the silence, the white giant halted – froze – again his outlines stood out clear and bold against the golden background.

"Now fall on, damn you!" cried Amalric hysterically. "I have bound you into your human shape! The black wizard spoke truly! It was the master word he gave me! Fall on, *Ollam-onga* – till you break the spell by feasting on my heart, you are no more than a man like me!"

With a roar that was like the gust of a black wind, the creature charged. Amalric sprang aside from the clutch of those hands whose strength was more than that of the whirlwind. A single taloned finger, spread wide and catching in his tunic, ripped the garment from him like a rotten rag as the monster plunged by. But Amalric, nerved to more than human quickness by the horror of the fight, wheeled and drove his sword through the thing's back, so that the point stood out a foot from the broad breast.

A fiendish howl of agony shook the tower; the monster whirled and rushed at Amalric, but the youth sprang aside and raced up the stairs to the dais. There he wheeled and catching up a marble seat, hurled it down upon the horror that was lumbering up the stairs. Full in the face the massive missile struck, carrying the fiend back down the steps. He rose, an awful sight, streaming blood and again essayed the stairs. In desperation Amalric lifted a jade bench whose weight wrenched a groan of effort from him, and hurled it.

Beneath the impact of the hurtling bulk Ollam-onga pitched back down the stair and lay among the marble shards, which were flooded with his blood. With a last desperate effort, he heaved himself up on his hands, eyes glazing, and throwing back his bloody head, voiced an awful cry. Amalric shuddered and recoiled from the abysmal horror of that scream. *And it was answered.* From somewhere in the air above the tower a faint medley of fiendish cries came back like an echo. Then the mangled white figure went limp among the blood-stained shards. And Amalric knew that one of the gods of Kush was no more. With the thought came blind, unreasoning horror.

In a fog of terror he rushed down the stair, shrinking from the thing that lay staring in the floor. The night seemed to cry out against him, aghast at the sacrilege. Reason, exultant over his triumph, was submerged in a flood of cosmic fear.

As he put foot on the head of the steps, he halted short. Up from the darkness Lissa came to him, her white arms outstretched, her eyes pools of horror.

"Amalric!" it was a haunting cry. He crushed her in his arms.

"I saw *It*," she whimpered – "dragging a dead man through the corridor. I screamed and fled; then when I returned, I heard you cry out, and knew you had gone to search for me in the red tower – "

"And you came to share my fate," his voice was almost inarticulate. Then as she tried to peer in trembling fascination past him, he covered her eyes with his hands and turned her about. Better that she should not see what lay on the crimson floor. As he half led, half carried her down the shadowed stairs, a glance over his shoulder showed him that a naked white figure lay no longer lay among the broken marble. The incantation had bound Ollam-onga into his human form in life, but not in death. Blindness momentarily assailed Amalric, then, galvanized into frantic haste, he hurried Lissa down the stairs and through the dark ruins.

He did not slacken pace until they reached the street where the camel and stallion huddled against one another. Quickly he mounted the girl on the camel, and he swung up on the stallion. Taking the lead-line, he headed straight for the broken wall. A few minutes later he breathed gustily. The open air of the desert cooled his blood; it was free of the scent of decay and hideous antiquity.

There was a small water-pouch hanging from his saddle bow. They had no food, and his sword was in the chamber in the red tower. He had not dared touch it. Without food and unarmed, they faced the desert; but its peril seemed less grim than the horror of the city behind them.

Without speaking they rode. Amalric headed south; somewhere in that direction there was a water hole. Just at dawn, as they mounted a crest of sand, he looked back toward Gazal, unreal in the pink light. And he stiffened and Lissa cried out. Out of a breach in the wall rode seven horsemen; their steeds were black, and the riders were cloaked in black from head to foot. There had been no horses in Gazal. Horror swept over Amalric, and turning, he urged their mounts on.

The sun rose, red, and then gold, and then a ball of white beaten flame. On and on the fugitives pressed, reeling with heat and fatigue, blinded by the glare. They moistened their lips with water from time to time. And behind at an even pace, rode seven black dots. Evening began to fall, and the sun reddened and lurched toward the desert rim. And a cold hand clutched Amalric's heart. The riders were closing in. As darkness came on, so came the black riders. Amalric glanced at Lissa, and a groan burst from him. His stallion stumbled and fell. The sun had gone down, the moon was blotted out suddenly by a bat-shaped shadow. In the utter darkness the stars glowed red, and behind him Amalric heard a rising rush as of an approaching wind. A black speeding clump bulked against the night, in which glinted sparks of awful light.

"Ride, girl!" he cried despairingly. "Go on – save yourself; it is me they want!"

For answer she slid down from the camel and threw her arms about him.

"I will die with you!"

Seven black shapes loomed against the stars, racing like the wind. Under the hoods shone balls of evil fire; flesh jaw bones seemed to clack together. Then there was an interruption; a horse swept past Amalric and the horse, a vague bulk in the unnatural darkness. There was the sound of an impact as the unknown steed caromed among the oncoming shapes. A horse screamed frenziedly, and a bull like voice bellowed in a strange tongue. From somewhere in the night a clamor of yells answered.

There was some sort of violent action taking place. Horse's hoofs stamped and clattered, there was the impact of savage blows, and the same stentorian voice was cursing lustily. Then the moon abruptly came out and lit a fantastic scene.

A man on a giant horse whirled, slashed and smote apparently at thin air, and from another direction swept a wild horde of riders, their curved swords flashing in the moon light. Away over the crest of a rise seven black figures were vanishing, their cloaks floating out like the wings of bats.

Amalric was swamped by wild men who leaped from their horses and swarmed around him. Sinewy naked arms pinioned him, fierce brown hawk-like faces snarled at him. Lissa screamed. Then the attackers were thrust right and left as the man on the great horse reined through the crowd. He bent from his saddle, glared closely at Amalric.

"The devil!" he roared; "Amalric the Aquilonian!"

"Conan!" Amalric exclaimed bewilderedly. "Conan! Alive!"

"More alive than you seem to be," answered the other. "By Crom, man you look as if all the devils in this desert had been hunting you through the night. What things were those pursuing you? I was riding around the camp my men had pitched, to make sure no enemies were in hiding, when the moon went out like a candle, and then I heard sounds of flight. I rode toward the sounds, and by Crom, I was among those devils before I knew what was happening. I had my sword in my hand and I laid about me – by Crom, their eyes blazed like fire in the dark! I know my edge bit them, but when the moon came out, they were gone like a puff of wind. Were they men or fiends?"

"Ghouls sent up from Hell," shuddered Amalric. "Ask me no more; some things are not to be discussed."

Conan did not press the matter, nor did he look incredulous. His beliefs included night fiends, ghosts, hobgoblins and dwarfs.

"Trust you to find a woman, even in a desert," he said, glancing at Lissa, who had crept to Amalric and was clinging close to him, glancing fearfully at the wild figures which hemmed them in.

"Wine!" roared Conan. "Bring flasks! Here!" He seized a leather flask from those thrust out to him, and placed it in Amalric's hand. "Give the girl a swig, and drink some yourself," he advised. "Then we'll put you on horses and take you to the camp. You need food, rest and sleep. I can see that."

A richly caparisoned horse was brought, rearing and prancing, and willing hands helped Amalric into the saddle; then the girl was handed up to him, and they moved off southward, surrounded by the wiry brown riders in their picturesque semi-nakedness. Conan rode ahead, humming a riding song of the mercenaries.

"Who is he?" whispered Lissa, her arms about her lover's neck; he was holding her on the saddle in front of him.

"Conan, the Cimmerian," muttered Amalric. "The man I wandered with in the desert after the defeat of the mercenaries. These are the men who struck him down. I left him lying under their spears, apparently dead. Now we meet him obviously in command of, and respected by them."

"He is a terrible man," she whispered.

He smiled. "You never saw a white-skinned barbarian before. He is a wanderer and a plunderer, and a slayer, but he has his own code of morals. I don't think we have anything to fear from him."

In his heart he was not sure. In a way, it might be said that he had forfeited Conan's comradeship when he had ridden away into the desert, leaving the Cimmerian senseless on the ground. But he had not known that Conan was not dead. Doubt haunted Amalric. Savagely loyal to his companions, the Cimmerian's wild nature saw no reason why the rest of the world should not be plundered. He lived by the sword. And Amalric suppressed a shudder as he thought of what might chance did Conan desire Lissa.

Later on, having eaten and drunk in the camp of the riders, Amalric sat by a small fire in front of Conan's tent; Lissa, covered with a silken cloak, slumbered with her curly head on his knees. And across from him the fire light played on Conan's face, interchanging lights and shadows.

"Who are these men?" asked the young Aquilonian.

"The riders of Tombalku," answered the Cimmerian.

"Tombalku!" exclaimed Amalric. "Then it is no myth!"

"Far from it!" agreed Conan. "When my accursed steed fell with me, I was knocked senseless, and when I recovered consciousness, the devils had me bound hand and foot. This angered me, so I snapped several of the cords they had me tied with, but they rebound them as fast as I could break them – never did I get a hand entirely free. But to them my strength seemed remarkable – "

Amalric gazed at Conan unspeaking. The man was tall and broad as Tilutan had been, without the black man's surplus flesh. He could have broken the Ghanata's neck with his naked hands.

"They decided to carry me to their city instead of killing me out of hand," Conan went on. "They thought a man like me should be a long time in dying by torture, and so give them sport. Well, they bound me on a horse without a saddle, and we went to Tombalku.

"There are two kings of Tombalku. They took me before them – a lean brown-skinned devil named Zehbeh, and a big fat negro who dozed on his ivory-tusk throne. They spoke a dialect I could understand a little, it being much like that of the western Mandingo who dwell on the coast. Zehbeh asked a brown priest, Daura, what should be done with me, and Daura cast dice made of sheep bone, and said I should be flayed alive before the altar of Jhil. Every one cheered and that woke the negro king.

"I spat on Daura and cursed him roundly, and the kings as well, and told them that if I was to be skinned, by Crom, I demanded a good bellyfull of wine before they began, and I damned them for thieves and cowards and sons of harlots.

"At this the black king roused and sat up and stared at me, and then he rose and shouted: "Amra!' and I knew him – Sakumbe, a Suba from the Black Coast, a fat adventurer I had known well in the days when I was a corsair along that coast. He trafficked in ivory, gold dust and slaves, and would cheat the devil out of his eye-teeth – well, when he knew me, he descended from his throne and embraced me for joy – the black, smelly devil – and took my cords off me with his own hands. Then he announced that I was Amra, the Lion, his friend, and that no harm should come to me. Then followed much discussion, because Zehbeh and Daura wanted my hide. But Sakumbe yelled for his witch-finder, Askia, and he came, all feathers and bells and snake-skins – a wizard of the Black Coast, and a son of the devil if there ever was one.

"Askia pranced and made incantations, and announced that Sakumbe was the chosen of Agujo, the Dark One, and all the black people of Tombalku shouted, and Zehbeh backed down.

"For the blacks in Tombalku are the real power. Several centuries ago the Aphaki, a Shemitish race, pushed into the southern desert and established the kingdom of Tombalku. They mixed with the desert-blacks and the result was a brown straight-haired race, which is still more white than black. They are the dominant caste in Tombalku, but they are in the minority, and a pure black king always sits on the throne beside the Aphaki ruler.

"The Aphaki conquered the nomads of the southwestern desert, and the negro tribes of the steppes which lie to the south of them. These riders, for instance, are Tibu, of mixed Stygian and negro blood.

"Well, Sakumbe, through Askia, is the real ruler of Tombalku. The Aphaki worship Jhil, but the blacks worship Ajujo the Dark One, and his kin. Askia came to Tombalku with Sakumbe, and revived the worship of Ajujo, which was crumbling because of the Aphaki priests. Askia made black magic which defeated the wizardry of the Aphaki, and the blacks hailed him as a prophet sent by the dark gods. Sakumbe and Askia wax as Zehbeh and Daura wane.

"Well, as I am Sakumbe's friend, and Askia spoke for me, the blacks received me with great applause. Sakumbe had Kordofo, the general of the horsemen, poisoned, and gave me his place, which delighted the blacks and exasperated the Aphaki.

"You will like Tombalku! It was made for men like us to loot! There are half a dozen powerful factions plotting and intriguing against each other – there are continual brawls in the taverns and streets, secret murders, mutilations, and executions. And there are women, gold, wine – all that a mercenary wants! And I am high in favor and power! By Crom, Amalric, you could not come at a better time! Why, what's the matter? You do not seem as enthusiastic as I remember you having once been in such matters."

"I crave your pardon, Conan," apologized Amalric. "I do not lack interest, but weariness and want of sleep overcomes me."

But it was not gold, women and intrigue that the Aquilonian was thinking, but of the girl who slumbered on his lap; there was no joy in the thought of taking her into such a welter of intrigue and blood as Conan had described. A subtle change had come over Amalric, almost without his knowledge.

Untitled Synopsis
(The Hour of the Dragon)

The plot began with four men in a chamber of a Nemedian castle bringing back to life a Stygian mummy, thousands of years old. One of the men was a powerful Nemedian baron with the ambitions of a king-maker. One was the younger brother of the king of Nemedia. One was a claimant to the throne of Aquilonia. One was a priest of Mitra who had been expelled from his order because of his studies of the forbidden arts of magic. The mummy was that of a sorcerer of long ago, an Hyborian of a kingdom which had been destroyed by the Nemedians, Aquilonians, and Argosseans. The name of this kingdom was Acheron, and its capital city was called Python. Many centuries before the people of Acheron, Hyborians more highly civilized than their neighbors to the east and the west, had been lords of an empire which included what was later southern Nemedia and Brythunia, most of Corinthia, most of Ophir, western Koth and the western lands of Shem, northern Argos, and eastern Aquilonia. With the overthrow and destruction of Acheron by its ruder western neighbors, their greatest sorcerer had fled to Stygia, living there until poisoned by a Stygian priest of Set the Old Serpent. Then he had been mummified with curious art, without removing any of his vital parts, and the mummy had been placed in a hidden temple. Thence, at the conspirators' instigation, it had been stolen by thieves from Zamora. The Nemedian baron's name was Amalric; the king's brother was named Tarascus; the Aquilonian claimant was named Valerius; the priest's name was Orastes; the sorcerer's name was Xaltotun. Valerius was a reckless young rogue, tall, yellow-haired, mocking at himself and everything else, but a courageous fighter. He was distantly related to that Aquilonian king destroyed by Conan the Cimmerian, when the latter took the throne of Aquilonia. That king had exiled him, and he had been roaming the world as a soldier of fortune until Amalric's plots had drawn him back. He was to aid the conspirators in placing Tarascus on the Nemedian throne, then they would set him on the throne of Aquilonia. Amalric was strongly built, dark, ruthless, with hidden designs of his own. He desired to set his puppets on their thrones, rule both, overthrow both, and finally place himself on the throne of the united countries. Tarascus was a small, darkish young man, crafty, courageous, sensual, but a puppet in Amalric's hands. Orastes was a large man with soft white hands, a dabbler in the black arts. Xaltotun, when brought to life by strange incantations, was a tall man with quick strong hands and strange magnetic eyes and thick black hair. He listened to their speech, as they explained to him all that had occurred since his death, and agreed to aid them. But, he said, before he could regain his full magical power, they must steal for him the jewel called the Heart of Ahriman, which was kept in a secret place in the kingdom of Aquilonia. This had been taken from him when Python fell, and so he had been forced to flee to Stygia. In his own heart the wizard planned to restore the ancient kingdom of Acheron. The descendants of the people of Acheron were more plentiful than men supposed, dwelling in the fastness of the hills, in communities in the great cities, and scattered throughout the kingdom as priests, menials, secretaries, and scribes. The jewel was stolen; the king of Nemedia was assassinated by black magic, and Tarascus was set on the throne. Then the armies of Nemedia moved against Aquilonia. In his tent in the night before the battle, Conan the Cimmerian dreamed a strange dream in which many of the past events of his life passed in review once more. He saw strange shapes and events, and woke in a sweat of fear to call his captains. Dawn was breaking and the hosts were in motion. A strange hooded figure appeared in the king's tent and Conan was stricken with a curious paralysis. He could not ride to battle, so they brought a common soldier from the ranks who much resembled him and put the king's armor on him, and he rode beneath the great lion banner. But he fell, fighting gloriously, and the Aquilonian host was broken and hurled in headlong defeat. Conan, lying helpless in his tent, was attacked by the Nemedian knights, his guard cut down. He fought with his sword, holding himself upright to the tent-pole, until Xaltotun overcame him by magic. He was put secretly into a chariot and secretly conveyed to the capital of Nemedia, for Amalric did not wish it known that it had not been the king who had fallen. He was thrown into the pits beneath the palace, where a giant ape attacked him. But a girl in the train of Tarascus gave Conan a dagger, with which he killed the beast and escaped. Coming into the palace of Tarascus to slay him, he saw the king give a jewel to a man and a bag of gold and order him to take the gem and throw it into the sea. This jewel, althought Conan did not know it, was the Heart of Ahriman, which Tarascus had stolen from the sorcerer because he feared him and had a dim inkling of what Xaltotun intended. Conan smote at Tarascus, but missed, and then, leaving the city, worked his way toward the Aquilonian border. Reaching the border, he learned that his people believed him dead, that the barons were at war with one another, and that Valerius, appearing on the eastern border with the Nemedian army, defeated a host sent against him by the barons, took the capital city and was acclaimed king by the mob, who feared a foreign invasion. Gunderland in the north, and Poitain in the south retained their independence, Gunderland partially and Poitain wholly, and southward Conan made his way, to join Count Trocero, his chancellor, who held the passes that lead down toward the plains of Zingara. But first he made his way to his capital which was in the hands of Valerius because an old witch, in the mountains of eastern Aquilonia, spoke cryptically to him of the Heart of Ahriman, and showed him visions in a crystal floating in smoke – of Zamorian thieves looting a Stygian temple, and stealing a flaming jewel from a subterranean cavern below the city. Thither Conan went and was admitted and aided by his loyal vassals, and going to the cavern, found the jewel gone and fought a fiendish battle with an unseen creature who guarded it. Escaping, he knew at last that the Heart of Ahriman was the gem Tarascus had given the man; but he secured horse and armor and travelled to Poitain where he found Trocero holding the mountain passes against Valerius. Meanwhile Xaltotun did not know of the loss of his jewel, because he kept it in a golden case for ever locked, and he worked his magic without stay. Only the greater magic needed the Heart of Ahriman. But Conan had been recognized in his capital and men rode after him, while others rode to Nemedia with the news. Conan fought a battle in the passes and with the Poitanians defeated the Nemedians. But Trocero did not have enough warriors to invade Aquilonia and defeat the Nemedians and the barons who espoused Valerius, and his people feared the magic of Xaltotun. They urged Conan to remain and rule them as a separate kingdom, and conquer Zingara, but he determined to follow the man who had taken the Heart of Ahriman. He rode toward the ports of Argos.

Notes on The Hour of the Dragon

First Day. (Day of battle.)
Conan at Valkia. Amalric, Tarascus, Valerius and Xaltotun at Valkia. Orastes at Belverus. Prospero on his way to Valkia.

That Night.
Conan was on his way to Belverus with Xaltotun. Amalric, Tarascus and Valerius were encamped in Valkia, their cavalry pursuing the fleeing Aquilonians through the hills. Prospero was falling back toward Tarantia. Orastes was in Belverus.

The Second Day.
Conan was a captive in Belverus. Xaltotun and Orastes were in Belverus. Tarascus was on his way from Valkia to Belverus. Amalric and Valerius were marching through the hills toward Tarantia. Prospero was approaching Tarantia.

That Night.
Conan was a captive in Belverus and escaped. Orastes and Xaltotun were in Belverus, Xaltotun sleeping the sleep of the black lotus of Stygia. Tarascus reached Belverus. Prospero arrived in Tarantia and found that news of the battle had preceded him. Amalric and Valerius camped in the plains of Aquilonia, devastating the countryside.

The Third Day.
Conan crossed the border and took refuge in the hills. Tarascus, wounded, was in Belverus, with Xaltotun and Orastes. The king's squire pursued Conan in the hills. That evening Prospero evacuated Tarantia. At sunset Amalric and Valerius entered the city, unopposed.

That Night.
Conan slept in the hut of Zelata, the witch. Tarascus and Orastes set out from Belverus to Tarantia. Amalric crowned Valerius king of Aquilonia in the great coronation hall of Tarantia. Xaltotun remained in Belverus.

THE FOURTH DAY.
Conan made his way through the hills toward Tarantia. Xaltotun remained at Belverus. Tarascus and Orastes were on their way to Tarantia. Amalric and Valerius were at Tarantia, receiving homage.

That Night.
Conan made his way through the devastated plains toward Tarantia. Xaltotun remained at Belverus. Tarascus and Orastes were on their way to Tarantia. Amalric and Valerius remained at Tarantia.

THE FIFTH DAY.
Conan, at evening, came within sight of Tarantia. Xaltotun remained at Belverus. Amalric with the Nemedians was devastating surrounding provinces. Tarascus and Orastes arrived at Tarantia. Valerius remained at Tarantia, paying old scores and confiscating property.

* * *

Xaltotun left Valkia at sunset, and arrived in Belverus before dawn. He travelled faster than the average man could travel. That means he made the journey in about twelve hours. It would take the average chariot fifteen, with a change of horses. A man on a good horse might make it in fourteen hours. If Conan left Belverus after midnight, say he was on the road at one o'clock and riding like hell, he had been riding six hours when the sun came up. He would still have eight hours to ride. He rested an hour, which made it eight o'clock. It would be about four o'clock when he reached the hills. He would really be taking a shorter cut, because he had left the road which wound toward the passes in the hills. Belverus lay nearer the border than Tarantia.

* * *

Conan was moving up the valley of the Shirki, a day and a night's hard marching from Tanasul; Amalric could reach Tanasul in little over a day's march. The Gundermen were advancing along the valley of Khor, about three days march from Tanasul; Tarascus was at Galparan, a day and night's march to the Pass of Falcons, and a little over a day's march from Tanasul.

* * *

THE FIRST DAY:
Tarascus at Galparan;
Amalric, Valerius and Xaltotun at the camp near Tanasul;
Conan to the southewest advancing along the Shirki;
The Gundermen north of the Goralian hills;

The First Night:
Tarascus at Galparan;
The other in camp; Xaltotun making magic;
Conan approaching Tanasul;
The Gundermen moving southward toward Tanasul;

THE SECOND DAY:
At dawn the courier reached Tarascus, who broke camp and reached Amalric's camp with his horsemen at sunset; the footmen arrived some hours later;
Amalric and his companions lay in camp, waiting for Tarascus;
Conan nearing Tanasul;
The Gundermen marching through the Goralian hills;

The Second Night:
Tarascus, Amalric, Valerius and Xaltotun lay in the camp in the plain;
Late that night Conan reached Tanasul and crossed and camped on the other side.
The Gundermen were camped further back in the hills.

THE THIRD DAY:
Tarascus, and the Nemedian host, marching toward Tanasul, learned that Conan had crossed; he pushed ahead with his horsemen, and arrived at Tanasul just at twilight;
Conan was camped in the Goralian hills;
The Gundermen were pushing southward swiftly;

The Third Night:
The Nemedians camped in the plain beside the river;
Conan camped in the hills;
The Gundermen reached his camp after nightfall.

Part of two nights
It took Conan a day and a night of marching to reach Tanasul;

* * *

Conan marched all the first day until late that night; camped that first night and set out before dawn; marched all the second day; reached Tanasul late the second night. Time: one whole day's march and part of two nights; would have taken another man two days and two nights.

The first day and night Amalric lay in camp, waiting for Tarascus, who took a whole day in getting there. He could reach Tanasul in a day's hard riding; with his host it required a day and part of a night.

If he had set out when he wished to, he would have reached the Shirki first, but Xaltotun wished him to wait for Tarascus.

Untitled Synopsis (A Witch Shall Be Born)

The story began with Taramis, Queen of Khauran, awaking in her chamber at the sight of a spot of light glowing on the velvet-tapestried wall. In that spot she saw the head of her sister, Salome, who had been carried into the desert shortly after her birth, to die, because she had the witch-mark upon her bosom – the blood-red crescent. In the conversation which followed it was explained that because, centuries before, a Queen of Khauran had cohabited with a pre-Adamite demon, every so often a witch would be born in the royal family. Salome said there had always been witches named Salome, and always would be. She, Taramis' twin sister, had been carried into the desert, but had been discovered by a Khitan magician travelling from Stygia in a carvan. He had recognized the witch mark and had taken her and brought her up, instructing her in many black arts. Now she had returned to seize the throne. Her master had driven her forth, because she lacked the cosmic scope of true wizardry, was merely a harlot of the black arts. She had fallen in with a Kothian adventurer who commanded an army of professional fighting men, Shemites from the western cities of Shem. This man had come to Khauran and asked the hand of Queen Taramis. He was at that time camped with his hosts outside the city walls. The gates were carefully guarded, for Taramis did not trust the man. Salome told Taramis that she had entered the palace secretly, by drugging all the queen's servants. She told her that she, Taramis, would be cast into a dungeon, and she, Salome, would reign in her place. The Kothian entered just then, and Salome cynically handed her sister over to be raped by him, while she went forth to give the soldiers at the gates orders to admit the Shemites.

The next scene was that of a young soldier being bandaged by his terrified sweetheart, as he told of the treachery. Queen Taramis had apparently given orders to her dumbfounded soldiers that the Shemites were to be admitted into the city. This was done, and she announced that she would make him king to reign beside her. The soldiers and populace rose, but only her guard were left in the city. These were cut down by the Shemites, except the captain of the guard, Conan the Cimmerian, who refused to believe that Taramis was Taramis. He swore it was some devil in her shape, and fought ferociously before being overpowered. The boy said that the Kothian was having him crucified outside the city wall. This happened; Conan fought off the vultures with his teeth, and attracted the attention of a bandit chief who was scouting near the walls in hopes of plunder. This was Olgerd Vladislav, a Zaporoskan, or *kozak*, who had wandered down from the steppes and established himself among the nomadic Shemitish tribes of the desert. He freed Conan and took him into his band, after a savage test of the Cimmerian's endurance.

In the meantime – as a letter from a savant visiting in Khauran showed – Salome, posing as Taramis, had abolished the worship of Ishtar, filled the temples with obscene images, made human sacrifices and placed in the shrine a hideous monster from the outer gulfs. The young soldier, convinced that Taramis was slain or imprisoned and a fraud reigning in her stead, haunted the palace and prisons disguised as a beggar, and Salome, having tortured her sister by showing her the head of a trusted councillor, tossed it to the beggar to dispose of, and unwittingly revealed the secret. He hurried to Conan with the news. Conan had in the meantime, wishing vengeance on the Kothian, raised a great army of nomads. Olgerd intended taking and sacking Khauran, but Conan deposed him, and announced his intention of rescuing Taramis and placing her back on the throne.

The young soldier rescued Taramis from prison, but they were driven into the temple by Salome. But Conan defeated the Kothian, swept into the city, destroyed the monster. The Kothian was crucified, and Taramis set back upon her throne.

Appendices

Hyborian Genesis Part II

Notes on the Creation of the Conan Stories

by Patrice Louinet

The year 1933 ended on a much more positive note than it had begun for Robert E. Howard. It had promised to be catastrophic. In 1932, Fiction House had ceased publication of Fight Stories and Action Stories, two magazines which had paid modestly but regularly, ensuring Howard of a meager yet regular income. The arrival of Strange Tales – a direct competitor to Weird Tales – which paid well, and on acceptance rather than publication, had been a compensation, but late in 1932 Howard had learned that this magazine was also going out of circulation. As 1933 began, he was left with only one regular market: Farnsworth Wright's magazines Magic Carpet Magazine, a fledgling quarterly, and Weird Tales. There was but one thing to do, and for a few weeks Howard literally deluged Weird Tales with submissions, with one clear aim: to sell as much as possible. Among the stories submitted were most of the inferior Conan stories, written with a visible need for a quick sale. It was only in the spring of 1933, with an impressive number of Conan stories awaiting publication in Wright's magazine (*Xuthal of the Dusk*, *Queen of the Black Coast*, *The Pool of the Black One*, *Iron Shadows in the Moon* and *Black Colossus*), that Howard began to devote his attentions to building other markets. Hiring Otis Adelbert Kline as his agent, the Texan spent most of the next few weeks trying to sell some more of his boxing yarns and dabbling in genres that were new to him: detective stories and westerns. He also began to seriously consider the question of the rights to his stories, and looked into the possibility of having short-story collections published in England.

October 1933 found Howard returning to Conan. Weird Tales had already published three of the five Conan stories in their backlog, as it was becoming evident that the character was a popular success. *The Devil in Iron*, completed circa October 1933, was a somewhat half-baked effort from a Howard who had not written a Conan story in six months, drawing heavily from the earlier Conan story, *Iron Shadows in the Moon.* Both tales showed Howard's debt to Harold Lamb, a pillar of Adventure, a publication whose influence on Howard was probably greater than that of Weird Tales.

If Howard was an early devotee of Weird Tales – we know he was already aware of the magazine's existence less than six months after it first appeared on the newsstands – his first love was clearly adventure fiction, much more than the tales of the weird. The Texan's discovery of Adventure was a cherished memory: "...Magazines were even more scarce than books. It was after I moved into 'town' (speaking comparatively) that I began to buy magazines. I well remember the first I ever bought. I was fifteen years old. I bought it one summer night when a wild restlessness in me would not let me keep still, and I had exhausted all the reading material on the place. I'll never forget the thrill it gave me. Somehow it had never occurred to me before that I could buy a magazine. It was an Adventure. I still have the copy. After that I bought Adventure for many years, though at times it cramped my resources to pay the price. It came out three times a month, then.... I skimped and saved from one magazine to the next; I'd buy one copy and have it charged, and when the next issue was out, I'd pay for the one for which I owed, and have the other one charged, and so on."

By 1921, when Howard discovered it, Adventure was a well-established magazine, one of the leading if not the leading fiction magazine of its times, hosting the talents of Talbot Mundy and Harold Lamb on a regular basis. Arthur D. Howden-Smith delivered tales of Viking adventures and Rafael Sabatini graced the magazine's pages for the first time in that summer of 1921. These authors would influence Robert E. Howard much more than any of the Weird Tales writers. Howard's interest in Adventure went beyond the mere reading of the stories: he had two letters published in the magazine in 1924 and corresponded semi-regularly with R.W. Gordon, who was in charge of its folk-song department. It was apparently Adventure which gave Howard the desire to become a writer: "I wrote my first story when I was fifteen, and sent it – to Adventure, I believe. Three years later I managed to break into Weird Tales. Three years of writing without selling a blasted line. (I never have been able to sell to Adventure; guess my first attempt cooked me with them for ever!)" These lines were written in the summer of 1933, a few weeks before the Texan was to start writing adventure fiction. Beyond the half-amused, half-exasperated tone Howard uses, one can feel his frustration at not having ever been published in the magazine. The entirety of Howard's surviving early output from 1922 and 1923 can be best described as a teenager's sincere attempts at emulating what he was reading in Adventure: he thus began – but never completed – a dozen stories featuring Frank Gordon, whose adventures were derived from Talbot Mundy and whose nickname – "El Borak, the Swift" – was borrowed from Sabatini.

Significantly enough, when Howard resumed writing adventure stories in October 1933, the process started with a resurrection as improbable as Xaltotun's in *The Hour of the Dragon*: the protagonist of his first mature adventure stories was Francis X. Gordon, "El Borak," a revamped version of his teen-age creation. He thus wasn't exploring new ground but bridging a gap of ten years. In the second Gordon story, *The Daughter of Erlik Khan*, Gordon explores the city of Yolgan, niched in a mysterious Oriental mountain, where the beautiful Yasmeena is held prisoner. In the Texan's next tale, the Conan story *The People of the Black Circle*, the mysterious Oriental mountain is called Yimsha and it is there that Conan rescues another beautiful Yasmina. As Howard had exclaimed just after reading his first

Mundy novels in 1923: "...Yasmini? She's some character, isn't she?"

Much has been written about the influence of Talbot Mundy on this particular Conan tale, but while Howard's source material for this story has yet to be identified, Mundy was very probably not part of it. It very much seems that Howard's background research for his "Eastern adventure" stories also furnished the background for the new Conan tales. In *The Devil in Iron*, for instance, Howard had changed the name of the king of Turan from Yildiz (in *Iron Shadows in the Moon*) to Yezdigerd. Much of the action of that story taking place on the isle of Xapur, it is quite probable that the names were derived from the historical Yezdigerd – a Persian king and a conqueror, just as Howard's character – and Shapur, his father. Yezdigerd returned in *The People of the Black Circle*, and with him several new elements of geography which Howard added to his Hyborian world with this story, such as the Himelian Mountains, Afghulistan and Vendhya.

The People of the Black Circle was Howard's longest Conan effort to date; it is a true, and successful, novella and not merely a "long short story." A tale of that length could not stand on Conan's shoulders alone, and Yasmina is a welcome change from some of the earlier stories' cringing women. However, it was in Khemsa that Howard created a memorable secondary character, torn between his loyalty to his masters and his love for Gitara, between his spiritual and his earthly cravings. For, as befits a story exploring the East and the West, *The People of the Black Circle* is a study on duality: a brother and a sister, one dead, the other alive; two antithetic couples, Conan and Yasmina versus Khemsa and Gitara (two couples in which rivalry for power is a significant factor in the relationship). But where the former are masters (hill chief and queen respectively), the latter are but servants of chiefs. The opposition between the primitive hillmen and the Seers of Yimsha, that is to say between the physical and the mental, was evidently nourished by the year-long debate on the subject which had occupied Howard and H. P. Lovecraft for most of the year 1933.

If the tale at times evokes Mundy's penchant for mysticism, Howard's treatment is entirely his own. In fact, there was probably little need for the Texan to look to Mundy to find inspiration for mysticism: he had bathed in it for years. More: once one has scratched away the Oriental trappings of the tale, what is revealed is a story that strangely touches on many points on Howard's family history. His father, Dr. Isaac M. Howard, was all his life interested in mysticism, yoga and hypnotism. He regularly practiced hypnotism on his patients, sometimes with a young Robert E. Howard present, and had annotated his copies of *The Hindu Science of Breath* and *Fourteen Lessons in Yogi Philosophy* by Yogi Ramacharaka. If Howard needed documentation on Eastern mysticism, he needn't reread Mundy, as he had a much better source of information under his own roof. The opening scene – recounting Yasmina's brother's death at her own hands – is another striking autobiographical example. On a literary plane, it invites comparison with several other tales, notably *Dermod's Bane*, in which a man is afflicted beyond reason by the death of his twin sister. In Howard's fiction, brothers and sisters often have to separate, and usually in painful conditions. The reasons for such an obsession may very well originate from a reported (though undocumented) miscarriage suffered by Howard's mother in 1908, when Howard was aged two. This would invite us to draw a parallel between Yasmina and Howard, both having experienced the loss of a sibling. However, and as usual in Howard's fiction, these biographical elements were soon diluted and distorted in the story the Texan had to tell in order to sell it to Farnsworth Wright. *The People of the Black Circle* is a particularly satisfying Conan story for all these reasons. The tale functions very well on an escapist level and is leagues ahead of standard pulp-fare plotting, but there is a definite depth and texture to all its aspects, which ranks it among the three or four best Conan stories Howard had written to date.

Farnsworth Wright must have been rather impressed with it since less than five months elapsed between its acceptance and the publication of the first part of the serialization. He was, however, not so pleased with the increasing liberties Howard was taking with his dialogue and the explicitness of certain situations, and in several instances severely toned down some of the Cimmerian's oaths and sexual allusions.

In early January 1934, as Howard was writing *The People of the Black Circle*, he at last received news of the story collection he had submitted to Denis Archer in England in June of the past year. The answer wasn't a positive one. If the editor had found the stories "exceedingly interesting," it was not enough: "The difficulty that arises about publication in book form, is the prejudice that is very strong over here just now against collections of short stories, and I find myself very reluctantly forced to return the stories to you. With this suggestion, however, that any time you find yourself able to produce a full-length novel of about 70,000–75,000 words along the lines of the stories, my allied company, Pawling and Ness Ltd., who deal with the lending libraries, and are able to sell a first edition of 5,000 copies, will be very willing to publish it."

With the exception of his partly autobiographical *Post Oaks and Sand Roughs* (1928), Howard had never completed a novel, though he was demonstrating he was learning the craft with *The People of the Black Circle*, whose final version runs 31,000 words. Many other writers would have stopped their efforts here, confronted with a publisher who took six months to answer, negatively at that, refusing a collection of stories which he had asked for in the first place. Later that month, however, Howard reported to August Derleth: "An English firm, after keeping a collection of my short stories for months, finally sent them back, saying that there was a prejudice over there just now against such collections – of short stories, I mean – and suggested that I write a full length novel for them. But I'm not overly enthusiastic about it, for I've been disappointed so much. Of course, I'll do my best."

Howard probably began working on the novel in February 1934, but he was to abandon the story a few weeks later.

Almuric – for this is very probably the novel Howard began to write for the British publisher – was abandoned midway, as he had written a first draft and the first half of the second one. This was to have to been Howard's third – and last – Yasmina/Yasmeena tale, after *The Daughter of Erlik Khan* and *The Devil in Iron*. Like her namesakes, this Yasmeena also lived in a strange mount: Yuthla. Why Howard insisted that his Yasmeenas/Yasminas dwell in "y" mountains will probably remain a mystery. The novel cannibalized several key scenes from the stories which had been initially submitted to the publisher. The winged Yagas of *Almuric*, for instance, definitely owed something to the winged creatures of the Solomon Kane story *Wings in the Night*. Howard was indeed making sure that his novel would be "along the lines of the stories" he had previously submitted. Nevertheless, Howard left *Almuric* incomplete for reasons that remain mysterious. (The novel would linger for several years, until it was eventually published in the pages of Weird Tales after Howard's death, completed by another writer).

After abandoning *Almuric*, Howard probably realized that it was only logical to make Conan the central character of his novel: the sale of *The People of the Black Circle* in late February or March 1934 showed him that he could write successfully at length about the character. Much more importantly the setting – the Hyborian Age – and the protagonist were very much in Howard's mind, and little if any work was needed to build a background for the intended novel. Lastly, Conan tales had also been included in the first batch of stories sent to Archer: he would, once again, be submitting material "along the lines" of what he had already proposed to the British publisher.

The surviving synopsis and 29-page draft of that first Conan effort are intriguing to say the least, a sharp departure from the other Conan stories. This "Tombalku" draft was begun and abandoned after Howard had finished *The People of the Black Circle* and abandoned *Almuric*, in all probability in mid-March 1934. Conan is not the protagonist of the story; that role falls to one Amalric (whose name evokes Almuric). Reading the synopsis and first draft, it is easy enough to see that there wasn't enough good material here to make a novel; there was in fact scant good material at all. The connection between the first part of the story and what would have been the Tombalku chapters is unconvincing, and clearly the story wasn't going anywhere. Howard soon realized it and abandoned this tale, too, to begin work on his third – final and successful – attempt at writing his novel: *The Hour of the Dragon*.

There was very little to salvage from Howard's two previous efforts. On the surface, there is indeed very little to show that the three stories were penned at about the same time: in *The Hour of the Dragon*, Conan briefly mentions a Ghanata knife, a tribe otherwise mentioned only in the unfinished Tombalku draft; in an early draft of the novel we are informed that Conan was once called "Iron Hand," the same nickname given Esau Cairn on the planet Almuric. There is also the mention of a "Prince Almuric" in *The Hour of the Dragon*, but this may have been derived more from his namesake in *Xuthal of the Dusk* – another prince who met his doom at the hands of Stygians – than from the novel of the same title.

One passage from the Tombalku story, however, may have inspired the Texan for the subject of his novel:

> One of the men, his face smooth and unlined, but his hair silver, was saying: "Aquilonia? There was an invasion – we heard – King Bragorus of Nemedia – how went the war?"
>
> "He was driven back," answered Amalric briefly, resisting a shudder. Nine hundred years had passed since Bragorus led his spearmen across the marches of Aquilonia.

Here was the springboard for the plot of *The Hour of the Dragon*: an invasion of Aquilonia by its neighbor Nemedia. The seven mysterious horsemen were also probably transformed into *The Hour of the Dragon*'s four sorcerors from Khitai. Amra, Conan's alias when he was a pirate among the black corsairs, also made the jump from the draft to the novel, and the theme of the rival kings is obviously an essential ingredient to the novel. Much of this material had already furnished the background to an early Conan story, *The Scarlet Citadel*, part of the initial lot of stories sent to England, which featured Conan as Amra and an invasion (from Koth and Ophir in this case). Xaltotun's resurrection is highly reminiscent of Thugra Khotan's, in *Black Colossus*, though this particular tale had not been among the lot sent to England in mid-1933.

Howard knew what he should do with *The Hour of the Dragon* and how he should be doing it: he was at the same time recycling several elements from his past Conan stories and trying to conquer a new readership. He had thus to present as much as possible of his Hyborian Age and its possibilities to his intended new readers, and also should have no compunction about recycling several elements from former Conan stories, since the British market was averse to publishing short stories. The reader would thus have hints of Stygia, of the Hyborian Age equivalents to the African kingdoms, would even get a glimpse – by way of the mysterious sorcerors – of the countries east of Vilayet, in a tale which remained, however, centered on the Hyborian countries he would be familiar with: the kingdoms corresponding to modern occidental Europe.

It had been a long time since Howard had written of Conan as a king and one could wonder why he chose to return to a theme which had long disappeared from his stories. The answer probably resides once again in the novel's intended market. The British public had always been keenly interested in the subject of mythical kings and so had been Howard himself: hadn't he, in *The Phoenix on the Sword*, written about a king who wins his battle aided by a magic sword quite similar to Excalibur? Hadn't he, in *The Scarlet Citadel*, written that the king is one with his kingdom, and that he who slays the king cuts the cords of the kingdom? Was King Conan ready to acknowledge his kinship with the most famous Celtic King of all, Arthur?

In *The Scarlet Citadel*, Conan's capture was achieved through treachery and his eventual victory was mostly a matter of superior military strategy. In the novel, Conan's paralysis has a distinctive supernatural origin and Howard insists on what has really transpired when Xaltotun prevented Conan from taking part in the battle. With Conan's paralysis, an essential link has been broken by magic: Conan has been severed from his army and it was this which led to its defeat. As Pallantides declares shortly thereafter: "Only [Conan] could have led us to victory this day." With the apparent death of Conan, king of Aquilonia, the unity and strength of Aquilonia disappears. As a partisan will later tell Conan, in words closely echoing the proverb from *The Scarlet Citadel*: "You were the cord that held the fagots together. When the cord was cut, the fagots fell apart." It is only Conan's presumed death that enables Valerius to get on the throne: "So long as Conan lives, he is a threat, a unifying factor for Aquilonia" declares Tarascus. "Only in unity is there strength," later echoes Conan. Valerius, in spite of his military victory, doesn't succeed in restoring the lost unity of the kingdom and obtaining the allegiance of the people. Echoes Conan: "It's one thing to seize a throne with the aid of its subjects and rule them with their consent. It's another to subjugate a foreign realm and rule it by fear." Conan appears to have been the rightful king to Aquilonia and only magic could defeat the unity that existed between him and his people.

It was not the Heart of Ahriman that brought about the defeat of Conan. The Heart is not an instrument of evil. Hadrathus, priest of Asura, later confirms that "against it the powers of darkness cannot stand, when it is in the hands of an adept… It restores life, and can destroy life. [Xaltotun] has stolen it, not to use it against his enemies, but to keep them from using it against him," and concluding with: "[The Heart] holds the destiny of Aquilonia." Why does the Heart hold the destiny of Aquilonia? At the beginning of the novel, we learn that the jewel "was hidden in a cavern below the temple of Mitra, in Tarantia." The symbolism is obvious: the Heart, as its name would suggest, was placed at the heart, in the center, of the kingdom. Furthermore, Mitraism is the Hyborian Age's closest equivalent to an organized religion, the official religion of Aquilonia, as well as the better structured of the Hyborian cults; hence its "central" position. Tarantia requires some discussing. In *The Scarlet Citadel*, the capital of Aquilonia is called Tamar; it is called Tarantia in the novel. Howard's changing of the name was no "egregious blunder" as certain editors would have it, but the result of a careful choice: Tarantia is derived from Tara, mystical and political capital of Ireland, seen as the heart of their kingdom by the Celts of Ireland: "You will not press the throne again unless you find the heart of your kingdom," says Zelata to Conan, to which he replies: "Do you mean the city of Tarantia?" The Heart is thus the mystical stone that symbolizes the exact center of the country, the symbol of the link that unites the people and the land to the king. Once this link is severed "the heart is gone from [the] kingdom." The consequences are dire and immediate for the people and the country:

> only embers and ashes showed where farm huts and villas had stood... A vast swath of desolation had been cut through the country from the foothills westward. Conan cursed as he rode thorough blackened expanses that had been rich fields, and saw the gaunt gable-ends of burned houses jutting out the sky. He moved through an empty and deserted land.

All this is perfectly logical, for in tales of the Grail the country becomes a barren land, the wasteland, from the moment the king cannot properly govern his kingdom anymore: the consequences of Conan's defeat at the hand of the conspirators go far beyond the capture and destitution of the Cimmerian. The problem in *The Hour of the Dragon* is that Conan seems at first unaware of the mystic bond which links him to his country. His will to get the throne back from his enemies is doomed from the start and even his most loyal subjects refuse to follow him in what they consider a suicidal enterprise. Only when Conan has understood everything can the quest begin: "What a fool I've been! The Heart of Ahriman! The heart of my kingdom! Find the heart of my kingdom, Zelata said."

It is thus at about the central point of the story that Howard's novel reveals itself as a quest, and more precisely as an Arthurian-like quest for the Grail. Behind the Arthurian legendry one finds the obsession of the Celts with the common king they historically never had, the one who was to unite the tribes against common foes. This king, a *rex*, as opposed to the Roman notion of *imperator*, permanent representative of a strong and centralized power, was most of the time a military leader. And what Howard is telling us is exactly that: Conan's quest for the Heart is a quest for the perfect way to fulfill his duty as a *rex* and not as an *imperator*, as a tyrant. This is clearly demonstrated in the exchange between Conan and Trocero in the middle section of the book:

"Then let us unite Zingara with Poitain," argued Trocero. "Half a dozen princes strive against each other, and the country is torn asunder by civil wars. We will conquer it, province by province, and add it to your dominions. Then with the aid of the Zingarans we will conquer Argos and Ophir. We will build an empire –"

Again Conan shook his head. "Let others dream imperial dreams. I but wish to hold what is mine. I have no desire to rule an empire welded together by blood and fire. It's one thing to seize a throne with the aid of its subjects and rule them with their consent. It's another to subjugate a foreign realm and rule it by fear. I don't wish to be another Valerius. No, Trocero, I'll rule all Aquilonia and no more, or I'll rule nothing." (pg. 168)

Whoever had the idea of retitling Howard's novel *Conan the Conqueror* had evidently not understood its theme: Conan is anything but a conqueror by nature. If Conan's kingship has to be envisioned as a conclusion of sorts to his life, then the lesson is one entirely different from what has been suggested for years: Conan the King has much less freedom and power (to act as he wants) than Conan the Cimmerian.

If Conan is an Arthur, we might wonder where his Guinevere is. The queen played a very special role in Celtic countries, and her absence in Howard's novel could seem surprising, at least to a reader unfamiliar with the Cimmerian. Many Weird Tales readers must have experienced a jolt when reading that Conan vowed to marry Zenobia at the end of the novel. One wonders, and indeed several critics have wondered, if Conan would be true to his word. We have no way to answer such a question, though we can note that Zenobia's crowning would bring the novel even closer to the Arthurian myth.

In fact each of the three women of the story – Zenobia, Zelata and Albiona – seem to embody part of the symbolic role assigned to the Arthurian queen. Zenobia (whose name was Sabina in the early drafts of the novel) is the one supposed to be married (soon) to the king. Zelata is in charge of the initiation aspects of the quest: she is the one who helps Conan understand the symbolism of the Heart of Ahriman, of the link between the king and his kingdom. Albiona was given a name and a rank which help us identify the three women of the novel as a composite picture of the Arthurian queen. She is of course a member of the nobility, but it is the etymology of her name which betrays her, for Albiona is derived from *alba*, latin for white. Arthur's wife was of distinct Celtic origin: *gwen*, the radical behind all the variants of the name of King Arthur's wife (Guinevere, Guenièvre, Gwenhwyfar, etc., Gaelic: *finn*) means white (and by extension: fair).

The Hyborian Age's equivalent to the quest for the Grail is then found in the ensuing chapters of the novel, when Conan has discovered the importance and the role of the Heart of Ahriman. These various picaresque episodes offer a succession of adventures and battles also found in most of the Arthurian texts. This is the origin for the episodes of the castle of Valbroso and the ghouls in the forest, of

Publio, of the ship's mutiny, of Khemi and of Akivasha, which, strictly speaking, don't add anything to the story, so much that Karl Wagner could suppose that one chapter may have been lost here in the transition between the English publisher and the pages of Weird Tales, a loss that no one would have noticed.

Conan's return to his throne begins with his securing of the Heart of Ahriman. This is achieved at the end of chapter 19: "[Conan] whirled about his head the great jewel, which threw off splashes of light that spotted the deck with golden fire." The next chapter opens: "Winter had passed from Aquilonia. Leaves sprang out on the limbs of trees, and the fresh grass smiled to the touch of the warm southern breezes." With the heart once back in proper hands, life is restored, the wasteland once more becomes a land of plenty, of the Grail: "But in the full flood of spring a sudden whisper passed over the sinking kingdom that woke the land to eager life." This image of the country returning to life with the riding back of the holders of the Grail irresistibly calls to mind a similar scene in John Boorman's *Excalibur*. Xaltotun's defeat is now but a matter of time. The conspirators are divided, while Conan's forces unite again. The restoration of the king and the land is now inevitable.

Howard was definitely writing his novel with his public in mind and it is probably not a coincidence that the story contains homages to British writers. The beginning of Sir Arthur Conan Doyle's *Sir Nigel* very probably furnished the idea for the plague episode in Howard's novel. More importantly, he was once more paying homage to one of his favorite playwrights, Shakespeare, whose *Hamlet* seems to have been very present with Howard at composition time: "There is method in his madness" in chapter 3 is a clear echo of the dramatist's most famous play. (Howard definitely wanted this phrase to appear in his novel, as it appeared in three instances in the second draft of the novel!) In fact, many of Howard's tales dealing with kingship invite comparison with the play. In the case of *The Hour of the Dragon*, the parallels are evident, with both tales centering on the exploits of a king (or would-be king) deposed by an usurper whom he would have thought an ally! Conan, dispossessed of his throne and dead (or believed so) had in fact all the qualities of the Danish ghost-king. Upon seeing Conan, whom he believes dead, a Poitanian soldier waxes Shakespearean and we could for a space believe ourselves on the battlements of Elsinore: "His breath hissed inward and his ruddy face paled. 'Avaunt!' he ejaculated. 'Why have you come back from the gray lands of death to terrify me? I was always your true liegeman in your lifetime –'"

The Hour of the Dragon is by far the Howard story for which we have the greatest number of draft pages. In addition to the 241 pages of the published version, 620 pages of drafts survive, while several hundred others (a carbon of the definitive version and at least one complete draft) were lost over the years. Howard wrote five versions of his story, with several parts of these rewritten two or three times. While he would tell others that the stories came easily to him, he was working at it much harder than he would care to admit. The story's synopsis provides an excellent sample of Howard's working method: running three dense single-spaced pages, it covers the first five chapters in minute detail with only a few variations from the published version, while the subsequent chapters are much less detailed and the second part of the novel not covered at all. Howard built his first drafts from this, testing his scenes and dialogues. Xaltotun's motivations for sparing Conan thus changed several times as Howard was writing his drafts and getting a better grasp of his characters and how they would act and interact when confronted with certain situations. The passage in which Tiberias sacrifices himself by leading Valerius and five thousand men to a deathly trap in the gorges was added in the last stages of writing, offering the reader some memorable moments and infusing the end of the novel with a sense of suspense and incertitude which it would otherwise be lacking.

The study of the typescripts shows that Howard didn't begin work on his Conan novel until after he had finished both *The People of the Black Circle* and a detective story received by his agent on March 10. Chances are that he didn't actually begin it until after he had sent another story to his agent circa March 17. It was only apt that such a novel was begun at the time of Saint Patrick's Day. Records show that Howard's agent didn't receive anything from him between March 19 and June 20. If we accept March 17, give or take a couple of days, as the beginning date of the writing of the novel, then *The Hour of the Dragon* was written in less than two months: on May 20, 1934, Howard wrote Denis Archer in England: "As you doubtless remember, in your letter of Jan. 9th, 1934, you suggested that I submit a full length novel, on the order of the weird short stories formerly submitted, to your allied company of Pawling & Ness Ltd. Under separate cover I am sending you a 75,000 word novel, entitled, *The Hour of the Dragon*, written according to your suggestions. Hoping it will prove acceptable..."

During those two months, Howard apparently didn't write any other story, concentrating all his efforts on his novel, with an estimated output of 5,000 words per day, seven days a week. On May 20, the day he sent the novel to England, Howard wrote four short letters. *The Hour of the Dragon* had occupied almost all of his time for those two months. Edgar Hoffmann Price's brief visit in April seems to have been the sole distraction during those two months. For someone who was not expecting much from the British market, two full months of work seems an awful lot. One suspects that Howard had much more faith and hope in his novel than he was ready to admit. He knew that if the novel was to be accepted – and published – it could be a major, perhaps *the* major, break for him.

As could be expected, Howard took a few days off in June: "Having completed several weeks of steady work, I'm knocking off a few hours for relaxation and to try to catch up with my correspondence which I've allowed to stack up outrageously." Howard took a short vacation and visited the Carlsbad caverns, which were to inspire him for one of his next Conan stories, but he soon found himself back to work and back to Conan. Only a few days had elapsed between the completion of *The People of the Black Circle* and the beginning of *The Hour of the Dragon.* The delay was very probably the same between *The Hour of the Dragon* and his next Conan story.

A Witch Shall Be Born was written in late May or early June 1934, probably in a matter of days. The tale was evidently intended to replenish Farnsworth Wright's stock of Conan stories. In April 1934, Wright had published *Iron Shadows in the Moon*, *Queen of the Black Coast* had followed in May, and Howard knew that *The Devil in Iron* and *The People of the Black Circle* were scheduled for the August 1934 and subsequent issues, leaving him with no new Conan stories awaiting publication in the pages of Weird Tales. This was a new situation for the Texan, since *Iron Shadows in the Moon* and *Queen of the Black Coast* had been written and sold in 1932. Wright was accepting Conan stories as fast as he could get them, and was now almost systematically granting them the privileges of the cover (*Queen of the Black Coast*, *The Devil in Iron*, *The People of the Black Circle*, and *A Witch Shall Be Born*, published in a seven-month span, were all cover-featured). Conan's popularity was growing, and the character was very probably attracting new readers to Weird Tales. Women wrote to the magazine, asking for more Conan, whom they envisioned, thanks in part to Wright's censoring hands, as a romantic barbarian. *A Witch Shall Be Born* required only two drafts before Howard was satisfied with it. That it matched Wright's expectations exactly there can be no doubt. In a letter to Robert H. Barlow dated July 5, 1934, Howard wrote: "Here, at last, is the ms. I promised you some time ago. *A Witch Shall Be Born.* It is my latest Conan story, and Mr. Wright says my best."

A Witch is hardly Howard's best, but it is a special Conan tale in the sense that it is at the same time a rather forgettable Conan story yet contains the most famous, or rather the most memorable scene of the entire series. Reading the story, one gets the impression that Howard was simply borrowing from that year's production to craft the tale. The monster at the end of the story seems to be a cousin to that in the last chapter of *Almuric.* Taramis and Salome remind us that Howard was fascinated with brothers and sisters (with another occurrence of painful separation at birth) and also remind us of Howard's interest in duality. Paranoia, a theme in Howard's work as early as the Kull story *The Shadow Kingdom* (1926–27), runs rampant through this tale, and Howard repeats that people aren't always what they seem to be. It is a frequent occurrence in Howard that evil lurks behind seemingly innocent features. In *A Witch Shall Be Born*, only Conan – and Howard? – seems to have all the facts. All other characters are as blind as Olgerd Vladislav to what has been taking place under their very eyes.

Conan, in *A Witch Shall Be Born*, is becoming a superhuman character. Howard was growing extremely confident with his creation as testifies the structure of the tale. We are here miles away from pulp formula: Conan – the protagonist – gives life to the entire story by being present in only two chapters. It is tempting to draw a parallel between Conan and what Howard thought he was achieving with the Conan series: The Texan knew he had a winner and that he could get away with almost everything, even not having the lead character in the story except in the central chapters. Conan dominates the whole story and this is made plain in the crucifixion scene. How can anybody kill a character – literarily or literally – who can survive such a scene as that one? For to write a crucifixion scene will automatically invite a Christic comparison. Conan probably became "immortal" with this scene and one wonders to what extent Howard wished it to be so. The story – average as it is – exudes Howard's confidence in his creation. It was accepted with relish by Farnsworth Wright, published on the heels of four consecutive issues of Weird Tales starring the Cimmerian, and once again won the cover. Howard had every reason to be confident.

At the beginning of 1933, Howard only had one regular market. In mid-1934, he was appearing in almost every issue of Weird Tales, had succeeded in making Action Stories a regular market, with a Howard story in each issue, thought he had another regular market in Jack Dempsey's Fight Magazine, was having stories published in several new and different magazines thanks to his agent Otis Adelbert Kline; furthermore, he thought he had just sold a novel to the British market.

It was an idyllic situation.

It wasn't to last long.

NOTES ON THE CONAN TYPESCRIPTS AND THE CHRONOLOGY

By Patrice Louinet

LIST OF THE EXTANT CONAN TYPESCRIPTS (*January–June 1934*)

The final drafts of the stories published in Weird Tales were probably destroyed after the story was typeset, and thus are no longer extant. The surviving typescript for *A Witch Shall Be Born* is the exception rather than the rule, unfortunately.

Regarding the terminology used: a draft is "incomplete" when we are missing at least one page; it is "unfinished" when Howard didn't finish the draft. Sometimes Howard would write a draft and rewrite only a portion of it; such drafts are subdivided with numerals (i.e., draft b2 recycles pages from draft b1).

We are particularly indebted to Glenn Lord for furnishing copies of the typescripts mentioned below, and to Terence McVicker for the copy of the typescript of *A Witch Shall Be Born.*

The People of the Black Circle

– synopsis, untitled, 2 pgs.
– draft a, untitled, 80 pgs.
– draft b1, incomplete and unfinished (pgs. 10-92; 94-98 + 47a of 98; numbered 10-28, 30, 30-98 in error; missing pg. 93; pg. 47a discarded in favor of 47b; pgs. 1-9 lost, pgs. 10-90 survive as carbon (and were reused in draft b2); pg. 91 survives as original and carbon; pg. 47a and pgs. 92 and 94-98 as originals)
– draft b2 (final Weird Tales version) was comprised of draft b1 pgs. 1-10 [lost], draft b1 pgs. 11-91 [survive as carbon], plus draft b2 pg. 92 [lost] and pgs. 93-98 [survive as carbon]

In addition to his drafts, Howard wrote the paragraphs which appeared before the second and third installment of the serialization in Weird Tales, summing up the events of the previous chapters. A total of ten pages survive, six as originals and four as carbons, the latter identical to the text appearing in Weird Tales.

Untitled story

– synopsis, untitled, 3 pgs.
– draft, untitled and unfinished, 29 pgs.

The Hour of the Dragon

– synopsis, untitled, 2 pgs.
– notes, 4 pgs.
– draft a, untitled, incomplete and unfinished (pgs. 1-7, 21-29, 31-119 of 119)
– draft b1, untitled, diminishing to part-story, part-synopsis 160 pgs. (numbered 1-70, 72-116, 118-162 in error)
– draft b2, incomplete and unfinished, diminishing to a synopsis, (re-uses draft b1 pgs. 1-150 plus part of pg. 151; pgs. 151-163, 165-169 of 169; numbered 151, 153, 153-163, 165-169 in error; missing pg. 164)
– draft c, untitled, unfinished and incomplete, (pgs. 1, 3-196 of 196; missing pg. 2; numbered 1-65, 67-196 in error)
– draft d1, incomplete (pgs. 210-229 of 229 pgs.; numbered 210-227, 229, 229 in error; pgs. 1-209 were reused for drafts d2 and d3 then later lost; pgs. 210-216 were also reused for draft d2 and were discarded)
– draft d2 (re-uses draft d1 pgs. 1-216; numbered 217-221, 227-237 of 237; there are no missing pgs. between 221 and 227 in spite of the numbering)
– draft d3 [lost: this draft was probably 236 pgs. long, among the papers sent to Otis Adelbert Kline after Howard's death and later lost; pgs. 1-209 came from draft d1; pgs. 210-236 were new]
– discarded pages from final draft (draft e): pgs. 1-4, 6, 9, 15-18, 24, 38-39, 46-50, 52, 55, 61, 70, 72 (2 different), 79-80, 85, 94, 96-99, 101, 111, 113, 117, 122, 128, 134-136, 170, 206, 211-213, 216-217, 221-223, 225-226, 228-229, 232-241 of 241 pgs. There is a strong possibility that these pages were discarded and revised when Howard prepared the novel for submission to Farnsworth Wright.
– draft e (final Weird Tales version) [lost: the carbon for this was probably among the papers sent to Otis Adelbert Kline after Howard's death and later lost]
– submission sheet to Denis Archer, with verse heading, 1 pg.

A Witch Shall Be Born

– synopsis, untitled, 1 pg.
– draft a (this draft was sent to Robert H. Barlow on 5 July 1934; the typescript is now in private hands; unfortunately, it hasn't been possible to examine the typescript for this edition.)
– draft b1, incomplete, 53 pgs. (pgs. 1-4, 6-52 survive as originals, pgs. 1-53 as carbon, with slight differences between the two.)
– draft b2 (final Weird Tales version: reuses draft b1, pgs. 1-52; pgs. 53-55 survive as originals, pgs. 54-55 as carbon [REH probably kept the wrong pg. 53 carbon in his files.])

Notes on the Original Howard Texts

The texts for this edition of Volume 2 of the Complete Conan of Cimmeria were prepared by Patrice Louinet, Rusty Burke and Dave Gentzel, with assistance from Glenn Lord. The stories have been checked either against Howard's original typescripts, copies of which were furnished by Glenn Lord and Terence McVicker, or the first published appearance if a typescript was unavailable. Drafts of Howard's stories, when extant, have also been checked to ensure the greatest accuracy. Every effort has been made to present the work of Robert E. Howard as faithfully as possible.

The study of the extant texts for *A Witch Shall Be Born* (Howard's original typescript, the carbon thereof and the Weird Tales text), showed conclusively that Farnsworth Wright, the editor of Weird Tales, had censored several passages in the Conan stories, particularly bits of dialogue and descriptions that he probably found too "explicit". Fortunately, carbons survive for most of the later Conan stories, often in complete or nearly-complete form. The comparison of the texts for which both carbon and original typescript survive shows that these are nearly identical. The only differences concern the titles, subtitles and chapter divisions of the stories, which are often – but not always – absent from the carbons. Additionally, a few typographical errors may have been fixed, or a word replaced by another. Unless the original typescripts ever surface, Howard's carbons offer by far the purest available text for many of the Conan stories.

Deviations from the original sources are detailed in these textual notes. In the following pages, page, line and word number are given as follows: 51.9.5, indicating page 51, ninth line, fifth word. Story titles, chapter numbers and titles, and breaks before and after chapter headings, titles and illustrations are not counted. The page/line number will be followed by the reading in the original source, or a statement indicating the type of change made. Punctuation changes are indicated by giving the immediately preceding word followed by the original punctuation.

The People of the Black Circle
Text taken from Howard's carbon, provided by Glenn Lord, and from the September, October and November 1934 issues of Weird Tales. The surviving carbon is incomplete, lacking pages 1-9 and 92 of a 98 page typescript; the missing pages (from the beginning to "she asked" (page 10, line 1) and from "so willingly" (74.26.13) to "repeated helplessly" (75.12.7) are taken from the Weird Tales appearance. Howard's chapters are untitled on the carbon; it is not known whether the subtitles are Howard's or Wright's. Changes from the Weird Tales text: 5.37.6: Sap; 7.6.13: Hills; 8.28.2: Majesty; 9.19.12: Skalos. 9.24.5: Majesty. Changes from Howard's carbon: 10.18.9: b; 9.30.13: "a" omitted; 11.17.13: Eastern; 12.20.12:

country-side; 12.25.9: Then; 15.10.7: sent led; 16.6.11: train; 16.9.9: unwanted; 17.4.2: of; 17.27.14: not of one of; 18.27.2: between; 20.10.7: excercise; 20.11.9: excercises; 21.17.6: 'the' absent from typescript; 22.2.10: 'star-light' hyphenated at line-break; 22.5.1: no comma after 'carelessly'; 22.22.6: quiesence; 22.36.3: when; 24.21.1: gripped; 25.14.10: hillsmen; 25.32.13: irrelevent; 25.35.8: liad; 28.9.9: into; 28.9.13: seem; 30.17.12: no comma after 'squatted' (typed to right edge of carbon); 30.23.5: Irakzai; 32.18.11: fore-finger; 33.20.1: asonished; 33.20.7: distended; 33.34.4: 'as' absent from original; 37.5.7: no comma after 'through'; 40.17.7: profferred; 40.24.10: hit; 40.25.2: supply; 41.7.5: comma after 'flight'; 41.26.7: 'north west'; 42.26.12: 'in' not in original; 42.28.7: what ever; 43.10.6: hypnostism; 44.34.4: hundred; 44.39.11: neophism; 45.1.12: excercise; 45.19.1: Raksha; 47.5.7: the top-left corner of the carbon is torn; 'He shook' and the 'l' of 'loose' are missing; the missing words appear in the Weird Tales version and the first draft; 47.16.3: river bed; 48.3.5: river bed; 48.27.6: traffick; 48.33.11: 'chief' not in original; 50.18.3: tough; 51.17.5: comma after 'than'; 51.32.10: gald; 51.37.14: herslf; 51.37.15: in; 52.3.3: scrutinised; 52.9.6: every; 53.7.7: 'to' not in original; 53.22.8: loosly; 53.24.13: onlique; 54.10.4: on; 55.2.15: comma instead of semi-colon after 'fingers'; 56.5.14: no comma after 'first'; 56.18.7: no comma after 'suddenly'; 56.27.8: 'stems' absent from original; the word appears in the Weird Tales text and in the first draft; 57.4.3: 'in' not in original; 58.10.11: wide braced; 59.10.11: infest; 59.26.1: 'did' not in original; 60.11.2: half blinded; 60.16.8: thunder storm; 60.17.1: nightning; 61.12.13: green robed; 61.15.3: 'as' not in original; 61.28.16: sheer walled; 62.32.8: 'in a' in original; 64.1.1: unprecendented; 64.31.14: black robed; 64.34.9: black robed; 65.35.8: no comma after 'mid-stride' in original; 66.12.9: reinacted; 66.24.11: suddeness; 66.27.6: 'if' not in original; 67.1.5: 'whether' not in original; 67.9.5: black robed; 67.9.9: no comma after 'convulsions' (typed to right edge of paper); 67.35.7: 'the' not in original; 68.7.9: his; 68.14.13: stars; 68.16.7: left hand; 70.2.11: half way; 70.8.1: sandal-wood; 72.1.1: He (there is no chapter transition at this point of Howard's carbon.); 72.8.15: hair; 73.5.11: dociley; 73.14.5: to; 73.38.1: His; 74.1.1: semi-colon instead of comma after 'Yes'. 77.9.6: left hand; 77.12.8: melee; 77.23.11: 'was' repeated; 77.29.13: van-guard; 78.12.2: accepting.

The Hour of the Dragon

Originally appeared in Weird Tales in five installments, December 1935 and January, February, March and April 1936. The verse heading did not appear in the magazine; it is taken from Howard's submission sheet for the novel prepared for British publisher Denis Archer in May 1934 (document provided by Glenn Lord). It is not known if the heading was included when the novel was sent to Weird Tales. There is no chapter 20 in the Weird Tales text: chapter 19 concluded the March 1936 installment, and the April installment began with chapter 21. A study of the drafts for the novel shows that this is a mistake in numbering rather than a missing chapter. 89.11.13: Zingarians; 133.22.13: not; 138.24.13: can not; 146.26.4: without; 156.32.11: intense; ('incense' in all surviving drafts); 166.8.7: Conon; 167.36.8: men; 172.13.5: 'from' not in original; 197.11.7: shoreline; 198.22.12: shoreline; 210.6.5: ceatures; 213.32.10: 'was' not in original; 244.16.13: men; 245.5.5: Gunderman.

A Witch Shall Be Born
Text taken from Howard's original typescript, provided by Terence McVicker; page 5 is absent from the typescript; the text for this page has been taken from Howard's carbon, provided by Glenn Lord. 257.12.2: 'herself' not in original; 258.21.8: coifure; 258.21.13: queen's; 258.22.12: boudior; 260.8.1: 'He' underlined; 260.14.1: 'He' underlined; 260.16.2: 'He' underlined; 260.20.1: pouring; 260.21.1: 'He' underlined; 260.24.2: 'He' underlined; 261.23.5: semi-colon after 'called'; 264.9.2: exclamation mark after 'slain'; 266.5.11: happens; 266.31.6: no hyphen in 'low-swinging'; 267.8.12: comma after 'rescue'; 267.36.9: minature; 268.28.14: tavern-floor; 270.34.7: no em-dash before 'he'; 270.35.1: comma instead of em-dash after 'nomads'; 272.2.5: 'to' not in original; 274.6.14: independance; 274.27.6: 'the' not in original; 276.6.1: from whence; 277.1.5: envelopes; 277.10.5: contemptously; 277.21.7: coifure; 277.37.11: permenently; 278.24.4: every; 278.32.7: silvered; 280.15.11: aubdible; 282.13.14: it; 282.14.15: it; 282.21.15: vizer; 282.28.8: 'a' not in original; 285.26.8: hoard; 290.10.14: protect; 291.2.2: thick; 291.15.4: semi-colon after 'merged'; 296.6.2: pillard; 296.36.2: cresent; 296.37.7: agonies; 300.5.2: there; 301.7.1: comma after 'compassion'.

Untitled synopsis (The People of the Black Circle)
Text taken from Howard's original typescript, provided by Glenn Lord. No changes have been made for this edition.

The Story thus Far... (The People of the Black Circle)
First page taken from Howard's carbon, provided by Glenn Lord. The second carbon was also in Howard's files but was in such bad condition that Glenn Lord had to retype it, respecting the original document's layout, text and eventual mistakes. The text for this edition is taken from Glenn Lord's retyping. No changes have been made for this edition.

Untitled synopsis (Amalric...)
Text taken from Howard's original typescript, provided by Glenn Lord. No changes have been made for this edition.

Untitled draft (Three men squatted…)
Text taken from Howard's original typescript, provided by Glenn Lord. No changes have been made for this edition.

Untitled synopsis (The Hour of the Dragon)
Text taken from Howard's original typescript, provided by Glenn Lord. No changes have been made for this edition.

Notes for The Hour of the Dragon
Text taken from Howard's original typescript, provided by Glenn Lord. No changes have been made for this edition.

Untitled synopsis (A Witch Shall Be Born)
Text taken from Howard's original typescript, provided by Glenn Lord. No changes have been made for this edition.

I am grateful to Jerry Tiritilli, Rick Bernal, Scott Gustafson, Geof Darrow, Larry Majewski and Tom Gianni. Their enthusiasm for art and fantasy has always been an inspiration. Also for their suggestions and insights, I'd like to thank the Keegan family, Barry Klugerman, Rick Vitone, Dave Burton, Mark Schultz and Al Wyman. Applause for Barbara and Jack Baum, if not for them, where would we be? Lastly, thanks to Marcelo Anciano. His vision of the Robert E. Howard/Wandering Star library is now considered a benchmark of quality in the publishing of fine books.

Gary Gianni

My thanks to the Wandering Star team for making it happen a second time. Marcelo, Stuart and Rusty: we did it! Thanks to Glenn Lord for his support of this project and his continuous help. These books couldn't exist without you. Thanks also to Terence McVicker for his generosity and his help with this volume. And very special thanks to Shelly and Valérie for letting the boys out of the chores when superior duty called.

Patrice Louinet

Many thanks to the Wandering Star team, particularly Patrice, Marcelo and Stuart, for yeoman effort into the wee smalls; to Glenn Lord for his years of effort on behalf of REH and for his hard work in assisting this project; and of course to Shelly, with much love – thanks for letting me out of the chores when the deadline looms!

Rusty Burke

I would like to thank Marcelo, Patrice and Rusty for being a pleasure to work with once again and Gary for revitalising my interest in Conan. Thanks also to Mandy and Emma for being patient and understanding, Fishburn Hedges for allowing me to use their design studio after hours and at weekends again (and again) and, finally, to Phil Watson with whom I used to exchange Howard books and Conan comics many, many years ago. *Cheers, Phil!*

Stuart Williams

When I first started these books I had no idea that I would be creating a library of illustrated books. I would like to thank all who have been involved in its conception and to the many artists who have been incredibly supportive of my endeavour: Al Williamson, Mike Mignola, Mark Schultz, Geof Darrow, Neil Gaiman, Bruce Timm, Frank Cho, Justin Sweet, Frank Frazetta, Jeff Jones and, of course, Gary Gianni. Very special thanks also to Jim Keegan, Stuart, Rusty and Patrice, my keystones, and not forgetting Ed Waterman, web designer supreme.

Marcelo Anciano